LE MORTE D'ARTHUR

VOLUME I

We cannot be certain of the identity of the author of *Le Morte D'Arthur* and several theories have been advanced as to his historical circumstances. However, the theory put forward by an American scholar, G. L. Kittredge, has prevailed. He claimed that the author was a Sir Thomas Malory or Maleore of Newbold Revell in Warwickshire, born in the first quarter of the fifteenth century, who spent the greatest part of the last twenty years of his life in prison. Contemporary accounts accuse him of a number of crimes, including attempted murder, rape and armed robbery and he is also credited with a couple of dramatic escapes from prison. Other records suggest that he was a fighting man rather than a criminal. He was certainly in the service of Richard Beauchamp, Earl of Warwick, and fought with him in the siege of Calais in 1436. It is not surprising that some scholars have found it difficult to reconcile this violent man with the author of these moral tales.

Another possible candidate is a Thomas Malory of Studley and Hutton in Yorkshire and it has been suggested that the language of the tales points to an author living north of Warwickshire.

It is generally accepted that the author was a member of the gentry and a Lancastrian who deeply mourned the passing of the age of chivalry. He describes himself as a 'knight-prisoner' and it is clear that he spent many years in prison and *Le Morte D'Arthur* was probably written while the author was incarcerated. It would seem that he had seen service in south-western France and it is possible that some of this book was written while he was held captive by Jacques d'Armagnac, who had an extensive Arthurian library. He is thought to have died around 1471.

•

John Lawlor was Professor of English Language and Literature at the University of Keele, and has held visiting appointments at the Folger Shakespeare Library, Brandeis University and the Universities of California, British Columbia and New Mexico. He is the author of *The Tragic Sense in Shakespeare*, *Piers Plowman: an Essay in Criticism* and *Chaucer*.

Janet Cowen is a lecturer in English at King's College, University of London.

[illegible]

Although the [illegible] of the identity of the author of [illegible] has been [illegible], it [illegible] accepted that [illegible] Thomas Malory [illegible] of Newbold Revell in Warwickshire [illegible] in the first quarter of the fifteenth century [illegible] of the last twenty years of his life in prison. [illegible] a number of crimes including attempted murder, [illegible] and [illegible] [illegible] prison. Other [illegible] a man better than a criminal. He was [illegible] Richard Beauchamp, Earl of Warwick, and [illegible] [illegible] in 1445. [illegible] this [illegible] with the author of [illegible].

[illegible] Thomas Malory of [illegible] Yorkshire [illegible]

[illegible] was [illegible] at the [illegible] of [illegible] [illegible] the book was [illegible] [illegible]

[illegible] Library of [illegible] and [illegible] University [illegible] [illegible]

[illegible]

SIR THOMAS MALORY

Le Morte D'Arthur

IN TWO VOLUMES

VOLUME I

EDITED BY JANET COWEN

WITH AN INTRODUCTION BY JOHN LAWLOR

PENGUIN BOOKS

Penguin Books Ltd, Harmondsworth, Middlesex, England
Viking Penguin Inc., 40 West 23rd Street, New York, New York 10010, U.S.A.
Penguin Books Australia Ltd, Ringwood, Victoria, Australia
Penguin Books Canada Limited, 2801 John Street, Markham, Ontario, Canada L3R 1B4
Penguin Books (N.Z.) Ltd, 182–190 Wairau Road, Auckland 10, New Zealand

—

Published in the Penguin English Library 1969
Reprinted 1973, 1975, 1976, 1977, 1978, 1979, 1981,
1982 (twice), 1983, 1984
Reprinted in Penguin Classics 1986 (twice)

—

—

Made and printed in Great Britain by
Hazell Watson & Viney Limited,
Member of the BPCC Group,
Aylesbury, Bucks
Set in Linotype Juliana

CONTENTS

Le Morte D'Arthur

INTRODUCTION

1

FACT and fiction, romantic impossibility and historical likelihood, are intertwined at many stages of Arthurian story. There is, to begin with, the richness and enigmatic quality of all things connected with Arthur – a beguilingly beautiful labyrinth (*Arturi regis ambages pulcerrime*) for Dante at the end of the thirteenth century, and a continuing attraction in the seventeenth for Milton, who thought he might find a theme fit for epic in a tale of Arthur 'moving wars beneath the earth'. That is one side, and a lasting side, of Arthurian story. In such reincarnations, we have *Rex quondam Rexque futurus*, the King who once was and who will be again: given the archetype, the appropriate magic follows. Who would have thought that a hero of this order might in fact be traced in history? Yet there is ground for believing in the existence of a victorious commander, a Briton of the later fifth century, leading a series of successful encounters with invaders (and, possibly, traitorous Britons)[1] – a glorious career which later generations thought of as ended not by external defeat but by dissension within the war-band. This is the Arthur who is first reflected in the pages of Geoffrey of Monmouth (1136): and it is this Arthur who continued to appeal to medieval English writers – a leader whose triumphant course ends in the lamentable division of his kingdom; he passes from men's sight as one whose glory is not overthrown but temporarily eclipsed. French writers, on the other hand, appear from the outset to be chiefly interested in one outstanding member of Arthur's company, Sir Lancelot; and in handling this theme they seize from the beginning on the tragic possibilities that lie in wait for chivalry when it is

1. See Kenneth Jackson, 'The Arthur of History', in *Arthurian Literature in the Middle Ages*, ed. R. S. Loomis, Oxford, 1959, pp. 1–11.

drawn aside from the only true quest, 'the seeking out of the high secrets and hidden things of Our Lord'. The Grail is the goal of man's highest endeavour; and by this standard Sir Lancelot, best of earthly knights, falls short. An English author who has before him both English and French tellings of Arthurian story is dealing with potentially irreconcilable material; and this point is central to all assessment of Malory's *Morte*. Since French sources bulk large in his work, Malory has been subject to what his best exponent has, with characteristic modesty, called 'almost a necessary evil', an English author edited by a French scholar;[1] and all learned debate must run the risk of strong, if latent, preconception in favour of an 'original' which Malory may be thought of as 'translating'. In this light he is always in danger of being judged, for good or ill, in terms of his faithfulness as an intermediary; his individuality as a writer is liable to be underrated or all but ignored.

Malory's individual being as a man, his historical identity, has provided a paradox, too. Since the 1890s, beginning with the skilful advocacy of the American scholar Kittredge, it has been generally accepted that the author was a certain Sir Thomas Malory or Maleore (with variant spellings) who lived at Newbold Revell in Warwickshire, soldiered at Calais in his youth under the great Richard Beauchamp, Earl of Warwick, and came to see in the decline of the Lancastrian fortunes a parallel with the overthrow of King Arthur's rule. He even gives Mordred, the insurgent in his story, a Yorkist-like army, drawn from south-eastern England. All very pleasing and probable, no doubt: but this Sir Thomas turns out, on later inquiry, to have been a prisoner, and his offences include armed assault and rape. Apologists have reminded us of the turbulent times in which he lived; but the rape with which Malory was charged cannot be explained away as a technicality in the forcible eviction of a tenant. Two

1. Eugène Vinaver, *The Works of Sir Thomas Malory*, Oxford, 2nd ed., 1967, p.x. Quotations from this edition are made with acknowledgements to the Clarendon Press.

offences were alleged, and the charge reads unambiguously *cum ea carnaliter concubuit.* This rather unpromising figure, then, appears to be the author of 'the noble and joyous historye of the grete conquerour and excellent kyng, Kyng Arthur'; and, to crown all, there came to light (at Winchester in 1934) a manuscript which showed clearly how the writer had set about his task. The work is divided into clearly-defined sections; a series of prayers for 'help' or 'deliverance', occurring throughout the book, amplify the single prayer that Caxton had printed at the end, and one of them makes it plain that the petitioner is 'a knyght presoner'; and one section (that on the Roman war, Caxton's Book V) is notably longer in the manuscript than in the printed text. By this single discovery we are given new information about the author; about the mode of composition; and, by implication, about the first editor, William Caxton, who published his edition in 1485.

This, of course, in turn raised other problems, and the effect was to suspend Malorian studies until a full text of the Winchester Manuscript was available. It appeared in 1947, as *The Works of Sir Thomas Malory*, edited by Eugène Vinaver, with a revised edition, based on a fresh collection and incorporating new matter in the Commentary, appearing in 1967. With the text of Winchester before them, scholars have begun to engage in lively discussion. In the field of interpretation, one matter has been strikingly dominant, the question of unity. Could Malory be said to have written a 'hoole book' or instead eight separate romances (hence the significance of Vinaver's title, *The Works of Sir Thomas Malory*)? As to the author himself, William Matthews has recently come forward with a vigorous claim for a Yorkshire Knight in place of Kittredge's 'ill-framed' candidate.[1] The debate, on these counts as on others, continues; and the general liveliness of interest in Arthurian matter can

1. *The Ill-Framed Knight*, Berkeley and Los Angeles, 1966. ('Ill-framed' reflects Vinaver's conjecture that the name 'Malory' derives from a nickname meaning 'ill-framed' or 'ill-set'.)

be seen from evidence as widely different as the musical *Camelot*, based on T. H. White's serio-comic re-shaping of Malory, *The Once and Future King*, and excavation, begun in 1966 and still continuing, at South Cadbury 'Castle', which appears to have been the base of a British ruler of some substance, whether Arthur or another. 'Camelot', according to John Leland, was a local name for it in the sixteenth century: and the name is perpetuated in the Camelot Research Committee which has charge of the work. As their President stirringly puts it, we may yet live to see 'another convergence of fact and tradition' similar to that which brought Troy and Mycenae out of legend into fact.[1] Leaving aside all further question of historical identity, Malory's no less than Arthur's, what shall we say of Malory's contribution to the legend, his labour to tell 'of Kyng Arthur and of his noble knyghts of the Rounde Table'?

2

Arthur, the monarch of a kingdom that falls by treachery, makes his first appearance in Geoffrey of Monmouth's History of the Kings of Britain, written in 1136. There he is at the height of success, ready to march into Italy having defeated the Roman army, when he hears of Mordred's treachery in seizing the throne and marrying the Queen. Arthur returns to Britain and is at first victorious against the rebels; but in the last battle (beside the river Camel, 'in Cornwall') though Mordred falls, Arthur himself is fatally wounded and, appointing a successor to the crown, he is taken to 'the island of Avallon for the healing of his wounds'. When this matter is first handled in French, all interest is focused not upon Arthur but upon Sir Lancelot. *Le Roman de Lancelot du Lac* (1225–30) consists of *Lancelot*, an account of the

1. Sir Mortimer Wheeler, in the Committee's leaflet 'Can *this* be Camelot?' As to the legend, readers of the Personal column of *The Times* were notified on 22 July 1955, 'I think I have identified the Holy Grail ...'

Quest for the Holy Grail, and the death of King Arthur; and this was later enlarged by the *Estoire del Graal* and the *Estoire de Merlin*. The focus, from the beginning, is firmly upon Lancelot; and his failure to achieve the Grail gives the measure of earthly chivalry. The son, Galahad, succeeds where Lancelot falls short. More important, from our present point of view, is the function of the *Mort Artu*, the section dealing with Arthur's defeat and death. It is there 'to describe Lancelot's final failure – that which occurred when he was called upon to save Arthur and his kingdom'.[1] The French Arthurian cycle establishes clearly the gap between earthly and spiritual. By this standard knights who have shown little secular prowess – Galahad, Bors, Perceval – shine forth: and Lancelot and Arthur are inevitably headed for disaster. The distinction is well summed up in terms first used by E. K. Chambers.[2] Corbenic (the castle where the Grail is achieved) predominates over Camelot (the region *par excellence* of the chivalric life). Readers who come to Arthurian story with this tradition (derived perhaps from Tennyson or from Wagner, rather than medieval writers) colouring their thoughts will find it difficult to know what Malory is about, and may find him unduly prosaic, insensitive to what they take to be the true import of his material. We must, however, remind ourselves that there is no one version of Arthurian material towards which all others must aspire.

In contrast with the French the earliest English versions of the story, Layamon's *Brut* (written in the closing years of the twelfth century) and the alliterative *Morte Arthur* (about 1360) tell the story simply, in terms of the chronicle tradition. Here, as in Geoffrey of Monmouth, the centre of attention is Arthur, and the story is of stark disaster overtaking his kingdom once loyalty is breached. There is only

1. Vinaver, *The Tale of the Death of King Arthur*, Oxford, 1955, p.x.

2. His essay 'Sir Thomas Malory', read to the English Association in 1922, is reprinted in *Sir Thomas Wyatt and some collected studies*, London, 1933, pp. 21–45.

one instance before Malory of an English writer working from a French source (the stanzaic *Le Morte Arthur*, dating from the late fourteenth century); and it is very noticeable that this writer disregards the link between the Grail and the Lancelot themes. He leaves his readers to confront the dire events of which Lancelot, Arthur and Guinevere are the victims. Like Lancelot's seven companions, now turned hermit, we must resign ourselves to things which pass our understanding:

> Off lancelot du lake telle I no more,
> But thus by-leve these ermytes sevyn;
> And yit is Arthur beryed thore,
> And quene Gaynour, as I yow nevyn;
> With monkes that ar Ryght of lore.
> They Rede and synge with mylde stevyn:
> 'Ihesu, that suffred woundes sore,
> Graunt us All the blysse of hevyn!'
> Amen.
>
> *Explycit le morte Arthur*

Here is something which, it may be argued, has qualities equal and opposite to those of the French romances. Where they provide explanation and continuity, the English writer presents unmitigated reality, what indubitably happened in all its sharpness. If he refers to Fortune's wheel – that convincing instrument of destiny – it is in terms that only underline cruel inevitability. The wheel turns in Arthur's nightmare before the last battle, and he falls into darkness (a 'blake water'), to be rent limb from limb by monsters. Here, then, is a version which, notwithstanding French sources, is graphically simple, leaving the audience free to make what they can of the connexions between what men are and the things that befall them. Malory, in his turn, must be allowed the same freedom; and if he does not link the Death of Arthur with the quest for the Grail and if he does not ex-

by-leve: leave. *ermytes sevyn*: the seven hermits.
yit: still, to this present day. *thore*: there.
nevyn: (name) tell, assure. *with mylde stevyn*: in hushed voices.

patiate on the meaning of Fortune's wheel, he may, so far from misunderstanding the superiority of Corbenic over Camelot, have contrived it that Corbenic becomes 'a province of Camelot'.[1] In that event, the chivalric life will not be explained from without, as a thing inferior to the spiritual order: it is to be 'reinterpreted', as Vinaver acutely notes, 'from within'.[2] The changes Malory makes can be treated under several heads – structure and incidental detail; the matter of love; and style, the choice and ordering of language. In all of these aspects we are concerned with an English writer pursuing his own course and, in the absence of any clear model, learning in the doing.

3

The essential structural difference between the French Arthurian prose cycle and Malory's work may be expressed as the difference between complex interweaving and a more sequential treatment.[3] In the French, no one section of the work exists in isolation from the next; ideally, 'each episode or group of episodes was to be either a continuation of what occurred earlier on, or an anticipation of what was yet to come, or both.'[4] An analogy from visual art may help. The French mode of narration may be thought of as a process of intertwining, the themes of the complex story being 'entwined, latticed, knotted or plaited' so that they resemble 'the themes in Romanesque ornament, caught in a constant movement of endless complexity'.[5] Malory's first and essential

1. Vinaver, *Malory*, Oxford, 1929, p. 84.

2. Vinaver, *The Tale of the Death of King Arthur*, p. xii.

3. C. S. Lewis argues that in Malory it is a matter of degree. 'To anyone who comes to his work fresh from modern literature its polyphonic character will be at first one of the most noticeable things about it' ('The English Prose *Morte*' in *Essays on Malory*, ed. J. A. W. Bennett, Oxford, 1963, pp. 7–28; p. 14).

4. Vinaver, *The Tale of the Death of King Arthur*, p. xix.

5. Vinaver, 'Form and meaning in Medieval Romance', Presidential Address, Modern Humanities Research Association, 1966, p. 17.

response to that complexity is to cut clear swaths, to establish lines of demarcation between major sections of the story. Whatever impact his work is to have will be sequential and cumulative; and since his eye is firmly upon the *Morte*, the unrelieved disaster (*Morte Arthur Saunz Guerdon*) of the death of Arthur and the passing of the goodly fellowship of the Round Table, the pattern of significance will have to become increasingly apparent in a rising tide of events and their inevitable train of consequence, not be immovably evident in any overriding system, however exalted. Certainly, the 'Tale of the Sankgreal' will have an honoured place, as 'a tale chronicled for one of the truest and one of the holiest that is in this world'. But that is all Malory's design allows. We must return to the plane of the earthly chivalry, and to the disaster that impends when Lancelot, the King's most redoubtable champion, is seen to be a man of fatally divided loyalties – first, as lover of Guinevere, then as the unwitting slayer of Gareth, brother of Lancelot's most faithful friend, Gawain. There is no need to credit Malory with great artistry. Faced with what might have seemed the threatening complexity of his French sources he very possibly reacted with healthy mistrust. But, equally, there is no question that as events draw near to the fated end he writes with greatest authority. He deserves the praise of having kept his eye on the object; of having at the very least felt his way through to the things that made coherent sense, and constituted a manifest warning, for him and for all Englishmen.

Malory began with a tale of King Arthur and the Roman Emperor Lucius, where Arthur stands forth as a veritable military hero – one who, in the language of the Winchester colophon, 'was Emperoure hymself thorow dygnyté of his hondys'. This, shortened, constitutes Caxton's Book V. Malory then went on to draw from the *Suite du Merlin* more material which gave background to this figure – his beginnings and some notable earlier exploits. This made up his 'Tale of King Arthur', which forms Caxton's Books I to IV.

It is thought that there was an interval of time before he resumed his work with 'The Noble Tale of Sir Launcelot' and the 'Tale of Sir Gareth' (Caxton VI and VII). There next lay in his path the formidable matter of the Tristram story and of the Grail, and here his powers were above all tested, before the culminating power and irresistible sequence of the last two sections of his work, the 'Book of Sir Launcelot and Queen Guinevere' and the conclusion of the whole in 'The most piteous tale of the Morte Arthur saunz guerdon'. Structurally, Malory's work gains pace and authority as it advances: *virisque adquirit eundo*. The design draws to a head; ambiguities and lesser things – among them, in this telling, the Grail quest itself – fall into place as total and irreversible loss threatens. In the end we are left with a kingdom and the values it epitomized breached from within:

> Things fall apart; the centre cannot hold;
> Mere anarchy is loosed upon the world.

This difference in structure is paralleled in a characteristic difference of tone, evident in the incidental detail of Malory's work as against the French. Most notably, the marvels cease to multiply: Malory prunes them, sometimes omitting, sometimes telescoping. He is less interested in a world where magic is evident in a dozen particulars than in the one detail that transforms the world we know. Here again it would be inept to press for conscious art over natural bent. All we can say is that Malory's preference is for singleness and simplicity over variety and multiplicity. The same is true of his preference for realistic, often homely, detail. For example, in the story of Tristram, he alters his source, in which Tristan's first falling in love arose from a desire to oust Palomides from Iseult's favours: now love is an unprompted growth. On the other hand, at the parting of the lovers, not even mentioned in the French, Malory adds detail: there is an effusion of grief ('comédie larmoyante', as Vinaver once severely called it) and the exchange of pledges. This has less the air of conscious realism than of an entire naturalness – an unstudied concern to handle matters that are within the narrator's range and, where opportunity offers, to establish their credibility in human terms. Such a narrator comes into his own when the matter lies within his own field of experience. The Grail quest in Malory has the air of a real expedition. The French writers may choose to have their eyes on higher things: but Malory's field expedition has to be financed. Malory's Guinevere sends to Bors, Hector and Lionel 'tresour ynough for theyr expencys': and when Guinevere's steadfastness in seeking the mad Lancelot is to be brought home to him, Sir Ector's words carry the stamp of truth: 'Hyt hath coste my lady the quene twenty thousand pounds the sekynge of you.'

If we call this quality prosaic, we must mean a habit of concentration on what is within the narrator's range, what he can, in this sense, be understood to vouch for. Arthur the King, the earthly chivalry in its accomplishments – what Spenser called 'derring doe' – this is the centre of his attention. When that world is to be destroyed he himself is the first to grieve; and then only Malory can find appropriate words for this Arthur:

> Wyte you well, my harte was never so hevy as hit ys now. And much more I am soryar for my good knyghtes losse than for the losse of my fayre quene; for quenys I myght have inow, but such a felyship of good knyghtes shall never be togydirs in no company.[1]

These are the priorities in Malory's handling of his material. The matter of love has therefore a subordinate interest; and on two occasions this is strikingly apparent. They deserve to be set out in full, as instances of Malory's own invention, without parallel in his sources, and as such directly expressive of his own characteristic temper.

1. Quotations in this Introduction follow the Winchester MS and are not modernized.

4

The first occurs early in Malory's career as a writer, if the account earlier given is correct. It is in 'The Noble Tale of Sir Launcelot du Lake', where Lancelot is about to take leave of a 'damesell' whom he has saved from 'dystresse'. Praising him as excelling all other knights for courtesy and 'meekness', the lady goes on:

'But one thyng, sir knyght, methynkes ye lak, ye that ar a knyght wyveles, that ye woll nat love som mayden other jantylwoman. For I cowde never here sey that ever ye loved ony of no maner of degré, and that is grete pyté. But hit is noysed that ye love quene Gwenyvere, and that she hath ordeyned by enchauntemente that ye shall never love none other but hir, nother none other damesell ne lady shall rejoyce you; where[fore] there be many in this londe, of hyghe astate and lowe, that make grete sorow.'

'Fayre damesell,' seyde sir Launcelot, 'I may nat warne peple to speke of me what hit pleasyth hem. But for to be a weddyd man, I thynke hit nat, for than I muste couche with hir and leve armys and turnamentis, batellys and adventures. And as for to sey to take my pleasaunce with peramours, that woll I refuse: in prencipall for drede of God, for knyghtes that bene adventures sholde nat be advoutrers nothir lecherous, for than they be nat happy nother fortunate unto the werrys; for other they shall be overcom with a sympler knyght than they be hemself, other ellys they shall sle by unhappe and hir cursednesse bettir men than they be hemself. And so who that usyth peramours shall be unhappy, and all thynge unhappy that is aboute them.'

And so sir Launcelot and she departed.

(*Works*, pp. 270–71; Caxton VI 10)

Here Sir Lancelot, the arch-exemplar of those who love *peramours*, is made to disclaim both marriage and adultery. What can this mean? We must turn to the context in which this Lancelot comes forward; and it is at once apparent that we are not dealing with the Lancelot of French romance. Malory has turned from Arthur, the pre-eminent figure, whose deeds are chronicled in the Roman War (Caxton,

Book V) to deal with the one who stands next in chivalrous prowess – a Sir Lancelot who 'encresed so mervaylously in worship and honoure' that 'therefore he is the fyrste knyght that the Frey[n]sh booke makyth me[n]cion of aftir kynge Arthure com frome Rome.' There is Lancelot's significance defined; and it has an appropriate consequence:

Wherefore quene Gwenyvere had hym in grete favoure aboven all other knyghtis, and so he loved the quene agayne aboven all other ladyes dayes of his lyff, and for hir he dud many dedys of armys and saved her from the fyre thorow his noble chevalry.

Guinevere honours Arthur's most proficient knight and he in response ('agayne') reveres her above all others, throughout his life ('dayes of his lyff'). Malory concludes the sentence with a glimpse of what those 'dayes of his lyff' will include – many feats of arms on her behalf and a rescue from the stake; but in the close we are firmly reminded of the source from which all springs, Lancelot's 'noble chevalry'. It cannot be maintained that the purpose of this Book is to show Lancelot setting out 'to prove himself . . . in order to win the approval of Guinevere, whom he already loves'.[1] Lancelot in fact, in the passage already quoted and in two others, is made to deny the rumour that he and Guinevere are lovers. Malory's mood in the present passage is proleptic: he brings into play his knowledge of where things will end. But the Lancelot who occupies the stage is Lancelot in his original brightness, 'the fyrste knyght . . . aftir kynge Arthure com frome Rome'. The criterion of excellence is one and the same for liege-lord and follower – 'armys and worshyp', 'prouesse and noble dedys', 'noble chevalry'.

Lancelot's response to the lady's questioning therefore places 'armys and turnamentis, batellys and adventures' in

1. This is the view of R. M. Lumiansky, 'Prelude to Adultery', in *Malory's Originality*, ed. Lumiansky, Baltimore, 1964, pp. 91–8. For Vinaver's rejection of this (in particular, the theory of a 'progressive development of the Lancelot-Guinevere relationship which runs through *Le Morte Darthur*'), see *Works*, 2nd edn., 1967, pp. 1413–14.

the forefront of proper endeavour. Marriage, in this light, is a renunciation. Do we have here, undeveloped as it is, a hint of the idiosyncratic and temperamental difference between Arthur and Lancelot? Lancelot stubbornly clings to his single state, as though it were the only one proper to 'adventurous' knighthood. Yet in King Arthur we do not have an inactive hero, married though he is.[1] At all events, it is not marriage but loving *peramours* that is condemned; and Lancelot's language is firm, modulating from solemnity ('in prencipall for drede of God') to simple certainty. The key to Malory's handling of the passage is in words that the modern reader may easily misread – 'happy', 'unhappe', and the repeated 'unhappy' which seals the conclusion. We must think of this in much stronger terms than the ordinary sense of 'happy' or 'unhappy' allows today. 'Mishap' is a step towards it, if we go beyond the sense of a minor slip to the gravity of ill-fortune, things going grievously and unalterably wrong. For example, Arthur, at the final parting of the ways, turns away from the traitor with the single exclamation, 'Alas, this unhappy day!' Even more strikingly, cause and effect are brought together in the one word when, after battle is joined, Arthur catches sight of Mordred:

'Now, gyff me my speare,' seyde kynge Arthure unto sir Lucan, 'for yondir I have aspyed the traytoure that all thys woo hath wrought.'

'Sir, latte hym be,' seyde sir Lucan, 'for he ys unhappy. And yf ye passe this unhappy day y[e] shall be ryght well revenged.'

It is this long prospect of 'unhappiness' which momentarily darkens the scene when Lancelot assures the lady 'who that usyth peramours shall be unhappy, and all thynge unhappy that is aboute them.' Lancelot is not yet the lover of Guinevere *peramours*; but what he asserts as established doctrine – a consequence which, since it cannot be set aside, has the force of destiny – will one day become a matter of disastrous

1. See R. T. Davies, 'The Worshipful Way in Malory', in *Patterns of Love and Courtesy*, ed. Lawlor, London, 1966, pp. 157–77; p. 162.

experience. Lancelot speaks more than he knows; Malory invests his words with tragic irony.

The second major instance of Malory dealing with the matter of love occurs in the penultimate section of the whole work, 'The Book of Sir Lancelot and Queen Guinevere'. Caxton places this section at the very end of Book XVIII (Chapter 25): but in any ordering, it is clearly designed to serve as prologue to what immediately follows – the events of 'the moneth of May' when Guinevere rides forth with 'ten knyghtes of the Table Rounde ... on-maynge into woodis and fyldis besydes Westemynster'. This time Malory speaks in his own person. He begins with the praise of 'the moneth of May ... whan every lusty harte begynnyth to blossom and to burgyne'. This, above all, is the time when 'lovers callyth to their mynde olde jantylnes and old servyse'. Things are gathering to a head in his story; but the new stage is rooted deep in the past. This prompts the next reflection. The seasons pass: 'grene summer' is followed in the natural order by 'wynter rasure' which 'dothe allway arace and deface grene summer'; and this, Malory affirms, is the pattern of 'unstable love in man and woman' –

> for in many persones there ys no stabylité; for [w]e may se all day, for a lytyll blaste of wyntres rasure, anone we shall deface and lay aparte trew love, for lytyll or nowght, that coste muche thynge. Thys ys no wysedome nother no stabylité, but hit ys fyeblenes of nature and grete disworshyp, whosomever usyth thys.

Here, again, modern usage may mislead. We must be on our guard against writing down 'stabylité' as a commonplace virtue. Much more, it is the highly prized characteristic of steadfastness, continuance in well-doing. 'Stability' in this sense is the great virtue of constancy. Its larger implications are evident enough for Malory. When 'the felyshyp of the Rounde Table ys brokyn' the foundation of order is gone; there will be, the Knights perceive, 'ever debate and stryff' in place of 'quyet and reste'. Lancelot is credited by them with 'a grete parte' in the achievement of order; and, in reply, Lancelot gives it its proper name: 'I wote well that in me was nat all the *stabilité* of thys realme, but in that I myght I ded my dever' (Caxton XX 17–18).

'Stability', then, is the great virtue, to be lamented in its passing. But in the present passage, Malory has a surprise in store. First, as on the earlier occasion, we must be told what true virtue consists in; 'vertuouse love' is therefore defined:

> lyke as May moneth flowryth and floryshyth in every mannes gardyne, so in lyke wyse lat every man of worshyp florysh hys herte in thys worlde: firste unto God, and nexte unto the joy of them that he promysed hys feythe unto; for there was never worshypfull man nor worshypfull woman but they loved one bettir than another; and worshyp in armys may never be foyled. But firste reserve the honoure to God, and secundely thy quarell muste com of thy lady. And such love I calle vertuouse love.

It is very different, Malory goes on, from experience of love 'nowadayes', when love is 'sone hote sone colde. Thys ys no stabylyté' –

> But the olde love was nat so. For men and women coude love togydirs seven yerys, and no lycoures lustis was betwyxte them, and than was love trouthe and faythefulnes. And so in lyke wyse was used such love in kynge Arthurs dayes.

So be it. Inconstancy appears as a national failing – 'a greate defaughte of us Englysshemen, for ther may no thynge us please no terme' (Caxton XXI 1). Malory's readers must therefore be willing to receive upon report what they cannot, in their latter age, experience for themselves. Where Malory had glanced forward in the earlier episode, from Lancelot's innocence to his later sufferings, here he makes his reader look back, to old times and the 'old love'. But here, as there, he comes to rest in the admirable qualities of his characters. Lancelot's 'noble chevalry', from which all was to spring, is now echoed in praise for Guinevere. Modern lovers will do well to recall the past:

And therefore all ye that be lovers, calle unto youre remembraunce the monethe of May, lyke as ded quene Gwenyver, for whom I make here a lytyll mencion, that whyle she lyved she was a trew lover, and therefor she had a good ende.

Guinevere is commended as a 'trew' lover, and 'truth' of course means 'stabylyté', constancy. Once again, in the 'bad' instance Malory dwells upon the redeeming feature. But it marks an advance in skill that this time the author pays tribute in his own person, making 'a lytyll mencion' that, poised at the end of his prologue, looks forward not only to the action immediately following ('So hit befelle in the moneth of May') but to the longer run of the whole story, the 'ende' that already begins to darken the horizon.

In both instances, Malory has called into play knowledge of events to come; and since they are dire events, in each instance a bright present is overshadowed. The effect is, of course, to heighten the sense of inevitability: momentarily, present and future lie in one focus. But that is not all. We end each time with the admirable qualities of the protagonists; and this most powerfully expresses the writer's sense that what is to come is a destiny from which no one, least of all the writer himself, can safeguard the persons of this story. Their lot is thus, in the ancient phrase, *soth ond sārlīc*, true and tragic. The shadow that falls is the shadow of events impending in the real world, not a foreseeable downfall in terms of a supernaturally-approved system. A narrative method which is sequential rather than 'polyphonic' encourages the writer to reach backward and forward. Given this method, time becomes especially the writer's medium – successive time, as contrasted with the continuum in which the interwoven method would place all persons and events, to make one grand design. This is an opportunity which Malory, moved especially by nostalgia, a reverence for that in the past which he would see revived in the present, is peculiarly fitted to take; and in the most successful parts of his work it sustains a sense of onward and irresistible force. Here we have two leading illustrations that in Malory's handling the story 'had to rely on its own resources and move by its own momentum'.[1]

5

What part is played in this by Malory's style? Vinaver, writing in 1929, when Malory's achievement seemed to him largely inexplicable in terms of content, concluded that the *Morte Darthur* rested securely on 'the mysterious power of style – the only immortal merit in the world of books'.[2] It is, in fact, a most insecure assumption that Malory has any one distinctive style. Like a good many fifteenth-century writers, he writes in one way when he is following his sources, another when he turns to address his 'gentle' readers. There is a further complication: as the source varies, so, too, does Malory. He can write in the ordinary, progressive manner of his French prose source; or, equally, in the strongly alliterative manner of the English poem which underlies the Roman War (Caxton V); or, again, he will echo the rhythms of the stanzaic *English Morte* (as in Caxton XX 19). A style? : it is really a question of styles. To illustrate, there is, firstly, the continuing manner of French prose:

And than the good man and sir Launcelot went into the chapell; and the good man toke a stole aboute hys neck and a booke, and than he conjoured on that booke. And with that they saw the fyende in an hydeous fygure, that there was no man so hardé-herted in the worlde but he sholde a bene aferde. Than seyde the fyende,

'Thou hast travayle me gretly. Now telle me what thou wolte with me.'

'I woll,' seyde the good man, 'that thou telle me how my felawe becam dede, and whether he be saved or dampned.'

Than he seyde with an horrible voice,

'He ys nat lost, but he ys saved !'

'How may that be?' seyde the good man. 'Hit semyth me that

1. Vinaver, *The Tale of the Death of King Arthur*, p. xxv.
2. Vinaver, *Malory*, p. 114.

he levith nat well, for he brake hys order for to were a sherte where he ought to were none, and who that trespassith ayenst oure [ordre] doth nat well.'

'Nat so,' seyde the fyende. 'Thys man that lyeth here was com of grete lynage . . .'

('The Quest of the Holy Grail', *Works*, pp. 925–6; cf Caxton XV 1)

Lors entre li preudoms en sa chappelle et prent ung livre et met une estole entour son col, *et puis vient hors* et commence a conjurer *l'ennemi*. Et *quant il a grant piece lut, il regarde et* voit l'ennemy en si hideuse fourme qu'il n'a si hardi homme en tout le monde qui *grand hide* n'en eust *et* paour. 'Tu me travailles trop,' fait l'ennemi, 'or me di que tu me veulz.' – 'Je veul,' fait il, 'que tu me dies comment cilz miens compains est mort, et [s]'il est perilz ou sauvez.' Lors parle *l'ennemi* a voix orrible *et espoventable* et dist; 'N'est mie perils, mais sauvés.' – 'Et comment puet ce estre?' fait li preudhoms. 'Il me semble *que tu me mentes, car ce ne me commande mie nostre order, ains le vee tout plainement* que nulx de nostre ordre ne veste chemise *de lin*; et qui *la vest, il* trespasse l'ordre. *Et qui en trespassant ordre muert*, ce n'est mie bien, *ce m'est avis*.' – 'A!' fait l'ennemi, '*je te diray comment il est alés de lui. Tu scés bien qu*'il fu *gentils homs et* de grant lignage . . .'

(Text from Vinaver, *Malory*, pp. 159–60)

The structure of each passage is essentially the same; but I have italicized in the French those words and phrases which Malory does not render, and it will be seen that his passage gathers force, until with the final disclosure all is swept aside that does not serve the bleak contrast of life and death: 'this man *that lyeth here* was com of grete lynage.'[1] Malory's style, in this type of passage, where he follows a French original, may certainly be said to make improvements in detail on his source – by compression and omission, as well as by telling addition. But in structure it is identical with the source – a prose which has the characteristic virtues and limitations of oral narration; clean, progressive, never worse than comfortably pedestrian and often strikingly laconic.

1. Caxton reads *that lyeth here dede*.

With other sources, the matter is very different, and then the effects can be strongly evident to every reader. Arthur's dream (Caxton V 4) is itself a kind of half-strangled alliterative poem, where the clashing phrases make the menace actual and all but overpowering:

As the kynge was in his cog and lay in his caban, he felle in a slumberyng and dremed how a dredfull dragon dud drenche much of his peple and com fleyng one wynge oute of the weste partyes. And his hede, hym semed, was enamyled with asure, and his shuldyrs shone as the golde, and his wombe was lyke mayles of a merveylous hew, and his tayle was fulle of tatyrs, and his feete were florysshed as hit were fyne sable. And his clawys were lyke clene golde, and an hydeouse flame of fyre there flowe oute of his mowth, lyke as the londe and the watir had flawmed all on fyre.

There the alliterative rhythms are plain for all to hear. Less obvious are the phrases which slip in from the stanzaic *Morte* and blend with those alliterative turns which are inseparable from a truly native English speech; as, 'ware and wyse', 'droupe and dare', with the occasional stride into full rhythm ('whyle we thus in holys us hyde'). Both kinds of alliterative effect are as different as could be from the quasi-ceremonious language in which Malory directly addresses his readers. The outstanding example of that is the passage already quoted, on 'wynter rasure' (Caxton XVIII 25). There the fifteenth-century disease of 'augmentation' is sadly evident both in the high-sounding latinate words ('constrayne', 'dyverce', 'neclygence', 'rasure', 'stabylité'), and in the intendedly elegant clusterings of synonyms ('to blossom and to burgyne', 'burgenyth and florysshyth', and the full measure of 'sprynglth, burgenyth, buddyth, and florysshyth'). It is a manner that in its quieter manifestations survives in Cranmer's Prayer book; the pattern 'arace and deface', 'deface and lay aparte', may recall 'acknowledge and confess', 'assemble and meet together', 'erred and strayed'. In both secular and religious writings, later readers have vainly striven to establish significant distinction between terms that were meant to make their impact not by subtlety of difference but by cumulative force.

It is easy to ridicule augmentation full-blown. From 'spryngith, burgenyth, buddyth, and florysshyth' it is but a step to the portentous Lord Berners, assuring his readers that he has 'volved, turned and read' those writings which he judged 'commodious, necessary and profitable', to the end that his gentle readers ('the noble gentlemen of England') might 'see, behold and read the high enterprises, famous acts and glorious deeds done and achieved by their valiant ancestors'.[1] Clearly, what we are told three times is true. Yet Berners is but one more writer who, like Malory, feels he must compose ornately for his appearance in person, but who writes a prose of unostentatious simplicity when he is following his French source. This disease of 'augmentation' in the end yields a pearl of great price. Hunting for – perhaps we should say, being haunted by – the more refined equivalent, the English writer can never be wholly unaware that English is a language in which apparent synonyms most often convey subtle gradations of mood or attitude rather than of meaning. The adoptions from French and Latin do not so much oust the native words as move them imperceptibly down a scale; and whereas that scale is originally conceived in terms of a hierarchical 'high' and 'low', it comes in the long run to be an instrument of highly effective nuance. The end-product is in the seventeenth century, when Browne can revivify a commonplace by saying that a man may be 'as content with six foot as the *moles* of Adrianus'.[2] There, in the contrast of two phrases, are the mighty and the humble made one in the grave. For a more complex example, we may hear Jeremy Taylor leading to the assertion that the triumph of the Christian Faith is miraculous (because otherwise inexplicable), by characterizing the Apostles as 'men of mean

1. Preface to *The Chronicles of Froissart*. On the other hand, the speech of John Ball (chap. CCCLXXXI) is outstandingly effective for its simplicity.

2. *Urn Burial*, chapter V.

breeding and illiberal arts'. It is the exact tone of polite incredulity: and so the sceptical listener has no inner defence against the final assault of plain language expressing unalterable fact, in 'the certainty of them that saw it, and the courage of them that died for it, and the multitude of them that believed it'.[1]

Malory's attemptedly solemn address to the reader (Caxton XVIII 25) has its moments of near unbalance: but in the end it, too, comes home to truth and simplicity. As in the major structuring of his story, so, too, in this; Malory has his eye on the object. His piece of 'high sentence' is not designed to glorify himself, but only to lead to the 'lytyll mencion' of Queen Guinevere: 'whyle she lyved she was a trew lover, and therefor she had a good ende.' Here, as in the quiet omissions and pruning of incidental detail, and in the treatment of adulterous passion, Malory succeeds because he holds to one purpose: to tell the story as it appears to him. He has his own 'stabylyté' and the reward is in the strength of his telling. For once, it is wholly appropriate that 'style' least of all reveals the author. C. S. Lewis put the matter with characteristic verve: 'If you were searching all literature for a man who might be described as "the opposite of Pater", Malory would be a strong candidate.'[2]

6

There is of course one man whom the 'augmented' manner calls vividly to mind, and that is Caxton, Malory's first publisher and, as we now know, his first editor. The discovery of the Winchester Manuscript brought clearly to light the fact of composition by distinct sections (as well as a difference in bulk between what Malory had written about Arthur versus the Emperor Lucius and Caxton's Book V). Caxton, we now

1. Sermon preached at the funeral of the Lord Primate (*Works*, London, 1844, VIII, 400).

2. 'The English Prose *Morte*' in *Essays on Malory*, ed. Bennett, p. 24.

see, took eight romances and made them into one book, making certain minor editorial changes (including the omission of all but one of the *explicits*, the first of which is the most revealing, for in it the writer took leave of the reader and left his work for others to continue), and creating certain confusions, or 'incongruities',[1] which arise from the effort to make a single book. In addition, he contributed a Preface which some readers may have taken too readily as a statement of Malory's intent. The question, however, remains whether the unity Caxton aimed for is largely factitious, or whether he has seized upon the essential characteristic of Malory's writings.

The debate has been joined and shows no sign of ending.[2] This clearly, is not the place to attempt to resolve it. But every reader of Malory's work may profit by the reminder that the last colophon of all speaks of two books ending together:

> Here is the ende of the hoole book of king Arthur and of his noble knyghtes of the Rounde Table, that whan they were hole togyders there was ever an hondred and forty. And here is the ende of *The Deth of Arthur*.[3]

Here, clearly, the writer claims that 'Two things are finished; this particular tale, and the whole book of which it is a part.'[4] But granted that, it is another question whether we can press for a close degree of congruence in all the parts of the 'hoole book'. What is certain is that the last two books display a high degree of – can we call it? – cogency; the sense, at the very least, of complex matter coming to a final resolu-

1. See Vinaver, *Works*, 2nd edn., 1967, p. xxxviii.

2. The two notable collections of critical essays have already been referred to: *Essays on Malory*, ed. J. A. W. Bennett; and *Malory's Originality*, ed. R. M. Lumiansky.

3. Only one of the two extant copies of Caxton (that in the Pierpont Morgan Library) preserves this colophon.

4. D. S. Brewer, 'the hoole book', in *Essays on Malory*, pp. 41–63; p. 61. On the problem set by the concept of 'unity', see Vinaver, *Works*, 2nd edn., 1967, pp. xli–li.

tion, and, at best (in the closing scenes of all) of an awful finality as inevitable destruction sets in – 'a grete angur and unhapp[e] that stynted nat tylle the floure of chyvalry of [alle] the worlde was destroyed and slayne'. Caxton, it appears, did not feel the almost gravitational pull of the *Morte* itself, the death of Arthur and the overthrowing of the earthly chivalry, as he certainly did not succumb to the attraction of a militant Arthur, the victorious King of Britain who successfully challenges the Roman Empire. Malory, we may say, adapting Cassio, is to be relished more in the soldier than in the scholar. Caxton was mildly concerned, too, at what Ascham was to call 'open manslaughter and bold bawdrye'. His counsel to the reader is plain: 'Doo after the good and leve the evyl, and it shal brynge you to good fame and renommee.' But for all that, Caxton grasped that the book he made was to be called the *Morte Darthur*, in spite of the obvious objection – 'Notwythstondyng it treateth of the byrth, lyf, and actes of the sayd kyng Arthur . . .' The *Morte*, Caxton sees, takes precedence, and the rest falls into shape –

> . . . his noble knyghtes of the rounde table, theyr meruayllous enquestes and adventures, thachyeuyng of the sangreal, & in thende the dolorous deth & departyng out of thys world of them al.

This has the right proportions: we begin and end with the great event towards which all tends and in virtue of which all has significance. Here is another Englishman who has his eye on what is of final importance: though for Caxton the centre of attention is not Arthur the exemplar of the military virtues, but Arthur the undoubted king, 'reputed and taken for one of the nine worthy, and the fyrst of the thre Crysten men'. So Caxton is entitled to his place as a maker of the English Arthuriad. The book he issues, 'by me deuyded in to XXI bookes chapytred', is the work that has been known to all those who, so far, have re-created 'Malory'. C. S. Lewis suggests that the true state of our 'English prose *Morte*', as he calls it, is to be likened to 'a great cathedral, where Saxon, Norman, Gothic, Renaissance, and Georgian elements all co-exist, and all grow together into something strange and admirable which none of its successive builders intended or foresaw'. In that tradition, Lewis argues, Caxton, too, was a builder: and 'the greatest service that he did the old fabric was one of demolition', in abridging 'the whole dreary business' of the Roman war.[1] The modern reader who is wholly intent on Malory, on seeing what he in fact wrote, and tracing out, it may be, his errors and false paths as well as his admitted triumphs, can now turn to Vinaver's irreproachable *Works of Sir Thomas Malory*. Those who wish to revisit the *Morte Darthur*, the book as Caxton shaped it, have their text in the present volume. Each party has its own pleasure and profit; and each can contribute to the common stock of perpetual interest in Arthurian story.

The Once and Future King and *Camelot* are one line of development. The Grail moves among men once more in Charles Williams's *War in Heaven* (1930); and Merlin, risen from the dead, is drawn into yet another battle against the forces of evil in C. S. Lewis's *That Hideous Strength* (1945). Who is to say that the beguiling stories interwoven with the great name of Arthur – *Arturi regis ambages pulcerrime* – will have no appeal for succeeding generations? Even where the source is not Malory, there is recognition of his distinctive appeal. *The Waste Land* is a highly individual response to Jessie Weston and to Frazer: but Eliot had read enough Malory to see Tennyson as 'Chaucer retold for children'.[2] John Cowper Powys, casting an ancient spell on modern Glastonbury, deals in a great mystery – 'that beautiful and terrible force by which the lies of great creative Nature give birth to truth that is to be'. But the language in which it is realized is inseparable from a sense of England and the English past:

1. *Essays on Malory*, pp. 25–6.

2. Herbert Howarth, *Notes on some figures behind* T. S. Eliot, London, 1965, p. 238.

> And John thought, 'I'm English and she's English and this is England.' ... And without formulating the thought in words he got the impression of the old anonymous ballads writ in northern dialect and full of cold winds and cold sword-points and cold spades and cold rivers; an impression wherein the chilly green grass and the peewits' cries made woman's love into a wild, stoical, romantic thing; and yet a thing calling out for bread and bed and candlelight.

The width and variety of response to Arthurian story, in authors French and English, named and anonymous, reinforces one truth that applies equally to Malory and to the authors of the French cycle, as it applies to all, medieval or modern, who take up the old stories. Each draws from the common store according to the measure of his understanding: *quicquid recipitur, recipitur ad modum recipientis.* What each in his turn makes is to be judged in its own light. The source itself remains undiminished.

EDITOR'S NOTE

THE text is based on Caxton's printed edition of 1485. The syntax of the original has been left unchanged, but the spelling has been modernized. Archaic forms have usually been kept, although some minor alterations have been made, as, e.g., in rendering *hem* (3rd person plural pronoun) as *them*, and in the past tenses of a few verbs. Obsolete words are explained in the Glossary and incorporate the same minor spelling changes as are made regularly elsewhere. Caxton's spellings of proper names have been harmonized. Modern punctuation and paragraphing have been used.

In commenting in the Notes on difficult points, I have occasionally referred to the readings of the Winchester Manuscript, which has been edited by Professor E. Vinaver as *The Works of Sir Thomas Malory*, Oxford, 1967 (second edition). My thanks are due to the Clarendon Press for permission to quote from this edition, to which I am greatly indebted. My thanks are also due to the Pierpont Morgan Library and the John Rylands Library for supplying microfilms of the two extant copies of Caxton's edition.

JANET COWEN

Le Morte D'Arthur

CAXTON'S ORIGINAL PREFACE

AFTER that I had accomplished and finished divers histories, as well of contemplation as of other historial and worldly acts of great conquerors and princes, and also certain books of examples and doctrine, many noble and divers gentlemen of this realm of England camen and demanded me, many and ofttimes, wherefore that I have not do made and imprint the noble history of the Sangrail, and of the most renowned Christian king, first and chief of the three best Christian and worthy, King Arthur, which ought most to be remembered among us English men tofore all other Christian kings.

For it is notoyrly known through the universal world that there be nine worthy and the best that ever were, that is to wit, three paynims, three Jews, and three Christian men. As for the paynims, they were tofore the Incarnation of Christ, which were named: the first, Hector of Troy, of whom the history is comen both in ballad and in prose; the second, Alexander the Great; and the third, Julius Caesar, Emperor of Rome, of whom the histories be well-known and had. And as for the three Jews, which also were tofore the Incarnation of our Lord, of whom the first was Duke Joshua, which brought the children of Israel into the land of behest, the second David, King of Jerusalem, and the third Judas Maccabaeus, of these three the Bible rehearseth all their noble histories and acts. And sith the said Incarnation have been three noble Christian men stalled and admitted through the universal world into the number of the nine best and worthy, of whom was first the noble Arthur, whose noble acts I purpose to write in this present book here following. The second was Charlemagne, or Charles the Great, of whom the history is had in many places both in French and in English; and the

do made: had made. *Sangrail*: Holy Grail. *tofore*: before.
notoryrly known: well known. *paynims*: pagans.
behest: promise. *sith*: since. *stalled*: put.

third and last was Godfrey of Bouillon,[1] of whose acts and life I made a book unto the excellent prince and king of noble memory, King Edward the Fourth.

The said noble gentlemen instantly required me to imprint the history of the said noble king and conqueror, King Arthur, and of his knights, with the history of the Sangrail, and of the death and ending of the said Arthur, affirming that I ought rather to imprint his acts and noble feats, than of Godfrey of Bouillon, or any of the other eight, considering that he was a man born within this realm, and king and emperor of the same; and that there be in French divers and many noble volumes of his acts, and also of his knights.

To whom I answered, that divers men hold opinion that there was no such Arthur, and that all such books as be made of him be but feigned and fables, because that some chronicles make of him no mention nor remember him nothing, ne of his knights.

Whereto they answered, and one in special said, that in him that should say or think that there was never such a king called Arthur might well be aretted great folly and blindness; for he said that there were many evidences of the contrary: first, ye may see his sepulture in the Monastery of Glastonbury; and also in *Polichronicon*,[2] in the fifth book, the sixth chapter, and in the seventh book the twenty-third chapter, where his body was buried, and after founden and translated into the said monastery. Ye shall see also in the history of Boccaccio, in his book *De Casu Principum*, part of his noble acts, and also of his fall. Also Galfridus in his British book[3] recounteth his life. And in divers places of England many remembrances be yet of him and shall remain perpetually, and also of his knights. First in the Abbey of Westminster, at Saint Edward's shrine, remaineth the print of his seal in red wax closed in beryl, in which is written: *Patricius, Arthurus, Britannie, Gallie, Germanie, Dacie, Imperator*. Item in the castle of Dover ye may see Gawain's skull and Craddock's mantle; at Winchester, the Round Table; in

ne: nor. *aretted*: counted. *item*: also.

other places, Launcelot's sword and many other things. Then all these things considered, there can no man reasonably gainsay but there was a king of this land named Arthur. For in all places, Christian and heathen, he is reputed and taken for one of the nine worthy, and the first of the three Christian men. And also he is more spoken of beyond the sea, more books made of his noble acts than there be in England, as well in Dutch, Italian, Spanish, and Greek, as in French. And yet of record remain in witness of him in Wales, in the town of Camelot, the great stones and marvellous works of iron lying under the ground, and royal vaults, which divers now living hath seen. Wherefore it is a marvel why he is no more renowned in his own country, save only it accordeth to the word of God, which saith that no man is accepted for a prophet in his own country.

Then, all these things foresaid alleged, I could not well deny but that there was such a noble king named Arthur, and reputed one of the nine worthy, and first and chief of the Christian men. And many noble volumes be made of him and of his noble knights in French, which I have seen and read beyond the sea, which be not had in our maternal tongue, but in Welsh be many and also in French and some in English, but no where nigh all. Wherefore, such as have late been drawn out briefly into English I have after the simple cunning that God hath sent to me, under the favour and correction of all noble lords and gentlemen, enprised to imprint a book of the noble histories of the said King Arthur, and of certain of his knights, after a copy unto me delivered, which copy Sir Thomas Malory did take out of certain books of French, and reduced it into English.

And I, according to my copy, have done set it in imprint, to the intent that noble men may see and learn the noble acts of chivalry, the gentle and virtuous deeds that some knights used in those days, by which they came to honour; and how they that were vicious were punished and oft put to shame and rebuke; humbly beseeching all noble lords and

cunning: ability. *enprised*: undertaken.

ladies, with all other estates, of what estate or degree they be of, that shall see and read in this said book and work, that they take the good and honest acts in their remembrance, and to follow the same, wherein they shall find many joyous and pleasant histories, and noble and renowned acts of humanity, gentleness, and chivalries. For herein may be seen noble chivalry, courtesy, humanity, friendliness, hardiness, love, friendship, cowardice, murder, hate, virtue, and sin. Do after the good and leave the evil, and it shall bring you to good fame and renown.

And for to pass the time this book shall be pleasant to read in; but for to give faith and believe that all is true that is contained herein, ye be at your liberty. But all is written for our doctrine, and for to beware that we fall not to vice ne sin, but to exercise and follow virtue, by which we may come and attain to good fame and renown in this life, and after this short and transitory life, to come unto everlasting bliss in heaven, the which he grant us that reigneth in heaven, the blessed Trinity. Amen.

Then to proceed forth in this said book, which I direct unto all noble princes, lords and ladies, gentlemen or gentlewomen, that desire to read or hear read of the noble and joyous history of the great conqueror and excellent king, King Arthur, sometime king of this noble realm, then called Britain: I, William Caxton, simple person, present this book following, which I have enprised to imprint; and treateth of the noble acts, feats of arms of chivalry, prowess, hardiness, humanity, love, courtesy and very gentleness, with many wonderful histories and adventures. And for to understand briefly the content of this volume, I have divided it into twenty-one books, and every book chaptered as hereafter shall by God's grace follow.

The first book shall treat how Uther Pendragon gat the noble conqueror King Arthur, and containeth twenty-eight chapters. The second book treateth of Balin the noble knight, and containeth nineteen chapters. The third book treateth of

gat: begot.

the marriage of King Arthur to Queen Guenever, with other matters, and containeth fifteen chapters. The fourth book, how Merlin was assotted, and of war made to King Arthur, and containeth twenty-nine chapters. The fifth book treateth of the conquest of Lucius the emperor, and containeth twelve chapters. The sixth book treateth of Sir Launcelot and Sir Lionel, and marvellous adventures, and containeth eighteen chapters. The seventh book treateth of a noble knight called Sir Gareth, and named by Sir Kay, Beaumains, and containeth thirty-six chapters. The eighth book treateth of the birth of Sir Tristram, the noble knight, and of his acts, and containeth forty-one chapters. The ninth book treateth of a knight named by Sir Kay, La Cote Male Taile, and also of Sir Tristram, and containeth forty-four chapters. The tenth book treateth of Sir Tristram and other marvellous adventures, and containeth eighty-eight chapters. The eleventh book treateth of Sir Launcelot and Sir Galahad, and containeth fourteen chapters. The twelfth book treateth of Sir Launcelot and his madness, and containeth fourteen chapters. The thirteenth book treateth how Galahad came first to King Arthur's court, and the quest how the Sangrail was begun, and containeth twenty chapters. The fourteenth book treateth of the quest of the Sangrail, and containeth ten chapters. The fifteenth book treateth of Sir Launcelot, and containeth six chapters. The sixteenth book treateth of Sir Bors and Sir Lionel his brother, and containeth seventeen chapters. The seventeenth book treateth of the Sangrail, and containeth twenty-three chapters. The eighteenth book treateth of Sir Launcelot and the queen, and containeth twenty-five chapters. The nineteenth book treateth of Queen Guenever and Launcelot, and containeth thirteen chapters. The twentieth book treateth of the piteous death of Arthur, and containeth twenty-two chapters. The twenty-first book treateth of his last departing, and how Sir Launcelot came to revenge his death, and containeth thirteen chapters. The sum is twenty-one books, which contain the sum of five hundred and seven chapters, as more plainly shall follow hereafter.

Book I

CHAPTER 1 : *First, How Uther Pendragon sent for the Duke of Cornwall and Igraine his wife, and of their departing suddenly again*

It befell in the days of Uther Pendragon, when he was king of all England, and so reigned, that there was a mighty duke in Cornwall that held war against him long time. And the duke was called the Duke of Tintagel. And so by means King Uther sent for this duke, charging him to bring his wife with him, for she was called a fair lady, and a passing wise, and her name was called Igraine.

So when the duke and his wife were comen unto the king, by the means of great lords they were accorded both. The king liked and loved this lady well, and he made them great cheer out of measure, and desired to have lain by her. But she was a passing good woman, and would not assent unto the king. And then she told the duke her husband, and said, 'I suppose that we were sent for that I should be dishonoured, wherefore, husband, I counsel you that we depart from hence suddenly, that we may ride all night unto our own castle.' And in like wise as she said so they departed, that neither the king nor none of his council were ware of their departing.

As soon as King Uther knew of their departing so suddenly, he was wonderly wroth. Then he called to him his privy council, and told them of the sudden departing of the duke and his wife. Then they advised the king to send for the duke and his wife by a great charge: 'And if he will not come at your summons, then may ye do your best, then have ye cause to make mighty war upon him.'

So that was done, and the messengers had their answers,

passing: exceedingly. *cheer*: entertainment.

and that was this shortly, that neither he nor his wife would not come at him. Then was the king wonderly wroth. And then the king sent him plain word again, and bad him be ready and stuff him and garnish him, for within forty days he would fetch him out of the biggest castle that he hath.

When the duke had this warning, anon he went and furnished and garnished two strong castles of his, of the which the one hight Tintagel, and the other castle hight Terrabil. So his wife Dame Igraine he put in the Castle of Tintagel, and himself he put in the Castle of Terrabil, the which had many issues and posterns out. Then in all haste came Uther with a great host, and laid a siege about the Castle of Terrabil. And there he pitched many pavilions, and there was great war made on both parties, and much people slain.

Then for pure anger and for great love of fair Igraine the King Uther fell sick. So came to the King Uther Sir Ulfius, a noble knight, and asked the king why he was sick.

'I shall tell thee,' said the king. 'I am sick for anger and for love of fair Igraine that I may not be whole.'

'Well, my lord,' said Sir Ulfius, 'I shall seek Merlin, and he shall do you remedy, that your heart shall be pleased.'

So Ulfius departed, and by adventure he met Merlin in a beggar's array, and there Merlin asked Ulfius whom he sought. And he said he had little ado to tell him.

'Well,' said Merlin, 'I know whom thou seekest, for thou seekest Merlin; therefore seek no farther, for I am he, and if King Uther will well reward me, and be sworn unto me to fulfil my desire, that shall be his honour and profit more than mine, for I shall cause him to have all his desire.'

'All this will I undertake,' said Ulfius, 'that there shall be nothing reasonable but thou shalt have thy desire.'

'Well,' said Merlin, 'he shall have his intent and desire. And therefore,' said Merlin, 'ride on your way, for I will not be long behind.'

stuff him and garnish him: make provision against a siege.

CHAPTER 2: *How Uther Pendragon made war on the Duke of Cornwall, and how by the mean of Merlin he lay by the Duchess and gat Arthur*

Then Ulfius was glad, and rode on more than a pace till that he came to King Uther Pendragon, and told him he had met with Merlin.

'Where is he?' said the king.

'Sir,' said Ulfius, 'he will not dwell long.'

Therewithal Ulfius was ware where Merlin stood at the porch of the pavilion's door. And then Merlin was bound to come to the king. When King Uther saw him, he said he was welcome.

'Sir,' said Merlin 'I know all your heart every deal. So ye will be sworn unto me as ye be a true king anointed, to fulfil my desire, ye shall have your desire.'

Then the king was sworn upon the four Evangelists.

'Sir,' said Merlin, 'this is my desire: the first night that ye shall lie by Igraine ye shall get a child on her, and when that is born, that it shall be delivered to me for to nourish there as I will have it; for it shall be your worship, and the child's avail as mickle as the child is worth.'

'I will well,' said the king, 'as thou wilt have it.'

'Now make you ready,' said Merlin, 'this night ye shall lie with Igraine in the Castle of Tintagel, and ye shall be like the duke her husband, Ulfius shall be like Sir Brastias, a knight of the duke's, and I will be like a knight that hight Sir Jordans, a knight of the duke's. But wait ye make not many questions with her nor her men, but say ye are diseased, and so hie you to bed, and rise not on the morn till I come to you, for the Castle of Tintagel is but ten miles hence.'

So this was done as they devised. But the Duke of Tintagel espied how the king rode from the siege of Terrabil, and

dwell: delay. *deal*: part. *worship*: honour. *mickle*: much.
hight: is called. *wait*: be careful. *diseased*: weary.
hie you: hurry.

therefore that night he issued out of the castle at a postern for to have distressed the king's host. And so, through his own issue, the duke himself was slain or-ever the king came at the Castle of Tintagel.

So after the death of the duke, King Uther lay with Igraine more than three hours after his death, and begat on her that night Arthur; and, or day came, Merlin came to the king, and bad him make him ready, and so he kissed the lady Igraine and departed in all haste. But when the lady heard tell of the duke her husband, and by all record he was dead or-ever King Uther came to her, then she marvelled who that might be that lay with her in likeness of her lord; so she mourned privily and held her peace.

Then all the barons by one assent prayed the king of accord betwixt the lady Igraine and him; the king gave them leave, for fain would he have been accorded with her. So the king put all the trust in Ulfius to entreat between them, so by the entreaty at the last the king and she met together.

'Now will we do well,' said Ulfius. 'Our king is a lusty knight and wifeless, and my lady Igraine is a passing fair lady; it were great joy unto us all, and it might please the king to make her his queen.'

Unto that they all well accorded and moved it to the king. And anon, like a lusty knight, he assented thereto with good will, and so in all haste they were married in a morning with great mirth and joy.

And King Lot of Lothian and of Orkney then wedded Margawse that was Gawain's mother, and King Nentres of the land of Garlot wedded Elaine. All this was done at the request of King Uther. And the third sister Morgan le Fay was put to school in a nunnery, and there she learned so much that she was a great clerk of necromancy, and after she was wedded to King Uriens of the land of Gore, that was Sir Uwain's le Blanchemains father.

or-ever: before. *fain*: gladly. *entreat*: negotiate.
and it might please: if it might please.

CHAPTER 3: *Of the birth of King Arthur and of his nurture*

Then Queen Agraine waxed daily greater and greater, so it befell after within half a year, as King Uther lay by his queen, he asked her, by the faith she ought to him, whose was the child within her body; then was she sore abashed to give answer.

'Dismay you not,' said the king, 'but tell me the truth, and I shall love you the better, by the faith of my body.'

'Sir,' said she, 'I shall tell you the truth. The same night that my lord was dead, the hour of his death, as his knights record, there came into my castle of Tintagel a man like my lord in speech and in countenance, and two knights with him in likeness of his two knights Brastias and Jordans, and so I went unto bed with him as I ought to do with my lord, and the same night, as I shall answer unto God, this child was begotten upon me.'

'That is truth,' said the king, 'as ye say; for it was I myself that came in the likeness, and therefore dismay you not, for I am father to the child;' and there he told her all the cause, how it was by Merlin's counsel. Then the queen made great joy when she knew who was the father of her child.

Soon came Merlin unto the king, and said, 'Sir, ye must purvey you for the nourishing of your child.'

'As thou wilt,' said the king, 'be it.'

'Well,' said Merlin, 'I know a lord of yours in this land, that is a passing true man and a faithful, and he shall have the nourishing of your child; and his name is Sir Ector, and he is a lord of fair livelihood in many parts in England and Wales; and this lord, Sir Ector, let him be sent for, for to come and speak with you, and desire him yourself, as he loveth you, that he will put his own child to nourishing to another woman, and that his wife nourish yours. And when

ought to him: owed him. *purvey*: provide.

the child is born let it be delivered to me at yonder privy postern unchristened.'

So like as Merlin devised it was done. And when Sir Ector was come he made fiance to the king for to nourish the child like as the king desired; and there the king granted Sir Ector great rewards. Then when the lady was delivered, the king commanded two knights and two ladies to take the child, bound in a cloth of gold, 'and that ye deliver him to what poor man ye meet at the postern gate of the castle.' So the child was delivered unto Merlin, and so he bare it forth unto Sir Ector, and made an holy man to christen him, and named him Arthur; and so Sir Ector's wife nourished him with her own pap.

CHAPTER 4: *Of the death of King Uther Pendragon*

Then within two years King Uther fell sick of a great malady. And in the meanwhile his enemies usurped upon him, and did a great battle upon his men, and slew many of his people.

'Sir,' said Merlin, 'ye may not lie so as ye do, for ye must to the field though ye ride on an horse-litter; for ye shall never have the better of your enemies but if your person be there, and then shall ye have the victory.'

So it was done as Merlin had devised, and they carried the king forth in an horse-litter with a great host toward his enemies. And at St Albans there met with the king a great host of the north. And that day Sir Ulfius and Sir Brastias did great deeds of arms, and King Uther's men overcame the northern battle and slew many people, and put the remnant to flight. And then the king returned unto London, and made great joy of his victory.

And then he fell passing sore sick, so that three days and three nights he was speechless; wherefore all the barons made great sorrow, and asked Merlin what counsel were best.

'There nis none other remedy,' said Merlin, 'but God will

fiance: promise. *northern battle*: northern battalion. *nis*: is not.

have his will. But look ye all, barons, be before King Uther to-morn, and God and I shall make him to speak.'

So on the morn all the barons with Merlin came tofore the king; then Merlin said aloud unto King Uther, 'Sir, shall your son Arthur be king, after your days, of this realm with all the appurtenance?'[1]

Then Uther Pendragon turned him, and said in hearing of them all, 'I give him God's blessing and mine, and bid him pray for my soul, and righteously and worshipfully that he claim the crown upon forfeiture of my blessing.' And therewith he yielded up the ghost, and then was he interred as longed to a king, wherefore the queen, fair Igraine, made great sorrow, and all the barons.

CHAPTER 5: *How Arthur was chosen king, and of wonders and marvels of a sword taken out of a stone by the said Arthur*

Then stood the realm in great jeopardy long while, for every lord that was mighty of men made him strong, and many weened to have been king. Then Merlin went to the Archbishop of Canterbury, and counselled him for to send for all the lords of the realm, and all the gentlemen of arms, that they should to London come by Christmas, upon pain of cursing; and for this cause: that Jehu, that was born on that night, that He would of his great mercy show some miracle, as He was come to be king of mankind, for to show some miracle who should be rightwise king of this realm. So the Archbishop, by the advice of Merlin, sent for all the lords and gentlemen of arms that they should come by Christmas even unto London. And many of them made them clean of their life, that their prayer might be the more acceptable unto God.

So in the greatest church of London (whether it were Paul's or not the French book maketh no mention) all the estates were long or day in the church for to pray. And when

longed: belonged. *weened*: thought.

matins and the first mass was done, there was seen in the churchyard, against the high altar, a great stone four square, like unto a marble stone, and in midst thereof was like an anvil of steel a foot on high, and therein stuck a fair sword naked by the point, and letters there were written in gold about the sword that saiden thus:–WHOSO PULLETH OUT THIS SWORD OF THIS STONE AND ANVIL, IS RIGHTWISE KING BORN OF ALL ENGLAND. Then the people marvelled, and told it to the Archbishop.

'I command,' said the Archbishop, 'that ye keep you within your church, and pray unto God still; that no man touch the sword till the high mass be all done.'

So when all masses were done all the lords went to behold the stone and the sword. And when they saw the scripture, some assayed, such as would have been king. But none might stir the sword nor move it.

'He is not here,' said the Archbishop, 'that shall achieve the sword, but doubt not God will make him known. But this is my counsel,' said the Archbishop, 'that we let purvey ten knights, men of good fame, and they to keep this sword.'

So it was ordained, and then there was made a cry, that every man should assay that would, for to win the sword. And upon New Year's Day the barons let make a jousts and a tournament, that all knights that would joust or tourney there might play. And all this was ordained for to keep the lords together and the commons, for the Archbishop trusted that God would make him known that should win the sword.

So upon New Year's Day, when the service was done, the barons rode unto the field, some to joust and some to tourney, and so it happed that Sir Ector, that had great livelihood about London, rode unto the jousts, and with him rode Sir Kay his son, and young Arthur that was his nourished brother; and Sir Kay was made knight at All Hallowmass afore. So as they rode to the jousts-ward, Sir Kay had lost his sword, for he had left it at his father's lodging, and so he prayed young Arthur for to ride for his sword.

let purvey: order to be appointed.

'I will well,' said Arthur, and rode fast after the sword. And when he came home the lady and all were out to see the jousting.

Then was Arthur wroth, and said to himself, 'I will ride to the churchyard, and take the sword with me that sticketh in the stone, for my brother Sir Kay shall not be without a sword this day.' So when he came to the churchyard, Sir Arthur alit and tied his horse to the stile, and so he went to the tent, and found no knights there, for they were at jousting; and so he handled the sword by the handles, and lightly and fiercely pulled it out of the stone, and took his horse and rode his way until he came to his brother Sir Kay, and delivered him the sword.

And as soon as Sir Kay saw the sword, he wist well it was the sword of the stone, and so he rode to his father Sir Ector, and said; 'Sir, lo here is the sword of the stone, wherefore I must be king of this land.'

When Sir Ector beheld the sword, he returned again and came to the church, and there they alit all three, and went into the church. And anon he made Sir Kay to swear upon a book how he came to that sword.

'Sir,' said Sir Kay, 'by my brother Arthur, for he brought it to me.'

'How gat ye this sword?' said Sir Ector to Arthur.

'Sir, I will tell you. When I came home for my brother's sword, I found nobody at home to deliver me his sword, and so I thought my brother Sir Kay should not be swordless, and so I came hither eagerly and pulled it out of the stone without any pain.'

'Found ye any knights about this sword?' said Sir Ector.

'Nay,' said Arthur.

'Now,' said Sir Ector to Arthur, 'I understand ye must be king of this land.'

'Wherefore I,' said Arthur, 'and for what cause?'

'Sir,' said Ector, 'for God will have it so, for there should never man have drawn out this sword, but he that shall be

lightly: easily. *wist*: knew.

rightwise king of this land. Now let me see whether ye can put the sword there as it was, and pull it out again.'

'That is no mastery,' said Arthur, and so he put it in the stone; therewithal Sir Ector assayed to pull out the sword and failed.

CHAPTER 6: *How King Arthur pulled out the sword divers times*

'Now assay,' said Sir Ector unto Sir Kay. And anon he pulled at the sword with all his might, but it would not be.

'Now shall ye assay,' said Sir Ector to Arthur.

'I will well,' said Arthur, and pulled it out easily. And therewithal Sir Ector knelt down to the earth, and Sir Kay.

'Alas,' said Arthur, 'my own dear father and brother, why kneel ye to me?'

'Nay, nay, my lord Arthur, it is not so, I was never your father nor of your blood, but I wot well ye are of an higher blood than I weened ye were.' And then Sir Ector told him all, how he was betaken him for to nourish him, and by whose commandment, and by Merlin's deliverance. Then Arthur made great dole when he understood that Sir Ector was not his father.

'Sir,' said Ector unto Arthur, 'will ye be my good and gracious lord when ye are king?'

'Else were I to blame,' said Arthur, 'for ye are the man in the world that I am most beholding to, and my good lady and mother your wife, that as well as her own hath fostered me and kept. And if ever it be God's will that I be king as ye say, ye shall desire of me what I may do, and I shall not fail you, God forbid I should fail you.'

'Sir,' said Sir Ector, 'I will ask no more of you, but that ye will make my son, your foster brother, Sir Kay, seneschal of all your lands.'

wot: know. *betaken*: entrusted. *dole*: lamentation.
seneschal: steward.

'That shall be done,' said Arthur, 'and more, by the faith of my body, that never man shall have that office but he, while he and I live.'

Therewithal they went unto the Archbishop, and told him how the sword was achieved, and by whom. And on Twelfth-day all the barons came thither, and to assay to take the sword, who that would assay. But there afore them all, there might none take it out but Arthur; wherefore there were many lords wroth, and said it was great shame unto them all and the realm, to be over-governed with a boy of no high blood born, and so they fell out at that time, that it was put off till Candlemas, and then all the barons should meet there again; but alway the ten knights were ordained to watch the sword day and night, and so they set a pavilion over the stone and the sword, and five always watched.

So at Candlemas many more great lords came thither for to have won the sword, but there might none prevail. And right as Arthur did at Christmas, he did at Candlemas, and pulled out the sword easily, whereof the barons were sore agrieved and put it off in delay till the high feast of Easter. And as Arthur sped before, so did he at Easter, yet there were some of the great lords had indignation that Arthur should be king, and put it off in a delay till the feast of Pentecost. Then the Archbishop of Canterbury by Merlin's providence let purvey then of the best knights that they might get, and such knights as Uther Pendragon loved best and most trusted in his days. And such knights were put about Arthur as Sir Baudwin of Britain, Sir Kay, Sir Ulfius, Sir Brastias. All these with many other, were always about Arthur, day and night, till the feast of Pentecost.

CHAPTER 7: *How King Arthur was crowned, and how he made officers*

And at the feast of Pentecost all manner of men assayed to pull at the sword that would assay, but none might prevail but Arthur, and pulled it out afore all the lords and commons that were there, wherefore all the commons cried at once, 'We will have Arthur unto our king; we will put him no more in delay, for we all see that it is God's will that he shall be our king, and who that holdeth against it, we will slay him.' And therewithal they kneeled at once, both rich and poor, and cried Arthur mercy because they had delayed him so long. And Arthur forgave them, and took the sword between both his hands, and offered it upon the altar where the Archbishop was, and so was he made knight of the best man that was there.

And so anon was the coronation made. And there was he sworn unto his lords and the commons for to be a true king, to stand with true justice from thenceforth the days of this life. Also then he made all lords that held of the crown to come in, and to do service as they ought to do. And many complaints were made unto Sir Arthur of great wrongs that were done since the death of King Uther, of many lands that were bereaved lords, knights, ladies, and gentlemen. Wherefore King Arthur made the lands to be given again unto them that ought them. When this was done, that the king had stablished all the countries about London, then he let make Sir Kay Seneschal of England; and Sir Baudwin of Britain was made constable; and Sir Ulfius was made chamberlain; and Sir Brastias was made warden to wait upon the north from Trent forwards, for it was that time the most part the king's enemies. But within few years after, Arthur won all the north, Scotland, and all that were under their obeissance. Also Wales, a part of it, held against Arthur, but he overcame them all, as he did the remnant, through the noble prowess of himself and his knights of the Round Table.[1]

ought them: owned them.

CHAPTER 8: *How King Arthur held in Wales, at a Pentecost, a great feast, and what kings and lords came to his feast*

Then the king removed into Wales, and let cry a great feast that it should be holden at Pentecost after the incoronation of him at the city of Caerleon. Unto the feast came King Lot of Lothian and of Orkney, with five hundred knights with him. Also there came to the feast King Uriens of Gore with four hundred knights with him. Also there came to that feast King Nentres of Garlot, with seven hundred knights with him. Also there came to the feast the King of Scotland with six hundred knights with him, and he was but a young man. Also there came to the feast a king that was called the King with the Hundred Knights, but he and his men were passing well beseen at all points. Also there came the King of Carados with five hundred knights.

And King Arthur was glad of their coming, for he weened that all the kings and knights had come for great love, and to have done him worship at his feast, wherefore the king made great joy, and sent the kings and knights great presents. But the kings would none receive, but rebuked the messengers shamefully, and said they had no joy to receive no gifts of a beardless boy that was come of low blood, and sent him word they would none of his gifts, but that they were come to give him gifts with hard swords betwixt the neck and the shoulders; and therefore they came thither, so they told to the messengers plainly, for it was great shame to all them to see such a boy to have a rule of so noble a realm as this land was. With this answer the messengers departed and told to King Arthur this answer. Wherefore, by the advice of his barons, he took him to a strong tower with five hundred good men with him; and all the kings aforesaid in a manner laid a siege tofore him, but King Arthur was well victualled.

And within fifteen days there came Merlin among them

holden: held. *well beseen*: good looking.

into the city of Caerleon. Then all the kings were passing glad of Merlin, and asked him, 'For what cause is that boy Arthur made your king?'

'Sirs,' said Merlin, 'I shall tell you the cause, for he is King Uther Pendragon's son, born in wedlock, gotten on Igraine, the Duke's wife of Tintagel.'

'Then is he a bastard,' they said all.

'Nay,' said Merlin, 'after the death of the duke, more than three hours, was Arthur begotten, and thirteen days after, King Uther wedded Igraine; and therefore I prove him he is no bastard, and who saith nay, he shall be king and overcome all his enemies; and, or he die, he shall be long king of all England, and have under his obeissance Wales, Ireland, and Scotland, and more realms than I will now rehearse.'

Some of the kings had marvel of Merlin's words, and deemed well that it should be as he said; and some of them laughed him to scorn, as King Lot; and more other called him a witch. But then were they accorded with Merlin, that King Arthur should come out and speak with the kings, and to come safe and to go safe, such surance there was made. So Merlin went unto King Arthur, and told him how he had done, and bad him fear not, 'but come out boldly and speak with them, and spare them not, but answer them as their king and chieftain, for ye shall overcome them all, whether they will or nill.'

CHAPTER 9: *Of the first war that King Arthur had, and how he won the field*

Then King Arthur came out of his tower, and had under his gown a jesseraunte of double mail, and there went with him the Archbishop of Canterbury, and Sir Baudwin of Britain, and Sir Kay, and Sir Brastias: these were the men of most worship that were with him. And when they were met

deemed: thought. *jesseraunte*: coat of armour.

there was no meekness, but stout words on both sides; but always King Arthur answered them, and said he would make them to bow and he lived. Wherefore they departed with wrath, and King Arthur bad keep them well, and they bad the king keep him well. So the king returned him to the tower again and armed him and all his knights.

'What will ye do?' said Merlin to the kings. 'Ye were better for to stint, for ye shall not here prevail though ye were ten so many.'

'Be we well advised to be afeared of a dream-reader?' said King Lot.

With that Merlin vanished away, and came to King Arthur, and bad him set on them fiercely. And in the meanwhile there were three hundred good men of the best that were with the kings, that went straight unto King Arthur and that comforted him greatly.

'Sir,' said Merlin to Arthur, 'fight not with the sword that ye had by miracle, till that ye see ye go unto the worse, then draw it out and do your best.'

So forthwithal King Arthur set upon them in their lodging. And Sir Baudwin, Sir Kay, and Sir Brastias slew on the right hand and on the left hand that it was marvel, and always King Arthur on horseback laid on with a sword, and did marvellous deeds of arms that many of the kings had great joy of his deeds and hardiness. Then King Lot brake out on the back side, and the King with the Hundred Knights, and King Carados, and set on Arthur fiercely behind him. With that Sir Arthur turned with his knights, and smote behind and before, and ever Sir Arthur was in the foremost press till his horse was slain underneath him. And therewith King Lot smote down King Arthur. With that his four knights received him and set him on horseback. Then he drew his sword Excalibur,[1] but it was so bright in his enemies' eyen, that it gave light like thirty torches. And therewith he put them aback, and slew much people. And then the commons of Caerleon arose with clubs and staves and slew many

stint: cease.

knights; but all the kings held them together with their knights that were left alive, and so fled and departed. And Merlin came unto Arthur, and counselled him to follow them no further.

CHAPTER 10: *How Merlin counselled King Arthur to send for King Ban and King Bors, and of their counsel taken for the war*

So after the feast and journey, King Arthur drew him unto London, and so by the counsel of Merlin, the king let call his barons to council, for Merlin had told the king that the six kings that made war upon him would in all haste be awroke on him and on his lands. Wherefore the king asked counsel at them all. They could no counsel give, but said they were big enough.

'Ye say well,' said Arthur; 'I thank you for your good courage, but will ye all that loveth me speak with Merlin? Ye know well that he hath done much for me, and he knoweth many things, and when he is afore you, I would that ye prayed him heartily of his best advice.' All the barons said they would pray him and desire him. So Merlin was sent for, and fair desired of all the barons to give them best counsel.

'I shall say you,' said Merlin, 'I warn you all, your enemies are passing strong for you, and they are good men of arms as be alive, and by this time they have gotten to them four kings more and a mighty duke; and unless that our king have more chivalry with him than he may make within the bounds of his own realm, and he fight with them in battle, he shall be overcome and slain.'

'What were best to do in this case?' said all the barons.

'I shall tell you,' said Merlin, 'mine advice: there are two brethren beyond the sea, and they be kings both and marvellous good men of their hands; and that one hight King Ban

awroke: avenged.

of Benwick, and that other hight King Bors of Gaul, that is France. And on these two kings warreth a mighty man of men, the King Claudas, and striveth with them for a castle, and great war is betwixt them; but this Claudas is so mighty of goods whereof he getteth good knights, that he putteth these two kings most part to[1] the worse; wherefore this is my counsel: that our king and sovereign lord send unto the kings Ban and Bors by two trusty knights with letters well devised, that and they will come and see King Arthur and his court, and so help him in his wars, that he will be sworn unto them to help them in their wars against King Claudas. Now, what say ye unto this counsel?' said Merlin.

'This is well counselled,' said the king and all the barons. Right so in all haste there were ordained to go two knights on the message unto the two kings. So were there made letters in the pleasant wise according unto King Arthur's desire.

Ulfius and Brastias were made the messengers, and so rode forth well horsed and well armed, and as the guise was that time, and so passed the sea and rode toward the city of Benwick. And there besides were eight knights that espied them, and at a strait passage they met with Ulfius and Brastias, and would have taken them prisoners; so they prayed them that they might pass, for they were messengers unto King Ban and Bors sent from King Arthur.

'Therefore,' said the eight knights, 'ye shall die or be prisoners, for we be knights of King Claudas.' And therewith two of them dressed their spears, and Ulfius and Brastias dressed their spears and ran together with great raundon and Claudas' knights brake their spears, and there to-held and bare the two knights out of their saddles to the earth, and so left them lying, and rode their ways. And the other six knights rode afore to a passage to meet with them again, and so Ulfius and Brastias smote other two down, and so passed on their ways. And at the fourth passage there met

guise: custom. *strait*: narrow. *dressed*: set in position.
raundon: force.

two for two, and both were laid unto the earth; so there was none of the eight knights but he was sore hurt or bruised.

And when they come to Benwick it fortuned there were both kings, Ban and Bors. And when it was told the kings that there were come messengers, there were sent unto them two knights of worship, the one hight Lionses, lord of the country of Payarne, and Sir Phariance, a worshipful knight. Anon they asked from whence they came, and they said from King Arthur, king of England; so they took them in their arms and made great joy each of other. But anon, as the two kings wist they were messengers of Arthur's, there was made no tarrying, but forthwith they spake with the knights, and welcomed them in the faithfullest wise, and said they were most welcome unto them before all the kings living. And therewith they kissed the letters and delivered them; and when Ban and Bors understood the letters, then they were more welcome than they were before.

And after the haste of the letters, they gave them this answer, that they would fulfil the desire of King Arthur's writing, and Ulfius and Brastias tarry there as long as they would, they should have such cheer as might be made them in those marches. Then Ulfius and Brastias told the king of the adventure at their passages of the eight knights.

'Ha! ah!' said Ban and Bors, 'they were my good friends. I would I had wist of them, they should not have escaped so.'

So Ulfius and Brastias had good cheer and great gifts as much as they might bear away, and had their answer by mouth and by writing, that those two kings would come unto Arthur in all the haste that they might.

So the two knights rode on afore, and passed the sea, and come to their lord, and told him how they had sped, whereof King Arthur was passing glad.

'At what time suppose ye the two kings will be here?'

'Sir,' said they, 'afore All Hallowmass.'

Then the king let purvey for a great feast, and let cry a great jousts. And by All Hallowmass the two kings were

let purvey: had preparations made. *let cry*: had announced.

come over the sea with three hundred knights well arrayed both for the peace and for the war. And King Arthur met with them ten mile out of London, and there was great joy as could be thought or made.

And on All Hallowmass at the great feast, sat in the hall the three kings, and Sir Kay Seneschal served in the hall, and Sir Lucan the Butler, that was Duke Corneus' son, and Sir Griflet, that was the son of Cardol; these three knights had the rule of all the service that served the kings. And anon, as they had washen and risen, all knights that would joust made them ready. By then they were ready on horseback there were seven hundred knights. And Arthur, Ban, and Bors, with the Archbishop of Canterbury, and Sir Ector, Kay's father, they were in a place covered with cloth of gold like an hall, with ladies and gentlewomen, for to behold who did best, and thereon to give judgement.

CHAPTER 11: *Of a great tourney made by King Arthur and the two Kings Ban and Bors, and how they went over the sea*

And King Arthur and the two kings let depart the seven hundred knights in two parties. And there were three hundred knights of the realm of Benwick and of Gaul turned on the other side. Then they dressed their shields, and began to couch their spears, many good knights. So Griflet was the first that met with a knight, one Ladinas, and they met so eagerly that all men had wonder; and they so fought that their shields fell to pieces, and horse and man fell to the earth; and both the French knight and the English knight lay so long that all men weened they had been dead.

When Lucan the Butler saw Griflet so lie, he horsed him again anon, and they two did marvellous deeds of arms with many bachelors. Also Sir Kay came out of an ambushment with five knights with him, and they six smote other six

couch: lower for attack. *bachelors*: young knights.

down. But Sir Kay did that day marvellous deeds of arms that there was none did so well as he that day. Then there came Ladinas and Gracian, two knights of France, and did passing well, that all men praised them. Then came there Sir Placidas, a good knight, and met with Sir Kay, and smote him down horse and man, wherefore Sir Griflet was wroth, and met with Sir Placidas so hard, that horse and man fell to the earth. But when the five knights wist that Sir Kay had a fall, they were wroth out of wit, and therewith each of them five bare down a knight.

When King Arthur and the two kings saw them begin wax wroth on both parties, they leapt on small hackneys, and let cry that all men should depart unto their lodging. And so they went home and unarmed them, and so to evensong and supper. And after, the three kings went into a garden, and gave the prize unto Sir Kay, and to Lucan the Butler, and unto Sir Griflet. And then they went unto council, and with them Gwenbaus, the brother unto Sir Ban and Bors, a wise clerk, and thither went Ulfius and Brastias, and Merlin. And after they had been in council, they went unto bed.

And on the morn they heard mass, and to dinner, and so to their council, and made many arguments what were best to do. At the last they were concluded, that Merlin should go with a token of King Ban, and that was a ring, unto his men and King Bors'; and Gracian and Placidas should go again and keep their castles and their countries, as for King Ban of Benwick, and King Bors of Gaul had ordained them, and so passed the sea and came to Benwick. And when the people saw King Ban's ring, and Gracian and Placidas, they were glad, and asked how the kings fared, and made great joy of their welfare and cording, and according unto the sovereign lords' desire, the men of war made them ready in all haste possible, so that they were fifteen thousand on horse and foot, and they had great plenty of victual with them, by Merlin's provision. But Gracian and Placidas were left to furnish and garnish the castles, for dread of King Claudas.

cording: agreement.

Right so Merlin passed the sea well victualled both by water and by land. And when he came to the sea he sent home the foot men again, and took no more with him but ten thousand men on horseback, the most part men of arms, and so shipped and passed the sea into England and landed at Dover. And through the wit of Merlin, he[1] led the host northward, the priviest way that could be thought, unto the Forest of Bedegraine, and there in a valley he lodged them secretly. Then rode Merlin unto Arthur and the two kings, and told them how he had sped, whereof they had great marvel, that man on earth might speed so soon, and go and come. So Merlin told them ten thousand were in the Forest of Bedegraine, well armed at all points. Then was there no more to say, but to horseback went all the host as Arthur had afore purveyed. So with twenty thousand he passed by night and day. But there was made such an ordinance afore by Merlin, that there should no man of war ride nor go in no country on this side Trent water, but if he had a token from King Arthur, where through the king's enemies durst not ride as they did tofore to espy.

CHAPTER 12: *How eleven kings gathered a great host against King Arthur*

And so within a little space the three kings came unto the Castle of Bedegraine, and found there a passing fair fellowship, and well beseen, wherof they had great joy, and victual they wanted none.

This was the cause of the northern host: that they were reared for the despite and rebuke the six kings had at Caerleon. And those six kings by their means, gat unto them five other kings; and thus they began to gather their people; and how they sware that for weal nor woe, they should not leave other, till they had destroyed Arthur. And then they made an oath. The first that began the oath was the Duke of

sped: got on. *leave other*: leave each other.

Cambenet, that he would bring with him five thousand men of arms, the which were ready on horseback. Then sware King Brandegoris of Strangore that he would bring five thousand men of arms on horseback. Then sware King Clarivaus of Northumberland he would bring three thousand men of arms. Then sware the King of the Hundred Knights, that was a passing good man and a young, that he would bring four thousand men of arms on horseback. Then there swore King Lot, a passing good knight, and Sir Gawain's father, that he would bring five thousand men of arms on horseback. Also there swore King Uriens, that was Sir Uwain's father, of the land of Gore, and he would bring six thousand men of arms on horseback. Also there swore King Idres of Cornwall, that he would bring five thousand men of arms on horseback. Also there swore King Cradelment to bring five thousand men on horseback. Also there swore King Agwisance of Ireland to bring five thousand men of arms on horseback. Also there swore King Nentres to bring five thousand men of arms on horseback. Also there swore King Carados to bring five thousand men of arms on horseback. So their whole host was of clean men of arms on horseback fifty thousand, and a-foot ten thousand, of good men's bodies. Then were they soon ready, and mounted upon horse and sent forth their fore-riders, for these eleven kings in their ways laid a siege unto the Castle of Bedegraine; and so they departed and drew toward Arthur, and left few to abide at the siege, for the Castle of Bedegraine was holden of King Arthur, and the men that were therein were Arthur's.

CHAPTER 13: *Of a dream of the King with the Hundred Knights*

So by Merlin's advice there were sent fore-riders to skim the country, and they met with the fore-riders of the north, and made them to tell which way the host came, and then

clean: excellent.

they told it to Arthur, and by King Ban and Bors' counsel they let burn and destroy all the country afore them, there they should ride.

The King with the Hundred Knights mette a wonder dream two nights afore the battle, that there blew a great wind, and blew down their castles and their towns, and after that came a water and bare it all away. All that heard of the sweven said it was a token of great battle. Then by counsel of Merlin, when they wist which way the eleven kings would ride and lodge that night, at midnight they set upon them, as they were in their pavilions. But the scout-watch by their host cried, 'Lords! at arms! for here be your enemies at your hand!'

CHAPTER 14: *How the eleven kings with their host fought against Arthur and his host, and many great feats of the war*

Then King Arthur and King Ban and King Bors, with their good and trusty knights, set on them so fiercely that he made them overthrow their pavilions on their heads, but the eleven kings, by manly prowess of arms, took a fair champaign, but there was slain that morrowtide ten thousand good men's bodies. And so they had afore them a strong passage, yet were they fifty thousand of hardy men. Then it drew toward day.

'Now shall ye do by mine advice,' said Merlin unto the three kings: 'I would that King Ban and King Bors, with their fellowship of ten thousand men, were put in a wood here beside, in an ambushment, and keep them privy, and that they be laid or the light of the day come, and that they stir not till ye and your knights have fought with them long. And when it is daylight, dress your battle even afore them and the passage, that they may see all your host, for then will they be the more hardy, when they see you but about

mette: dreamed. *sweven*: dream. *champaign*: field.
strong passage: difficult way.

twenty thousand, and cause them to be the gladder to suffer you and your host to come over the passage.' All the three kings and the whole barons said that Merlin said passingly well, and it was done anon as Merlin had devised.

So on the morn, when either host saw other, the host of the north was well comforted. Then to Ulfius and Brastias were delivered three thousand men of arms, and they set on them fiercely in the passage, and slew on the right hand and on the left hand that it was wonder to tell. When that the eleven kings saw that there was so few a fellowship did such deeds of arms, they were ashamed and set on them again fiercely. And there was Sir Ulfius' horse slain under him, but he did marvellously well on foot. But the Duke Eustace of Cambenet and King Clarivaus of Northumberland were alway grievous on Ulfius. Then Brastias saw his fellow fared so withal, he smote the duke with a spear, that horse and man fell down. That saw King Clarivaus and returned unto Brastias, and either smote other so that horse and man went to the earth, and so they lay long astonied, and their horses' knees brast to the hard bone.

Then came Sir Kay the Seneschal with six fellows with him, and did passing well. With that came the eleven kings, and there was Griflet put to the earth, horse and man, and Lucan the Butler, horse and man, by King Brandegoris, and King Idres, and King Agwisance. Then waxed the medley passing hard on both parties.

When Sir Kay saw Griflet on foot, he rode on King Nentres and smote him down, and led his horse unto Sir Griflet, and horsed him again. Also Sir Kay with the same spear smote down King Lot, and hurt him passing sore. That saw the King with the Hundred Knights, and ran unto Sir Kay and smote him down, and took his horse, and gave him King Lot, whereof he said 'Gramercy'. When Sir Griflet saw Sir Kay and Lucan the Butler on foot, he took a sharp spear,

fared so withal: treated in such a way. *astonied*: stunned.
brast: burst. *medley*: conflict. *Gramercy*: many thanks.

great and square, and rode to Pinel, a good man of arms, and smote horse and man down, and then he took his horse, and gave him unto Sir Kay.

Then King Lot saw King Nentres on foot, he ran unto Melot de la Roche, and smote him down, horse and man, and gave King Nentres the horse, and horsed him again. Also the King of the Hundred Knights saw King Idres on foot, then he ran unto Gwinas de Bloi, and smote him down, horse and man, and gave King Idres the horse, and horsed him again; and King Lot smote down Clariance de la Forest Savage, and gave the horse unto Duke Eustace. And so when they had horsed the kings again they drew them all eleven kings together, and said they would be revenged of the damage that they had taken that day.

The meanwhile came in Sir Ector with an eager countenance, and found Ulfius and Brastias on foot, in great peril of death, that were foul defiled under horse feet. Then King Arthur as a lion ran unto King Cradelment of North Wales, and smote him through the left side, that the horse and the king fell down; and then he took the horse by the rein, and led him unto Ulfius, and said, 'Have this horse, mine old friend, for great need hast thou of horse.'

'Gramercy,' said Ulfius.

Then Sir Arthur did so marvellously in arms, that all men had wonder. When the King with the Hundred Knights saw King Cradelment on foot, he ran unto Sir Ector, that was well horsed, Sir Kay's father, and smote horse and man down, and gave the horse unto the king, and horsed him again; and when King Arthur saw the king ride on Sir Ector's horse, he was wroth and with his sword he smote the king on the helm, that a quarter of the helm and shield fell down, and the sword carved down unto the horse's neck, and so the king and the horse fell down to the ground. Then Sir Kay came unto Sir Morganor, seneschal with the King of the Hundred Knights, and smote him down, horse and man, and led the horse unto his father, Sir Ector; then Sir Ector ran unto a knight, hight

defiled: afflicted.

Lardans, and smote horse and man down, and led the horse unto Sir Brastias, that great need had of an horse, and was greatly defiled. When Brastias beheld Lucan the Butler, that lay like a dead man under the horse's feet, and ever Sir Griflet did marvellously for to rescue him, and there were always fourteen knights on Sir Lucan, and then Brastias smote one of them on the helm, that it went to the teeth, and he rode to another and smote him, that the arm flew into the field; then he went to the third and smote him on the shoulder, that shoulder and arm flew in the field. And when Griflet saw rescues, he smote a knight on the temples, that head and helm went to the earth, and Griflet took the horse of that knight, and led him unto Sir Lucan, and bad him mount upon the horse and revenge his hurts. For Brastias had slain a knight tofore and horsed Griflet.

CHAPTER 15: *Yet of the same battle*

Then Lucan saw King Agwisance, that late had slain Moris de la Roche,[1] and Lucan ran to him with a short spear that was great, that he gave him such a fall, that the horse fell down to the earth. Also Lucan found there on foot Bellias of Flanders and Sir Gwinas, two hardy knights, and in that woodness that Lucan was in, he slew two bachelors and horsed them again. Then waxed the battle passing hard on both parties, but Arthur was glad that his knights were horsed again, and then they fought together, that the noise and sound rang by the water and the wood. Wherefore King Ban and King Bors made them ready and dressed their shields and harness, and they were so courageous that many knights shook and bevered for eagerness.

All this while Lucan, and Gwinas, and Brian, and Bellias of Flanders, held strong medley against six kings, that was King Lot, King Nentres, King Brandegoris, King Idres, King Uriens, and King Agwisance. So with the help of Sir Kay and

woodness: madness. *bevered*: trembled. *eagerness*: fierceness.

of Sir Griflet they held these six kings hard, that unnethe they had any power to defend them. But when Sir Arthur saw the battle would not be ended by no manner, he fared wood as a lion, and steered his horse here and there, on the right hand, and on the left hand, that he stint not till he had slain twenty knights. Also he wounded King Lot sore on the shoulder and made him to leave that ground, for Sir Kay and Griflet did with King Arthur there great deeds of arms.

Then Ulfius, and Brastias, and Sir Ector encountered against the Duke Eustace, and King Cradelment, and King Clarivaus of Northumberland, and King Carados, and against the King with the Hundred Knights. So these knights encountered with these kings, that they made them to avoid the ground. Then King Lot made great dole for his damages and his fellows, and said unto the ten kings, 'But if ye will do as I devise we shall be slain and destroyed. Let me have the King with the Hundred Knights, and King Agwisance, and King Idres, and the Duke of Cambenet, and we five kings will have fifteen thousand men of arms with us, and we will go apart while ye six kings hold medley with twelve thousand; and we see that ye have foughten with them long, then will we come on fiercely, and else shall we never match them,' said King Lot, 'but by this mean.' So they departed as they here devised, and six kings made their party strong against Arthur, and made great war long.

In the meanwhile brake the ambushment of King Ban and King Bors, and Lionses and Phariance had the avant-guard, and they two knights met with King Idres and his fellowship, and there began a great medley of breaking of spears, and smiting of swords, with slaying of men and horses, and King Idres was near at discomfiture. That saw Agwisance the king, and put Lionses and Phariance in point of death; for the Duke of Cambenet came on withal with a great fellowship, so these two knights were in great danger of their lives that they were fain to return, but always they rescued themselves and their fellowship marvellously. When King Bors

unnethe: scarcely. *fared*: behaved. *avoid*: leave.

saw those knights put aback, it grieved him sore; then he came on so fast that his fellowship seemed as black as Inde.

When King Lot had espied King Bors, he knew him well, then he said, 'O Jehu, defend us from death and horrible maims! For I see well we be in great peril of death; for I see yonder a king, one of the most worshipfullest men, and the best knights[2] of the world be inclined unto his fellowship.'

'What is he?' said the King with the Hundred Knights.

'It is,' said King Lot, 'King Bors of Gaul; I marvel how they come into this country without witting of us all.'

'It was by Merlin's advice,' said the knight.

'As for him,' said King Carados, 'I will encounter with King Bors, and ye will rescue me when mister is.'

'Go on,' said they all, 'we will do all that we may.'

Then King Carados and his host rode on a soft pace, till that they come as nigh King Bors as bow-draught, then either battle let their horse run as fast as they might. And Bleoberis[3] that was godson unto King Bors he bare his chief standard, that was a passing good knight.

'Now shall we see,' said King Bors, 'how these northern Britons can bear the arms;' and King Bors encountered with a knight, and smote him throughout with a spear that he fell dead unto the earth, and after drew hiss word and did marvellous deeds of arms, that all parties had great wonder thereof. And his knights failed not, but did their part, and King Carados was smitten to the earth. With that came the King with the Hundred Knights and rescued King Carados mightily by force of arms, for he was a passing good knight of a king, and but a young man.

CHAPTER 16

By then came into the field King Ban as fierce as a lion, with bands of green and thereupon gold.

'Ha! ah!' said King Lot, 'we must be discomfit, for yonder

maims: wounds. *witting*: knowledge. *mister*: need.

I see the most valiant knight of the world, and the man of the most renown, for such two brethren as is King Ban and King Bors are not living, wherefore we must needs void or die; and but if we avoid manly and wisely there is but death.'

When King Ban came into the battle, he came in so fiercely that the strokes redounded again from the wood and the water; wherefore King Lot wept for pity and dole that he saw so many good knights take their end. But through the great force of King Ban they made both the northern battles that were departed burtled together for great dread, and the three kings and their knights slew on ever, that it was pity on to behold that multitude of the people that fled.

But King Lot, and King of the Hundred Knights, and King Morganor gathered the people together passing knightly, and did great prowess of arms, and held the battle all that day, like hard. When the King of the Hundred Knights beheld the great damage that King Ban did, he thrust unto him with his horse, and smote him high upon the helm, a great stroke, and stonied him sore. Then King Ban was wroth with him, and followed on him fiercely; the other saw that, and cast up his shield, and spurred his horse forward, but the stroke of King Ban fell down and carved a cantel off the shield, and the sword slid down by the hauberk behind his back, and cut through the trapper of steel and the horse even in two pieces, that the sword felt the earth. Then the King of the Hundred Knights voided the horse lightly, and with his sword he broached the horse of King Ban through and through. With that King Ban voided lightly from the dead horse, and then King Ban smote at the other so eagerly, and smote him on the helm, that he fell to the earth. Also in that ire he felled King Morganor, and there was great slaughter of good knights and much people.

By then came into the press King Arthur, and found King Ban standing among dead men and dead horse, fighting on foot as a wood lion, that there came none nigh him as far as

dole: sorrow. *like hard*: equally hard. *cantel*: piece.
trapper: trapping. *lightly*: quickly. *broached*: pierced.

he might reach with his sword but he caught a grievous buffet; whereof King Arthur had great pity. And Arthur was so bloody, that by his shield there might no man know him, for all was blood and brains on his sword. And as Arthur looked by him he saw a knight that was passingly well horsed, and therewith Sir Arthur ran to him, and smote him on the helm, that his sword went unto his teeth, and the knight sank down to the earth dead, and anon Arthur took the horse by the rein, and led him unto King Ban, and said, 'Fair brother, have this horse, for ye have great mister thereof, and me repenteth sore of your great damage.'

'It shall be soon revenged,' said King Ban, 'for I trust in God mine eure is not such but some of them may sore repent this.'

'I will well,' said Arthur, 'for I see your deeds full actual; nevertheless, I might not come at you at that time.'

But when King Ban was mounted on horseback, then there began new battle the which was sore and hard, and passing great slaughter. And so through great force King Arthur, King Ban, and King Bors made their knights a little to withdraw them. But alway the eleven kings with their chivalry never turned back; and so withdrew them to a little wood, and so over a little river, and there they rested them, for on the night they might have no rest on the field. And then the eleven kings and knights put them on a heap all together, as men adread and out of all comfort. But there was no man might pass them, they held them so hard together both behind and before, that King Arthur had marvel of their deeds of arms, and was passing wroth.

'Ah, Sir Arthur,' said King Ban and King Bors, 'blame them not, for they do as good men ought to do.'

'For, by my faith,' said King Ban, 'they are the best fighting men, and knights of most prowess, that ever I saw or heard speak of, and those eleven kings are men of great worship; and if they were longing unto you there were no king

eure: fortune.

under the heaven had such eleven knights, and of such worship.'

'I may not love them,' said Arthur, 'they would destroy me.'

'That wot we well,' said King Ban and King Bors, 'for they are your mortal enemies, and that hath been proved aforehand, and this day they have done their part, and that is great pity of their wilfulness.'

Then all the eleven kings drew them together, and then said King Lot, 'Lords, ye must other ways than ye do, or else the great loss is behind; ye may see what people we have lost, and what good men we lose, because we wait always on these foot-men, and ever in saving of one of the foot-men we lose ten horsemen for him; therefore this is mine advice: let us put our foot-men from us, for it is near night, for the noble Arthur will not tarry on the foot-men, for they may save themselves, the wood is near hand. And when we horsemen be together, look every each of you kings let make such ordinance that none break upon pain of death. And who that seeth any man dress him to flee, lightly that he be slain, for it is better that we slay a coward, than through a coward all we to be slain. How say ye?' said King Lot, 'Answer me all ye kings.'

'It is well said,' quoth King Nentres; so said the King of the Hundred Knights; the same said the King Carados, and King Uriens; so did King Idres and King Brandegoris: and so did King Cradelment, and the Duke of Cambenet; the same said King Clarivaus and King Agwisance, and sware they would never fail other, neither for life nor for death. And whoso that fled, but did as they did, should be slain. Then they amended their harness, and righted their shields, and took new spears and set them on their thighs, and stood still as it had been a plumb of wood.

plumb: block.

CHAPTER 17: *Yet more of the said battle, and how it was ended by Merlin*

When Sir Arthur and King Ban and Bors beheld them and all their knights, they praised them much for their noble cheer of chivalry, for the hardiest fighters that ever they heard or saw. With that, there dressed them a forty noble knights, and said unto the three kings, they would break their battle; these were their names: Lionses, Phariance, Ulfius, Brastias, Ector, Kay, Lucan the Butler, Griflet le Fise de Dieu, Moris de la Roche, Gwinas de Bloi, Brian de la Forest Savage, Bellias, Morians of the Castle of Maidens, Flannedrius of the Castle of Ladies, Annecians that was King Bors' godson, a noble knight, Ladinas de la Rouse, Emerause, Caulas, Gracian le Castlein, one Blois de la Case, and Sir Colgrevaunce de Gore. All these knights rode on afore with spears on their thighs, and spurred their horses mightily as the horses might run. And the eleven kings with part of their knights rushed with their horses as fast as they might with their spears, and there they did on both parts marvellous deeds of arms. So came into the thick of the press, Arthur, Ban, and Bors, and slew down right on both hands, that their horses went in blood up to the fetlocks. But ever the eleven kings and their host was ever in the visage of Arthur. Wherefore Ban and Bors had great marvel, considering the great slaughter that there was, but at the last they were driven aback over a little river.

With that came Merlin on a great black horse, and said unto Arthur, 'Thou hast never done, hast thou not done enough? Of three score thousand this day has thou left alive but fifteen thousand, and it is time to say "Ho!" For God is wroth with thee, that thou wilt never have done, for yonder eleven kings at this time will not be overthrown, but and thou tarry on them any longer, thy fortune will turn and they shall increase. And therefore withdraw you unto your lodging, and rest you as soon as ye may, and reward your

cheer: appearance.

good knights with gold and with silver, for they have well deserved it; there may no riches be too dear for them, for of so few men as ye have, there were never men did more of prowess than they have done today, for ye have matched this day with the best fighters of the world.'

'That is truth,' said King Ban and Bors.

'Also,' said Merlin, 'withdraw you where ye list, for this three year I dare undertake they shall not dere you; and by then ye shall hear new tidings.' And then Merlin said unto Arthur, 'These eleven kings have more on hand than they are ware of, for the Saracens are landed in their countries, more than forty thousand, that burn and slay, and have laid siege at the Castle Wandesborow, and make great destruction; therefore dread you not this three year. Also, sir, all the goods that be gotten at this battle, let it be searched, and when ye have it in your hands, let it be given freely unto these two kings, Ban and Bors, that they may reward their knights withal; and that shall cause strangers to be of better will to do you service at need. Also ye be able to reward your own knights of your own goods whensomever it liketh you.'

'It is well said,' quoth Arthur, 'and as thou hast devised, so shall it be done.'

When it was delivered to Ban and Bors, they gave the goods as freely to their knights as freely as it was given to them. Then Merlin took his leave of Arthur and of the two kings, for to go and see his master Bleise, that dwelt in Northumberland; and so he departed and came to his master, that was passing glad of his coming.

And there he told how Arthur and the two kings had sped at the great battle, and how it was ended, and told the names of every king and knight of worship that was there. And so Bleise wrote the battle word by word, as Merlin told him how it began, and by whom, and in likewise how it was ended, and who had the worse. All the battles that were done in Arthur's days, Merlin did his master Bleise do write; also he did do

did his master Bleise do write: told his master Bleise to write.
shall not dere you: shall not harm you.

write all the battles that every worthy knight did of Arthur's court.

After this Merlin departed from his master and came to King Arthur, that was in the Castle of Bedegraine, that was one of the castles that standen in the Forest of Sherwood. And Merlin was so disguised that King Arthur knew him not, for he was all befurred in black sheep skins, and a great pair of boots, and a bow and arrows, in a russet gown, and brought wild geese in his hand, and it was on the morn after Candlemas day; but King Arthur knew him not.

'Sir,' said Merlin unto the king, 'will ye give me a gift?'

'Wherefore,' said King Arthur, 'should I give thee a gift, churl?'

'Sir,' said Merlin, 'ye were better to give me a gift that is not in your hand than to lose great riches, for here in the same place there the great battle was, is great treasure hid in the earth.'

'Who told thee so, churl?' said Arthur.

'Merlin told me so,' said he.

Then Ulfius and Brastias knew him well enough, and smiled. 'Sir,' said these two knights, 'it is Merlin that so speaketh unto you.'

Then King Arthur was greatly abashed, and had marvel of Merlin, and so had King Ban and King Bors, and so they had great disport at him.

So in the meanwhile there came a damosel that was an earl's daughter: his name was Sanam, and her name was Lionors, a passing fair damosel; and so she came thither for to do homage, as other lords did after the great battle. And King Arthur set his love greatly upon her, and so did she upon him, and the king had ado with her, and gat on her a child: his name was Borre, that was after a good knight, and of the Table Round.

Then there came word that the King Rience of North Wales made great war on King Leodegrance of Camelerd, for the which thing Arthur was wroth, for he loved him

damosel: maiden.

well, and hated King Rience, for he was alway against him. So by ordinance of the three kings that were sent home unto Benwick, all they would depart for dread of King Claudas: and Phariance, and Antemes, and Gracian, and Lionses of Payarne, with the leaders of those that should keep the king's lands.

CHAPTER 18: *How King Arthur, King Ban, and King Bors rescued King Leodegrance, and other incidents*

And then King Arthur, and King Ban, and King Bors departed with their fellowship, a twenty thousand, and came within six days into the country of Camelerd, and there rescued King Leodegrance, and slew there much people of King Rience, unto the number of ten thousand men, and put him to flight.

And then had these three kings great cheer of King Leodegrance, that thanked them of their great goodness, that they would revenge him of his enemies; and there had Arthur the first sight of Guenever, the king's daughter of Camelerd, and ever after he loved her. After, they were wedded, as it telleth in the book. So, briefly to make an end, they took their leave to go into their own countries, for King Claudas did great destruction on their lands.

'Then' said Arthur, 'I will go with you.'

'Nay,' said the kings, 'ye shall not at this time, for ye have much to do yet in these lands, therefore we will depart, and with the great goods that we have gotten in these lands by your gifts, we shall wage good knights and withstand the King Claudas' malice, for by the grace of God, and we have need we shall send to you for your succour; and if ye have need, send for us, and we will not tarry, by the faith of our bodies.'

'It shall not,' said Merlin, 'need that these two kings come again in the way of war, but I know well King Arthur may

wage: pay.

not be long from you, for within a year or two ye shall have great need, and then shall he revenge you on your enemies, as ye have done on his. For these eleven kings shall die all in a day, by the great might and prowess of arms of two valiant knights,' (as it telleth after) 'their names be Balin le Savage, and Balan, his brother, that be marvellous good knights as be any living.'

Now turn we to the eleven kings that returned unto a city that hight Sorhaute, the which city was within King Uriens', and there they refreshed them as well as they might, and made leeches search their wounds, and sorrowed greatly for the death of their people.

With that there came a messenger and told how there was comen into their lands people that were lawless as well as Saracens, a forty thousand, 'and have burnt and slain all the people that they may come by, without mercy, and have laid siege on the Castle of Wandesborow.'

'Alas,' said the eleven kings, 'here is sorrow upon sorrow, and if we had not warred against Arthur as we have done, he would soon revenge us; as for King Leodegrance, he loveth Arthur better than us, and as for King Rience, he hath enough to do with Leodegrance, for he hath laid siege unto him.' So they consented together to keep all the marches of Cornwall, of Wales, and of the north.

So first, they put King Idres in the city of Nantes in Brittany, with four thousand men of arms, to watch both the water and the land. Also they put in the city of Windesan, King Nentres of Garlot, with four thousand knights to watch both on water and on land. Also they had of other men of war more than eight thousand, for to fortify all the fortresses in the marches of Cornwall. Also they put more knights in all the marches of Wales and Scotland, with many good men of arms, and so they kept them together the space of three year, and ever allied them with mighty kings and dukes and lords. And to them fell King Rience of North Wales, the which was a mighty man of men, and Nero that was a mighty

leeches: physicians.

man of men. And all this while they furnished them and garnished them of good men of arms, and victual, and of all manner of habiliment that pretendeth to the war, to avenge them for the battle of Bedegraine, as it telleth in the book of adventures following.

~

CHAPTER 19: *How King Arthur rode to Caerleon, and of his dream, and how he saw the Questing Beast*

Then after the departing of King Ban and of King Bors, King Arthur rode unto Caerleon. And thither came to him King Lot's wife, of Orkney, in manner of a message, but she was sent thither to espy the court of King Arthur; and she came richly beseen, with her four sons Gawain, Gaheris, Agravain, and Gareth, with many other knights and ladies. For she was a passing fair lady, wherefor the king cast great love unto her, and desired to lie by her. So they were agreed, and he begat upon her Mordred, and she was his sister, on the mother side, Igraine. So there she rested her a month, and at the last departed.

Then the king dreamed a marvellous dream whereof he was sore adread. But all this time King Arthur knew not that King Lot's wife was his sister. Thus was the dream of Arthur:

Him thought there was come into this land griffins and serpents, and him thought they burnt and slew all the people in the land, and then him thought he fought with them, and they did him passing great harm, and wounded him full sore, but at the last he slew them.

When the king awaked, he was passing heavy of his dream, and so to put it out of thoughts, he made him ready with many knights to ride on hunting. As soon as he was in the forest the king saw a great hart afore him.

'This hart will I chase,' said King Arthur, and so he spurred the horse, and rode after long, and so by fine force oft he was

pretendeth: pertains.

like to have smitten the hart; whereas the king had chased the hart so long, that his horse had lost his breath, and fell down dead; then a yeoman fetched the king another horse. So the king saw the hart ambushed, and his horse dead; he set him down by a fountain, and there he fell in great thoughts.

And as he sat so, him thought he heard a noise of hounds, to the sum of thirty. And with that the king saw coming toward him the strangest beast that ever he saw or heard of. So the beast went to the well and drank, and the noise was in the beast's belly like unto the questing of thirty couple hounds; but all the while the beast drank there was no noise in the beast's belly; and therewith the beast departed with a great noise, whereof the king had great marvel. And so he was in a great thought, and therewith he fell asleep.

Right so there came a knight afoot unto Arthur and said, 'Knight full of thought and sleepy, tell me if thou sawest a strange beast pass this way.'

'Such one saw I,' said King Arthur, 'that is past two mile; what would ye with the beast?' said Arthur.

'Sir, I have followed that beast long time, and killed mine horse, so would God I had another to follow my quest.'

Right so came one with the king's horse, and when the knight saw the horse, he prayed the king to give him the horse: 'for I have followed this quest this twelvemonth, and either I shall achieve him, or bleed of the best blood of my body.'

Pellinor, that time king, followed the Questing Beast, and after his death Sir Palomides followed it.

CHAPTER 20: *How King Pellinor took Arthur's horse and followed the Questing Beast, and how Merlin met with Arthur*

'Sir knight,' said the king 'leave that quest and suffer me to have it, and I will follow it another twelvemonth.'

'Ah, fool,' said the knight unto Arthur, 'it is in vain thy desire, for it shall never be achieved but by me, or my next kin.' Therewith he start unto the king's horse and mounted into the saddle, and said, 'Gramercy, this horse is my own.'

'Well,' said the king, 'thou mayst take mine horse by force, but and I might prove thee whether thou were better on horseback or I.'[1]

'Well,' said the knight, 'seek me here when thou wilt, and here nigh this well thou shalt find me,' and so passed on his way.

Then the king sat in a study, and bad his men fetch his horse as fast as ever they might. Right so came by him Merlin like a child of fourteen year of age, and saluted the king, and asked him why he was so pensive.

'I may well be pensive' said the king, 'for I have seen the marvellest sight that ever I saw.'

'That know I well,' said Merlin, 'as well as thyself, and of all thy thoughts, but thou art but a fool to take thought, for it will not amend thee. Also I know what thou art, and who was thy father, and of whom thou were begotten; King Uther Pendragon was thy father, and begat thee on Igraine.'

'That is false' said King Arthur, 'How shouldest thou know it, for thou art not so old of years to know my father?'

'Yes,' said Merlin, 'I know it better than ye or any man living.'

'I will not believe thee,' said Arthur, and was wroth with the child.

So departed Merlin, and came again in the likeness of an old man of fourscore year of age, whereof the king was right glad, for he seemed to be right wise. Then said the old man, 'Why are ye so sad?'

'I may well be heavy,' said Arthur, 'for many things. Also here was a child, and told me many things that meseemeth he should not know, for he was not of age to know my father.'

'Yes,' said the old man, 'the child told you truth, and more would he have told you and ye would have suffered him. But ye have done a thing late that God is displeased with you, for ye have lain by your sister, and on her ye have gotten a child that shall destroy you and all the knights of your realm.'

'What are ye,' said Arthur, 'that tell me these tidings?'

'I am Merlin, and I was he in the child's likeness.'

'Ah,' said King Arthur, 'ye are a marvellous man, but I marvel much of thy words that I must die in battle.'

'Marvel not,' said Merlin, 'for it is God's will your body to be punished for your foul deeds. But I may well be sorry,' said Merlin, 'for I shall die a shameful death to be put in the earth quick, and ye shall die a worshipful death.' And as they talked this, came one with the king's horse, and so the king mounted on his horse, and Merlin on another, and so rode unto Caerleon.

And anon the king asked Ector and Ulfius how he was begotten, and they told him Uther Pendragon was his father and Queen Igraine his mother.[2] Then he said to Merlin, 'I will that my mother be sent for, that I may speak with her; and if she say so herself, then will I believe it.'

In all haste, the queen was sent for, and she came and brought with her Morgan le Fay, her daughter, that was as fair a lady as any might be, and the king welcomed Igraine in the best manner.

CHAPTER 21: *How Ulfius apeached Queen Igraine, Arthur's mother, of treason; and how a knight came and desired to have the death of his master revenged*

Right so came Ulfius, and said openly that the king and all might hear that wer efeasted that day, 'Ye are the falsest lady of the world, and the most traitress unto the king's person.'

'Beware,' said Arhur, 'what thou sayest; thou speakest a great word.'

'I am well ware,' said Ulfius, 'what I speak, and here is my glove to prove it upon any man that will say the contrary, that this Queen Igraine is causer of your great damage, and of your great war. For, and she would have uttered it in the life of King Uther Pendragon, of the birth of you, and how ye were begotten, ye had never had the mortal wars that ye have had; for the most part of your barons of your realm knew never whose son ye were, nor of whom ye were begotten; and she that bare you of her body should have made it known openly in excusing of her worship and yours, and in likewise to all the realm, wherefore I prove her false to God and to you and to all your realm, and who will say the contrary I will prove it on his body.'

Then spake Igraine and said, 'I am a woman and I may not fight, but rather than I should be dishonoured, there would some good man take my quarrel. More,' she said, 'Merlin knoweth well, and ye Sir Ulfius, how King Uther came to me in the Castle of Tintagel in the likeness of my lord, that was dead three hours tofore, and thereby gat a child that night upon me. And after the thirteenth day King Uther wedded me, and by his commandment when the child was born it was delivered unto Merlin and nourished by him, and so I saw the child never after, nor wot not what is his name, for I knew him never yet.'

And there Ulfius said to the queen, 'Merlin is more to blame than ye.'

'Well I wot,' said the queen, 'I bare a child by my lord King Uther, but I wot not where he is become.'

Then Merlin took the king by the hand, saying, 'This is your mother.' And therewith Sir Ector bare witness how he nourished him by Uther's commandment. And therewith King Arthur took his mother, Queen Igraine, in his arms and kissed her, and either wept upon other. And then the king let make a feast that lasted eight days.

Then on a day there come in the court a squire on horseback, leading a knight before him wounded to the death, and told him how there was a knight in the forest had reared up a pavilion by a well, 'and hath slain my master, a good knight, his name was Miles; wherefore I beseech you that my master may be buried, and that some knight may revenge my master's death.' Then the noise was great of that knight's death in the court, and every man said his advice.

Then came Griflet that was but a squire, and he was but young, of the age of the King Arthur, so he besought the king for all his service that he had done him, to give him the order of knighthood.

CHAPTER 22: *How Griflet was made knight, and jousted with a knight*

'Thou art full young and tender of age,' said Arthur, 'for to take so high an order on thee.'

'Sir,' said Griflet, 'I beseech you make me knight.'

'Sir,' said Merlin, 'it were great pity to lose Griflet, for he will be a passing good man when he is of age, abiding with you the term of his life. And if he adventure his body with yonder knight at the fountain, it is in great peril if ever he come again, for he is one of the best knights of the world, and the strongest man of arms.'

'Well,' said Arthur. So at the desire of Griflet the king made him knight.

'Now,' said Arthur unto Sir Griflet, 'sithen I have made you knight thou must give me a gift.'

'What ye will,' said Griflet.

'Thou shalt promise me by the faith of thy body, when thou has jousted with the knight at the fountain, whether it fall ye be on foot or on horseback, that right so ye shall come again unto me without making any more debate.'

'I will promise you,' said Griflet, 'as you desire.'

Then took Griflet his horse in great haste, and dressed his shield and took a spear in his hand, and so he rode a great wallop till he came to the fountain, and thereby he saw a rich pavilion, and thereby under a cloth stood a fair horse well saddled and bridled, and on a tree a shield of divers colours and a great spear. Then Griflet smote on the shield with the butt of his spear, that the shield fell down to the ground.

wallop: gallop.

With that the knight came out of the pavilion, and said, 'Fair knight, why smote ye down my shield?'

'For I will joust with you,' said Griflet.

'It is better ye do not,' said the knight, 'for ye are but young, and late made knight, and your might is nothing to mine.'

'As for that,' said Griflet, 'I will joust with you.'

'That is me loth,' said the knight, 'but sithen I must needs, I will dress me thereto. Of whence be ye?' said the knight.

'Sir, I am of Arthur's court.'

So the two knights ran together that Griflet's spear all to-shivered; and therewithal he smote Griflet through the shield and the left side, and brake the spear that the truncheon stuck in his body, that horse and knight fell down.

CHAPTER 23: *How twelve knights came from Rome and asked truage for this land of Arthur, and how Arthur fought with a knight*

Then the knight saw him lie so on the ground; he alit, and was passing heavy, for he weened he had slain him. And then he unlaced his helm and gat him wind, and so with the truncheon he set him on his horse and gat him wind, and so betook him to God, and said he had a mighty heart, and if he might live he would prove a passing good knight. And so Sir Griflet rode to the court, where great dole was made for him. But through good leeches he was healed and saved.

Right so came into the court twelve knights, and were aged men, and they came from the Emperor of Rome, and they asked of Arthur truage for this realm, other else the emperor would destroy him and his land.

'Well,' said King Arthur, 'ye are messengers, therefore ye may say what ye will, other else ye should die therefore. But this is mine answer: I owe the emperor no truage, nor none will I hold him, but on a fair field I shall give him my truage

that is me loth: I am reluctant. *other else*: or else. *truage*: tribute.

that shall be with a sharp spear, or else with a sharp sword, and that shall not be long, by my father's soul, Uther Pendragon.'

And therewith the messengers departed passingly wroth, and King Arthur as wroth, for in evil time came they then; for the king was passingly wroth for the hurt of Sir Griflet. And so he commanded a privy man of his chamber that or it be day his best horse and armour, with all that longeth unto his person, be without the city or tomorrow day. Right so or tomorrow day he met with his man and his horse, and so mounted up and dressed his shield and took his spear, and bad his chamberlain tarry there till he came again.

And so Arthur rode a soft pace till it was day, and then was he ware of three churls chasing Merlin, and would have slain him. Then the king rode unto them, and bad them: 'Flee, churls!' then were they afeared when they saw a knight, and fled.

'O Merlin,' said Arthur, 'here hadst thou been slain for all thy crafts had I not been.'

'Nay,' said Merlin, 'not so, for I could save myself and I would; and thou art more near thy death than I am, for thou goest to the deathward, and God be not thy friend.'

So as they went thus talking they came to the fountain, and the rich pavilion there by it. Then King Arthur was ware where sat a knight armed in a chair.

'Sir knight,' said Arthur, 'for what cause abidest thou here, that there may no knight ride this way but if he joust with thee?' said the king. 'I rede thee leave that custom,' said Arthur.

'This custom,' said the knight, 'have I used and will use maugre who saith nay, and who is grieved with my custom let him amend it that will.'

'I will amend it,' said Arthur.

'I shall defend thee,' said the knight.

Anon he took his horse and dressed his shield and took a

rede: advise *maugre*: in spite of.

spear, and they met so hard either in other's shields, that all to-shivered their spears. Therewith anon Arthur pulled out his sword.

'Nay, not so,' said the knight; 'it is fairer,' said the knight, 'that we twain run more together with sharp spears.'

'I will well,' said Arthur, 'and I had any more spears.'

'I have enow,' said the knight; so there came a squire and brought two good spears, and Arthur chose one and he another.

So they spurred their horses and came together with all their mights,[1] that either brake their spears to their hands. Then Arthur set hand on his sword.

'Nay,' said the knight, 'ye shall do better, ye are a passing good jouster as ever I met withal, and once for the love of the high order of knighthood let us joust once again.'

'I assent me,' said Arthur.

Anon there were brought two great spears, and every knight gat a spear, and therewith they ran together that Arthur's spear all to-shivered. But the other knight hit him so hard in midst of the shield, that horse and man fell to the earth, and therewith Arthur was eager, and pulled out his sword, and said, 'I will assay thee, sir knight, on foot, for I have lost the honour on horseback.'

'I will be on horseback,' said the knight.

Then was Arthur wroth, and dressed his shield toward him with his sword drawn. When the knight saw that, he alit, for him thought no worship to have a knight at such avail, he to be on horseback and he on foot, and so he alit and dressed his shield unto Arthur. And there began a strong battle with many great strokes, and so hewed with their swords that the cantels flew in the fields, and much blood they bled both, that all the place there as they fought was overbled with blood, and thus they fought long and rested them, and then they went to the battle again, and so hurtled together like two rams that either fell to the earth. So at the last they smote together that both their swords met even

enow: enough. *avail*: advantage.

together. But the sword of the knight smote King Arthur's sword in two pieces, wherefore he was heavy. Then said the knight unto Arthur, 'Thou art in my danger whether me list to save thee or slay thee, and but thou yield thee as overcome and recreant, thou shalt die.'

'As for death,' said King Arthur, 'welcome be it when it cometh, but to yield me unto thee as recreant I had lever die than to be so shamed.'

And wherewithal the king leapt unto Pellinor, and took him by the middle and threw him down, and rased off his helm. When the knight felt that, he was adread, for he was a passing big man of might, and anon he brought Arthur under him, and rased off his helm and would have smitten off his head.

CHAPTER 24: *How Merlin saved Arthur's life, and threw an enchantment upon King Pellinor and made him to sleep*

Therewithal came Merlin and said, 'Knight, hold thy hand, for and thou slay that knight thou puttest this realm in the greatest damage that ever was realm: for this knight is a man of more worship than thou wotest of.'

'Why, who is he?' said the knight.

'It is King Arthur.'

Then would he have slain him for dread of his wrath, and heaved up his sword, and therewith Merlin cast an enchantment to the knight, that he fell to the earth in a great sleep. Then Merlin took up King Arthur, and rode forth on the knight's horse.

'Alas!' said Arthur, 'What has thou done, Merlin? Hast thou slain this good knight by thy crafts? There liveth not so worshipful a knight as he was; I had lever than the stint of my land a year that he were alive.'

'Care ye not,' said Merlin, 'for he is wholer than ye; for

danger: power. *me list*: it pleases me. *recreant*: surrendering. *lever*: rather. *rased*: tore.

he is but asleep, and will awake within three hours. I told you,' said Merlin, 'what a knight he was; here had ye been slain had I not been. Also there liveth not a bigger knight than he is one, and he shall hereafter do you right good service; and his name is Pellinor, and he shall have two sons that shall be passing good men; save one, they shall have no fellow of prowess and of good living, and their names shall be Percival of Wales and Lamorak of Wales, and he shall tell you the name of your own son begotten of your sister that shall be the destruction of all this realm.'

CHAPTER 25: *How Arthur by the mean of Merlin gat Excalibur his sword of the Lady of the Lake*

Right so the king and he departed, and went until an hermit that was a good man and a great leech. So the hermit searched all his wounds and gave him good salves; so the king was there three days, and then were his wounds well amended that he might ride and go, and so departed.

And as they rode, Arthur said, 'I have no sword.'

'No force,' said Merlin, 'hereby is a sword that shall be yours, and I may.'

So they rode till they came to a lake, the which was a fair water and broad, and in the midst of the lake Arthur was ware of an arm clothed in white samite, that held a fair sword in that hand.

'Lo!' said Merlin, 'yonder is that sword that I spake of.'

With that they saw a damosel going upon the lake.

'What damosel is that?' said Arthur.

'That is the Lady of the Lake,' said Merlin; 'and within that lake is a rock, and therein is as fair a place as any on earth, and richly beseen; and this damosel will come to you anon, and then speak ye fair to her that she will give you that sword.'

'No *force*': 'That does not matter.' *samite*: a rich silk material.

Anon withal came the damosel unto Arthur, and saluted him, and he her again.

'Damosel,' said Arthur, 'what sword is that, that yonder the arm holdeth above the water? I would it were mine, for I have no sword.'

'Sir Arthur, king,' said the damosel, 'that sword is mine, and if ye will give me a gift when I ask it you, ye shall have it.'

'By my faith,' said Arthur, 'I will give you what gift ye will ask.'

'Well!' said the damosel, 'Go ye into yonder barge, and row yourself to the sword, and take it and the scabbard with you, and I will ask my gift when I see my time.'

So Sir Arthur and Merlin alit and tied their horses to two trees, and so they went into the ship, and when they came to the sword that the hand held, Sir Arthur took it up by the handles, and took it with him, and the arm and the hand went under the water, and so came unto the land and rode forth, and then Sir Arthur saw a rich pavilion.

'What signifieth yonder pavilion?'

'It is the knight's pavilion,' said Merlin, 'that ye fought with last, Sir Pellinor; but he is out, he is not there. He hath ado with a knight of yours that hight Egglame, and they have foughten together, but at the last Egglame fled, and else he had been dead, and he hath chased him even to Caerleon, and we shall meet with him anon in the highway.'

'That is well said,' said Arthur, 'now have I a sword, now will I wage battle with him, and be avenged on him.'

'Sir, ye shall not so,' said Merlin, 'for the knight is weary of fighting and chasing, so that ye shall have no worship to have ado with him; also he will not be lightly matched of one knight living, and therefore it is my counsel, let him pass, for he shall do you good service in short time, and his sons after his days. Also ye shall see that day in short space, ye shall be right glad to give him your sister to wed.'

'When I see him, I will do as ye advise me,' said Arthur.

Then Sir Arthur looked on the sword, and liked it passing well.

'Whether liketh you better,' said Merlin, 'the sword or the scabbard?'

'Me liketh better the sword,' said Arthur.

'Ye are more unwise,' said Merlin, 'for the scabbard is worth ten of the swords, for whiles ye have the scabbard upon you, ye shall never lose no blood be ye never so sore wounded, therefore keep well the scabbard always with you.'

So they rode unto Caerleon, and by the way they met with Sir Pellinor; but Merlin had done such a craft, that Pellinor saw not Arthur, and he passed by without any words.

'I marvel,' said Arthur, 'that the knight would not speak.'

'Sir,' said Merlin, 'he saw you not, for and he had seen you, ye had not lightly departed.'

So they came unto Caerleon, whereof his knights were passing glad. And when they heard of his adventures, they marvelled that he would jeopard his person so, alone. But all men of worship said it was merry to be under such a chieftain, that would put his person in adventure as other poor knights did.

CHAPTER 26: *How tidings came to Arthur that King Rience had overcome eleven kings, and how he desired Arthur's beard to purfle his mantle*

This meanwhile came a messenger from King Rience of North Wales, and king he was of all Ireland, and of many isles. And this was his message, greeting well King Arthur in this manner wise, saying that King Rience had discomfit and overcome eleven kings, and every each of them did him homage, and that was this, they gave him their beards clean flayed off, as much as there was; wherefore the messenger came for King Arthur's beard. For King Rience had purfled a mantle with kings' beards, and there lacked one place of

whether: which of the two. *purfled*: trimmed.

the mantle; wherefore he sent for his beard, or else he would enter into his lands and burn and slay, 'and never leave till he have the head and the beard.'

'Well,' said Arthur, 'thou hast said thy message, the which is the most villainous and lewdest message that ever man heard sent unto a king; also thou mayest see my beard is full young yet to make a purfle of it. But tell thou thy king this: I owe him none homage, ne none of mine elders, but or it be long to, he shall do me homage on both knees, or else he shall lose his head, by the faith of my body, for this is the most shamefulest message that ever I heard speak of. I have espied thy king met never yet with worshipful man, but tell him, I will have his head without he do me homage.'

Then the messenger departed.

'Now is there any here,' said Arthur, 'that knoweth King Rience?'

Then answered a knight that hight Naram, 'Sir, I know the king well; he is a passing good man of his body, as few be living, and a passing proud man, and sir, doubt ye not he will make war on you with a mighty puissance.'

'Well,' said Arthur, 'I shall ordain for him in short time.'

CHAPTER 27: *How all the children were sent for that were born on May-day, and how Mordred was saved*

Then King Arthur let send for all the children born on May-day, begotten of lords and born of ladies; for Merlin told King Arthur that he that should destroy him should be born in May-day, wherefore he sent for them all, upon pain of death; and so there were found many lords' sons, and all were sent unto the king, and so was Mordred sent by King Lot's wife, and all were put in a ship to the sea, and some were four weeks old, and some less.

And so by fortune the ship drove unto a castle, and was all to-riven, and destroyed the most part, save that Mordred

lewdest: most boorish. *puissance*: power. *ordain*: arrange.

was cast up, and a good man found him, and nourished him till he was fourteen year old, and then he brought him to the court, as it rehearseth afterward, toward the end of the Death of Arthur.

So many lords and barons of this realm were displeased, for their children were so lost, and many put the wite on Merlin more than on Arthur; so what for dread and for love, they held their peace.

But when the messenger came to King Rience, then was he wood out of measure, and purveyed him for a great host, as it rehearseth after in the book of Balin le Savage, that followeth next after, how by adventure Balin gat the sword.

Explicit Liber Primus

wite: blame.

Book II

CHAPTER 1: *Of a damosel which came girt with a sword for to find a man of such virtue to draw it out of the scabbard*

After the death of Uther Pendragon reigned Arthur his son, the which had great war in his days for to get all England into his hand. For there were many kings within the realm of England, and in Wales, Scotland, and Cornwall.

So it befell on a time when King Arthur was at London, there came a knight and told the king tidings how that the King Rience of North Wales had reared a great number of people, and were entered into the land, and burnt and slew the king's true liege people.

'If this be true,' said Arthur, 'it were great shame unto mine estate but that he were mightily withstood.'

'It is truth,' said the knight, 'for I saw the host myself.'

'Well,' said the king, 'let make a cry, that all the lords, knights, and gentlemen of arms should draw unto a castle' (called Camelot in those days) 'and there the king would let make a council-general and a great jousts.'

So when the king was come thither with all his baronage, and lodged as they seemed best, there was come a damosel the which was sent on message from the great lady Lile of Avelion. And when she came before King Arthur, she told from whom she came, and how she was sent on message unto him for these causes. Then she let her mantle fall that was richly furred; and then was she girt with a noble sword whereof the king had marvel, and said, 'Damosel, for what cause are ye girt with that sword? It beseemeth you not.'

'Now shall I tell you,' said the damosel. 'This sword that I

***beseemeth*:** befits.

am girt withal doth me great sorrow and cumberance, for I may not be delivered of this sword but by a knight, but he must be a passing good man of his hands and of his deeds, and without villainy or treachery, and without treason. And if I may find such a knight that hath all these virtues, he may draw out this sword out of the sheath, for I have been at King Rience's, it was told me there were passing good knights, and he and all his knights have assayed it and none can speed.'

'This is a great marvel,' said Arthur, 'if this be sooth; I will myself assay to draw out the sword, not presuming upon myself that I am the best knight, but that I will begin to draw at your sword in giving example to all the barons that they shall assay every each one after other when I have assayed it.'

Then Arthur took the sword by the sheath and by the girdle and pulled at it eagerly, but the sword would not out.

'Sir,' said the damosel, 'you need not to pull half so hard, for he that shall pull it out shall do it with little might.'

'Ye say well,' said Arthur; 'now assay ye all my barons.'

'But beware ye be not defiled with shame, treachery ne guile; then it will not avail,' said the damosel, 'for he must be a clean knight without villainy, and of a gentle strain of father side and mother side.'

Most of all the barons of the Round Table that were there at that time assayed all by row,, but there might none speed; wherefore the damosel made great sorrow out of measure, and said, 'Alas; I weened in this court had been the best knights without treachery or treason.'

'By my faith,' saith Arthur, 'here are good knights, as I deem, as any be in the world, but their grace is not to help you, wherefore I am displeased.'

sooth: true.

CHAPTER 2: *How Balin, arrayed like a poor knight, pulled out the sword, which afterward was cause of his death*

Then fell it so that time there was a poor knight with King Arthur, that had been prisoner with him half a year and more for slaying of a knight, the which was cousin unto King Arthur. The name of this knight was called Balin, and by good means of the barons he was delivered out of prison, for he was a good man named of his body, and he was born in Northumberland; and so he went privily into the court, and saw this adventure, whereof it raised his heart, and would assay it as other knights did, but for he was poor and poorly arrayed he put him not far in press; but in his heart he was fully assured to do as well, if his grace happed him, as any knight that there was. And as the damosel took her leave of Arthur and of all the barons, so departing, this knight Balin called unto her, and said,

'Damosel, I pray you of your courtesy, suffer me as well to assay as these lords; though that I be so poorly clothed, in my heart meseemeth I am fully assured as some of these other, and meseemeth in my heart to speed right well.'

The damosel beheld the poor knight, and saw he was a likely man, but for his poor arrayment she thought he should be of no worship without villainy or treachery. And then she said unto the knight, 'Sir, it needeth not to put me to more pain or labour, for it seemeth not you to speed thereas other have failed.'

'Ah! fair damosel,' said Balin, 'worthiness, and good tatches, and good deeds, are not only in arrayment, but manhood and worship is hid within man's person, and many a worshipful knight is not known unto all people, and therefore worship and hardiness is not in arrayment.'

'By God,' said the damosel, 'ye say sooth; therefore ye shall assay to do what ye may.'

Then Balin took the sword by the girdle and sheath, and

in press: in the crowd. *tatches*: qualities.

drew it out easily; and when he looked on the sword it pleased him much. Then had the king and all the barons great marvel that Balin had done that adventure; many knights had great despite at Balin.

'Certes,' said the damosel, 'this is a passing good knight, and the best that ever I found, and most of worship without treason, treachery, or villainy, and many marvels shall he do. Now, gentle and courteous knight, give me the sword again.'

'Nay,' said Balin, 'for this sword will I keep, but it be taken from me with force.'

'Well,' said the damosel, 'ye are not wise to keep the sword from me, for ye shall slay with the sword the best friend that ye have, and the man that ye most love in the world, and the sword shall be your destruction.'

'I shall take the adventure,' said Balin, 'that God will ordain me, but the sword ye shall not have at this time, by the faith of my body.'

'Ye shall repent it within short time,' said the damosel, 'for I would have the sword more for your avail than for mine, for I am passing heavy for your sake; for ye will not believe that sword shall be your destruction, and that is great pity.' With that the damosel departed, making great sorrow.

Anon after, Balin sent for his horse and armour, and so would depart from the court, and took his leave of King Arthur.

'Nay,' said the king, 'I suppose ye will not depart so lightly from this fellowship, I suppose ye are displeased that I have showed you unkindness. Blame me the less, for I was misinformed against you, but I weened ye had not been such a knight as ye are of worship and prowess, and if ye will abide in this court among my fellowship, I shall so advance you as ye shall be pleased.'

'God thank your highness,' said Balin, 'your bounty and highness may no man praise half to the value; but at this time I must needs depart, beseeching you alway of your good grace.'

adventure: fortune.

'Truly,' said the king, 'I am right wroth for your departing; I pray you, fair knight, that ye tarry not long, and ye shall be right welcome to me, and to my barons, and I shall amend all miss that I have done against you.'

'God thank your great lordship,' said Balin, and therewith made him ready to depart.

Then the most part of the knights of the Round Table said that Balin did not this adventure all only by might, but by witchcraft.

CHAPTER 3: *How the Lady of the Lake demanded the knight's head that had won the sword, or the maiden's head*

The meanwhile that this knight was making him ready to depart, there came into the court a lady that hight the Lady of the Lake. And she came on horseback, richly beseen, and saluted King Arthur, and there asked him a gift that he promised her when she gave him the sword.

'That is sooth,' said Arthur, 'a gift I promised you, but I have forgotten the name of my sword that ye gave me.'

'The name of it,' said the lady, 'is Excalibur, that is as much to say as Cut-steel.'

'Ye say well,' said the king, 'ask what ye will and ye shall have it, and it lie in my power to give it.'

'Well,' said the lady, 'I ask the head of the knight that hath won the sword, or else the damosel's head that brought it; I take no force though I have both their heads, for he slew my brother, a good knight and a true, and that gentlewoman was causer of my father's death.'

'Truly,' said King Arthur, 'I may not grant neither of their heads with my worship, therefore ask what ye will else, and I shall fulfil your desire.'

'I will ask none other thing,' said the lady.

When Balin was ready to depart, he saw the Lady of the Lake, that by her means had slain Balin's mother, and he had sought her three years; and when it was told him that she asked his head of King Arthur, he went to her straight and said, 'Evil be you found; ye would have my head, and therefore ye shall lose yours,' and with his sword lightly he smote off her head before King Arthur.

'Alas, for shame!' said Arthur. 'Why have ye done so? Ye have shamed me and all my court, for this was a lady that I was beholden to, and hither she came under my safe-conduct; I shall never forgive you that trespass.'

'Sir,' said Balin, 'me forthinketh of your displeasure, for this same lady was the untruest lady living, and by enchantment and sorcery she hath been the destroyer of many good knights, and she was causer that my mother was burnt, through her falsehood and treachery.'

'What cause soever ye had,' said Arthur, 'ye should have forborne her in my presence; therefore, think not the contrary, ye shall repent it, for such another despite had I never in my court; therefore withdraw you out of my court in all haste that ye may.'

Then Balin took up the head of the lady, and bare it with him to his hostelry, and there he met with his squire, that was sorry he had displeased King Arthur, and so they rode forth out of the town.

'Now,' said Balin, 'we must depart. Take thou this head and bear it to my friends, and tell them how I have sped, and tell my friends in Northumberland that my most foe is dead. Also tell them how I am out of prison, and what adventure befell me at the getting of this sword.'

'Alas!' said the squire, 'ye are greatly to blame for to displease King Arthur.'

'As for that,' said Balin, 'I will hie me in all the haste that I may to meet with King Rience and destroy him, either else to die therefore; and if it may hap me to win him, then will King Arthur be my good and gracious lord.'

'Where shall I meet with you?' said the squire.

'In King Arthur's court,' said Balin. So his squire and he departed at that time.

Then King Arthur and all the court made great dole and

me forthinketh: I regret.

had shame of the death of the Lady of the Lake. Then the king buried her richly.

CHAPTER 4: *How Merlin told the adventure of this damosel*

At that time there was a knight, the which was the King's son of Ireland, and his name was Lanceor, the which was an orgulous knight, and counted himself one of the best of the court, and he had great despite at Balin for the achieving of the sword, that any should be accounted more hardy, or more of prowess. And he asked King Arthur if he would give him leave to ride after Balin and to revenge the despite that he had done.

'Do your best,' said Arthur, 'I am right wroth with Balin;[1] I would he were quit of the despite that he hath done to me and to my court.'

Then this Lanceor went to his hostelry to make him ready. In the meanwhile came Merlin unto the court of King Arthur, and there was told him the adventure of the sword, and the death of the Lady of the Lake.

'Now shall I say you,' said Merlin, 'this same damosel that here standeth, that brought the sword unto your court, I shall tell you the cause of her coming: she was the falsest damosel that liveth.'

'Say not so,' said they.

'She hath a brother, a passing good knight of prowess and a full true man; and this damosel loved another knight that held her to paramour. And this good knight her brother met with the knight that held her to paramour, and slew him by force of his hands. When this false damosel understood this, she went to the Lady Lile of Avelion, and besought her of help, to be avenged on her own brother.

orgulous: proud. *quit of*: repayed for.

CHAPTER 5: *How Balin was pursued by Sir Lanceor, knight of Ireland, and how he jousted and slew him*

'And so this Lady Lile of Avelion took her this sword that she brought with her, and told there should no man pull it out of the sheath but if he be one of the best knights of this realm, and he should be hard and full of prowess, and with that sword he should slay her brother. This was the cause that the damosel came into this court. I know it as well as ye. Would God she had not comen into this court, but she came never in fellowship of worship to do good, but always great harm. And that knight that hath achieved the sword shall be destroyed by that sword, for the which will be great damage for there liveth not a knight of more prowess than he is, and he shall do unto you, my lord Arthur, great honour and kindness; and it is great pity he shall not endure but a while, for of his strength and hardiness I know not his match living.'

So the knight of Ireland armed him at all points, and dressed his shield on his shoulder, and mounted upon horseback, and took his spear in his hand, and rode after a great pace, as much as his horse might go. And within a little space on a mountain he had a sight of Balin, and with a loud voice he cried, 'Abide, knight, for ye shall abide whether ye will or nill, and the shield that is tofore you shall not help.'

When Balin heard the noise, he turned his horse fiercely, and said, 'Fair knight, what will ye with me, will ye joust with me?'

'Yea,' said the Irish knight, 'therefore come I after you.'

'Peradventure,' said Balin, 'it had been better to have held you at home, for many a man weeneth to put his enemy to a rebuke, and oft it falleth to himself. Of what court be ye sent from?' said Balin.

'I am come from the court of King Arthur,' said the knight

took her: gave her. *damage*: grief.

of Ireland, 'that come hither for to revenge the despite ye did this day to King Arthur and to his court.'

'Well,' said Balin, 'I see well I must have ado with you; that me forthinketh for to grieve King Arthur, or any of his court; and your quarrel is full simple,' said Balin, 'unto me, for the lady that is dead did me great damage, and else would I have been loth as any knight that liveth for to slay a lady.'

'Make you ready,' said the knight Lanceor, 'and dress you unto me, for that one shall abide in the field.'

Then they took their spears, and came together as much as their horses might drive, and the Irish knight smote Balin on the shield, that all went shivers of his spear, and Balin hit him through the shield, and the hauberk perished, and so pierced through his body and the horse's croup, and anon turned his horse fiercely, and drew out his sword, and wist not that he had slain him; and then he saw him lie as a dead corpse.

CHAPTER 6: *How a damosel, which was love to Lanceor, slew herself for love, and how Balin met with his brother Balan*

Then he looked by him, and was ware of a damosel that came riding[1] full fast as the horse might ride, on a fair palfrey. And when she espie dthat Lanceor was slain, she made sorrow out of measure, and said, 'O Balin, two bodies thou hast slain and one heart, and two hearts in one body, and two souls thou hast lost.' And therewith she took the sword from her love that lay dead, and fell to the ground in a swoon.

And when she arose she made great dole out of measure, the which sorrow grieved Balin passingly sore, and he went unto her for to have taken the sword out of her hand, but she held it so fast he might not take it out of her hand unless he should have hurt her, and suddenly she set the pommel to the ground, and rove herself through the body.

When Balin espied her deeds, he was passing heavy in his heart, and ashamed that so fair a damosel had destroyed herself for the love of his death. 'Alas,' said Balin, 'me repenteth sore the death of this knight, for the love of this damosel, for there was much true love betwixt them both,' and for sorrow might not longer behold him, but turned his horse and looked toward a great forest.

And there he was ware, by the arms, of his brother Balan. And when they were met they put off their helms and kissed together, and wept for joy and pity.

Then Balan said, 'I little weened to have met with you at this sudden adventure; I am right glad of your deliverance of your dolorous prisonment, for a man told me, in the Castle of Four Stones, that ye were delivered, and that man had seen you in the court of Wing Arthur, and therefore I came hither into this country, for here I supposed to find you.'

Anon the knight Balin told hiss brother of his adventure of the sword, and of the death of the Lady of the Lake, and how King Arthur was displeased with him. 'Wherefore he sent this knight after me, that lieth here dead, and the death of this damosel grieveth me sore.'

'So doth it me,' said Balan, 'but ye must take the adventure that God will ordain you.'

'Truly,' said Balin, 'I am right heavy that my lord Arthur is displeased with me, for he is the most worshipful knight that reigneth now on earth, and his love will I get or else I will put my life in adventure, for the King Rience lieth at a siege at Castle Terrabil, and thither will we draw in all haste, to prove our worship and prowess upon him.'

'I will well,' said Balan, 'that we do, and we will help each other as brethren ought to do.'

CHAPTER 7: *How a dwarf reproved Balin for the death of Lanceor, and how King Mark of Cornwall found them, and made a tomb over them*

'Now go we hence,' said Balin, 'and well be we met.'

The meanwhile as they talked, there came a dwarf from the city of Camelot on horseback, as much as he might, and found the dead bodies, wherefore he made great dole, and pulled out his hair for sorrow, and said, 'Which of you knights have done this deed?'

'Whereby askest thou it?' said Balan.

'For I would wit it,' said the dwarf.

'It was I,' said Balin, 'that slew this knight in my defendant, for hither he came to chase me, and other I must slay him or he me; and this damosel slew herself for his love, which repenteth me, and for her sake I shall owe all women the better love.'

'Alas,' said the dwarf, 'thou hast done great damage unto thyself, for this knight that is here dead was one of the most valiantest men that lived, and trust well, Balin, the kin of this knight will chase you through the world till they have slain you.'

'As for that,' said Balan, 'I fear not greatly, but I am right heavy that I have displeased my lord King Arthur, for the death of this knight.'

So as they talked together, there came a king of Cornwall riding, the which hight King Mark. And when he saw these two bodies dead, and understood how they were dead, by the two knights above said, then made the king great sorrow for the true love that was betwixt them, and said, 'I will not depart till I have on this earth made a tomb.' And there he pitched his pavilions and sought through all the country to find a tomb, and in a church they found one was fair and rich, and then the king let put them both in the earth, and put the tomb upon them, and wrote the names of them both

defendant: defence.

on the tomb, how: HERE LIETH LANCEOR THE KING'S SON OF IRELAND, THAT AT HIS OWN REQUEST WAS SLAIN BY THE HANDS OF BALIN; and how: HIS LADY, COLOMBE, AND PARAMOUR, SLEW HERSELF WITH HER LOVE'S SWORD FOR DOLE AND SORROW.

CHAPTER 8: *How Merlin prophesied that two the best knights of the world should fight there, which were Sir Lancelot and Sir Tristram*

The meanwhile as this was a-doing, in came Merlin to King Mark, seeing all his doing, said, 'Here shall be in this same place the greatest battle betwixt two knights that was or ever shall be, and the truest lovers, and yet none of them shall slay other.' And there Merlin wrote their names upon the tomb with letters of gold that should fight in that place, whose names were Launcelot de Lake, and Tristram.

'Thou art a marvellous man,' said King Mark unto Merlin, 'that speakest of such marvels; thou art a boistous man and an unlikely to tell of such deeds. What is thy name?' said King Mark.

'At this time,' said Merlin, 'I will not tell, but at that time when Sir Tristram is taken with his sovereign lady, then ye shall hear and know my name, and at that time ye shall hear tidings that shall not please you.' Then said Merlin to Balin, 'Thou hast done thyself great hurt, because that thou savest not this lady that slew herself, that might have saved her and thou wouldest.'

'By the faith of my body,' said Balin, 'I might not save her, for she slew herself suddenly.'

'Me repenteth,' said Merlin, 'because of the death of that lady thou shalt strike a stroke most dolorous that ever man struck, except the stroke of Our Lord, for thou shalt hurt the truest knight and the man of most worship that now liveth, and through that stroke three kingdoms shall be in

boistous: unsophisticated.

great poverty, misery and wretchedness twelve year, and the knight shall not be whole of that wound many years.'

Then Merlin took his leave of Balin. And Balin said, 'If I wist it were sooth that ye say I should do such perilous deed as that, I would slay myself to make thee a liar.'

Therewith Merlin vanished away suddenly. And then Balin and his brother took their leave of King Mark.

'First,' said the king, 'tell me your name.'

'Sir,' said Balan, 'ye may see he beareth two swords, thereby ye may call him the Knight with the Two Swords.'

And so departed King Mark unto Camelot to King Arthur, and Balin took the way toward King Rience; and as they rode together they met with Merlin disguised, but they knew him not.

'Whither ride you?' said Merlin.

'We have little to do,' said the two knights, 'to tell thee.'

'But what is thy name?' said Balin.

'At this time,' said Merlin, 'I will not tell it thee.'

'It is evil seen,' said the knights, 'that thou art a true man, that thou wilt not tell thy name.'

'As for that,' said Merlin, 'be it as it be may, I can tell you wherefore ye ride this way, for to meet King Rience; but it will not avail you without ye have my counsel.'

'Ah!' said Balin, 'ye are Merlin; we will be ruled by your counsel.'

'Come on,' said Merlin, 'ye shall have great worship, and look that ye do knightly, for ye shall have great need.'

'As for that,' said Balan, 'dread you not, we will do what we may.'

evil seen: hard to see.

CHAPTER 9: *How Balin and his brother, by the counsel of Merlin, took King Rience and brought him to King Arthur*

Then Merlin lodged them in a wood among leaves beside the highway, and took off the bridles of their horses and put them to grass and laid them down to rest them till it was nigh midnight. Then Merlin bad them rise, and make them ready, for the king was nigh them, that was stolen away from his host with a three score horses of his best knights, and twenty of them rode tofore to warn the Lady de Vance that the king was coming, for that night King Rience should have lain with her.

'Which is the king?' said Balin.

'Abide,' said Merlin, 'here in a strait way ye shall meet with him;' and therewith he showed Balin and his brother where he rode.

Anon Balin and his brother met with the king, and smote him down, and wounded him fiercely, and laid him to the ground; and there they slew on the right hand and the left hand, and slew more than forty of his men, and the remnant fled. Then went they again to King Rience and would have slain him had he not yielded him unto their grace. Then said he thus:

'Knights full of prowess, slay me not, for by my life ye may win, and by my death ye shall win nothing.'

Then said these two knights, 'Ye say sooth and truth,' and so laid him on an horse-litter.

With that Merlin was vanished, and came to King Arthur aforehand, and told him how his most enemy was taken and discomfited.

'By whom?' said King Arthur.

'By two knights,' said Merlin, 'that would please your lordship, and tomorrow ye shall know what knights they are.'

Anon after came the Knight with the Two Swords and Balan his brother, and brought with them King Rience of

strait: narrow.

North Wales, and there delivered him to the porters, and charged them with him; and so they two returned again in the dawning of the day.

King Arthur came then to King Rience, and said, 'Sir king, ye are welcome. By what adventure come ye hither?'

'Sir,' said King Rience, 'I came hither by an hard adventure.'

'Who won you?' said King Arthur.

'Sir,' said the king, 'the Knight with the Two Swords and his brother, which are two marvellous knights of prowess.'

'I know them not,' said Arthur, 'but much I am beholden to them.'

'Ah,' said Merlin, 'I shall tell you: it is Balin that achieved the sword, and his brother Balan, a good knight, there liveth not a better of prowess and of worthiness, and it shall be the greatest dole of him that ever I knew of knight, for he shall not long endure.'

'Alas,' said King Arthur, 'that is great pity; for I am much beholding unto him, and I have ill deserved it unto him for his kindness.'

'Nay,' said Merlin, 'he shall do much more for you, and that shall ye know in haste. But, sir, are ye purveyed?' said Merlin, 'for to-morn the host of Nero, King Rience's brother, will set on you or noon with a great host, and therefore make you ready, for I will depart from you.'

CHAPTER 10: *How King Arthur had a battle against Nero and King Lot of Orkney, and how King Lot was deceived by Merlin, and how twelve kings were slain*

Then King Arthur made ready his host in ten battles, and Nero was ready in the field afore the Castle Terrabil with a great host, and he had ten battles, with many more people than Arthur had. Then Nero had the vanguard with the most part of his people. And Merlin came to King Lot of the Isle of Orkney, and held him with a tale of prophecy, till

Nero and his people were destroyed. And there Sir Kay the Seneschal did passingly well, that the days of his life the worship went never from him; and Sir Hervis de Revel did marvellous deeds with King Arthur, and King Arthur slew that day twenty knights and maimed forty. At that time came in the Knight with the Two Swords and his brother Balan, but they two did so marvellously that the king and all the knights marvelled of them, and all they that beheld them said they were sent from heaven as angels, or devils from hell; and King Arthur said himself they were the best knights that ever he saw, for they gave such strokes that all men had wonder of them.

In the meanwhile came one to King Lot, and told him while he tarried there Nero was destroyed and slain with all his people.

'Alas,' said King Lot, 'I am ashamed, for by my default there is many a worshipful man slain, for and we had been together there had been none host under the heaven that had been able for to have matched with us; this faiter with his prophecy hath mocked me.'

(All that did Merlin, for he knew well that and King Lot had been with his body there at the first battle, King Arthur had been slain, and all his people destroyed; and well Merlin knew the one of the kings should be dead that day, and loth was Merlin that any of them both should be slain; but of the twain, he had lever King Lot had been slain than King Arthur.)

'Now what is best to do?' said King Lot of Orkney. 'Whether is me better to treat with King Arthur or to fight, for the greater part of our people are slain and destroyed?'

'Sir,' said a knight, 'set on Arthur for they are weary and forfoughten and we be fresh.'

'As for me,' said King Lot, 'I would every knight would do his part as I would do mine.'

And then they advanced banners and smote together and

faiter: imposter. *forfoughten*: wearied with fighting.

all to-shivered their spears; and Arthur's knights, with the help of the Knight with the Two Swords and his brother Balan put King Lot and his host to the worse. But always King Lot held him in the foremost front, and did marvellous deeds of arms, for all his host was borne up by his hands, for he abode all knights. Alas he might not endure, the which was great pity, that so worthy a knight as he was one should be overmatched, that of late time afore had been a knight of King Arthur's, and wedded the sister of King Arthur; and for King Arthur lay by King Lot's wife, the which was Arthur's sister, and gat on her Mordred, therefore King Lot held against Arthur.

So therc was a knight that was called the Knight with the Strange Beast, and at that time his right name was called Pellinor, the which was a good man of prowess, and he smote a mighty stroke at King Lot as he fought with all his enemies, and he failed of his stroke, and smote the horse's neck, that he fell to the ground with King Lot; and therewith anon Pellinor smote him a great stroke through the helm and head unto the brows. And then all the host of Orkney fled for the death of King Lot, and there were slain many mothers' sons. But King Pellinor bare the wite of the death of King Lot, wherefore Sir Gawain revenged the death of his father the tenth year after he was made knight, and slew King Pellinor with his own hands.

Also there were slain at that battle twelve kings on the side of King Lot with Nero, and all were buried in the Church of Saint Stephen's in Camelot, and the remnant of knights and of other were buried in a great rock.

CHAPTER 11: *Of the interment of twelve kings, and of the prophecy of Merlin how Balin should give the Dolorous Stroke*

So at the interment came King Lot's wife Margawse with her four sons, Gawain, Agravain, Gaheris, and Gareth. Also

abode: withstood.

there came thither King Uriens, Sir Uwain's father, and Morgan le Fay his wife that was King Arthur's sister. All these came to the interment.

But of all these twelve kings, King Arthur let make the tomb of King Lot passing richly, and made his tomb by his own; and then Arthur let make twelve images of laton and copper, and over-gilt it with gold, in the sign of twelve kings, and each one of them held a taper of wax that burnt day and night; and King Arthur was made in sign of a figure standing above them with a sword drawn in his hand, and all the twelve figures had countenance like unto men that were overcome.

All this made Merlin by his subtle craft, and there he told the king, 'When I am dead these tapers shall burn no longer, and soon after the adventures of the Sangrail shall come among you and be achieved.' Also he told Arthur how 'Balin the worshipful knight shall give the Dolorous Stroke, whereof shall fall great vengeance.'

'Oh, where is Balin and Balan and Pellinor?' said King Arthur.

'As for Pellinor,' said Merlin, 'he will meet with you soon; and as for Balin he will not be long from you; but the other brother will depart, ye shall see him no more.'

'By my faith,' said Arthur, 'they are two marvellous knights, and namely Balin passeth of prowess of any knight that ever I found, for much beholden I am unto him; would God he would abide with me.'

'Sir,' said Merlin, 'look ye keep well the scabbard of Excalibur, for ye shall lose no blood while ye have the scabbard upon you, though ye have as many wounds upon you as ye may have.' (So after, for great trust, Arthur betook the scabbard to Morgan le Fay his sister, and she loved another knight better than her husband King Uriens or King Arthur, and she would have had Arthur her brother slain, and therefore she let make another scabbard like it by enchantment, and gave the scabbard Excalibur to her love; and the knight's

laton: mixed metal. *namely*: especially.

name was called Accolon, that after had near slain King Arthur.) After this Merlin told unto King Arthur of the prophecy that there should be a great battle beside Salisbury, and Mordred his own son should be against him. Also he told him that Bagdemagus was his cousin, and germain unto King Uriens.

CHAPTER 12: *How a sorrowful knight came tofore Arthur, and how Balin fetched him, and how that knight was slain by a knight invisible*

Within a day or two King Arthur was somewhat sick, and he let pitch his pavilion in a meadow, and there he laid him down on a pallet to sleep, but he might have no rest. Right so he heard a great noise of an horse, and therewith the king looked out at the porch of the pavilion, and saw a knight coming even by him making great dole.

'Abide, fair sir,' said Arthur, 'and tell me wherefore thou makest this sorrow.'

'Ye may little amend me,' said the knight, and so passed forth to the Castle of Meliot.

Anon after there came Balin, and when he saw King Arthur he alit off his horse, and came to the king on foot, and saluted him.

'By my head,' said Arthur, 'ye be welcome. Sir, right now came riding this way a knight making great mourn, for what cause I cannot tell; wherefore I would desire of you of your courtesy and of your gentleness to fetch again that knight either by force or else by his good will.'

'I will do more for your lordship than that,' said Balin; and so he rode more than a pace, and found the knight with a damosel in a forest, and said, 'Sir knight, ye must come with me unto King Arthur, for to tell him of your sorrow.'

'That will I not,' said the knight, 'for it will scathe me greatly, and do you none avail.'

'Sir,' said Balin, 'I pray you make you ready, for ye must

scathe: hurt.

go with me, or else I must fight with you and bring you by force, and that were me loth to do.'

'Will ye be my warrant,' said the knight, 'and I go with you?'

'Yea,' said Balin, 'or else I will die therefore.'

And so he made him ready to go with Balin, and left the damosel still. And as they were even afore King Arthur's pavilion, there came one invisible, and smote this knight that went with Balin throughout the body with a spear.

'Alas,' said the knight, 'I am slain under your conduct with a knight called Garlon; therefore take my horse that is better than yours, and ride to the damosel, and follow the quest that I was in as she will lead you, and revenge my death when ye may.'

'That shall I do,' said Balin, 'and that I make a vow unto knighthood;' and so he departed from this knight with great sorrow.

So King Arthur let bury this knight richly, and made a mention on his tomb, how there was slain Herlews le Berbeus, and by whom the treachery was done, the knight Garlon. But ever the damosel bare the truncheon of the spear with her that Sir Herlews was slain withal.

CHAPTER 13: *How Balin and the damosel met with a knight which was in likewise slain, and how the damosel bled for the custom of a castle*

So Balin and the damosel rode into a forest, and there met with a knight that had been on hunting, and that knight asked Balin for what cause he made so great sorrow.

'Me list not to tell you,' said Balin.

'Now,' said the knight, 'and I were armed as ye be I would fight with you.'

'That should little need,' said Balin, 'I am not afeared to tell you,' and told him all the cause how it was.

'Ah,' said the knight, 'is this all? Here I ensure you by

the faith of my body never to depart from you while my life lasteth.'

And so they went to the hostelry and armed them, and so rode forth with Balin. And as they came by an hermitage even by a churchyard, there came the knight Garlon invisible, and smote this knight, Perin de Mountbeliard, through the body with a spear.

'Alas,' said the knight, 'I am slain by this traitor knight that rideth invisible.'

'Alas,' said Balin, 'it is not the first despite he hath done me.' And there the hermit and Balin buried the knight under a rich stone and a tomb royal.

And on the morn they found letters of gold written, how: SIR GAWAIN SHALL REVENGE HIS FATHER'S DEATH, KING LOT, ON THE KING PELLINOR.

Anon after this Balin and the damosel rode till they came to a castle, and there Balin alit, and he and the damosel went to go into the castle, and anon as Balin came within the castle's gate the portcullis fell down at his back, and there fell many men about the damosel, and would have slain her. When Balin saw that, he was sore aggrieved, for he might not help the damosel; and then he went up into the tower, and leapt over the walls into the ditch, and hurt him not; and anon he pulled out his sword and would have foughten with them. And they all said nay, they would not fight with him, for they did nothing but the old custom of the castle, and told him how their lady was sick, and had lain many years, and she might not be whole but if she had a dish of silver full of blood of a clean maid and a king's daughter; 'and therefore the custom of the castle is, there shall no damosel pass this way but she shall bleed of her blood in a silver dish full.'

'Well,' said Balin, 'she shall bleed as much as she may bleed, but I will not lose the life of her whiles my life lasteth.'

And so Balin made her to bleed by her good will, but her blood halp not the lady. And so he and she rested there all

clean: pure. *halp*: helped.

night, and had there right good cheer, and on the morn they passed on their ways. And as it telleth after in the Sangrail, that Sir Percival's sister halp that lady with her blood, whereof she was dead.

CHAPTER 14: *How Balin met with that knight named Garlon at a feast, and there he slew him to have his blood to heal therewith the son of his host*

Then they rode three or four days and never met with adventure, and by hap they were lodged with a gentleman that was a rich man and well at ease. And as they sat at their supper Balin heard one[1] complain grievously by him in a chair. 'What is this noise?' said Balin.

'Forsooth,' said his host, 'I will tell you. I was but late at a jousting, and there I jousted with a knight that is brother unto King Pellam, and twice smote I him down, and then he promised to quit me on my best friend; and so he wounded my son, that cannot be whole till I have of that knight's blood, and he rideth alway invisible, but I know not his name.'

'Ah!' said Balin, 'I know that knight, his name is Garlon, he hath slain two knights of mine in the same manner, therefore I had lever meet with that knight than all the gold in this realm, for the despite he hath done me.'

'Well,' said his host, 'I shall tell you, King Pellam of Listinoise hath made do cry in all this country a great feast that shall be within these twenty days, and no knight may come there but if he bring his wife with him, or his paramour; and that knight, your enemy and mine, ye shall see that day.'

'Then I behote you,' said Balin, 'part of his blood to heal your son withal.'

'We will be forward to-morn,' said his host.

So on the morn they rode all three toward Pellam, and they had fifteen days' journey or they came thither; and that same day began the great feast. And so they alit and stabled

behote: promise.

their horses, and went into the castle; but Balin's host might not be let in because he had no lady.

Then Balin was well received and brought unto a chamber and unarmed him, and there were brought him robes to his pleasure, and would have had Balin leave his sword behind him.

'Nay,' said Balin, 'that do I not, for it is the custom of my country a knight always to keep his weapon with him, and that custom will I keep, or else I will depart as I came.' Then they gave him leave to wear his sword, and so he went unto the castle, and was set among knights of worship, and his lady afore him.

Soon Balin asked a knight, 'Is there not a knight in this court whose name is Garlon?'

'Yonder he goeth,' said a knight, 'he with the black face; he is the marvellest knight that is now living, for he destroyeth many good knights, for he goeth invisible.'

'Ah well,' said Balin, 'is that he?' Then Balin advised him long: 'If I slay him here I shall not scape, and if I leave him now, peradventure I shall never meet with him again at such a steven and much harm he will do and he live.'

Therewith this Garlon espied that this Balin beheld him, and then he came and smote Balin on the face with the back of his hand, and said, 'Knight, why beholdest thou me so? For shame therefore, eat thy meat and do that thou came for.'

'Thou sayest sooth,' said Balin, 'this is not the first despite that thou hast done me, and therefore I will do that I came for,' and rose up fiercely and clave his head to the shoulders. 'Give me the truncheon,' said Balin to his lady, 'wherewith he slew your knight.' Anon she gave it him, for alway she bare the truncheon with her. And therewith Balin smote him through the body, and said openly, 'With that truncheon thou hast slain a good knight, and now it sticketh in thy body.'

And then Balin called unto him his host, saying, 'Now may ye fetch blood enough to heal your son withal.'

advised him: considered to himself. *steven*: occasion.

CHAPTER 15: *How Balin fought with King Pellam, and how his sword brake, and how he gat a spear wherewith he smote the Dolorous Stroke*

Anon all the knights arose from the table for to set on Balin, and King Pellam himself arose up fiercely, and said, 'Knight, hast thou slain my brother? Thou shalt die therefore or thou depart.'

'Well,' said Balin, 'do it yourself.'

'Yes,' said King Pellam, 'there shall no man have ado with thee but myself, for the love of my brother.'

Then King Pellam caught in his hand a grim weapon and smote eagerly at Balin; but Balin put his sword betwixt his head and the stroke, and therewith his sword brast in sunder.[1] And when Balin was weaponless he ran into a chamber for to seek some weapon, and so from chamber to chamber, and no weapon he could find, and always King Pellam after him. And at the last he entered into a chamber that was marvellously well dight and richly, and a bed arrayed with cloth of gold the richest that might be thought, and one lying therein, and thereby stood a table of clean gold with four pillars of silver that bare up the table, and upon the table stood a marvellous spear strangely wrought.

And when Balin saw that spear, he gat it in his hand and turned him to King Pellam, and smote him passingly sore with that spear, that King Pellam fell down in a swoon, and therewith the castle roof and walls brake and fell to the earth, and Balin fell down so that he might not stir foot nor hand. And so the most part of the castle, that was fall down through that Dolorous Stroke, lay upon Pellam and Balin three days.[2]

dight: arranged.

CHAPTER 16: *How Balin was delivered by Merlin, and saved a knight that would have slain himself for love*

Then Merlin came thither and took up Balin, and gat him a good horse, for his was dead, and bad him ride out of that country.

'I would have my damosel,' said Balin.

'Lo,' said Merlin, 'where she lieth dead.'

[1]And King Pellam lay so, many years sore wounded, and might never be whole till Galahad the Haut Prince healed him in the quest of the Sangrail, for in that place was part of the blood of Our Lord Jesus Christ, that Joseph of Arimathea brought into this land, and there himself lay in that rich bed. And that was the same spear that Longius smote Our Lord to the heart. And King Pellam was nigh of Joseph's kin, and that was the most worshipful man that lived in those days, and great pity it was of his hurt, for through that stroke, turned to great dole, tray and tene.

Then departed Balin from Merlin, and said, 'In this world we meet never no more.' So he rode forth through the fair countries and cities, and found the people dead, slain on every side. And all that were alive cried, 'O Balin, thou hast caused great damage in these countries; for the dolorous stroke thou gavest unto King Pellam, three countries are destroyed, and doubt not but the vengeance will fall on thee at the last.'

When Balin was past those countries he was passing fain. So he rode eight days or he met with adventure. And at the last he came into a fair forest in a valley, and was ware of a tower, and there beside he saw a great horse of war, tied to a tree, and there beside sat a fair knight on the ground and made great mourning, and he was a likely man, and a well made. Balin said, 'God save you, why be ye so heavy? Tell me and I will amend it, and I may to my power.'

'Sir knight,' said he again, 'thou doest me great grief, for I

tray: sorrow. *tene*: grief. *fain*: glad.

was in merry thoughts, and now thou puttest me to more pain.'

Balin went a little from him, and looked on his horse; then heard Balin him say thus: 'Ah, fair lady, why have ye broken my promise, for thou promisest me to meet me here by noon, and I may curse thee that ever ye gave me this sword, for with this sword I slay myself,' and pulled it out. And therewith Balin start unto him and took him by the hand.

'Let go my hand,' said the knight, 'or else I shall slay thee.'

'That shall not need,' said Balin, 'for I shall promise you my help to get you your lady, and ye will tell me where she is.'

'What is your name?' said the knight.

'My name is Balin le Savage.'

'Ah, sir, I know you well enough, ye are the Knight with the Two Swords, and the man of most prowess of your hands living.'

'What is your name?' said Balin.

'My name is Garnish of the Mount, a poor man's son, but by my prowess and hardiness a duke hath made me knight, and gave me lands; his name is Duke Hermel, and his daughter is she that I love, and she me, as I deemed.'

'How far is she hence?' said Balin.

'But six mile,' said the knight.

'Now ride we hence,' said these two knights. So they rode more than a pace, till that they came to a fair castle well walled and ditched.

'I will into the castle,' said Balin, 'and look if she be there.'

So he went in and searched from chamber to chamber, and found her bed, but she was not there. Then Balin looked into a fair little garden, and under a laurel tree he saw her lie upon a quilt of green samite and a knight in her arms, fast halsing either other, and under their heads grass and herbs. When Balin saw her lie so with the foulest knight that ever he saw, and she a fair lady, then Balin went through all the chambers again, and told the knight how he found her as

halsing: embracing.

she had slept fast, and so brought him in the place there she lay fast sleeping.

CHAPTER 17: *How that knight slew his love and a knight lying by her, and after, how he slew himself with his own sword, and how Balin rode toward a castle where he lost his life*

And when Garnish beheld her so lying, for pure sorrow his mouth and nose brast out on bleeding, and with his sword he smote off both their heads, and then he made sorrow out of measure, and said, 'O Balin, much sorrow hast thou brought unto me, for haddest thou not showed me that sight I should have passed my sorrow.'

'Forsooth,' said Balin, 'I did it to this intent that it should better thy courage, and that ye might see and know her falsehood, and to cause you to leave love of such a lady; God knoweth I did none other but as I would ye did to me.'

'Alas,' said Garnish, 'now is my sorrow double that I may not endure, now have I slain that I most loved in all my life;' and therewith suddenly he rove himself on his own sword unto the hilts.

When Balin saw that, he dressed him thenceward, lest folk would say he had slain them; and so he rode forth, and within three days he came by a cross, and thereon were letters of gold written, that said, IT IS NOT FOR NO KNIGHT ALONE TO RIDE TOWARD THIS CASTLE.

Then saw he an old hoar gentleman coming toward him, that said, 'Balin le Savage, thou passest thy bounds to come this way, therefore turn again and it will avail thee.' And he vanished away anon; and so he heard an horn blow as it had been the death of a beast. 'That blast,' said Balin, 'is blown for me, for I am the prize and yet am I not dead.'

Anon withal he saw an hundred ladies and many knights, that welcomed him with fair semblant, and made him passing good cheer unto his sight, and led him into the castle, and there was dancing and minstrelsy and all manner of joy.

Then the chief lady of the castle said, 'Knight with the Two Swords, ye must have ado and joust with a knight hereby that keepeth an island, for there may no man pass this way, but he must joust or he pass.'

'That is an unhappy custom,' said Balin, 'that a knight may not pass this way but if he joust.'

'Ye shall not have ado but with one knight,' said the lady.

'Well,' said Balin, 'since I shall, thereto I am ready, but travelling men are oft weary and their horses too; but though my horse be weary my heart is not weary. I would be fain there my death should be.'

'Sir,' said a knight to Balin, 'methinketh your shield is not good, I will lend you a bigger, thereof I pray you.'

And so he took the shield that was unknown and left his own, and so rode unto the island, and put him and his horse in a great boat; and when he came on the other side he met with a damosel, and she said, 'O knight Balin, why have ye left your own shield? Alas ye have put yourself in great danger, for by your shield ye should have been known; it is great pity of you as ever was of knight, for of thy prowess and hardiness thou hast no fellow living.'

'Me repenteth,' said Balin, 'that ever I came within this country, but I may not turn now again for shame, and what adventure shall fall to me, be it life or death, I will take the adventure that shall come to me.' And then he looked on his armour, and understood he was well armed, and therewith blessed him and mounted upon his horse.

CHAPTER 18: *How Balin met with his brother Balan, and how each of them slew other unknown, till they were wounded to death*

Then afore him he saw come riding out of a castle a knight, and his horse trapped all red, and himself in the same colour. When this knight in the red beheld Balin, him thought it

blessed him: crossed himself.

should be his brother Balin because of his two swords, but because he knew not his shield he deemed it was not he. And so they aventred their spears and came marvellously fast together, and they smote other in the shields, but their spears and their course were so big that it bare down horse and man that they lay both in a swoon.

But Balin was bruised sore with the fall of his horse, for he was weary of travel. And Balan was the first that rose on foot and drew his sword, and went toward Balin, and he arose and went against him; but Balan smote Balin first, and he put up his shield and smote him through the shield and tamed his helm. Then Balin smote him again with that unhappy sword, and well nigh had felled his brother Balan, and so they fought there together till their breaths failed.

Then Balin looked up to the castle and saw the towers stand full of ladies. So they went unto battle again, and wounded every each other dolefully, and then they breathed ofttimes, and so went unto battle that all the place there as they fought was blood red. And at that time there was none of them both but they had either smitten other seven great wounds, so that the least of them might have been the death of the mightiest giant in this world.

Then they went to battle again so marvellously that doubt it was to hear of that battle for the great blood-shedding, and their hauberks unnailed, that naked they were on every side.

At last Balan the younger brother withdrew him a little and laid him down. Then said Balin le Savage, 'What knight art thou? For or now I found never no knight that matched me.'

'My name is,' said he, 'Balan, brother unto the good knight, Balin.'

'Alas,' said Balin, 'that ever I should see this day,' and therewith he fell backward in a swoon.

Then Balan yede on all four feet and hands, and put off the helm of his brother, and might not know him by the visage

aventred: set in position. *tamed*: pierced. *doubt*: a fearful thing.
yede: went.

it was so full hewn and bled; but when he awoke he said, 'O Balan, my brother, thou hast slain me and I thee, wherefore all the wide world shall speak of us both.'

'Alas,' said Balan, 'that ever I saw this day, that through mishap I might not know you, for I espied well your two swords, but because ye had another shield I deemed ye had been another knight.'

'Alas,' said Balin, 'all that made an unhappy knight in the castle, for he caused me to leave mine own shield to our both's destruction, and if I might live I would destroy that castle for ill customs.'

'That were well done,' said Balan, 'for I had never grace to depart from them since that I came hither, for here it happed me to slay a knight that kept this island, and since might I never depart, and no more should ye, brother, and ye might have slain me as ye have, and escaped yourself with the life.'

Right so came the lady of the tower with four knights and six ladies and six yeomen unto them, and there she heard how they made their moan either to other, and said, 'We came both out of one tomb, that is to say one mother's belly, and so shall we lie both in one pit.' So Balan prayed the lady of her gentleness, for his true service, that she would bury them both in that same place there the battle was done. And she granted them with weeping it should be done richly in the best manner.

'Now, will ye send for a priest, that we may receive our sacrament, and receive the blessed body of Our Lord Jesus Christ?'

'Yea,' said the lady, 'it shall be done;' and so she sent for a priest and gave them their rites.

'Now,' said Balin, 'when we are buried in one tomb, and the mention made over us how two brethren slew each other, there will never good knight nor good man see our tomb but they will pray for our souls.'

And so all the ladies and gentlewomen wept for pity. Then

all that made an unhappy knight in the castle: 'a wretched knight in the castle caused all that.'

anon Balan died, but Balin died not till the midnight after, and so were they buried both, and the lady let make a mention of Balan how he was there slain by his brother's hands, but she knew not Balin's name.

CHAPTER 19: *How Merlin buried them both in one tomb, and of Balin's sword*

In the morn came Merlin and let write Balin's name on the tomb with letters of gold: that: HERE LIETH BALIN LE SAVAGE THAT WAS THE KNIGHT WITH TWO SWORDS, AND HE THAT SMOTE THE DOLOROUS STROKE.

Also Merlin let make there a bed, that there should never man lie therein but he went out of his wit, yet Launcelot de Lake fordid that bed through his noblesse.

And anon after Balin was dead, Merlin took his sword, and took off the pommel and set on another pommel. So Merlin bad a knight that stood afore him handle that sword, and he assayed, and he might not handle it. Then Merlin laughed.

'Why laugh ye?' said the knight.

'This is the cause,' said Merlin: 'there shall never man handle this sword but the best knight of the world, and that shall be Sir Launcelot or else Galahad his son, and Launcelot with this sword shall slay the man that in the world he loved best, that shall be Sir Gawain.'

All this he let write in the pommel of the sword. Then Merlin let make a bridge of iron and of steel into that island, and it was but half a foot broad, and there shall never man pass that bridge, nor have hardiness to go over, but if he were a passing good man and a good knight without treachery or villainy. Also the scabbard of Balin's sword Merlin left it on this side the island that Galahad should find it. Also Merlin let make by his subtlety that Balin's sword was put in a marble stone standing upright as great as a mill stone, and the stone

fordid: rendered powerless.

hoved always above the water and did many years, and so by adventure it swam down the stream to the city of Camelot, that is in English Winchester. And that same day Galahad the Haut Prince[1] came with King Arthur, and so Galahad brought with him the scabbard and achieved the sword that was there in the marble stone hoving upon the water. And on Whitsunday he achieved the sword as it is rehearsed in the book of Sangrail.

Soon after this was done Merlin came to King Arthur and told him of the Dolorous Stroke that Balin gave to King Pellam, and how Balin and Balan fought together the marvellest battle that ever was heard of, and how they were buried both in one tomb.

'Alas,' said King Arthur, 'this is the greatest pity that ever I heard tell of two knights, for in the world I know not such two knights.'

Thus endeth the tale of Balin and of Balan, two brethren born in Northumberland, good knights.

Sequitur iii. liber

hoved: remained.

Book III

CHAPTER 1: *How King Arthur took a wife, and wedded Guenever, daughter to Leodegrance, king of the land of Camelerd, with whom he had the Round Table*

In the beginning of Arthur, after he was chosen king by adventure and by grace, for the most part of the barons knew not that he was Uther Pendragon's son, but as Merlin made it openly known, but yet many kings and lords held great war against him for that cause, but well Arthur overcame them all, for the most part the days of his life he was ruled much by the counsel of Merlin. So it fell on a time King Arthur said unto Merlin, 'My barons will let me have no rest, but needs I must take a wife, and I will none take but by thy counsel and by thine advice.'

'It is well done,' said Merlin, 'that ye take a wife, for a man of your bounty and noblesse should not be without a wife. Now is there any that ye love more than another?'

'Yea,' said King Arthur, 'I love Guenever the King's daughter Leodegrance, of the land of Camelerd, the which holdeth in his house the Table Round that ye told he had of my father Uther. And this damosel is the most valiant and fairest lady that I know living, or yet that ever I could find.'

'Sir,' said Merlin, 'as of her beauty and fairness she is one of the fairest alive, but and ye loved her not so well as ye do, I should find you a damosel of beauty and of goodness that should like you and please you, and your heart were not set; but there as a man's heart is set, he will be loth to return.'

'That is truth,' said King Arthur.

But Merlin warned the king covertly that Guenever was

bounty: excellence.

not wholesome for him to take to wife, for he warned him that Launcelot should love her, and she him again; and so he turned his tale to the adventures of Sangrail. Then Merlin desired of the king for to have men with him that should enquire of Guenever, and so the king granted him, and Merlin went forth unto King Leodegrance of Camelerd, and told him of the desire of the king that he would have unto his wife Guenever his daughter.

'That is to me,' said King Leodegrance, 'the best tidings that ever I heard, that so worthy a king of prowess and noblesse will wed my daughter. And as for my lands, I will give him, wist I it might please him, but he hath lands enow, him needeth none, but I shall send him a gift shall please him much more, for I shall give him the Table Round, the which Uther Pendragon gave me, and when it is full complete, there is an hundred knights and fifty. And as for an hundred good knights I have myself, but I fault fifty, for so many have been slain in my days.'

And so Leodegrance delivered his daughter Guenever unto Merlin, and the Table Round with the hundred knights, and so they rode freshly, with great royalty, what by water and what by land, till that they came nigh unto London.

CHAPTER 2: *How the knights of the Round Table were ordained and their sieges blessed by the Bishop of Canterbury*

When King Arthur heard of the coming of Guenever and the hundred knights with the Table Round, then King Arthur made great joy for her coming, and that rich present, and said openly, 'This fair lady is passing welcome unto me, for I have loved her long, and therefore there is nothing so leve to me. And these knights with the Round Table pleasen me more than right great riches.'

And in all haste the king let ordain for the marriage and the coronation in the most honourable wise that could be

fault: lack. *sieges*: seats. *leve*: pleasing.

devised. 'Now, Merlin,' said King Arthur, 'go thou and espy me in all this land fifty knights which be of most prowess and worship.'

Within short time Merlin had found such knights that should fulfil twenty and eight knights,[1] but no more he could find. Then the Bishop of Canterbury was fetched, and he blessed the sieges with great royalty and devotion, and there set the eight and twenty knights in their sieges.

And when this was done Merlin said, 'Fair sirs, you must all arise and come to King Arthur for to do him homage; he will have the better will to maintain you.'

And so they arose and did their homage, and when they were gone Merlin found in every sieges letters of gold that told the knights' names that had sitten therein. But two sieges were void.

And so anon came young Gawain and asked the king a gift.

'Ask,' said the king, 'and I shall grant it you.'

'Sir, I ask that ye will make me knight that same day ye shall wed fair Guenever.'

'I will do it with a good will,' said King Arthur, 'and do unto you all the worship that I may, for I must by reason ye are mine nephew, my sister's son.'

CHAPTER 3: *How a poor man riding upon a lean mare desired of King Arthur to make his son knight*

Forthwithal there came a poor man into the court, and brought with him a fair young man of eighteen year of age riding upon a lean mare; and the poor man asked all men that he met, 'Where shall I find King Arthur?'

'Yonder he is,' said the knights, 'wilt thou anything with him?'

'Yea,' said the poor man, 'therefore I came hither.'

Anon as he came before the king, he saluted him and said, 'O King Arthur, the flower of all knights and kings, I beseech

Jesu save thee. Sir, it was told me that at this time of your marriage ye would give any man the gift that he would ask, out except that were unreasonable.'

'That is truth,' said the king, 'such cries I let make, and that will I hold, so it appair not my realm nor mine estate.'

'Ye say well and graciously,' said the poor man. 'Sir, I ask nothing else but that ye will make my son here a knight.'

'It is a great thing thou askest of me,' said the king. 'What is thy name?' said the king to the poor man.

'Sir, my name is Aries the cowherd.'

'Whether cometh this of thee or of thy son?' said the king.

'Nay, sir,' said Aries, 'this desire cometh of my son and not of me, for I shall tell you I have thirteen sons, and all they will fall to what labour I put them, and will be right glad to do labour, but this child will not labour for me, for anything that my wife or I may do, but always he will be shooting or casting darts, and glad for to see battles and to behold knights, and always day and night he desireth of me to be made a knight.'

'What is thy name?' said the king unto the young man.

'Sir, my name is Tor.'

The king beheld him fast, and saw he was passingly well-visaged and passingly well made of his years. 'Well,' said King Arthur unto Aries the cowherd, 'fetch all thy sons afore me that I may see them.'

And so the poor man did, and all were shapen much like the poor man. But Tor was not like none of them all in shape ne in countenance, for he was much more than any of them.

'Now,' said King Arthur unto the cowherd, 'where is the sword he shall be made knight withal?'

'It is here,' said Tor.

'Take it out of the sheath,' said the king, 'and require me to make you a knight.'

Then Tor alit off his mare and pulled out his sword, kneeling, and requiring the king that he would make him knight, and that he might be a knight of the Table Round.

appair: impair.

'As for a knight I will make you,' and therewith smote him in the neck with the sword, saying, 'Be ye a good knight, and so I pray to God so ye may be, and if ye be of prowess and of worthiness ye shall be a knight of the Table Round. Now Merlin,' said Arthur, 'say whether this Tor shall be a good knight or no.'

'Yea, sir, he ought to be a good knight, for he is comen of as good a man as any is alive, and of king's blood.'

'How so, sir?' said the king.

'I shall tell you,' said Merlin. 'This poor man, Aries the cowherd, is not his father, he is nothing sib to him, for King Pellinor is his father.'

'I suppose nay,' said the cowherd.

'Fetch thy wife afore me,' said Merlin, 'and she shall not say nay.'

Anon the wife was fetched, which was a fair housewife, and there she answered Merlin full womanly, and there she told the king and Merlin that when she was a maid, and went to milk kine, there met with her a stern knight, 'and half by force he had my maidenhead, and at that time he begat my son Tor, and he took away from me my greyhound that I had that time with me, and said that he would keep the greyhound for my love.'

'Ah,' said the cowherd, 'I weened not this, but I may believe it well, for he had never no tatches of me.'

'Sir,' said Tor unto Merlin, 'dishonour not my mother.'

'Sir,' said Merlin, 'it is more for your worship than hurt, for your father is a good man and a king, and he may right well advance you and your mother, for ye were begotten or ever she was wedded.'

'That is truth,' said the wife.

'It is the less grief unto me,' said the cowherd.

sib: related.

CHAPTER 4: *How Sir Tor was known for son of King Pellinor, and how Gawain was made knight*

So on the morn King Pellinor came to the court of King Arthur, which had great joy of him, and told him of Tor, how he was his son, and how he had made him knight at the request of the cowherd. When Pellinor beheld Tor, he pleased him much. So the king made Gawain knight, but Tor was the first he made at the feast.

'What is the cause,' said King Arthur, 'that there be two places void in the sieges?'

'Sir,' said Merlin, 'there shall no man sit in those places but they shall be of most worship. But in the Siege Perilous there shall no man sit therein but one, and if there be any so hardy to do it he shall be destroyed, and he that shall sit there shall have no fellow.'

And therewith Merlin took King Pellinor by the hand, and in the one hand next the two sieges and the Siege Perilous he said, in open audience, 'This is your place and best ye are worthy to sit therein of any that is here.'

Thereat sat Sir Gawain in great envy and told Gaheris his brother, 'Yonder knight is put to great worship, the which grieveth me sore, for he slew our father King Lot, therefore I will slay him,' said Gawain, 'with a sword that was sent me that is passing trenchant.'

'Ye shall not so,' said Gaheris, 'at this time, for at this time I am but a squire, and when I am made knight I will be avenged on him, and therefore, brother, it is best ye suffer till another time, that we may have him out of the court, for, and we did so we should trouble this high feast.'

'I will well,' said Gawain, 'as ye will.'

CHAPTER 5: *How at the feast of the wedding of King Arthur to Guenever, a white hart came into the hall, and thirty couple hounds, and how a brachet pinched the hart which was taken away.*

Then was the high feast made ready, and the king was wedded at Camelot unto Dame Guenever in the Church of Saint Stephen's, with great solemnity. And as every man was set after his degree, Merlin went to all the knights of the Round Table, and bad them sit still, that none of them remove, 'for ye shall see a strange and a marvellous adventure.'

Right so as they sat there came running in a white hart into the hall, and a white brachet next him, and thirty couple of black running hounds came after with a great cry, and the hart went about the Table Round as he went by other boards, the white brachet bit him by the buttock and pulled out a piece, wherethrough the hart leapt a great leap and overthrew a knight that sat at the board side, and therewith the knight arose and took up the brachet, and so went forth out of the hall, and took his horse and rode his way with the brachet.

Right so anon came in a lady on a white palfrey, and cried aloud to King Arthur, 'Sir, suffer me not to have this despite, for the brachet was mine that the knight led away.'

'I may not do therewith,' said the king.

With this there came a knight riding all armed on a great horse, and took the lady away with him with force, and ever she cried and made great dole. When she was gone the king was glad, for she made such a noise.

'Nay,' said Merlin, 'ye may not leave these adventures so lightly, for these adventures must be brought again or else it would be disworship to you and to your feast.'

'I will,' said the king, 'that all be done by your advice.'

'Then,' said Merlin, 'let call Sir Gawain, for he must bring again the white hart. Also, sir, ye must let call Sir Tor, for he must bring again the brachet and the knight, or else slay him. Also let call King Pellinor, for he must bring again the lady and the knight, or else slay him. And these three knights shall do marvellous adventures or they come again.'

Then were they called all three as it rehearseth afore, and every each of them took his charge, and armed them surely. But Sir Gawain had the first request, and therefore we will begin at him.

CHAPTER 6: *How Sir Gawain rode for to fetch again the hart, and how two brethren fought each against other for the hart*

Sir Gawain rode more than a pace, and Gaheris his brother that rode with him instead of a squire to do him service. So as they rode they saw two knights fight on horseback passing sore, so Sir Gawain and his brother rode betwixt them, and asked them for what cause they fought so.

The one knight answered and said, 'We fight for a simple matter, for we two be two brethren born and begotten of one man and of one woman.'

'Alas,' said Sir Gawain, 'why do ye so?'

'Sir,' said the elder, 'there came a white hart this way this day, and many hounds chased him, and a white brachet was alway next him, and we understood it was adventure made for the high feast of King Arthur, and therefore I would have gone after to have won me worship; and here my younger brother said he would go after the hart, for he was better knight than I; and for this cause we fell at debate, and so we thought to prove which of us both was better knight.'

'This is a simple cause,' said Sir Gawain; 'uncouth men ye should debate withal, and no brother with brother; therefor but if ye will do by my counsel I will have ado with you, that is, ye shall yield you unto me, and that ye go unto King Arthur and yield you unto his grace.'

'Sir knight,' said the two brethren, 'we are forfoughten

and much blood have we lost through our wilfulness, and therefore we would be loth to have ado with you.'

'Then do as I will have you,' said Sir Gawain.

'We will agree to fulfil your will; but by whom shall we say that we be thither sent?'

'Ye may say, "by the knight that followeth the quest of the hart that was white." Now what is your name?' said Gawain.

'Sorlouse of the Forest,' said the elder.

'And my name is,' said the younger, 'Brian of the Forest.'

And so they departed and went to the king's court, and Sir Gawain on his quest. And as Gawain followed the hart by the cry of the hounds, even afore him there was a great river, and the hart swam over; and as Sir Gawain would follow after, there stood a knight over the other side, and said, 'Sir knight, come not over after this hart but if thou wilt joust with me.'

'I will not fail as for that,' said Sir Gawain, 'to follow the quest that I am in,' and so made his horse to swim over the water.

And anon they gat their spears and ran together full hard; but Sir Gawain smote him off his horse, and then he turned his horse and bad him yield him.

'Nay,' said the knight, 'not so, though thou have the better of me on horseback. I pray thee, valiant knight, alight afoot and match we together with swords.'

'What is your name?' said Sir Gawain.

'Alardin of the Isles,' said the other.

Then either dressed their shields and smote together, but Sir Gawain smote him so hard through the helm that it went to the brains, and the knight fell down dead.

'Ah!' said Gaheris, 'that was a mighty stroke of a young knight.'

CHAPTER 7: *How the hart was chased into a castle and there slain, and how Gawain slew a lady*

Then Gawain and Gaheris rode more than a pace after the white hart, and let slip at the hart three couple of greyhounds, and so they chase the hart into a castle, and in the chief place of the castle they slew the hart. Sir Gawain and Gaheris followed after. Right so there came a knight out of a chamber with a sword drawn in his hand and slew two of the greyhounds, even in the sight of Sir Gawain, and the remnant he chased them with his sword out of the castle.

And when he came again, he said, 'O my white hart, me repenteth that thou art dead, for my sovereign lady gave thee to me, and evil have I kept thee, and thy death shall be dear bought and I live.'

And anon he went into his chamber and armed him, and came out fiercely, and there met he with Sir Gawain.

'Why have ye slain my hounds?' said Sir Gawain, 'for they did but their kind, and lever I had ye had wroken your anger upon me than upon a dumb beast.'

'Thou sayest truth,' said the knight, 'I have avenged me on thy hounds, and so I will on thee or thou go.'

Then Sir Gawain alit afoot and dressed his shield, and struck together mightily, and clave their shields, and stoned their helms, and brake their hauberks that the blood ran down to their feet. At last Sir Gawain smote the knight so hard that he fell to the earth, and then he cried mercy, and yielded him, and besought him as he was a knight and gentleman, to save his life.

'Thou shalt die,' said Sir Gawain, 'for slaying of my hounds.'

'I will make amends,' said the knight, 'unto my power.'

Sir Gawain would no mercy have but unlaced his helm to have stricken off his head. Right so came his lady out of a

kind**:** nature. ***wroken*****:** avenged.

chamber and fell over him, and so he smote off her head by misadventure.

'Alas,' said Gaheris, 'that is foul and shamefully done, that shame shall never from you; also ye should give mercy unto them that ask mercy, for a knight without mercy is without worship.'

Sir Gawain was so stonied of the death of this fair lady that he wist not what he did, and said unto the knight, 'Arise, I will give thee mercy.'

'Nay, nay,' said the knight, 'I take no force of mercy now, for thou hast slain my love and my lady that I loved best of all earthly thing.'

'Me sore repenteth it,' said Sir Gawain, 'for I thought to strike unto thee. But now thou shalt go unto King Arthur and tell him of thine adventures, and how thou art overcome by the knight that went in the quest of the white hart.'

'I take no force,' said the knight, 'whether I live or I die;' but so for dread of death he swore to go unto King Arthur, and he made him to bear one greyhound before him on his horse, and another behind him.

'What is your name,' said Sir Gawain, 'or we depart?'

'My name is,' said the knight, 'Ablamor of the Marsh.'

So he departed toward Camelot.

CHAPTER 8: *How four knights fought against Sir Gawain and Gaheris, and how they were overcome, and their lives saved at the request of four ladies*

And Sir Gawai went into the castle, and made him ready to lie there all night, and would have unarmed him.

'What will ye do,' said Gaheris, 'will ye unarm you in this country? Ye may think ye have many enemies here.'

They had not sooner said that word but there came four knights well armed, and assailed Sir Gawain hard, and said unto him, 'Thou new-made knight, thou hast shamed thy

I take no force of: I do not care about.

knighthood, for a knight without mercy is dishonoured. Also thou hast slain a fair lady to thy great shame to the world's end, and doubt thou not thou shalt have great need of mercy or thou depart from us.'

And therewith one of them smote Sir Gawain a great stroke that nigh he fell to the earth, and Gaheris smote him again sore, and so they were on the one side and on the other, that Sir Gawain and Gaheris were in jeopardy of their lives; and one with a bow, an archer, smote Sir Gawain through the arm that it grieved him wonderly sore.

And as they should have been slain, there came four fair ladies, and besought the knights of grace for Sir Gawain; and goodly at request of the ladies they gave Sir Gawain and Gaheris their lives, and made them to yield them as prisoners. Then Gawain and Gaheris made great dole.

'Alas!' said Sir Gawain, 'mine arm grieveth me sore, I am like to be maimed;' and so made his complaint piteously.

Early on the morrow there came to Sir Gawain one of the four ladies that had heard all his complaint, and said, 'Sir knight, what cheer?'

'Not good,' said he.

'It is your own default,' said the lady, 'for ye have done a passing foul deed in the slaying of the lady, the which will be great villainy unto you. But be ye not of King Arthur's kin?' said the lady.

'Yes truly,' said Sir Gawain.

'What is your name?' said the lady, 'Ye must tell it me or ye pass.'

'My name is Gawain, the King Lot of Orkney's son, and my mother is King Arthur's sister.'

'Ah! then are ye nephew unto King Arthur,' said the lady, 'and I shall so speak for you that ye shall have conduct to go to King Arthur for his love.'

And so she departed and told the four knights how their prisoner was King Arthur's nephew, 'and his name is Sir Gawain, King Lot's son of Orkney.' And they gave him the hart's head because it was in his quest. Then anon they delivered Sir Gawain under this promise, that he should bear the dead lady with him in this manner: the head of her was hanged about his neck, and the whole body of her lay before him on his horse's mane.

Right so rode he forth unto Camelot. And anon as he was come, Merlin desired of King Arthur that Sir Gawain should be sworn to tell of all his adventures, and how he slew the lady, and how he would give no mercy unto the knight, wherethrough the lady was slain. Then the king and the queen were greatly displeased with Sir Gawain for the slaying of the lady.

And there by ordinance of the queen there was set a quest of ladies on Sir Gawain, and they judged him for ever while he lived to be with all ladies, and to fight for their quarrels; and that ever he should be courteous, and never to refuse mercy to him that asketh mercy. Thus was Gawain sworn upon the four Evangelists that he should never be against lady ne gentlewoman, but if he fought for a lady and his adversary fought for another. And thus endeth the adventure of Sir Gawain that he did at the marriage of King Arthur. Amen.

CHAPTER 9: *How Sir Tor rode after the knight with the brachet, and of his adventure by the way*

Then Sir Tor was ready, he mounted upon his horseback, and rode after the knight with the brachet. So as he rode he met with a dwarf suddenly that smote his horse on the head with a staff, that he went backward his spear length.

'Why dost thou so?' said Sir Tor.

'For thou shalt not pass this way, but if thou joust with yonder knights of the pavilions.' Then was Tor ware where two pavilions were, and great spears stood out, and two shields hung on trees by the pavilions.

'I may not tarry,' said Sir Tor, 'for I am in a quest that I must needs follow.'

ordinance: command. *quest*: judgement.

'Thou shalt not pass,' said the dwarf, and therewithal he blew his horn.

Then there came one armed on horseback, and dressed his shield, and came fast toward Tor, and he dressed him against him, and so ran together that Tor bare him from his horse. And anon the knight yielded him to his mercy. 'But, sir, I have a fellow in yonder pavilion that will have ado with you anon.'

'He shall be welcome,' said Sir Tor.

Then was he ware of another knight coming with great raundon, and each of them dressed to other, that marvel it was to see; but the knight smote Sir Tor for a great stroke in midst of the shield that his spear all to-shivered. And Sir Tor smote him through the shield below of the shield, that it went through the cost of the knight, but the stroke slew him not. And therewith Sir Tor alit and smote him on the helm a great stroke, and therewith the knight yielded him and besought him of mercy.

'I will well,' said Sir Tor, 'but thou and thy fellow must go unto King Arthur, and yield you prisoners unto him.'

'By whom shall we say are we thither sent?'

'Ye shall say "by the knight that went in the quest of the knight that went with the brachet." Now, what be your two names?' said Sir Tor.

'My name is,' said the one, 'Sir Felot of Langduk.'

'And my name is,' said the other, 'Sir Petipace of Winchelsea.'

'Now go ye forth,' said Sir Tor, 'and God speed you and me.'

Then came the dwarf and said unto Sir Tor, 'I pray you give me a gift.'

'I will well,' said Sir Tor, 'ask.'

'I ask no more,' said the dwarf, 'but that ye will suffer me to do you service, for I will serve no more recreant knights.'

'Take an horse,' said Sir Tor, 'and ride on with me.'

'I wot ye ride after the knight with the white brachet, and I shall bring you there he is,' said the dwarf.

cost: side.

And so they rode throughout a forest, and at the last they were ware of two pavilions even by a priory with two shields, and the one shield was enewed with white, and the other shield was red.

CHAPTER 10: *How Sir Tor found the brachet with a lady, and how a knight assailed him for the said brachet*

Therewith Sir Tor alit and took the dwarf his glaive, and so he came to the white pavilion, and saw three damosels lie in it, on[1] one pallet sleeping, and so he went to the other pavilion, and found a lady lying sleeping therein, but there was the white brachet that bayed at her fast, and therewith the lady yede out of the pavilion and all her damosels. But anon as Sir Tor espied the white brachet, he took her by force and took her to the dwarf.

'What, will ye so,' said the lady, 'take my brachet from me?'

'Yea,' said Sir Tor, 'this brachet have I sought from King Arthur's court hither.'

'Well,' said the lady, 'knight, ye shall not go far with her, but that ye shall be met and grieved.'

'I shall abide what adventure that cometh by the grace of God,' and so mounted upon his horse, and passed on his way toward Camelot; but it was so near night he might not pass but little further.

'Know ye any lodging?' said Tor.

'I know none,' said the dwarf, 'but here besides is an hermitage, and there ye must take lodging as ye find.'

And within a while they came to the hermitage and took lodging; and was there grass, oats and bread for their horses; soon it was sped, and full hard was their supper; but there they rested them all night till on the morn, and heard a mass devoutly, and took their leave of the hermit, and Sir Tor

enewed: coloured. *brachet*: bitch-hound. *sped*: finished.

prayed the hermit to pray for him. He said he would, and betook him to God, and so mounted upon horseback and rode towards Camelot a long while.

With that they heard a knight call loud that came after them, and he said, 'Knight, abide, and yield my brachet that thou took from my lady.'

Sir Tor returned again, and beheld him how he was a seemly knight and well horsed, and well armed at all points; then Sir Tor dressed his shield, and took his spear in his hands, and the other came fiercely upon him, and smote both horse and man to the earth. Anon they arose lightly and drew their swords as eagerly as lions, and put their shields afore them, and smote through the shields, that the cantels fell off both parties. Also they tamed their helms that the hot blood ran out, and the thick mails of their hauberks they carved and rove in sunder that the hot blood ran to the earth, and both they had many wounds and were passing weary.

But Sir Tor espied that the other knight fainted, and then he sued fast upon him, and doubled his strokes, and gart him go to the earth on the one side. Then Sir Tor bad him yield him.

'That will I not,' said Abelleus, 'while my life lasteth and the soul is within my body, unless that thou wilt give me the brachet.'

'That will I not do,' said Sir Tor, 'for it was my quest to bring again thy brachet, thee, or both.'

CHAPTER 11: *How Sir Tor overcame the knight, and how he lost his head at the request of a lady*

With that came a damosel riding on a palfrey as fast as she might drive, and cried with a loud voice unto Sir Tor.

'What will ye with me?' said Sir Tor.

'I beseech thee,' said the damosel, 'for King Arthur's love, give me a gift; I require thee gentle knight, as thou art a gentleman.'

sued: followed. *gart*: caused.

'Now,' said Tor, 'ask a gift and I will give it you.'

'Gramercy,' said the damosel; 'now I ask the head of the false knight Abelleus, for he is the most outrageous knight that liveth, and the greatest murderer.'

'I am loth,' said Sir Tor, 'of that gift I have given you; let him make amends in that he hath trespassed unto you.'

'Now,' said the damosel, 'he may not, for he slew mine own brother afore mine own eyen, that was a better knight than he, and he had had grace; and I kneeled half an hour afore him in the mire for to save my brother's life, that had done him no damage, but fought with him by adventure of arms, and so for all that I could do he struck off his head; wherefore I require thee, as thou art a true knight, to give me my gift, or else I shall shame thee in all the court of King Arthur; for he is the falsest knight living, and a great destroyer of good knights.'

Then when Abelleus heard this, he was more afeared, and yielded him and asked mercy.

'I may not now,' said Sir Tor, 'but if I should be found false of my promise; for while I would have taken you to mercy ye would none ask but if ye had the brachet again that was my quest.'

And therewith he took off his helm, and he arose and fled, and Sir Tor after him, and smote off his head quite.

'Now sir,' said the damosel, 'it is near night; I pray you come and lodge with me here at my place, it is here fast by.'

'I will well,' said Sir Tor, for his horse and he had fared evil since they departed from Camelot.

And so he rode with her, and had passing good cheer with her; and she had a passing fair old knight to her husband that made him passing good cheer, and well eased both his horse and he. And on the morn he heard his mass, and brake his fast, and took his leave of the knight and of the lady, that besought him to tell him his name.

'Truly,' he said, 'my name is Sir Tor that was late made

knight, and this was the first quest of arms that ever I did, to bring again that this knight Abelleus took away from King Arthur's court.'

'O fair knight,' said the lady and her husband, 'and ye come here in our marches, come and see our poor lodging, and it shall be always at your commandment.'

So Sir Tor departed and came to Camelot on the third day by noon, and the king and the queen and all the court was passing fain of his coming, and made great joy that he was come again; for he went from the court with little succour, but as King Pellinor his father gave him an old courser, and King Arthur gave him armour and a sword, and else had he none other succour, but rode so forth himself alone. And then the king and the queen by Merlin's advice made him to swear to tell of his adventures, and so he told and made proofs of his deeds as it is afore rehearsed, wherefore the king and the queen made great joy.

'Nay, nay,' said Merlin, 'these be but japes to that he shall do; for he shall prove a noble knight of prowess, as good as any is living, and gentle and courteous, and of good tatches, and passing true of his promise, and never shall outrage.'

Wherethrough Merlin's words King Arthur gave him an earldom of lands that fell unto him. And here endeth the quest of Sir Tor, King Pellinor's son.

CHAPTER 12: *How King Pellinor rode after the lady and the knight that led her away, and how a lady desired help of him, and how he fought with two knights for that lady, of whom he slew the one at the first stroke*

Then King Pellinor armed him and mounted upon his horse, and rode more than a pace after the lady that the knight led away. And as he rode in a forest, he saw in a valley a damosel sit by a well, and a wounded knight in her arms, and Pellinor saluted her.

And when she was ware of him, she cried overloud, 'Help me, knight, for Christ's sake, King Pellinor.'

And he would not tarry, he was so eager in his quest, and ever she cried an hundred times after help. When she saw he would not abide, she prayed unto God to send him as much need of help as she had, and that he might feel it or he died. So, as the book telleth, the knight there died that there was wounded, wherefore the lady for pure sorrow slew herself with his sword.

As King Pellinor rode in that valley he met with a poor man, a labourer.

'Sawest thou not,' said Pellinor, 'a knight riding and leading away a lady?'

'Yea,' said the man, 'I saw that knight, and the lady that made great dole. And yonder beneath in a valley there shall ye see two pavilions, and one of the knights of the pavilions challenged that lady of that knight, and said she was his cousin near, wherefore he should lead her no farther. And so they waged battle in that quarrel, the one said he would have her by force, and the other said he would have the rule of her, because he was her kinsman, and would lead her to her kin. For this quarrel he left them fighting. And if ye will ride a pace ye shall find them fighting, and the lady was beleft with the two squires in the pavilions.'

'God thank thee,' said King Pellinor.

Then he rode a wallop till he had a sight of the two pavilions, and the two knights fighting. Anon he rode unto the pavilions, and saw the lady that was his quest, and said, 'Fair lady, ye must go with me unto the court of King Arthur.'

'Sir knight,' said the two squires that were with her, 'yonder are two knights that fight for this lady, go thither and depart them, and be agreed with them, and then may ye have her at your pleasure.'

'Ye say well,' said King Pellinor.

And anon he rode betwixt them, and departed them, and asked them the causes why that they fought.

'Sir knight,' said the one, 'I shall tell you: this lady is my kinswoman nigh, mine aunt's daughter, and when I heard her complain that she was with him maugre her head, I waged battle to fight with him.'

'Sir knight,' said the other, whose name was Hontzlake of Wentland,[1] 'and this lady I gat by my prowess of arms this day at Arthur's court.'

'That is untruly said,' said King Pellinor, 'for ye came in suddenly there as we were at the high feast, and took away this lady or any man might make him ready, and therefore it was my quest to bring her again and you both, or else the one of us to abide in the field; therefore the lady shall go with me, or I will die for it, for I have promised it King Arthur. And therefore fight ye no more, for none of you shall have no part of her at this time, and if ye list to fight for her, fight with me, and I will defend her.'

'Well,' said the knights, 'make you ready, and we shall assail you will all our power.'

And as King Pellinor would have put his horse from them, Sir Hontzlake rove his horse through with a sword, and said, 'Now art thou on foot as well as we are.'

When King Pellinor espied that his horse was slain, lightly he leapt from his horse and pulled out his sword, and put his shield afore him, and said, 'Knight, keep well thy head, for thou shalt have a buffet for the slaying of my horse.'

So King Pellinor gave him such a stroke upon the helm that he clave the head down to the chin, that he fell to the earth dead.

CHAPTER 13: *How King Pellinor gat the lady and brought her to Camelot to the court of King Arthur*

And then he turned him to the other knight that was sore wounded. But when he saw the other's buffet, he would not fight, but kneeled down and said, 'Take my cousin the lady

maugre her head: despite all she could do. *keep*: guard.

with you at your request, and I require you, as ye be a true knight, put her to no shame nor villainy.'

'What,' said King Pellinor, 'will ye not fight for her?'

'No, sir,' said the knight, 'I will not fight with such a knight of prowess as ye be.'

'Well,' said Pellinor, 'ye say well; I promise you she shall have no villainy by me, as I am true knight. But now me lacketh an horse,' said Pellinor, 'but I will have Hontzlake's horse.'

'Ye shall not need,' said the knight, 'for I shall give you such an horse as shall please you, so that ye will lodge with me, for it is near night.'

'I will well,' said King Pellinor, 'abide with you all night.'

And there he had with him right good cheer, and fared of the best with passing good wine, and had merry rest that night. And on the morn he heard a mass and dined; and then was brought him a fair bay courser, and King Pellinor's saddle set upon him.

'Now, what shall I call you?' said the knight, 'inasmuch as ye have my cousin at your desire of your quest.'

'Sir, I shall tell you, my name is King Pellinor of the Isles and knight of the Table Round.'

'Now I am glad,' said the knight, 'that such a noble man shall have the rule of my cousin.'

'Now, what is your name?' said Pellinor, 'I pray you tell me.'

'Sir, my name is Sir Meliot of Logris, and this lady my cousin hight Nimue, and the knight that was in the other pavilion is my sworn brother, a passing good knight, and his name is Brian of the Isles,[1] and he is full loth to do wrong, and full loth to fight with any man, but if he be sore sought on, so that for shame he may not leave it.'

'It is marvel,' said Pellinor, 'that he will not have ado with me.'

'Sir, he will not have ado with no man but if it be at his request.'

'Bring him to the court,' said Pellinor, 'one of these days.'

'Sir, we will come together.'

'And ye shall be welcome,' said Pellinor, 'to the court of King Arthur, and greatly allowed for your coming.'

And so he departed with the lady, and brought her to Camelot. So as they rode in a valley it was full of stones, and there the lady's horse stumbled and threw her down, that her arm was sore bruised and near she swooned for pain.

'Alas sir,' said the lady, 'mine arm is out of lith, wherethrough I must needs rest me.'

'Ye shall well,' said King Pellinor. And so he alit under a fair tree where was fair grass, and he put his horse thereto, and so laid him under the tree and slept till it was nigh night. And when he awoke he would have ridden.

'Sir,' said the lady, 'it is so dark that ye may as well ride backward as forward.'

So they abode still and made there their lodging. Then Sir Pellinor put off his armour; then a little afore midnight they heard the trotting of an horse.

'Be ye still,' said King Pellinor, 'for we shall hear of some adventure.'

CHAPTER 14: *How on the way he heard two knights, as he lay by night in a valley, and of other adventures*

And therewith he armed him. So right even afore him there met two knights, the one came froward Camelot, and the other from the north, and either saluted other.

'What tidings at Camelote?' said the one.

'By my head,' said the other, 'there have I been and espied the court of King Arthur, and there is such a fellowship they may never be broken, and well-nigh all the world holdeth with Arthur, for there is the flower of chivalry. Now for this cause I am riding into the north, to tell our chieftains of the fellowship that is withholden with King Arthur.'

allowed: commended. *lith*: joint.

'As for that,' said the other knight, 'I have brought a remedy with me, that is the greatest poison that ever ye heard speak of, and to Camelot will I with it, for we have a friend right nigh King Arthur, and well cherished, that shall poison King Arthur; for so he hath promised our chieftains, and received great gifts for to do it.'

'Beware,' said the other knight, 'of Merlin, for he knoweth all things by the devil's craft.'

'Therefore will I not let it,' said the knight. And so they departed in sunder.

Anon after Pellinor made him ready, and his lady, and rode toward Camelot; and as they came by the well thereas the wounded knight was and the lady, there he found the knight, and the lady eaten with lions or wild beasts, all save the head, wherefore he made great sorrow, and wept passing sore, and said, 'Alas! her life might I have saved, but I was so fierce in my quest therefore I would not abide.'

'Wherefore make ye such dole?' said the lady.

'I wot not,' said Pellinor, 'but my heart mourneth sore of the death of her, for she was a passing fair lady and a young.'

'Now, will ye do by mine advice?' said the lady. 'Take this knight and let him be buried in an hermitage, and then take the lady's head and bear it with you unto Arthur.'

So King Pellinor took this dead knight on his shoulders, and brought him to the hermitage, and charged the hermit with the corpse, that service should be done for the soul; 'and take his harness for your pain.'

'It shall be done,' said the hermit, 'as I will answer unto God.'

CHAPTER 15: *How when he was comen to Camelot he was sworn upon a book to tell the truth of his quest*

And therewith they departed, and came thereas the head of the lady lay with a fair yellow hair, that grieved King Pelli-

let: cease.

nor passingly sore when he looked on it, for much he cast his heart on the visage. And so by noon they came to Camelot; and the king and the queen were passing fain of his coming to the court. And there he was made to swear upon the four Evangelists, to tell the truth of his quest from the one to the other.

'Ah ! Sir Pellinor,' said Queen Guenever, 'ye were greatly to blame that ye saved not this lady's life.'

'Madam,' said Pellinor, 'ye were greatly to blame and ye would not save your own life and ye might, but, save your pleasure, I was so furious in my quest that I would not abide, and that repenteth me, and shall the days of my life.'

'Truly,' said Merlin, 'ye ought sore to repent it, for that lady was your own daughter begotten on the Lady of the Rule, and that knight that was dead was her love, and should have wedded her, and he was a right good knight of a young man, and would have proved a good man, and to this court was he coming, and his name was Sir Miles of the Launds, and a knight came behind him and slew him with a spear, and his name is Loraine le Savage, a false knight and a coward; and she for great sorrow and dole slew herself with his sword, and her name was Elaine. And because ye would not abide and help her, ye shall see your best friend fail you when ye be in the greatest distress that ever ye were or shall be. And that penance God hath ordained you for that deed, that he that ye shall most trust to of any man alive, he shall leave you there ye shall be slain.'

'Me forthinketh,' said King Pellinor, 'that this shall me betide, but God may fordo well destiny.'

[1]Thus, when the quest was done of the white hart, the which followed Sir Gawain, and the quest of the brachet, followed of Sir Tor, Pellinor's son, and the quest of the lady that the knight took away, the which King Pellinor at that time followed, then the king stablished all his knights, and gave them that were of lands not rich, he gave them lands, and charged them never to do outrageousity nor murder, and always to flee treason; also, by no mean to be cruel, but to

give mercy unto him that asketh mercy, upon pain of forfeiture of their worship and lordship of King Arthur for evermore; and always to do ladies, damosels, and gentlewomen succour, upon pain of death. Also, that no man take no battles in a wrongful quarrel for no law, ne for no world's goods. Unto this were all the knights sworn of the Table Round, both old and young. And every year were they sworn at the high feast of Pentecost.

Explicit the Wedding of King Arthur

Sequitur quartus liber

Book IV

CHAPTER 1: *How Merlin was assotted and doted on one of the Ladies of the Lake, and how he was shut in a rock under a stone and there died*

So after these quests of Sir Gawain, Sir Tor, and King Pellinor, it fell so that Merlin fell in a dotage on the damosel that King Pellinor brought to court, and she was one of the damosels of the lake, that hight Nimue. But Merlin would let have her no rest, but always he would be with her. And ever she made Merlin good cheer till she had learned of him all manner thing that she desired; and he was assotted upon her, that he might not be from her.

So on a time he told King Arthur that he should not dure long, but for all his crafts he should be put in the earth quick, and so he told the king many things that should befall, but always he warned the king to keep well his sword and the scabbard, for he told him how the sword and the scabbard should be stolen by a woman from him, that he most trusted. Also he told King Arthur that he should miss him, 'Yet had ye lever than all your lands to have me again.'

'Ah,' said the king, 'since ye know of your adventure, purvey for it, and put away by your crafts that misadventure.'

'Nay,' said Merlin, 'it will not be.' So he departed from the king.

And within a while the Damosel of the Lake departed, and Merlin went with her evermore wheresomever she went. And ofttimes Merlin would have had her privily away by his subtle crafts; then she made him to swear that he should never do none enchantment upon her if he would have his will. And so he sware; so she and Merlin went over the sea unto the land of Benwick, thereas King Ban was king that had great war against King Claudas, and there Merlin spake with King Ban's wife, a fair lady and a good, and her name was Elaine, and there he saw young Launcelot. There the queen made great sorrow for the mortal war that King Claudas made on her lord and on her lands.

'Take none heaviness,' said Merlin, 'for this same child within this twenty year shall revenge you on King Claudas, that all Christendom shall speak of it; and this same child shall be the most man of worship of the world, and his first name is Galahad, that know I well,' said Merlin, 'and since ye have confirmed him Launcelot.'

'That is truth,' said the queen, 'his first name was Galahad. O Merlin,' said the queen, 'shall I live to see my son such a man of prowess?'

'Yea, lady, on my peril ye shall see it, and live many winters after.'

And so soon after the lady and Merlin departed, and by the way Merlin showed her many wonders, and came into Cornwall. And always Merlin lay about the lady to have her maidenhood, and she was ever passing weary of him, and fain would have been delivered of him, for she was afeared of him because he was a devil's son, and she could not beskift him by no mean.

And so on a time it happed that Merlin showed to her in a rock whereas was a great wonder, and wrought by enchantment, that went under a great stone. So by her subtle working she made Merlin to go under that stone to let her wit of the marvels there, but she wrought so there for him that he came never out for all the craft he could do. And so she departed and left Merlin.

beskift: be rid of.

CHAPTER 2: *How five kings came into this land to war against King Arthur, and what counsel Arthur had against them*

And as King Arthur rode to Camelot, and held there a great feast with mirth and joy, so soon after he returned unto Cardol, and there came unto Arthur new tidings that the King of Denmark, and the King of Ireland that was his brother, and the King of the Vale, and the King of Soleyse, and the King of the Isle of Longtains, all these five kings with a great host were entered into the land of King Arthur, and burnt and slew clean afore them, both cities and castles, that it was pity to hear.

'Alas,' said King Arthur, 'yet had I never rest one month since I was crowned king of this land. Now shall I never rest till I meet with those kings in a fair field, that I make mine avow; for my true liege people shall not be destroyed in my default, go with me who will, and abide who that will.'

Then the king let write unto King Pellinor, and prayed him in all haste to make him ready with such people as he might lightliest rear and hie him after in all haste. All the barons were privily wroth that the king would depart so suddenly; but the king by no mean would abide, but made writing unto them that were not there, and bad them hie after him, such as were not at that time in the court.

Then the king came to Queen Guenever, and said, 'Lady make you ready, for ye shall go with me, for I may not long miss you, ye shall cause me to be the more hardy, what adventure so befall me; I will not wit my lady to be in no jeopardy.'

'Sir,' said she, 'I am at your commandment, and shall be ready what time so ye be ready.'

So on the morn the king and the queen departed with such fellowship as they had, and came into the north, into a forest beside Humber, and there lodged them.

When the word and tiding came unto the five kings above

clean: completely.

said, that Arthur was beside Humber in a forest, there was a knight, brother unto one of the five kings, that gave them this counsel:

'Ye know well that Sir Arthur hath the flower of chivalry of the world with him, as it is proved by the great battle he did with the eleven kings; and therefore hie unto him night and day till that we be nigh him, for the longer he tarrieth the bigger he is, and we ever the weaker; and he is so courageous of himself that he is come to the field with little people, and therefore let us set upon him or day and we shall slay down; of his knights there shall none escape.'

CHAPTER 3: *How King Arthur had ado with them and overthrew them, and slew the five kings and made the remnant to flee*

Unto this counsel these five kings assented, and so they passed forth with their host through North Wales, and came upon Arthur by night, and set upon his host as the king and his knights were in their pavilions. King Arthur was unarmed, and had lain him to rest with his Queen Guenever.

'Sir,' said Sir Kay, 'it is not good we be unarmed.'

'We shall have no need,' said Sir Gawain and Sir Griflet, that lay in a little pavilion by the king.

With that they heard a great noise, and many cried, 'Treason, treason!'

'Alas,' said King Arthur, 'we be betrayed! Unto arms, fellows,' then he cried. So they were armed anon at all points.

Then came there a wounded knight unto the king, and said, 'Sir, save yourself and my lady the queen, for our host is destroyed, and much people of ours slain.'

So anon the king and the queen and the three knights took their horses, and rode toward Humber to pass over it, and the water was so rough that they were afraid to pass over.

'Now may ye choose,' said King Arthur, 'whether ye will

slay down: destroy completely.

abide and take the adventure on this side, for and ye be taken they will slay you.'

'It were me lever,' said the queen, 'to die in the water than to fall in your enemies' hands and there be slain.'

And as they stood so talking, Sir Kay saw the five kings coming on horseback by themself alone, with their spears in their hands even toward them.

'Lo,' said Sir Kay, 'yonder be the five kings; let us go to them and match them.'

'That were folly,' said Sir Gawain, 'for we are but three and they be five.'

'That is truth,' said Sir Griflet.

'No force,' said Sir Kay, 'I will undertake two of them, and then may ye three undertake for the other three.'

And therewithal, Sir Kay let his horse run as fast as he might, and struck one of them through the shield and the body a fathom, that the king fell to the earth stark dead. That saw Sir Gawain and ran unto another king so hard that he smote him through the body. And therewithal King Arthur ran to another, and smote him through the body with a spear, that he fell to the earth dead. Then Sir Griflet ran unto the fourth king, and gave him such a fall that his neck brake. Anon Sir Kay ran unto the fifth king, and smote him so hard on the helm that the stroke clave the helm and the head to the earth.

'That was well stricken,' said King Arthur, 'and worshipfully hast thou hold thy promise; therefore I shall honour thee while that I live.' And therewithal they set the queen in a barge into Humber; but always Queen Guenever praised Sir Kay for his deeds, and said, 'What lady that ye love, and she love you not again she were greatly to blame; and among ladies,' said the queen, 'I shall bear your noble fame, for ye spake a great word, and fulfilled it worshipfully.' And therewith the queen departed.

Then the king and the three knights rode into the forest, for there they supposed to hear of them that were escaped; and there he found the most part of his people, and told them all how the five kings were dead. 'And therefore let us hold us together till it be day, and when their host have espied that their chieftains be slain, they will make such dole that they shall not more help themself.'

And right so as the king said, so it was; for when they found the five kings dead, they made such dole that they fell from their horses. Therewithal came King Arthur but with a few people, and slew on the left hand and on the right hand, that well-nigh there escaped no man, but all were slain to the number of thirty thousand. And when the battle was all ended, the king kneeled down and thanked God meekly. And then he sent for the queen, and soon she was come, and she made great joy of the overcoming of that battle.

CHAPTER 4: *How the battle was finished or he came, and how the king founded an abbey where the battle was*

Therewithal came one to King Arthur, and told him that King Pellinor was within three mile with a great host.

And he said, 'Go unto him, and let him understand how we have sped.'

So within a while King Pellinor came with a great host, and saluted the people and the king, and there was great joy made on every side. Then the king let search how much people of his party there was slain; and there were found but little past two hundred men slain and eight knights of the Table Round in their pavilions.

Then the king let rear and devise in the same place thereas the battle was done a fair abbey, and endowed it with great livelihood, and let it call the Abbey of La Beale Adventure. But when some of them came into their countries, thereof the five kings were kings, and told them how they were slain, there was made great dole. And all King Arthur's enemies, as the King of North Wales, and the kings of the North, wist of the battle; they were passing heavy. And so the king returned unto Camelot in haste.

And when he was come to Camelot he called King Pellinor unto him, and said, 'Ye understand well that we have lost eight knights of the best of the Table Round, and by your advice we will choose eight again of the best we may find in this court.'

'Sir,' said Pellinor, 'I shall counsel you after my conceit the best: there are in your court full noble knights both of old and young; and therefore by mine advice ye shall choose half of the old and half of the young.'

'Which be the old?' said King Arthur.

'Sir,' said King Pellinor, 'meseemeth that King Uriens that hath wedded your sister Morgan le Fay, and the King of the Lake, and Sir Hervis de Revel, a noble knight, and Sir Galagars, the fourth.'

'This is well devised,' said King Arthur, 'and right so shall it be. Now, which are the four young knights?' said Arthur.

'Sir,' said Pellinor, 'the first is Sir Gawain, your nephew, that is as good a knight of his time as any is in this land; and the second as meseemeth best is Sir Griflet le Fise de Dieu, that is a good knight and full desirous in arms, and who may see him live he shall prove a good knight; and the third as meseemeth is well to be one of the knights of the Round Table, Sir Kay the Seneschal, for many times he hath done full worshipfully, and now at your last battle he did full honourably for to undertake to slay two kings.'

'By my head,' said Arthur, 'he is best worthy to be a knight of the Round Table of any that ye have rehearsed, and he had done no more prowess in his life days.'

CHAPTER 5: *How Sir Tor was made knight of the Round Table, and how Bagdemagus was displeased*

'Now,' said King Pellinor, 'I shall put to you two knights, and ye shall choose which is most worthy, that is Sir Bagdemagus, and Sir Tor, my son. But because Sir Tor is my son I may not praise him, but else, and he were not my son, I durst say that of his age there is not in this land a better knight than he is, nor of better conditions and loth to do any wrong, and loth to take any wrong.'

'By my head,' said Arthur, 'he is a passing good knight as any ye spake of this day, that wot I well,' said the king, 'for I have seen him proved, but he sayeth little and he doth much more, for I know none in all this court and he were as well born on his mother side as he is on your side, that is like him of prowess and of might: and therefore I will have him at this time, and leave Sir Bagdemagus till another time.'

So when they were so chosen by the assent of all the barons, so were there founden in their sieges every knights' names that here are rehearsed; and so were they set in their sieges, whereof Sir Bagdemagus was wonderly wroth, that Sir Tor was advanced afore him, and therefore suddenly he departed from the court, and took his squire with him, and rode long in a forest till they came to a cross, and there alit and said his prayers devoutly. The meanwhile his squire found written upon the cross, that Bagdemagus should never return unto the court again, till he had won a knight's body of the Round Table, body for body.

'Lo, sir,' said his squire, 'here I find writing of you, therefore I rede you return again to the court.'

'That shall I never,' said Bagdemagus, 'till men speak of me great worship, and that I be worthy to be a knight of the Round Table.'

And so he rode forth, and there by the way he found a branch of an holy herb that was the sign of the Sangrail,[1] and no knight found such tokens but he were a good liver.

So, as Sir Bagdemagus rode to see many adventures, it happed him to come to the rock thereas the Lady of the Lake had put Merlin under the stone, and there he heard him make great dole; whereof Sir Bagdemagus would have holpen him, and went unto the great stone, and he was so heavy that an hundred men might not lift it up. When Merlin wist he was there, he bad leave his labour, for all was in vain, for he might never be holpen but by her that put him there.

And so Bagdemagus departed and did many adventures, and proved after a full good knight, and came again to the court and was made knight of the Round Table.

So on the morn there fell new tidings and other adventures.

CHAPTER 6: *How King Arthur, King Uriens, and Sir Accolon of Gaul, chased an hart, and of their marvellous adventure*

Then it befell that Arthur and many of his knights rode on hunting into a great forest, and it happed King Arthur, King Uriens, and Sir Accolon of Gaul, followed a great hart, for they three were well horsed, and so they chased so fast that within a while they three were then ten mile from their fellowship. And at the last they chased so sore that they slew their horses underneath them. Then were they all three on foot, and ever they saw the hart afore them passing weary and ambushed.

'What will we do?' said King Arthur, 'We are hard bestad.'

'Let us go on foot,' said King Uriens, 'till we may meet with some lodging.'

Then were they ware of the hart that lay on a great water bank, and a brachet biting on his throat, and more other hounds came after. Then King Arthur blew the prize and dight the hart.

Then the king looked about the world, and saw afore him in a great water a little ship, all apparelled with silk down to the water, and the ship came right unto them and landed on the sands. Then Arthur went to the bank and looked in, and saw none earthly creature therein.

'Sirs,' said the king, 'come thence, and let us see what is in this ship.'

So they went in all three, and found it richly behanged with cloth of silk. By then it was dark night, and there suddenly were about them an hundred torches set upon all the

hard bestad: hard pressed. *prize*: capture.

sides of the ship boards, and it gave great light; and therewithal there came out twelve fair damosels and saluted King Arthur on their knees, and called him by his name, and said he was right welcome, and such cheer as they had he should have of the best. The king thanked them fair. Therewithal they led the king and his two fellows into a fair chamber, and there was a cloth laid richly beseen of all that longed unto a table, and there were they served of all wines and meats that they could think; of that the king had great marvel, for he fared never better in his life as for one supper.

And so when they had supped at their leisure, King Arthur was led unto a chamber, a richer beseen chamber saw he never none, and so was King Uriens served, and led into such another chamber, and Sir Accolon was led into the third chamber passing richly and well beseen; and so were they laid in their beds easily. And anon they fell asleep, and slept marvellously sore all the night.

And on the morrow King Uriens was in Camelot abed in his wife's arms, Morgan le Fay. And when he awoke he had great marvel, how he came there, for on the even afore he was two days' journey from Camelot. And when King Arthur awoke he found himself in a dark prison, hearing about him many complaints of woeful knights.

CHAPTER 7: *How Arthur took upon him to fight to be delivered out of prison, and also for to deliver twenty knights that were in prison*

'What are ye that so complain?' said King Arthur.

'We be here twenty knights, prisoners,' said they, 'and some of us have lain here seven year, and some more and some less.'

'For what cause?' said Arthur.

'We shall tell you,' said the knights. 'This lord of this castle, his name is Sir Damas, and he is the falsest knight that liveth, and full of treason, and a very coward as any liveth, and he hath a younger brother, a good knight of prowess, his name is Sir Ontzlake, and this traitor Damas, the elder brother will give him no part of his livelihood, but as Sir Ontzlake keepeth through prowess of his hands, and so he keepeth from him a full manor and a rich, and therein Sir Ontzlake dwelleth worshipfully, and is well beloved of all people. And this Sir Damas, our master is as evil beloved, for he is without mercy, and he is a coward, and great war hath been betwixt them both, but Ontzlake hath ever the better, and ever he proffereth Sir Damas to fight for the livelihood, body for body, but he will not do; other else to find a knight to fight for him. Unto that Sir Damas hath granted to find a knight, but he is so evil beloved and hated, that there nis never a knight will fight for him. And when Damas saw this, that there was never a knight would fight for him, he hath daily lain await with many knights with him, and taken all the knights in this country to see and espy their adventures, he hath taken them by force and brought them to his prison. And so he took us severally as we rode on our adventures, and many good knights have died in this prison for hunger, to the number of eighteen knights. And if any of us all that here is, or hath been, would have foughten with his brother Ontzlake, he would have delivered us, but for because this Damas is so false and so full of treason we would never fight for him to die for it. And we be so lean for hunger that unnethe we may stand on our feet.'

'God deliver you, for his mercy,' said Arthur.

Anon, therewithal there came a damosel unto Arthur, and asked him, 'What cheer?'

'I cannot say,' said he.

'Sir,' said she, 'and ye will fight for my lord, ye shall be delivered out of prison, and else ye escape never the life.'

'Now,' said Arthur, 'that is hard, yet had I lever to fight with a knight than to die in prison; with this,' said Arthur, 'I may be delivered and all these prisoners, I will do the battle.'

'Yes,' said the damosel.

'I am ready,' said Arthur, 'and I had horse and armour.'

'Ye shall lack none,' said the damosel.

'Meseemeth, damosel, I should have seen you in the court of Arthur.'

'Nay,' said the damosel, 'I came never there. I am the lord's daughter of this castle.'

Yet was she false, for she was one of the damosels of Morgan le Fay.

Anon she went unto Sir Damas, and told him how he would do battle for him, and so he sent for Arthur. And when he came he was well coloured, and well made of his limbs, that all knights that saw him said it were a pity that such a knight should die in prison. So Sir Damas and he were agreed that he should fight for him upon this covenant, that all other knights should be delivered; and unto that was Sir Damas sworn unto Arthur, and also to do the battle to the uttermost. And with that all the twenty knights were brought out of the dark prison into the hall, and delivered, and so they all abode to see the battle.

CHAPTER 8: *How Accolon found himself by a well, and he took upon him to do battle against Arthur*

Now turn we unto Accolon of Gaul, that when he awoke he found himself by a deep well-side, within half a foot, in great peril of death. And there came out of that fountain a pipe of silver, and out of that pipe ran water all on high in a stone of marble. When Sir Accolon saw this, he blessed him and said, 'Jesu save my lord King Arthur, and King Uriens, for these damosels in this ship have betrayed us, they were devils and no women; and if I may escape this misadventure, I shall destroy all where I may find these false damosels that usen enchantments.'

Right with that there came a dwarf with a great mouth and a flat nose, and saluted Sir Accolon, and said how he came from Queen Morgan le Fay, 'and she greeteth you well, and biddeth you be of strong heart, for ye shall fight to-morn with a knight at the hour of prime, and therefore she hath sent you here Excalibur, Arthur's sword, and the scabbard, and she biddeth you as ye love her, that ye do the battle to the uttermost, without any mercy, like as ye had promised her when ye spake together in private; and what damosel that bringeth her the knight's head, which ye shall fight withal, she will make her a queen.'

'Now I understand you well,' said Accolon, 'I shall hold that I have promised her now I have the sword. When saw ye my lady Queen Morgan le Fay?'

'Right late,' said the dwarf.

Then Accolon took him in his arms and said, 'Recommend me unto my lady queen, and tell her all shall be done that I have promised her, and else I will die for it. Now I suppose,' said Accolon, 'she hath made all these crafts and enchantment for this battle.'

'Ye may well believe it,' said the dwarf.

Right so there came a knight and a lady with six squires, and saluted Accolon, and prayed him for to arise, and come and rest him at his manor. And so Accolon mounted upon a void horse, and went with the knight unto a fair manor by a priory, and there he had passing good cheer.

Then Sir Damas sent unto his brother Sir Ontzlake, and bad make him ready by to-morn at the hour of prime, and to be in the field to fight with a good knight, for he had founden a good knight that was ready to do battle at all points. When this word came unto Sir Ontzlake he was passing heavy, for he was wounded a little tofore through both his thighs with a spear, and made great dole; but as he was wounded he would have taken the battle on hand. So it happed at that time, by the means of Morgan le Fay, Accolon was with Sir Ontzlake lodged; and when he heard of that battle, and how Ontzlake was wounded, he said that he would fight for him, because Morgan le Fay had sent him Excalibur and the sheath for to fight with the knight on the morn: this was the cause Sir

Accolon took the battle on hand. Then Sir Ontzlake was passing glad, and thanked Sir Accolon with all his heart that he would do so much for him. And therewithal Sir Ontzlake sent word unto his brother Sir Damas, that he had a knight that for him should be ready in the field by the hour of prime.

So on the morn Sir Arthur was armed and well horsed, and asked Sir Damas, 'When shall we to the field?'

'Sir,' said Sir Damas, 'ye shall hear mass.'

And so Arthur heard a mass, and when mass was done there came a squire on a great horse, and asked Sir Damas if his knight were ready, 'for our knight is ready in the field.'

Then Sir Arthur mounted upon horseback, and there were all the knights and commons of that country; and so by all advices there were chosen twelve good men of the country for to wait upon the two knights.

And right as Arthur was on horseback there came a damosel from Morgan le Fay, and brought unto Sir Arthur a sword like unto Excalibur, and the scabbard, and said unto Arthur, 'Morgan le Fay sendeth here your sword for great love.'

And he thanked her, and weened it had been so, but she was false, for the sword and the scabbard was counterfeit, and brittle, and false.

CHAPTER 9: *Of the battle between King Arthur and Accolon*

And then they dressed them on both parts of the field, and let their horses run so fast that either smote other in the midst of the shield with their spear's head, that both horse and man went to the earth; and then they start up both, and pulled out their swords.

The meanwhile that they were thus at the battle, came the damosel of the lake into the field, that put Merlin under the stone; and she came thither for love of King Arthur, for she knew how Morgan le Fay had so ordained that King Arthur should have been slain that day, and therefore she came to save his life.

And so they went eagerly to the battle, and gave many great strokes, but always Arthur's sword bit not like Accolon's sword; but for the most part, every stroke that Accolon gave he wounded sore Arthur, that it was marvel he stood, and always his blood fell from him fast. When Arthur beheld the ground so sore be-bled he was dismayed, and then he deemed treason that his sword was changed; for his sword bit not steel as it was wont to do, therefore he dread him sore to be dead, for ever him seemed that the sword in Accolon's hand was Excalibur, for at every stroke that Accolon struck he drew blood on Arthur.

'Now, knight,' said Accolon unto Arthur, 'keep thee well from me.'

But Arthur answered not again, and gave him such a buffet on the helm that he made him to stoop, nigh falling down to the earth. Then Sir Accolon withdrew him a little, and came on with Excalibur on high, and smote Sir Arthur such a buffet that he fell nigh to the earth. Then were they wroth both, and gave each other many sore strokes, but always Sir Arthur lost so much blood that it was marvel he stood on his feet, but he was so full of knighthood that knightly he endured the pain. And Sir Accolon lost not a deal of blood, therefore he waxed passing light, and Sir Arthur was passing feeble, and weened verily to have died; but for all that he made countenance as though he might endure, and held Accolon as short as he might. But Accolon was so bold because of Excalibur that he waxed passing hardy. But all men that beheld him said they saw never knight fight so well as Arthur did considering the blood that he bled.

So was all the people sorry for him, but the two brethren would not accord; then always they fought together as fierce knights, and Sir Arthur withdrew him a little for to rest him, and Sir Accolon called him to battle and said, 'It is no time for me to suffer thee to rest.' And therewith he came fiercely upon Arthur, and Sir Arthur was wroth for the blood that he had lost, and smote Accolon on high upon the helm, so mightily, that he made him nigh to fall to the earth; and therewith Arthur's sword brast at the cross, and fell in the grass among the blood, and the pommel and the sure handles he held in his hands. When Sir Arthur saw that, he was in great fear to die, but always he held up his shield and lost no ground, nor bated no cheer.

CHAPTER 10: *How King Arthur's sword that he fought with brake, and how he recovered of Accolon his own sword Excalibur, and overcame his enemy*

Then Sir Accolon began with words of treason, and said, 'Knight, thou art overcome, and mayst not endure, and also thou art weaponless, and thou has lost much of thy blood, and I am full loth to slay thee, therefore yield thee to me as recreant.'

'Nay,' said Sir Arthur, 'I may not so, for I have promised to do the battle to the uttermost, by the faith of my body, while me lasteth the life, and therefore I had lever to die with honour than to live with shame; and if it were possible for me to die an hundred times, I had lever to die so oft than yield me to thee; for though I lack weapon, I shall lack no worship, and if thou slay me weaponless that shall be thy shame.'

'Well,' said Accolon, 'as for the shame I will not spare, now keep thee from me, for thou art but a dead man.'

And therewith Accolon gave him such a stroke that he fell nigh to the earth, and would have had Arthur to have cried him mercy. But Sir Arthur pressed unto Accolon with his shield, and gave him with the pommel in his hand such a buffet that he went three strides aback.

When the damosel of the lake beheld Arthur, how full of prowess his body was, and the false treason that was wrought for him to have had him slain, she had great pity that so good a knight and such a man of prowess should so be

bated no cheer: did not look dismayed.

destroyed. And at the next stroke Sir Accolon struck him such a stroke that by the damosel's enchantment the sword Excalibur fell out of Accolon's hand to the earth.

And therewithal Sir Arthur lightly leapt to it, and gat it in his hand, and forthwithal he knew that it was his sword Excalibur, and said, 'Thou hast been from me all too long, and much damage hast thou done me;' and therewith he espied the scabbard hanging by his side, and suddenly he start to him and pulled the scabbard from him, and threw it from him as far as he might throw it. 'O knight,' said Arthur, 'this day hast thou done me great damage with this sword; now are ye come unto your death, for I shall not warrant you but ye shall as well be rewarded with this sword or ever we depart as thou hast rewarded me, for much pain have ye made me to endue, and much blood have I lost.'

And therewith Sir Arthur rushed on him with all his might and pulled him to the earth, and then rushed off his helm, and gave him such a buffet on the head that the blood came out at his ears, his nose, and his mouth.

'Now will I slay thee,' said Arthur.

'Slay me ye may well,' said Accolon, 'and it please you, for ye are the best knight that ever I found, and I see well that God is with you. But for I promised to do this battle,' said Accolon, 'to the uttermost, and never to be recreant while I lived, therefore shall I never yield me with my mouth, but God do with my body what He will.'

Then Sir Arthur remembered him, and thought he should have seen this knight.

'Now tell me,' said Arthur, 'or I will slay thee, of what country art thou, and of what court?'

'Sir knight,' said Sir Accolon, 'I am of the court of King Arthur, and my name is Accolon of Gaul.'

Then was Arthur more dismayed than he was beforehand; for then he remembered him of his sister Morgan le Fay, and of the enchantment of the ship. 'O sir knight,' said he, 'I pray

rushed off: dragged off.

you tell me who gave you this sword, and by whom ye had it.'

CHAPTER 11: *How Accolon confessed the treason of Morgan le Fay, King Arthur's sister, and how she would have done slay him*

Then Sir Accolon bethought him, and said, 'Woe worth this sword, for by it have I gotten my death.'

'It may well be,' said the king.

'Now, sir,' said Accolon, 'I will tell you: this sword hath been in my keeping the most part of this twelvemonth; and Morgan le Fay, King Uriens' wife, sent it me yesterday by a dwarf, to this intent, that I should slay King Arthur, her brother. For ye shall understand King Arthur is the man in the world that she most hateth, because he is most of worship and of prowess of any of her blood. Also she loveth me out of measure as paramour, and I her again; and if she might bring about to slay Arthur by her crafts, she would slay her husband King Uriens lightly, and then had she me devised to be king in this land, and so to reign, and she to be my queen; but that is now done,' said Accolon, 'for I am sure of my death.'

'Well,' said Sir Arthur, 'I feel by you ye would have been king in this land. It had been great damage to have destroyed your lord,' said Arthur.

'It is truth,' said Accolon, 'but now I have told you truth, wherefore I pray you tell me of whence ye are, and of what court?'

'O Accolon,' said King Arthur, 'now I let thee wit that I am King Arthur, to whom thou hast done great damage.'

When Accolon heard that he cried aloud, 'Fair, sweet lord, have mercy on me, for I knew not you.'

'O Sir Accolon,' said King Arthur, 'mercy shalt thou have, because I feel by thy words at this time thou knowest not my person; but I understand well by thy words that thou hast agreed to the death of my person, and therefore thou art a traitor; but I wit thee the less, for my sister Morgan le Fay by her false crafts made thee to agree and consent to her false lusts, but I shall be sore avenged upon her and I live, that all Christendom shall speak of it. God knoweth I have honoured her and worshipped her more than all my kin, and more have I trusted her than mine own wife and all my kin after.'

Then Sir Arthur called the keepers of the field, and said, 'Sirs, cometh hither, for here are we two knights that have foughten unto a great damage unto us both, and like each one of us to have slain other, if it had happed so; and had any of us known other, here had been no battle, nor stroke stricken.'

Then all aloud cried Accolon unto all the knights and men that were then there gathered together, and said to them in this manner. 'O lords, this noble knight that I have foughten withal, the which me sore repenteth, is the most man of prowess, of manhood, and of worship in the world, for it is himself King Arthur, our alther liege lord, and with mishap and with misadventure have I done this battle with the king and lord that I am holden withal.'

CHAPTER 12: *How Arthur accorded the two brethren, and delivered the twenty knights, and how Sir Accolon died*

Then all the people fell down on their knees and cried King Arthur mercy.

'Mercy shall ye have,' said Arthur. 'Here may ye see what adventures befallen ofttime of errant knights, how that I have foughten with a knight of mine own unto my great damage and his both. But sirs, because I am sore hurt, and he both, and I had great need of a little rest, ye shall understand the opinion betwixt you two brethren:

'As to thee, Sir Damas, for whom I have been champion and won the field of this knight, yet will I judge because ye,

wit: blame. *our alther*: of us all.

Sir Damas, are called an orgulous knight, and full of villainy, and not worth of prowess of your deeds, therefore I will that ye give unto your brother all the whole manor with the appurtenance, under this form, that Sir Ontzlake hold the manor of you, and yearly to give you a palfry to ride upon, for that will become you better to ride on than upon a courser. Also I charge thee, Sir Damas, upon pain of death, that thou never distress no knights errant that ride on their adventure. And also that thou restore these twenty knights that thou hast long kept prisoners, of all their harness, that they be content for; and if any of them come to my court and complain of thee, by my head thou shalt die therefore. Also, Sir Ontzlake, as to you, because ye are named a good knight, and full of prowess, and true and gentle in all your deeds, this shall be your charge. I will give you that in all goodly haste ye come unto me and my court, and ye shall be a knight of mine, and if your deeds be thereafter I shall so prefer you, by the grace of God, that ye shall in short time be in ease for to live as worshipfully as your brother Sir Damas.'

'God thank your largeness of your goodness and of your bounty, I shall be from henceforward at all times at your commandment; for, sir,' said Sir Ontzlake, 'as God would, as I was hurt but late with an adventurous knight through both my thighs, that grieved me sore, and else had I done this battle with you.'

'God would,' said Arthur, 'it had been so, for then had not I been hurt as I am. I shall tell you the cause why: for I had not been hurt as I am, had not been mine own sword, that was stolen from me by treason; and this battle was ordained aforehand to have slain me, and so it was brought to the purpose by false treason, and by false enchantment.'

'Alas,' said Sir Ontzlake, 'that is a great pity that ever so noble a man as ye are of your deeds and prowess, that any man or woman might find in their hearts to work any treason against you.'

'I shall reward them,' said Arthur, 'in short time, by the

grace of God. Now, tell me,' said Arthur, 'how far am I from Camelot?'

'Sir, ye are two days' journey therefrom.'

'I would fain be at some place of worship,' said Sir Arthur, 'that I might rest me.'

'Sir,' said Sir Ontzlake, 'hereby is a rich abbey of your elders' foundation, of nuns, but three mile hence.'

So the king took his leave of all the people, and mounted upon horseback, and Sir Accolon with him. And when they were come to the abbey, he let fetch leeches and search his wounds and Accolon's both; but Sir Accolon died within four days, for he had bled so much blood that he might not live, but King Arthur was well recovered.

So when Accolon was dead he let send him on an horse-bier with six knights unto Camelot, and said, 'Bear him to my sister Morgan le Fay, and say that I send her him to a present, and tell her I have my sword Excalibur and the scabbard.'

So they departed with the body.

CHAPTER 13: *How Morgan would have slain Sir Uriens her husband, and how Sir Uwain her son saved him*

The meanwhile Morgan le Fay had weened King Arthur had been dead. So on a day she espied King Uriens lay in his bed sleeping. Then she called unto her a maiden of her counsel, and said, 'Go fetch me my lord's sword, for I saw never better time to slay him than now.'

'O madam,' said the damosel, 'and ye slay my lord ye can never escape.'

'Care not you,' said Morgan le Fay, 'for now I see my time in the which it is best to do it, and therefore hie thee fast and fetch me the sword.'

Then the damosel departed, found Sir Uwain sleeping upon a bed in another chamber, so she went unto Sir Uwain, and awaked him, and bad him, 'Arise, and wait on my lady your mother, for she will slay the king your father sleeping in his bed, for I go to fetch his sword.'

'Well,' said Sir Uwain, 'go on your way, and let me deal.'

Anon the damosel brought Morgan the sword with quaking hands, and lightly took the sword, and pulled it out, and went boldly unto the bed's side, and awaited how and where she might slay him best.

And as she lifted up the sword to smite, Sir Uwain leapt unto his mother, and caught her by the hand, and said, 'Ah, fiend, what wilt thou do? And thou were not my mother, with this sword I should smite off thy head. Ah', said Sir Uwain, 'men saith that Merlin was begotten of a devil, but I may say an earthly devil bare me.'

'O fair son, Uwain, have mercy upon me, I was tempted with a devil, wherefore I cry thee mercy; I will never more do so; and save my worship and discover me not.'

'On this covenant,' said Sir Uwain, 'I will forgive it you, so ye will never be about to do such deeds.'

'Nay, son,' said she, 'and that I make you assurance.'

CHAPTER 14: *How Queen Morgan le Fay made great sorrow for the death of Accolon, and how she stole away the scabbard from Arthur*

Then came tidings unto Morgan le Fay that Accolon was dead, and his body brought unto the church, and how King Arthur had his sword again. But when Queen Morgan wist that Accolon was dead, she was so sorrowful that near her heart to-brast. But because she would not it were known, outward she kept her countenance, and made no semblant of sorrow. But well she wist and she abode till her brother Arthur came thither, there should no gold go for her life. Then she went unto Queen Guenever, and asked her leave to ride into the country.

'Ye may abide,' said Queen Guenever, 'till your brother the king come home.'

'I may not,' said Morgan le Fay, 'for I have such hasty tidings, that I may not tarry.'

'Well,' said Guenever, 'ye may depart when ye will.'

So early on the morn, or it was day, she took her horse and rode all that day and most part of the night, and on the morn by noon she came to the same abbey of nuns whereas lay King Arthur; and she knowing he was there, she asked where he was. And they answered how he had laid him in his bed to sleep, for he had had but little rest these three nights.

'Well,' said she, 'I charge you that none of you awake him till I do,' and then she alit off her horse, and thought for to steal away Excalibur his sword.

And so she went straight unto his chamber, and no man durst disobey her commandment, and there she found Arthur asleep in his bed, and Excalibur in his right hand naked. When she saw that, she was passing heavy that she might not come by the sword without she had awaked him, and then she wist well she had been dead. Then she took the scabbard and went her way on horseback.

When the king awoke and missed his scabbard, he was wroth, and he asked who had been there, and they said his sister, Queen Morgan had been there, and had put the scabbard under her mantle and was gone.

'Alas,' said Arthur, 'falsely ye have watched me.'

'Sir,' said they all, 'we durst not disobey your sister's commandment.'

'Ah,' said the king, 'let fetch the best horse may be found, and bid Sir Ontzlake arm him in all haste, and take another good horse and ride with me.'

So anon the king and Ontzlake were well armed, and rode after this lady, and so they came by a cross and found a cowherd, and they asked the poor man if there came any lady late riding that way.

'Sir,' said this poor man, 'right late came a lady riding with a forty horses, and to yonder forest she rode.'

Then they spurred their horses, and followed fast, and

within a while Arthur had a sight of Morgan le Fay, then he chased as fast as he might. When she espied him following her, she rode a greater pace through the forest till she came to a plain, and when she saw she might not escape, she rode unto a lake thereby, and said, 'Whatsover come of me, my brother shall not have this scabbard.' And then she let throw the scabbard in the deepest of the water so it sank, for it was heavy of gold and precious stones. Then she rode into a valley where many great stones were, and when she saw she must be overtake, she shaped herself, horse and man, by enchantment unto a great marble stone.

Anon withal came Sir Arthur and Sir Ontzlake whereas the king might know his sister and her men, and one knight from another. 'Ah,' said the king, 'here may ye see the vengeance of God, and now am I sorry that this misadventure is befall.' And then he looked for the scabbard, but it would not be found, so he returned to the abbey there he came from.

So when Arthur was gone she turned all into the likeness as she and they were before, and said, 'Sirs, now may we go where we will.'

CHAPTER 15: *How Morgan le Fay saved a knight that should have been drowned, and how King Arthur returned home again*

Then said Morgan, 'Saw ye Arthur, my brother?'

'Yea,' said her knights, 'right well, and that ye should have found and we might have stirred from one stead, for by his armyvestal[1] countenance he would have caused us to have fled.'

'I believe you,' said Morgan.

Anon after as she rode she met a knight leading another knight on his horse before him, bound hand and foot, blindfold, to have drowned him in a fountain. When she saw this

stead: place.

knight so bound, she asked him, 'What will ye do with that knight?'

'Lady,' said he, 'I will drown him.'

'For what cause?' she asked.

'For I found him with my wife, and she shall have the same death anon.'

'That were pity,' said Morgan le Fay. 'Now, what say ye, knight, is it truth that he saith of you?' she said to the knight that should be drowned.

'Nay truly, madam, he saith not right on me.'

'Of whence be ye,' said Morgan le Fay, 'and of what country?'

'I am of the court of King Arthur, and my name is Manassen, cousin unto Accolon of Gaul.'

'Ye say well,' said she, 'and for the love of him ye shall be delivered, and ye shall have your adversary in the same case ye be in.'

So Manassen was loosed and the other knight bound. And anon Manassen unarmed him, and armed himself in his harness, and so mounted on horseback, and the knight afore him, and so threw him into the fountain and drowned him. And then he rode unto Morgan again, and asked if she would anything unto King Arthur.

'Tell him that I rescued thee, not for the love of him but for the love of Accolon, and tell him I fear him not while I can make me and them that be with me in likeness of stones; and let him wit I can do much more when I see my time.'

And so she departed into the country of Gore, and there was she richly received, and made her castles and towns passing strong, for always she dread much King Arthur.

When the king had well rested him at the abbey, he rode unto Camelot, and found his queen and his barons right glad of his coming. And when they heard of his strange adventures as is afore rehearsed, then all had marvel of the falsehood of Morgan le Fay; many knights wished her burnt. Then came Manassen to court and told the king of his adventure.

'Well,' said the king, 'she is a kind sister; I shall so be avenged on her and I live, that all Christendom shall speak of it.'

So on the morn there came a damosel from Morgan to the king, and she brought with her the richest mantle that ever was seen in that court, for it was set as full of precious stones as one might stand by another, and there were the richest stones that ever the king saw. And the damosel said, 'Your sister sendeth you this mantle, and desireth that ye should take this gift of her; and in what thing she hath offended you, she will amend it at your own pleasure.'

When the king beheld this mantle it pleased him much, but he said but little.

CHAPTER 16: *How the Damosel of the Lake saved King Arthur from a mantle which should have burnt him*

With that came the Damosel of the Lake unto the king, and said, 'Sir, I must speak with you in private.'

'Say on,' said the king, 'what ye will.'

'Sir,' said the damosel, 'put not on you this mantle till ye have seen more, and in no wise let it not come on you nor on no knight of yours till ye command the bringer thereof to put it upon her.'

'Well,' said King Arthur, 'it shall be done as ye counsel me.'

And then he said unto the damosel that came from his sister, 'Damosel, this mantle that ye have brought me, I will see it upon you.'

'Sir,' she said, 'It will not beseem me to wear a king's garment.'

'By my head,' said Arthur, 'ye shall wear it or it come on my back, or any man's that here is.'

And so the king made it to be put upon her, and forthwithal she fell down dead, and never more spake word after, and burnt to coals.

Then was the king wonderly wroth, more than he was toforehand, and said unto King Uriens, 'My sister, your wife, is alway about to betray me, and well I wot either ye, or my nephew, your son, is of counsel with her to have me destroyed; but as for you,' said the king to King Uriens, 'I deem not greatly that ye be of her counsel, for Accolon confessed to me by his own mouth, that she would have destroyed you as well as me, therefore I hold you excused; but as for your son, Sir Uwain, I hold him suspect, therefore I charge you put him out of my court.'

So Sir Uwain was discharged. And when Sir Gawain wist that, he made him ready to go with him, and said, 'Whoso banisheth my cousin-germain shall banish me.'

So they two departed, and rode into a great forest, and so they came to an abbey of monks, and there were well lodged. But when the king wist that Sir Gawain was departed from the court, there was made great sorrow among all the estates. 'Now,' said Gaheris, Gawain's brother, 'we have lost two good knights for the love of one.'

So on the morn they heard their masses in the abbey, and so they rode forth till that they came to a great forest. Then was Sir Gawain ware in a valley by a turret, twelve fair damosels, and two knights armed on great horses, and the damosels went to and fro by a tree. And then was Sir Gawain ware how there hung a white shield on that tree, and ever as the damosels came by it they spit upon it, and some threw mire upon the shield.

CHAPTER 17: *How Sir Gawain and Sir Uwain met with twelve fair damosels, and how they complained on Sir Marhaus*

Then Sir Gawain and Sir Uwain went and saluted them, and asked why they did that despite to the shield.

'Sirs,' saiden the damosels, 'we shall tell you. There is a knight in this country that oweth this white shield, and he is a passing good man of his hands, but he hateth all ladies and gentlewomen, and therefore we do all this despite to the shield.'

'I shall say you,' said Sir Gawain, 'it beseemeth evil a good knight to despise all ladies and gentlewomen, and peradventure though he hate you he hath some certain cause,[1] and peradventure he loveth in some other places ladies and gentlewomen, and to be loved again, and he be such a man of prowess as ye speak of. Now, what is his name?'

'Sir,' said they, 'his name is Marhaus, the King's son of Ireland.'

'I know him well,' said Sir Uwain, 'he is a passing good knight as any is alive, for I saw him once proved at a jousts where many knights were gathered, and that time there might no man withstand him.'

'Ah!' said Sir Gawain, 'damosels, methinketh ye are to blame, for it is to suppose, he that hung that shield there, he will not be long therefrom, and then may those knights match him on horseback, and that is more your worship than thus; for I will abide no longer to see a knight's shield dishonoured.'

And therewith Sir Uwain and Gawain departed a little from them, and then were they ware where Sir Marhaus came riding on a great horse straight toward them. And when the twelve damosels saw Sir Marhaus they fled into the turret as they were wild, so that some of them fell by the way.

Then the one of the knights of the tower dressed his shield, and said on high, 'Sir Marhaus, defend thee.' And so they ran together that the knight brake his spear on Marhaus, and Marhaus smote him so hard that he brake his neck and the horse's back. That saw the other knight of the turret, and dressed him toward Marhaus, and they met so eagerly together that the knight of the turret was soon smitten down, horse and man, stark dead.

CHAPTER 18: *How Sir Marhaus jousted with Sir Gawain and Sir Uwain, and overthrew them both*

And then Sir Marhaus rode unto his shield, and saw how it was defouled, and said, 'Of this despite I am a part avenged, but for her love that gave me this white shield I shall wear thee, and hang mine where thou was;' and so he hanged it about his neck. Then he rode straight unto Sir Gawain and to Sir Uwain, and asked them what they did there. They answered him that they came from King Arthur's court for to see adventures.

'Well,' said Sir Marhaus, 'here am I ready, an adventurous knight that will fulfil any adventure that ye will desire;' and so departed from them, to fetch his range.

'Let him go,' said Sir Uwain unto Sir Gawain, 'for he is a passing good knight as any is living; I would not by my will that any of us were matched with him.'

'Nay,' said Sir Gawain, 'not so, it were shame to us were he not assayed, were he never so good a knight.'

'Well,' said Sir Uwain, 'I will assay him afore you, for I am more weaker than ye, and if he smite me down then may ye revenge me.'

So these two knights came together with great raundon, that Sir Uwain smote Sir Marhaus that his spear brast in pieces on the shield, and Sir Marhaus smote him so sore that horse and man he bare to the earth, and hurt Sir Uwain on the left side. Then Sir Marhaus turned his horse and rode toward Gawain with his spear, and when Sir Gawain saw that, he dressed his shield, and they aventred their spears, and they came together with all the might of their horses, that either knight smote other so hard in midst of their shields, but Sir Gawain's spear brake, but Sir Marhaus' spear held; and therewith Sir Gawain and his horse rushed down to the earth.

And lightly Sir Gawain rose on his feet, and pulled out his sword, and dressed him toward Sir Marhaus on foot, and Sir

Marhaus saw that, and pulled out his sword and began to come to Sir Gawain on horseback.

'Sir knight,' said Sir Gawain, 'alight on foot, or else I will slay thy horse.'

'Gramercy,' said Sir Marhaus, 'of your gentleness ye teach me courtesy, for it is not for one knight to be on foot, and the other on horseback.'

And therewith Sir Marhaus set his spear against a tree and alit and tied his horse to a tree, and dressed his shield, and either came unto other eagerly, and smote together with their swords that their shields flew in cantels, and they bruised their helms and their hauberks, and wounded either other.

But Sir Gawain from it passed nine of the clock waxed ever stronger and stronger, for then it came to the hour of noon, and thrice his might was increased. All this espied Sir Marhaus and had great wonder how his might increased, and so they wounded other passing sore. And then when it was past noon, and when it drew toward evensong, Sir Gawain's strength feebled, and waxed passing faint that unnethes he might dure any longer, and Sir Marhaus was then bigger and bigger.

'Sir knight,' said Sir Marhaus, 'I have well felt that ye are a passing good knight and a marvellous man of might as ever I felt any, while it lasteth, and our quarrels are not great, and therefore it were pity to do you hurt, for I feel ye are passing feeble.'

'Ah,' said Sir Gawain, 'gentle knight, ye say the word that I should say.'

And therewith they took off their helms, and either kissed other, and there they swore together either to love other as brethren. And Sir Marhaus prayed Sir Gawain to lodge with him that night. And so they took their horses, and rode toward Sir Marhaus' house.

And as they rode by the way, 'Sir knight,' said Sir Gawain, 'I have marvel that so valiant a man as ye be love no ladies ne damosels.'

bruised: shattered.

'Sir,' said Sir Marhaus, 'they name me wrongfully those that give me that name, but well I wot it be the damosels of the turret that so name me, and other such as they be. Now shall I tell you for what cause I hate them: for they be sorceresses and enchanters many of them, and be a knight never so good of his body and full of prowess as man may be, they will make him a stark coward to have the better of him, and this is the principal cause that I hate them. And to all good ladies and gentlewomen I owe my service as a knight ought to do.'

As the book rehearseth in French, there were many knights that overmatched Sir Gawain, for all the thrice might that he had: Sir Launcelot de Lake, Sir Tristram, Sir Bors de Ganis, Sir Percival, Sir Pelleas, and Sir Marhaus, these six knights had the better of Sir Gawain.

Then within a little while they came to Sir Marhaus' place, which was in a little priory, and there they alit, and ladies and damosels unarmed them, and hastily looked to their hurts, for they were all three hurt. And so they had all three good lodging with Sir Marhaus, and good cheer, for when he wist that they were King Arthur's sister's sons he made them all the cheer that lay in his power, and so they sojourned there a seven-night, and were well eased of their wounds, and at the last departed.

'Now,' said Sir Marhaus, 'we will not depart so lightly, for I will bring you through the forest;' and rode day by day well a seven days or they found any adventure.

At the last they came into a great forest, that was named the country and forest of Arroy, and the country of strange adventures.

'In this country,' said Sir Marhaus, 'came never knight since it was christened, but he found strange adventures.'

And so they rode, and came into a deep valley full of stones, and thereby they saw a fair stream of water; above thereby was the head of the stream a fair fountain, and three damosels sitting thereby. And then they rode to them, and either saluted other, and the eldest had a garland of gold about her head, and she was three score winter of age or more, and her hair was white under the garland. The second damosel was of thirty winter of age, with a circlet of gold about her head. The third damosel was but fifteen year of age, and a garland of flowers about her head. When these knights had so beheld them, they asked them the cause why they sat at that fountain.

'We be here,' said the damosels, 'for this cause: if we may see any errant knights, to teach them unto strange adventures; and ye be three knights that seeken adventures, and we be three damosels and therefore each one of you must choose one of us; and when ye have done so we will lead you unto three highways, and there each of you shall choose a way and his damosel with him. And this day twelvemonth ye must meet here again, and God send you your lives, and thereto ye must plight your troth.'

'This is well said,' said Sir Marhaus.

CHAPTER 19: *How Sir Marhaus, Sir Gawain, and Sir Uwain met the damosels, and each of them took one*

'Now shall every each of us choose a damosel. I shall tell you,' said Sir Uwain, 'I am the youngest and most weakest of you both, therefore I will have the eldest damosel, for she hath seen much, and can best help me when I have need, for I have most need of help of you both.'

'Now,' said Sir Marhaus, 'I will have the damosel of thirty winter age, for she falleth best to me.'

'Well,' said Sir Gawain, 'I thank you, for ye have left me the youngest and the fairest, and she is most levest to me.'

Then every damosel took her knight by the reins of his bridle, and brought him to the three ways, and there was their oath made to meet at the fountain that day twelvemonth and they were living, and so they kissed and departed, and every each knight set his lady behind him. And Sir Uwain took the way that lay west, and Sir Marhaus took the way that lay south, and Sir Gawain took the way that lay north.

Now will we begin at Sir Gawain, that held that way till that he came unto a fair manor, where dwelled an old knight and a good householder, and there Sir Gawain asked the knight if he knew any adventures in that country.

'I shall show you some to-morn,' said the old knight, 'and that marvellous.'

So, on the morn they rode into the forest of adventures till they came to a laund, and thereby they found a cross, and as they stood and hoved, there came by them the fairest knight and the seemliest man that ever they saw, making the greatest dole that ever man made. And then he was ware of Sir Gawain, and saluted him, and prayed God to send him much worship.

'As to that,' said Sir Gawain, 'gramercy; also I pray to God that he send you honour and worship.'

'Ah,' said the knight, 'I may lay that aside, for sorrow and shame cometh to me after worship.'

CHAPTER 20: *How a knight and a dwarf strove for a lady*

And therewith he passed unto the one side of the laund; and on the other side saw Sir Gawain ten knights that hoved still and made[1] them ready with their shields and spears against that one knight that came by Sir Gawain. Then this one knight aventred a great spear, and one of the ten knights encountered with him, but this woeful knight smote him so hard that he fell over his horse's tail. So this same dolorous knight served them all, that at the leastway he smote down horse and man, and all he did with one spear; and so when they were all ten on foot, they went to that one knight, and he stood stone still, and suffered them to pull him down off his horse, and bound him hand and foot and tied him under the horse's belly, and so led him with them.

lust: wish.

'O Jesu!' said Sir Gawain, 'this is a doleful sight, to see the yonder knight so to be entreated, and it seemeth by the knight that he suffereth them to bind him so, for he maketh no resistance.'

'No,' said his host, 'that is truth, for and he would, they all were too weak so to do him.'

'Sir,' said the damosel unto Sir Gawain, 'meseemeth it were your worship to help that dolorous knight, for methinketh he is one of the best knights that ever I saw.'

'I would do for him,' said Sir Gawain, 'but it seemeth he will have no help.'

'Then,' said the damosel, 'methinketh ye have no lust to help him.'

Thus as they talked they saw a knight on the other side of the laund all armed save the head. And on the other side there came a dwarf on horseback all armed save the head, with a great mouth and a short nose; and when the dwarf came nigh he said, 'Where is the lady should meet us here?'

And therewithal she came forth out of the wood. And then they began to strive for the lady; for the knight said he would have her, and the dwarf said he would have her.

'Will we do well?' said the dwarf. 'Yonder is a knight at the cross, let us put it both upon him, and as he deemeth so shall it be.'

'I will well,' said the knight.

And so they went all three unto Sir Gawain and told him wherefore they strove.

'Well, sirs,' said he, 'will ye put the matter in my hand?'

'Yea,' they said both.

'Now damosel,' said Sir Gawain, 'ye shall stand betwixt them both, and whether ye list better to go to, he shall have you.'

And when she was set between them both, she left the knight and went to the dwarf, and the dwarf took her and went his way singing, and the knight went his way with great mourning.

lust: wish.

Then came there two knights all armed, and cried on high, 'Sir Gawain, knight of King Arthur's, make thee ready in all haste and joust with me.'

So they ran together, that either fell down, and then on foot they drew their swords, and did full actually.

The meanwhile the other knight went to the damosel, and asker her why she abode with that knight, 'and if ye would abide with me, I will be your faithful knight.'

'And with you will I be,' said the damosel, 'for with Sir Gawain I may not find in mine heart to be with him; for now here was one knight scomfit ten knights, and at the last he was cowardly led away and therefore let us two go whilst they fight.'

And Sir Gawain fought with that other knight long, but at the last they accorded both. And then the knight prayed Sir Gawain to lodge with him that night.

So as Sir Gawain went with this knight he asked him, 'What knight is he in this country that smote down the ten knights? For when he had done so manfully he suffered them to bind him hand and foot, and so led him away.'

'Ah,' said the knight, 'that is the best knight I trow in the world, and the most man of prowess, and he hath been served so as he was even more than ten times, and his name hight Sir Pelleas, and he loveth a great lady in this country and her name is Ettard. And so when he loved her there was cried in this country a great jousts three days, and all the knights of this country were there and gentlewomen, and who that proved him the best knight should have a passing good sword and a circlet of gold, and the circlet the knight should give it to the fairest lady that was at the jousts. And this knight Sir Pelleas was the best knight that was there, and there were five hundred knights, but there was never man that ever Sir Pelleas met withal but he struck him down, or else from his horse; and every day of three days he struck down twenty knights, therefore they gave him the prize. And forthwithal he went thereas the lady Ettard was, and gave

scomfit: defeated. *trow*: believe.

her the circlet, and said openly she was the fairest lady that there was, and that would he prove upon any knight that would say nay.

CHAPTER 21: *How King Pelleas suffered himself to be taken prisoner because he would have a sight of his lady, and how Sir Gawain promised him for to get to him the love of his lady*

'And so he chose her for his sovereign lady, and never to love other but her, but she was so proud that she had scorn of him, and said that she would never love him though he would die for her. Wherefore all ladies and gentlewomen had scorn of her that she was so proud, for there were fairer than she, and there was none that was there but and Sir Pelleas would have proffered them love, they would have loved him for his noble prowess. And so this knight promised the lady Ettard to follow her into this country, and never to leave her till she loved him. And thus he is here the most part nigh her, and lodged by a priory, and every week she sendeth knights to fight with him. And when he hath put them to the worse, then will he suffer them wilfully to take him prisoner, because he would have a sight of this lady. And always she doth him great despite, for sometime she maketh her knights to tie him to his horse's tail, and some to bind him under the horse's belly; thus in the most shamefullest wise that she can think he is brought to her. And all she doth it for to cause him to leave this country, and to leave his loving; but all this cannot make him to leave, for and he would have fought on foot he might have had the better of the ten knights as well on foot as on horseback.'

'Alas,' said Sir Gawain, 'it is great pity of him; and after this night I will seek him tomorrow, in this forest, to do him all the help I can.'

So on the morn Sir Gawain took his leave of his host Sir Carados, and rode into the forest; and at the last he met with

Sir Pelleas, making great moan out of measure, so each of them saluted other, and asked him why he made such sorrow. And as it is above rehearsed, Sir Pelleas told Sir Gawain: 'But always I suffer her knights to fare so with me as ye saw yesterday, in trust at the last to win her love, for she knoweth well all her knights should not lightly win me, and me list to fight with them to the uttermost. Wherefore and I loved her not so sore, I had lever die an hundred times, and I might die so oft, rather than I would suffer that despite; but I trust she will have pity upon me at the last, for love causeth many a good knight to suffer to have his intent, but alas I am unfortunate.' And therewith he made so great dole and sorrow that unnethe he might hold him on horseback.

'Now,' said Sir Gawain, 'leave your mourning and I shall promise you by the faith of my body to do all that lieth in my power to get you the love of your lady, and thereto I will plight you my troth.'

'Ah,' said Sir Pelleas, 'of what court are ye? Tell me, I pray you, my good friend.'

And then Sir Gawain said, 'I am of the court of King Arthur, and his sister's son, and King Lot of Orkney was my father, and my name is Sir Gawain.'

And then he said, 'My name is Sir Pelleas, born in the Isles, and of many isles I am lord, and never have I loved lady nor damosel till now in an unhappy time. And, sir knight, since ye are so nigh cousin unto King Arthur, and a king's son, therefore betray me not but help me, for I may never come by her but by some good knight, for she is in a strong castle here, fast by within this four mile, and over all this country she is lady of. And so I may never come to her presence, but as I suffer her knights to take me, and but if I did so that I might have a sight of her, I had been dead long or this time. And yet fair word had I never of her, but when I am brought tofore her she rebuketh me in the foulest manner, and then they take my horse and harness and putten me out of the gates, and she will not suffer me to eat nor drink; and always I offer me to be her prisoner, but that she will not suffer me, for I would desire no more, what pains so ever I had, so that I might have a sight of her daily.'

'Well,' said Sir Gawain, 'all this shall I amend and ye will do as I shall devise: I will have your horse and your armour, and so will I ride unto her castle and tell her that I have slain you, and so shall I come within her to cause her to cherish me, and then shall I do my true part that ye shall not fail to have the love of her.'

CHAPTER 22: *How Sir Gawain came to the Lady Ettard and lay by her, and how Sir Pelleas found them sleeping*

And therewith Sir Gawain plight his troth unto Sir Pelleas to be true and faithful unto him; so each one plight their troth to other, and so they changed horses and harness, and Sir Gawain departed, and came to the castle whereas stood the pavilions of this lady without the gate.

And as soon as Ettard had espied Sir Gawain she fled in toward the castle.

Sir Gawain spake on high, and bad her abide, for he was not Sir Pelleas; 'I am another knight that have slain Sir Pelleas.'

'Do off your helm,' said the Lady Ettard, 'that I may see your visage.'

And so when she saw that it was not Sir Pelleas, she made him alight and led him unto her castle, and asked him faithfully whether he had slain Sir Pelleas. And he said her yea, and told her his name was Sir Gawain of the court of King Arthur, and his sister's son.

'Truly,' said she, 'that is great pity, for he was a passing good knight of his body, but of all men alive I hated him most, for I could never be quit of him; and for ye have slain him I shall be your woman, and to do anything that might please you.' So she made Sir Gawain good cheer.

Then Sir Gawain said that that he loved a lady and by no mean she would love him.

'She is to blame,' said Ettard, 'and she will not love you, for ye that be so well born a man, and such a man of prowess, there is no lady in the world too good for you.'

'Will ye,' said Sir Gawain, 'promise me to do all that ye may, by the faith of your body, to get me the love of my lady?'

'Yea, sir,' said she, 'and that I promise you by the faith of my body.'

'Now,' said Sir Gawain, 'it is yourself that I love so well, therefore I pray you hold your promise.'

'I may not choose,' said the Lady Ettard, 'but if I should be forsworn;' and so she granted him to fulfil all his desire.

So it was then in the month of May that she and Sir Gawain went out of the castle and supped in a pavilion, and there was made a bed, and there Sir Gawain and the Lady Ettard went to bed together, and in another pavilion she laid her damosels, and in the third pavilion she laid part of her knights, for then she had no dread of Sir Pelleas. And there Sir Gawain lay with her in that pavilion two days and two nights.

And on the third day, in the morning early Sir Pelleas armed him, for he had never slept since Sir Gawain departed from him; for Sir Gawain had promised him by the faith of his body, to come to him unto his pavilion by that priory within the space of a day and a night. Then Sir Pelleas mounted upon horseback, and came to the pavilions that stood without the castle, and found in the first pavilion three knights in three beds, and three squires lying at their feet. Then went he to the second pavilion and found four gentlewomen lying in four beds. And then he yede to the third pavilion and found Sir Gawain lying in bed with his Lady Ettard, and either clipping other in arms, and when he saw that his heart wellnigh brast for sorrow, and said, 'Alas! that ever a knight should be found so false;' and then he took his horse and might not abide no longer for pure sorrow.

And when he had ridden nigh half a mile he turned

clipping: embracing.

again and thought to slay them both; and when he saw them both so lie sleeping fast, unnethe he might hold him on horseback for sorrow, and said thus to himself: 'Though this knight be never so false, I will never slay him sleeping, for I will never destroy the high order of knighthood;' and therewith he departed again.

And or he had ridden half a mile he returned again, and thought then to slay them both, making the greatest sorrow that ever man made. And when he came to the pavilions he tied his horse unto a tree, and pulled out his sword naked in his hand, and went to them thereas they lay, and yet he thought it were shame to slay them sleeping, and laid the naked sword overthwart both their throats, and so took his horse and rode his way.

And when Sir Pelleas came to his pavilions he told his knights and his squires how he had sped, and said thus to them: 'For your true and good service ye have done me I shall give you all my goods, for I will go unto my bed and never arise until I am dead. And when that I am dead I charge you that ye take the heart out of my body and bear it her betwixt two silver dishes, and tell her how I saw her lie with the false knight Sir Gawain.' Right so Sir Pelleas unarmed himself, and went unto his bed making marvellous dole and sorrow.

Then Sir Gawain and Ettard awoke of their sleep, and found the naked sword overthwart their throats, then she knew well it was Sir Pelleas' sword.

'Alas!' said she to Sir Gawain, 'ye have betrayed me and Sir Pelleas both, for ye told me ye had slain him, and now I know well it is not so, he is alive. And if Sir Pelleas had been as uncourteous to you as ye have been to him ye had been a dead knight. But ye have deceived me and betrayed me falsely, that all ladies and damosels may beware by you and me.'

And therewith Sir Gawain made him ready, and went into the forest.

So it happed then that the Damosel of the Lake, Nimue, met

with a knight of Sir Pelleas, that went on his foot in the forest making great dole, and she asked him the cause. And so the woeful knight told her how his master and lord was betrayed through a knight and a lady, and how 'he will never arise out of his bed till he be dead.'

'Bring me to him,' said she anon, 'and I will warrant his life he shall not die for love, and she that hath caused him so to love, she shall be in as evil plight as he is or it be long to, for it is no joy of such a proud lady that will have no mercy of such a valiant knight.'

Anon that knight brought her unto him, and when she saw him lie in his bed, she thought she saw never so likely a knight; and therewith she threw an enchantment upon him, and he fell asleep.

And therewhile she rode unto the Lady Ettard, and charged no man to awake him till she came again. So within two hours she brought the Lady Ettard thither, and both ladies found him asleep.

'Lo,' said the Damosel of the Lake, 'ye ought to be ashamed for to murder such a knight.' And therewith she threw such an enchantment upon her that she loved him sore that well nigh she was out of her mind.

'O Lord Jesu,' said the Lady Ettard, 'how is it befallen unto me that I love now him that I have most hated of any man alive?'

'That is the rightwise judgement of God,' said the damosel.

And then anon Sir Pelleas awaked and looked upon Ettard; and when he saw her he knew her, and then he hated her more than any woman alive, and said, 'Away, traitress, come never in my sight.'

And when she heard him say so, she wept and made great sorrow out of measure.

CHAPTER 23: *How Sir Pelleas loved no more Ettard by mean of the Damosel of the Lake, whom he loved ever after*

'Sir knight Pelleas,' said the Damosel of the Lake, 'take your horse and come forth with me out of this country, and ye shall love a lady that shall love you.'

'I will well,' said Sir Pelleas, 'for this lady Ettard hath done me great despite and shame,' and there he told her the beginning and ending, and how he had purposed never to have arisen, till that he had been dead. 'And now such grace God hath sent me, that I hate her as much as ever I loved her, thanked be Our Lord Jesus!'

'Thank me,' said the Damosel of the Lake.

Anon Sir Pelleas armed him, and took his horse, and commanded his men to bring after his pavilions, and his stuff where the Damosel of the Lake would assign.

So the Lady Ettard died for sorrow, and the Damosel of the Lake rejoiced Sir Pelleas, and loved together during their life days.

CHAPTER 24: *How Sir Marhaus rode with the damosel, and how he came to the Duke of the South Marches*

Now turn we unto Sir Marhaus, that rode with the damosel of thirty winter of age, southward. And so they came into a deep forest, and by fortune they were nighted, and rode long in a deep way, and at the last they came unto a courtelage, and there they asked harbour.

But the man of the courtelage would not lodge them for no treaties that they could treat, but thus much the good man said: 'And ye will take the adventure of your lodging, I shall bring you there ye shall be lodged.'

'What adventure is that that I shall have for my lodging?' said Sir Marhaus.

courtelage: court-yard.

'Ye shall wit when ye come there,' said the good man.

'Sir, what adventure so it be, bring me thither I pray thee.' said Sir Marhaus; 'for I am weary, my damosel, and my horse.'

So the good man went and opened the gate, and within an hour he brought him unto a fair castle, and then the poor man called the porter, and anon he was let into the castle, and so he told the lord how he brought him a knight errant and a damosel that would be lodged with him.

'Let him in,' said the lord, 'it may happen he shall repent that they took their lodging here.'

So Sir Marhaus was let in with torchlight, and there was a goodly sight of young men that welcomed him. And then his horse was led into the stable, and he and the damosel were brought into the hall, and there stood a mighty duke and many goodly men about him. Then this lord asked him what he hight, and from whence he came, and with whom he dwelt.

'Sir,' he said, 'I am a knight of King Arthur's and knight of the Table Round,[1] and my name is Sir Marhaus, and born I am in Ireland.'

And then said the duke to him, 'That me sore repenteth; the cause is this: for I love not thy lord nor none of thy fellows of the Table Round; and therefore ease thyself this night as well as thou mayest, for as to-morn I and my six sons shall match with you.'

'Is there no remedy but that I must have ado with you and your six sons at once?' said Sir Marhaus.

'No,' said the duke, 'for this cause I made mine avow, for Sir Gawain slew my seven sons in a recounter, therefore I made mine avow, there should never knight of King Arthur's court lodge with me, or come thereas I might have ado with him, but that I would have a revenging of my sons' death.'

'What is your name?' said Sir Marhaus; 'I require you tell me, and it please you.'

'Wit thou well I am the Duke of South Marches.'

'Ah,' said Sir Marhaus, 'I have heard say that ye have been

long time a great foe unto my lord Arthur and to his knights.'

'That shall ye feel to-morn,' said the duke.

'Shall I have ado with you?' said Sir Marhaus.

'Yea,' said the duke, 'thereof shalt thou not choose, and therefore take you to your chamber, and ye shall have all that to you longeth.'

So Sir Marhaus departed and was led to a chamber, and his damosel was led unto her chamber. And on the morn the duke sent unto Sir Marhaus and bad make him ready. And so Sir Marhaus arose and armed him, and then there was a mass sung afore him, and brake his fast, and so mounted on horseback in the court of the castle there they should do the battle. So there was the duke all ready on horseback, clean armed, and his six sons by him, and every each had a spear in his hand, and so they encountered, whereas the duke and his two sons brake their spears upon him, but Sir Marhaus held up his spear and touched none of them.

CHAPTER 25: *How Sir Marhaus fought with the duke and his six sons and made them to yield them*

Then came the four sons by couple, and two of them brake their spears, and so did the other two. And all this while Sir Marhaus touched them not. Then Sir Marhaus ran to the duke, and smote him with his spear that horse and man fell to the earth, and so he served his sons; and then Sir Marhaus alit down and bad the duke yield him or else he would slay him.

And then some of his sons recovered, and would have set upon Sir Marhaus; then Sir Marhaus said to the duke, 'Cease thy sons, or else I will do the uttermost to you all.'

Then the duke saw he might not escape the death, he cried to his sons, and charged them to yield them to Sir Marhaus; and they kneeled all down and put the pommels of their swords to the knight, and so he received them. And then they halp up their father, and so by their communal assent promised to Sir Marhaus never to be foes unto King Arthur, and thereupon at Whitsuntide after, to come, he and his sons, and put them in the king's grace.

Then Sir Marhaus departed, and within two days his damosel brought him whereas was a great tournament that the Lady de Vawse had cried. And who that did best should have a rich circlet of gold worth a thousand bezants. And there Sir Marhaus did so nobly that he was renowned, and had sometime down forty knights, and so the circlet of gold was rewarded him.

Then he departed from thence with great worship; and so within seven nights his damosel brought him to an earl's place, his name was the Earl Fergus, that after was Sir Tristram's knight; and this earl was but a young man, and late come into his lands, and there was a giant fast by him that hight Taulurd, and he had another brother in Cornwall that hight Taulas, that Sir Tristram slew when he was out of his mind. So this earl made his complaint unto Sir Marhaus, that there was a giant by him that destroyed all his lands, and how he durst nowhere ride nor go for him.

'Sir,' said the knight, 'whether useth he to fight, on horseback or on foot?'

'Nay,' said the earl, 'there may no horse bear him.'

'Well,' said Sir Marhaus, 'then will I fight with him on foot.'

So on the morn Sir Marhaus prayed the earl that one of his men might bring him whereas the giant was; and so he was, for he saw him sit under a tree of holly, and many clubs of iron and gisarmes about him.

So this knight dressed him to the giant, putting his shield afore him, and the giant took an iron club in his hand, and at the first stroke he clave Sir Marhaus' shield in two pieces. And there he was in great peril, for the giant was a wily fighter, but at last Sir Marhaus smote off his right arm above the elbow. Then the giant fled and the knight after him, and

bezants: gold coins. *gisarmes*: battle-axes.

so he drove him into a water, but the giant was so high that he might not wade after him. And then Sir Marhaus made the Earl Fergus' man to fetch him stones, and with those stones the knight gave the giant many sore knocks, till at the last he made him fall down into the water, and so was he there dead.

Then Sir Marhaus went unto the giant's castle, and there he delivered twenty-four ladies and twelve knights out of the giant's prison, and there he had great riches without number, so that the days of his life he was never poor man. Then he returned to the Earl Fergus, the which thanked him greatly, and would have given him half his lands, but he would none take.

So Sir Marhaus dwelled with the earl nigh half a year, for he was sore bruised with the giant, and at the last he took his leave. And as he rode by the way, he met with Sir Gawain and Sir Uwain, and so by adventure he met with four knights of Arthur's court, the first was Sir Sagramore le Desirous, Sir Ozana, Sir Dodinas le Savage, and Sir Felot of Listinoise; and there Sir Marhaus with one spear smote down these four knights, and hurt them sore. So he departed to meet at his day aforeset.

CHAPTER 26: *How Sir Uwain rode with the damosel of sixty year of age, and how he gat the prize at tourneying*

Now turn we unto Sir Uwain, that rode westward with his damosel of three score winter of age, and she brought him there as was a tournament nigh the march of Wales. And at that tournament Sir Uwain smote down thirty knights, therefore was given him the prize, and that was a gerfalcon, and a white steed trapped with cloth of gold. So then Sir Uwain did many adventures by the means of the old damosel, and so she brought him to a lady that was called the Lady of the Rock, the which was much courteous.

So there were in the country two knights that were brethren, and they were called two perilous knights, the one knight hight Sir Edward of the Red Castle, and the other Sir Hugh of the Red Castle; and these two brethren had disherited the Lady of the Rock of a barony of lands by their extortion. And as this knight was lodged with this lady she made her complaint to him of these two knights.

'Madam,' said Sir Uwain, 'they are to blame, for they do against the high order of knighthood, and the oath that they made; and if it like you I will speak with them, because I am a knight of King Arthur's, and I will entreat them with fairness; and if they will not, I shall do battle with them, and in the defence of your right.'

'Gramercy,' said the lady, 'and thereas I may not acquit you, God shall.'

So on the morn the two knights were sent for, that they should come thither to speak with the Lady of the Rock, and wit ye well they failed not, for they came with an hundred horse. But when this lady saw them in this manner so big, she would not suffer Sir Uwain to go out to them upon no surety ne for no fair language, but she made him speak with them over a tower. But finally these two brethren would not be entreated, and answered that they would keep that they had.

'Well,' said Sir Uwain, 'then will I fight with one of you, and prove that ye do this lady wrong.'

'That will we not,' said they, 'for and we do battle, we two will fight with one knight at once, and therefore if ye will fight so, we will be ready at what hour ye will assign. And if ye win us in battle the lady shall have her lands again.'

'Ye say well,' said Sir Uwain, 'therefore make you ready so that ye be here tomorn in the defence of the lady's right.'

CHAPTER 27: *How Sir Uwain fought with two knights and overcame them*

So was there sikerness made on both parties that no treason should be wrought on neither party; so then the knights departed and made them ready, and that night Sir Uwain had great cheer.

And on the morn he arose early and heard mass, and brake his fast, and so he rode unto the plain without the gates, where hoved the two brethren abiding him. So they rode together passing sore, that Sir Edward and Sir Hugh brake their spears upon Sir Uwain. And Sir Uwain smote Sir Edward that he fell over his horse and yet his spear brast not. And then he spurred his horse and came upon Sir Hugh and ovethrew him, but they soon recovered and dressed their shields and drew their swords and bad Sir Uwain alight and do his battle to the uttemost.

Then Sir Uwain devoided his horse suddenly, and put his shield afore him and drew his sword, and so they dressed together, and either gave other such strokes, and there these two brethren wounded Sir Uwain passing grievously that the Lady of the Rock weened he should have died. And thus they fought together five hours as men raged out of reason. And at the last Sir Uwain smote Sir Edward upon the helm such a stroke that his sword carved unto his canel bone, and then Sir Hugh abated his courage, but Sir Uwain pressed fast to have slain him. That saw Sir Hugh; he kneeled down and yielded him to Sir Uwain. And he of his gentleness received his sword, and took him by the hand, and went into the castle together.

Then the Lady of the Rock was passing glad, and the other brother made great sorrow for his brother's death. Then the lady was restored of all her lands, and Sir Hugh was commanded to be at the court of King Arthur at the next feast of Pentecost. So Sir Uwain dwelt with the lady nigh

sikerness: assurance. *devoided*: dismounted from.

half a year, for it was long or he might be whole of his great hurts.

And so when it drew nigh the term-day that Sir Gawain, Sir Marhaus, and Sir Uwain should meet at the cross-way, then every knight drew him thither to hold his promise that they had made; and Sir Marhaus and Sir Uwain brought their damosels with them, but Sir Gawain had lost his damosel as it is afore rehearsed.

CHAPTER 28: *How at the year's end all three knights with their three damosels met at the fountain*

Right so at the twelvemonths' end they met all three knights at the fountain and their damosels, but the damosel that Sir Gawain had could say but little worship of him. So they departed from the damosels and rode through a great forest, and there they met with a messenger that came from King Arthur, that had sought them well nigh a twelvemonth throughout all England, Wales, and Scotland, and charged if ever he might find Sir Gawain and Sir Uwain to bring them to the court again. And then were they all glad, and so prayed they Sir Marhaus to ride with them to the king's court.

And so within twelve days they came to Camelot, and the king was passing glad of their coming, and so was all the court. Then the king made them to swear upon a book to tell him all their adventures that had befall them that twelvemonth, and so they did. And there was Sir Marhaus well-known, for there were knights that he had matched aforetime, and he was named one of the best knights living.

Against the feast of Pentecost came the Damosel of the Lake and brought with her Sir Pelleas; and at that high feast there was great jousting of knights, and of all knights that were at that jousts, Sir Pelleas had the prize, and Sir Marhaus was named the next; but Sir Pelleas was so strong there might but few knights sit him a buffet with a spear. And at that next feast Sir Pelleas and Sir Marhaus were made knights of the Table Round, for there were two sieges void, for two knights were slain that twelvemonth, and great joy had King Arthur of Sir Pelleas and of Sir Marhaus.

But Pelleas loved never after Sir Gawain, but as he spared him for the love of King Arthur; but ofttimes at jousts and tournaments Sir Pelleas quit Sir Gawain, for so it rehearseth in the book of French. So Sir Tristram many days after fought with Sir Marhaus in an island, and there they did a great battle, but at the last Sir Tristram slew him, so Sir Tristram was wounded that unnethe he might recover, and lay at a nunnery half a year. And Sir Pelleas was a worshipful knight, and was one of the four that achieved the Sangrail;[1] and the Damosel of the Lake made by her means that never he had ado with Sir Launcelot de Lake, for where Sir Launcelot was at any jousts or any tournament, she would not suffer him be there that day, but if it were on the side of Sir Launcelot.

Explicit Liber Quartus.
Incipit Liber Quintus.

Book V

CHAPTER 1: *How twelve aged ambassadors of Rome came to King Arthur to demand truage for Britain*

When King Arthur had after long war rested, and held a royal feast and Table Round with his allies of kings, princes, and noble knights all of the Round Table, there came into his hall, he sitting on his throne royal, twelve ancient men, bearing each of them a branch of olive, in token that they came as ambassadors and messengers from the Emperor Lucius, which was called at that time, Dictator or Procuror of the Public Weal of Rome; which said messengers, after their entering and coming into the presence of King Arthur, did to him their obeisance in making to him reverence, said to him in this wise:

'The high and mighty Emperor Lucius sendeth to the King of Britain greeting, commanding thee to acknowledge him for thy lord, and to send him the truage due of this realm unto the Empire, which thy father and other tofore thy precessors have paid as is of record, and thou as rebel not knowing him as thy sovereign, withholdest and retainest contrary to the statutes and decrees made by the noble and worthy Julius Cesar, conqueror of this realm, and first Emperor of Rome. And if thou refuse his demand and commandment, know thou for certain that he shall make strong war against thee, thy realms and lands, and shall chastise thee and thy subjects, that it shall be example perpetual unto all kings and princes, for to deny their truage unto that noble empire which domineth upon the universal world.'

Then when they had showed the effect of their message, the king commanded them to withdraw them, and said he

domineth: holds sway.

should take advice of council and give to them an answer. Then some of the young knights, hearing this their message, would have run on them to have slain them, saying that it was a rebuke to all the knights there being present to suffer them to say so to the king. And anon the king commanded that none of them, upon pain of death, to missay them ne do them any harm, and commanded a knight to bring them to their lodging; 'and see that they have all that is necessary and requisite for them, with the best cheer, and that no dainty be spared, for the Romans be great lords, and though their message please me not nor my court, yet I must remember mine honour.'

After this the king let call all his lords and knights of the Round Table to counsel upon this matter, and desired them to say their advice.

Then Sir Cador of Cornwall spake first and said, 'Sir, this message liketh me well, for we have many days rested us and have been idle, and now I hope ye shall make sharp war on the Romans, where I doubt not we shall get honour.'

'I believe well,' said Arthur, 'that this matter pleaseth thee well, but these answers may not be answered, for the demand grieveth me sore, for truly I will never pay truage to Rome, wherefore I pray you to counsel me. I have understand that Belinus and Brenius, kings of Britain, have had the empire in their hands many days, and also Constantine the son of Heleine, which is an open evidence that we owe no tribute to Rome, but of right we that be descended of them have right to claim the title of the empire.'

CHAPTER 2: *How the kings and lords promised to King Arthur aid and help against the Romans*

Then answered King Agwisance of Scotland, 'Sir, ye ought of right to be above all other kings, for unto you is none like ne pareil in Christendom, of knighthood ne of dignity, and

pareil: equal.

I counsel you never to obey the Romans, for when they reigned on us they distressed our elders, and put this land to great extortions and tailles, wherefore I make here mine avow to avenge me on them; and for to strength your quarrel I shall furnish twenty thousand good men of war, and wage them on my costs, which shall await on you with myself when it shall please you.'

And the King of Little Britain granted him to the same thirty thousand; wherefore King Arthur thanked them. And then every man agreed to make war, and to aid after their power, that is to wit, the Lord of West Wales promised to bring thirty thousand men, and Sir Uwain, Sir Idrus his son, with their cousins, promised to bring thirty thousand. Then Sir Launcelot with all other promised in likewise every man a great multitude. And when King Arthur understood their courages and good wills he thanked them heartily, and after let call the ambassadors to hear their answer. And in presence of all his lords and knights he said to them in this wise:

'I will that ye return unto your lord and Procuror of the Common Weal for the Romans, and say ye to him, of his demand and commandment I set nothing, and that I know of no truage ne tribute that I owe to him, ne to none earthly prince, Christian ne heathen; but I pretend to have and occupy the sovereignty of the empire, wherein I am entitled by the right of my predecessors, sometime kings of this land; and say to him that I am delibered and fully concluded, to go with mine army with strength and power unto Rome, by the grace of God, to take possession in the empire and subdue them that be rebel. Wherefore I command him and all them of Rome, that incontinent they make to me their homage, and to acknowledge me for their Emperor and Governor, upon pain that shall ensue.'

And then he commanded his treasurer to give to them great and large gifts, and to pay all their dispenses, and assigned Sir Cador to convey them out of the land.

tailles: taxes. *delibered*: considered. *incontinent*: forthwith.

And so they took their leave and departed, and took their shipping at Sandwich, and passed forth by Flanders, Almain, the mountains, and all Italy, until they came unto Lucius. And after the reverence made, they made relation of their answer, like as ye tofore have heard.

When the Emperor Lucius had well understand their credence, he was sore moved as he had been all araged, and said, 'I had supposed that Arthur would have obeyed to my commandment, and have served you himself, as him well beseemed or any other king to do.'

'O Sir,' said one of the senators, 'let be such vain words, for we let you wit that I and my fellows were full sore afeared to behold his countenance. I fear me ye have made a rod for yourself, for he intendeth to be lord of this empire, which sore is to be doubted if he come, for he is all another man than ye ween, and holdeth the most noble court of the world; all other kings ne princes may not compare unto his noble mainten. On New Year's Day we saw him in his estate, which was the royallest that ever we saw, for he was served at his table with nine kings, and the noblest fellowship of other princes, lords, and knights that be in the world, and every knight approved and like a lord, and holdeth Table Round; and in his person the most manly man that liveth, and is like to conquer all the world, for unto his courage it is too little. Wherefore I advise you to keep well your marches and straits in the mountains; for certainly he is a lord to be doubted.'

'Well,' said Lucius, 'before Easter I suppose to pass the mountains, and so forth into France, and there bereave him his lands with Genoese and other mighty warriors of Tuscany and Lombardy. And I shall send for them all that be subjects and allied to the empire of Rome to come to mine aid,' and forthwith sent old wise knights unto these countries following:

First to Ambage and Arrage, to Alexandria, to India, to Armenia, whereas the river of Euphrates runneth into Asia,

credence: message. *mainten*: manner of life.

to Africa, and Europe the Large, to Ertayne and Elamye, to Araby, Egypt, and to Damascus, to Damietta and Cayer, to Cappadocia, to Tarsus, Turkey, Pontus and Pamphylia to Syria and Galatia. And all these were subject to Rome and many more, as Greece, Cyprus, Macedonia, Calabria, Cateland,[1] Portugal, with many thousands of Spaniards. Thus all these kings, dukes, and admirals, assembled about Rome, with sixteen kings at once, with great multitude of people.

When the emperor understood their coming he made ready his Romans and all the people between him and Flanders. Also he had gotten with him fifty giants which had been engendered of fiends; and they were ordained to guard his person, and to break the front of the battle of King Arthur.

And thus departed from Rome, and came down the mountains for to destroy the lands that Arthur had conquered, and came unto Cologne, and besieged a castle thereby, and won it soon, and stuffed it with two hundred Saracens or Infidels, and after destroyed many fair countries which Arthur had won of King Claudas. And thus Lucius came with all his host which were disperpled sixty mile in breadth, and commanded them to meet with him in Burgundy, for he purposed to destroy the realm of Little Britain.

CHAPTER 3: *How King Arthur held a Parliament at York, and how he ordained how the realm should be governed in his absence*

Now leave we of Lucius the Emperor and speak we of King Arthur, that commanded all them of his retinue to be ready at the utas of Hilary for to hold a Parliament at York. And at that Parliament was concluded to arrest all the navy of the land, and to be ready within fifteen days at Sandwich, and there he showed to his army how he purposed to conquer the empire which he ought to have of right.

And there he ordained two governors of this realm, that is

disperpled: dispersed. *utas*: octave, eighth day after festival.

to say, Sir Baudwin of Britain, for to counsel to the best, and Sir Constantine, son to Sir Cador of Cornwall, which after the death of Arthur was king of this realm.[1] And in the presence of all his lords he resigned the rule of the realm and Guenever his queen to them, wherefore Sir Launcelot was wroth, for he left Sir Tristram with King Mark for the love of Beale Isoud.

Then the Queen Guenever made great sorrow for the departing of her lord and other, and swooned in such wise that the ladies bare her into her chamber.

Thus the king with his great army departed, leaving the queen and realm in the governance of Sir Baudwin and Constantine. And when he was on his horse he said with an high voice, 'If I die in this journey I will that Sir Constantine be mine heir and king crowned of this realm as next of my blood,' and after departed and entered into the sea at Sandwich with all his army, with a great multitude of ships, galleys, cogs, and dromonds, sailing on the sea.

CHAPTER 4: *How King Arthur being shipped and lying in his cabin had a marvellous dream and of the exposition thereof*

And as the king lay in his cabin in the ship, he fell in a slumbering and dreamed a marvellous dream: him seemed that a dreadful dragon did drown much of his people, and he came flying out of the west, and his head was enamelled with azure, and his shoulders shone as gold, his belly like mails of a marvellous hue, his tail full of tatters, his feet full of fine sable, and his claws like fine gold; and an hideous flame of fire flew out of his mouth, like as the land and water had flamed all of fire. After, him seemed there came out of the orient a grimly boar all black in a cloud, and his paws as big as a post; he was rugged looking roughly, he was the foulest beast that ever man saw, he roared and

cogs: broadly built ships. *dromonds*: large ships.

roamed so hideously that it were marvel to hear. Then the dreadful dragon advanced him and came in the wind like a falcon giving great strokes on the boar, and the boar hit him again with his grizzly tusks that his breast was all bloody, and that the hot blood made all the sea red of his blood. Then the dragon flew away all on an height, and came down with such a swough, and smote the boar on the ridge, which was ten foot large from the head to the tail, and smote the boar all to powder both flesh and bones, that it flittered all abroad on the sea.

And therewith the king awoke anon, and was sore abashed of this dream, and sent anon for a wise philosopher, commanding to tell him the signification of his dream.

'Sir,' said the philosopher, 'the dragon that thou dreamedst of betokeneth thine own person that sailest here, and the colours of his wings be thy realms that thou hast won, and his tail which is all to-tattered signifieth the noble knights of the Round Table; and the boar that the dragon slew coming from the clouds betokeneth some tyrant that tormenteth the people, or else thou art like to fight with some giant thyself, being horrible and abominable, whose peer ye saw never in your days, wherefore of this dreadful dream doubt thee nothing, but as a conqueror come forth thyself.'

Then after this soon they had sight of land, and sailed till they arrived at Barflete in Flanders, and when they were there he found many of his great lords ready, as they had been commanded to await upon him.

CHAPTER 5: *How a man of the country told to him of a marvellous giant, and how he fought and conquered him*

Then came to him an husbandman of the country, and told him how there was in the country of Constantine, beside Brittany, a great giant which had slain, murdered and de-

swough: swoop.

voured much people of the country, and had been sustained seven year with the children of the commons of that land, 'insomuch that all the children be all slain and destroyed; and now late he hath taken the Duchess of Brittany as she rode with her meyne, and hath led her to his lodging which is in a mountain, for to ravish and lie by her to her life's end, and many people followed her, more than five hundred, but all they might not rescue her, but they left her shrieking and crying lamentably, wherefore I suppose that he hath slain her in fulfilling his foul lust of lechery. She was wife unto thy cousin Sir Howell, whom we call full nigh of thy blood. Now, as thou [art] a rightful king, have pity on this lady, and revenge us all as thou art a noble conqueror.'

'Alas,' said King Arthur, 'this is a great mischief, I had lever than the best realm that I have that I had been a furlong way tofore him for to have rescued that lady. Now, fellow,' said King Arthur, 'canst thou bring me thereas this giant haunteth?'

'Yea, sir,' said the good man, 'look yonder whereas thou seest those two great fires, there shalt thou find him, and more treasure than I suppose is in all France.'

When the king had understanden this piteous case, he returned into his tent. Then he called to him Sir Kay and Sir Bedevere, and commanded them secretly to make ready horse and harness for himself and them twain, for after evensong he would ride on pilgrimage with them two only unto Saint Michael's mount. And then anon he made him ready, and armed him at all points, and took his horse and his shield.

And so they three departed thence and rode forth as fast as ever they might till that they came to the fore-land of that mount. And there they alighted, and the king commanded them to tarry there, for he would himself go up into that mount. And so he ascended up into that hill till he came to a great fire, and there he found a careful widow wringing her hands and making great sorrow, sitting by a grave new made. And then King Arthur saluted her, and demanded of her

meyne: retinue.

wherefore she made such lamentation, to whom she answered and said,

'Sir knight, speak soft, for yonder is a devil, if he hear thee speak he will come and destroy thee; I hold thee unhappy; what dost thou here in this mountain? For if ye were such fifty as ye be, ye were not able to make resistance against this devil: here lieth a duchess dead, the which was the fairest of all the world, wife to Sir Howell, Duke of Brittany; he hath murdered her in forcing her, and hath slit her unto the navel.'

'Dame,' said the king, 'I come from the noble conqueror King Arthur, for to treat with that tyrant for his liege people.'

'Fie on such treaties,' said she, 'he setteth not by the king ne by no man else; but and if thou have brought Arthur's wife, dame Guenever, he shall be gladder than thou hadst given to him half France. Beware, approach him not too nigh, for he hath vanquished fifteen kings, and hath made him a coat full of precious stones enbroidered with their beards, which they sent him to have his love for salvation of their people at this last Christmas. And if thou wilt, speak with him at yonder great fire at supper.'

'Well,' said Arthur, 'I will accomplish my message for all your fearful words;' and went forth by the crest of that hill, and saw where he sat at supper gnawing on a limb of a man, baking his broad limbs by the fire, and breechless, and three fair damosels turning three broaches whereon were broached twelve young children late born, like young birds. When King Arthur beheld that piteous sight he had great compassion on them, so that his heart bled for sorrow, and hailed him saying in this wise:

'He that all the world wieldeth give thee short life and shameful death; and the devil have thy soul. Why hast thou murdered these young innocent children, and murdered this duchess? Therefore arise and dress thee, thou glutton, for this day shall thou die of my hand.'

Then the glutton anon start up, and took a great club in

his hand, and smote at the king that his coronal fell to the earth. And the king hit him again that he carve his belly and cut off his genitors, that his guts and his entrails fell down to the ground. Then the giant threw away his club, and caught the king in his arms that he crushed his ribs. Then the three maidens kneeled down and called to Christ for help and comfort of Arthur. And then Arthur weltered and wrung, that he was other while under and another time above. And so weltering and wallowing they rolled down the hill till they came to the sea mark, and ever as they so weltered Arthur smote him with his dagger. And it fortuned they came to the place whereas the two knights were and kept Arthur's horse; then when they saw the king fast in the giant's arms they came and loosed him.

And then the king commanded Sir Kay to smite off the giant's head, and to set it upon a truncheon of a spear, and bear it to Sir Howell, and tell him that his enemy was slain; 'and after let this head be bounden to a barbican that all the people may see and behold it; and go ye two up to the mountain, and fetch me my shield, my sword, and the club of iron; and as for the treasure, take ye it, for ye shall find there good out of number; so I have the kirtle and the club I desire no more. This was the fiercest giant that ever I met with, save one in the mount of Araby, which I overcame, but this was greater and fiercer.'

Then the knights fetched the club and the kirtle, and some of the treasure they took to themself, and returned again to the host. And anon this was known through all the country, wherefore the people came and thanked the king.

And he said again, 'Give the thank to God, and depart the goods among you.' And after that King Arthur said and commanded his cousin Howell, that he should ordain for a church to be builded on the same hill in the worship of Saint Michael.

And on the morn the king removed with his great battle, and came into Champagne and in a valley, and there they pitched their tents; and the king being set at his dinner, there came in two messengers, of whom that one was Marshal of France, and said to the king that the emperor was entered into France, and had destroyed a great part, and was in Burgundy, and had destroyed and made great slaughter of people, and burnt towns and boroughs; 'wherefore, if thou come not hastily, they must yield up their bodies and goods.'

CHAPTER 6: *How King Arthur sent Sir Gawain and other to Lucius, and how they were assailed and escaped with worship*

Then the king did do call Sir Gawain, Sir Bors, Sir Lionel, and Sir Bedevere, and commanded them to go straight to Sir Lucius, 'and say ye to him that hastily he remove out of my land; and if he will not, bid him make him ready to battle and not distress the poor people.'

Then anon these noble knights dressed them to horseback, and when they came to the green wood, they saw many pavilions set in a meadow, of silk of divers colours, beside a river, and the emperor's pavilion was in the middle with an eagle displayed above. To the which tent our knights rode toward, and ordained Sir Gawain and Sir Bors to do the message, and left in a bushment Sir Lionel and Sir Bedevere.

And then Sir Gawain and Sir Bors did their message, and commanded Lucius, in Arthur's name to avoid his land, or shortly to address him to battle. To whom Lucius answered and said, 'Ye shall return to your lord, and say ye to him that I shall subdue him and all his lands.'

Then Sir Gawain was wroth and said, 'I had lever than all France fight against thee.'

'And so had I,' said Sir Bors, 'lever than all Brittany or Burgundy.'

Then a knight named Sir Gainus, nigh cousin to the emperor, said, 'Lo, how these Britons be full of pride and boast, and they brag as though they bare up all the world.'

bushment: ambush.

Then Sir Gawain was sore grieved with these words, and pulled out his sword and smote off his head. And therewith turned their horses and rode over waters and through woods till they came to their bushment, whereas Sir Lionel and Sir Bedevere were hoving.

The Romans followed fast after, on horseback and on foot, over a champaign unto a wood; then Sir Bors turned his horse and saw a knight came fast on, whom he smote through the body with a spear that he fell dead down to the earth; then came Caliburn one of the strongest of Pavie, and smote down many of Arthur's knights. And when Sir Bors saw him do so much harm, he addressed toward him, and smote him through the breast, that he fell down dead to the earth. Then Sir Feldenak thought to revenge the death of Gainus upon Sir Gawain, but Sir Gawain was ware thereof, and smote him on the head, which stroke stinted not till it came to his breast.

And then he returned and came to his fellows in the bushment. And there was a recounter, for the bushment brake on the Romans, and slew and hew down the Romans, and forced the Romans to flee and return, whom the noble knights chased unto their tents.

Then the Romans gathered more people, and also foot-men came on, and there was a new battle, and so much people that Sir Bors and Sir Berel were taken. But when Sir Gawain saw that, he took with him Sir Idrus the good knight, and said he would never see King Arthur but if he rescued them, and pulled out Galatine his good sword, and followed them that led those two knights away; and he smote him that led Sir Bors, and took Sir Bors from him and delivered him to his fellows. And Sir Idrus in likewise rescued Sir Berel.

Then began the battle to be great, that our knights were in great jeopardy, wherefore Sir Gawain sent to King Arthur for succour, and that he hie him, 'for I am sore wounded, and that our prisoners may pay good out of number.'

And the messenger came to the king and told him his message. And anon the king did do assemble his army, but anon, or he departed, the prisoners were comen, and Sir Gawain and his fellows gat the field and put the Romans to flight, and after returned and came with their fellowship in such wise that no man of worship was lost of them, save that Sir Gawain was sore hurt. Then the king did do ransack his wounds and comforted him.

And thus was the beginning of the first journey of the Britons and Romans, and there were slain of the Romans more than ten thousand, and great joy and mirth was made that night in the host of King Arthur. And on the morn he sent all the prisoners into Paris under the guard of Sir Launcelot, with many knights, and of Sir Cador.

CHAPTER 7: *How Lucius sent certain spies in a bushment for to have taken his knights being prisoners, and how they were letted*

Now turn we to the Emperor of Rome, which espied that these prisoners should be sent to Paris, and anon he sent to lie in a bushment certain knights and princes with sixty thousand men, for to rescue his knights and lords that were prisoners.

And so on the morn as Launcelot and Sir Cador, chieftains and governors of all them that conveyed the prisoners, as they should pass through a wood, Sir Launcelot sent certain knights to espy if any were in the woods to let them. And when the said knights came into the wood, anon they espied and saw the great ambushment, and returned and told Sir Launcelot that there lay in await for them three score thousand Romans.

And then Sir Launcelot with such knights as he had, and men of war to the number of ten thousand, put them in array, and met with them and fought with them manly, and slew and dretched many of the Romans, and slew many knights and admirals of the party of the Romans and Saracens; there

did do ransack his wounds: had his wounds examined.
letted: hindered. *dretched*: harassed.

was slain the king of Lyly and three great lords, Aliduke, Herawd, and Heringdale. But Sir Launcelot fought so nobly that no man might endure a stroke of his hand, but where he came he showed his prowess and might, for he slew down right on every side; and the Romans and Saracens fled from him as the sheep from the wolf or from the lion, and put them all that abode alive to flight.

And so long they fought that tidings came to King Arthur, and anon he graithed him and came to the battle, and saw his knights how they had vanquished the battle, he embraced them knight by knight in his arms, and said, 'Ye be worthy to wield all your honour and worship; there was never king save myself that had so noble knights.'

'Sir,' said Cador, 'there was none of us failed other, but of the prowess and manhood of Sir Launcelot were more than wonder to tell, and also of his cousins which did that day many noble feats of war.' And also Sir Cador told who of his knights were slain, as Sir Berel, and other Sir Moris and Sir Maurel, two good knights.

Then the king wept, and dried his eyen with a kerchief, and said, 'Your courage had near hand destroyed you, for though ye had returned again, ye had lost no worship; for I call it folly, knights to abide when they be overmatched.'

'Nay,' said Launcelot and the other, 'for once shamed may never be recovered.'

CHAPTER 8: *How a senator told to Lucius of their discomfiture, and also of the great battle between Arthur and Lucius*

Now leave we King Arthur and his noble knights which had won the field, and had brought their prisoners to Paris, and speak we of a senator which escaped from the battle, and came to Lucius the emperor, and said to him,

'Sir emperor, I advise thee for to withdraw thee. What dost thou here? Thou shalt win nothing in these marches

graithed: prepared.

but great strokes out of all measure, for this day one of Arthur's knights was worth in the battle an hundred of ours.'

'Fie on thee,' said Lucius, 'thou speakest cowardly; for thy words grieve me more than all the loss that I had this day.' And anon he sent forth a king, which hight Sir Leomie, with a great army, and bad him hie him fast tofore, and he would follow hastily after.

King Arthur was warned privily, and sent his people to Sessoine, and took up the towns and castles from the Romans. Then the king commanded Sir Cador to take the rearward, and to take with him certain knights of the Round Table, 'And Sir Launcelot, Sir Bors, Sir Kay, Sir Marrok, with Sir Marhaus, shall await on our person.' Thus the King Arthur disperpled his host in divers parties, to the end that his enemies should not escape.

When the emperor was entered into the vale of Sessoine, he might see where King Arthur was embattled and his banner displayed; and he was beset round about with his enemies, that needs he must fight or yield him, for he might not flee, but said openly unto the Romans, 'Sirs, I admonish you that this day ye fight and acquit you as men, and remember how Rome domineth and is chief and head over all the earth and universal world, and suffer not these Britons this day to abide against us;' and therewith he did command his trumpets to blow the bloody sounds, in such wise that the ground trembled and dindled.

Then the battles approached and shove and shouted on both sides, and great strokes were smitten on both sides, many men overthrown, hurt, and slain; and great valiances, prowesses and appertices of war were that day showed, which were over long to recount the noble feats of every man, for they should contain an whole volume. But in especial, King Arthur rode in the battle exhorting his knights to do well, and himself did as nobly with his hands as was possible a man to do; he drew out Excalibur his sword, and awaited

dindled: trembled. *appertices*: feats.

ever whereas the Romans were thickest and most grieved his people, and anon he addressed him on that part, and hew and slew down right, and rescued his people; and he slew a great giant named Galapas, which was a man of an huge quantity and height; he shorted him and smote off both his legs by the knees, saying, 'Now art thou better of a size to deal with than thou were,' and after smote off his head. There Sir Gawain fought nobly and slew three admirals in that battle. And so did all the knights of the Round Table.

Thus the battle between King Arthur and Lucius the Emperor endured long. Lucius had on his side many Saracens which were slain. And thus the battle was great, and oftsides that one party was at a fordeal and anon at an afterdeal, which endured so long till at the last King Arthur espied where Lucius the Emperor fought, and did wonder with his own hands.

And anon he rode to him. And either smote other fiercely, and at last Lucius smote Arthur thwart the visage, and gave him a large wound. And when King Arthur felt himself hurt, anon he smote him again with Excalibur that it cleft his head, from the summit of his head, and stinted not till it came to his breast. And then the emperor fell down dead and there ended his life. And when it was known that the emperor was slain, anon all the Romans with all their host put them to flight, and King Arthur with all his knights followed the chase, and slew down right all them that they might attain.

And thus was the victory given to King Arthur, and the triumph; and there were slain on the party of Lucius more than a hundred thousand. And after King Arthur did do ransack the dead bodies, and did do bury them that were slain of his retinue, every man according to the estate and degree that he was of. And them that were hurt he let the surgeons do search their hurts and wounds, and commanded to spare no salves ne medicines till they were whole.

Then the king rode straight to the place where the Emperor

oftsides: often. *fordeal*: advantage. *afterdeal*: disadvantage.

Lucius lay dead, and with him he found slain the Sultan of Syria, the King of Egypt and of Ethiopia, which were two noble kings, with seventeen other kings of divers regions, and also sixty senators of Rome, all noble men, whom the king did do balm and gum with many good gums aromatic, and after did do cere them in sixty fold of cered cloth of sendal, and laid them in chests of lead, because they should not chafe ne savour, and upon all these bodies their shields with their arms and banners were set, to the end they should be known of what country they were.

And after he found three senators which were alive, to whom he said, 'For to save your lives I will that ye take these dead bodies, and carry them with you unto great Rome, and present them to the Potestate on my behalf, showing him my letters, and tell them that I in my person shall hastily be at Rome. And I suppose the Romans shall beware how they shall demand any tribute of me. And I command you to say when ye shall come to Rome, to the Potestate and all the Council and Senate, that I send to them these dead bodies for the tribute that they have demanded. And if they be not content with these, I shall pay more at my coming, for other tribute owe I none, ne none other will I pay. And methinketh this sufficeth for Britain, Ireland and all Almain with Germany. And furthermore, I charge you to say to them, that I command them upon pain of their heads never to demand tribute ne tax of me ne of my lands.'

Then with this charge and commandment, the three senators aforesaid departed with all the said dead bodies, laying the body of Lucius in a car covered with the arms of the Empire all alone; and after alway two bodies of kings in a chariot, and then the bodies of the senators after them, and so went toward Rome, and showed their legation and message to the Potestate and Senate, recounting the battle done in France, and how the field was lost and much people and innumerable slain. Wherefore they advised them in no wise to move no more war against that noble conqueror Arthur, 'for

cere: wax. *sendal*: fine cloth.

his might and prowess is most to be doubted, seeing the noble kings and great multitude of knights of the Round Table, to whom none earthly prince may compare.'

CHAPTER 9: *How Arthur, after he had achieved the battle against the Romans, entered into Almain, and so into Italy*

Now turn we unto King Arthur and his noble knights, which, after the great battle achieved against the Romans, entered into Lorraine, Brabant and Flanders, and sithen returned into Haut Almain, and so over the mountains into Lombardy, and after, into Tuscany wherein was a city which in no wise would yield themself ne obey, wherefore King Arthur besieged it, and lay long about it, and gave many assaults to the city; and they within defended them valiantly.

Then, on a time, the king called Sir Florence, a knight, and said to him they lacked victual, 'And not far from hence be great forests and woods, wherein be many of mine enemies with much bestial. I will that thou make thee ready and go thither in foraging, and take with thee Sir Gawain my nephew, Sir Wisshard, Sir Clegis, Sir Cleremond, and the Captain of Cardiff with other, and bring with you all the beasts that ye there can get.'

And anon these knights made them ready, and rode over holts and hills, through forests and woods, till they came into a fair meadow full of fair flowers and grass; and there they rested them and their horses all that night.

And in the springing of the day in the next morn, Sir Gawain took his horse and stole away from his fellowship, to seek some adventures. And anon he was ware of a man armed, walking his horse easily by a wood's side, and his shield laced to his shoulder, sitting on a strong courser, without any man saving a page bearing a mighty spear. The knight bare in his shield three griffins of gold, in sable carbuncle, the chief of silver. When Sir Gawain espied this gay

bestial**:** cattle.

knight, he fewtered his spear, and rode straight to him, and demanded of him from whence that he was.

That other answered and said he was of Tuscany, and demanded of Sir Gawain, 'What, profferest thou, proud knight, thee so boldly? Here gettest thou no prey, thou mayest prove when thou wilt, for thou shalt be my prisoner or thou depart.'

Then said Gawain, 'Thou avauntest thee greatly and speakest proud words, I counsel thee for all thy boast that thou make thee ready, and take thy gear to thee, tofore greater grame fall to thee.'

CHAPTER 10: *Of a battle done by Gawain against a Saracen, which after was yielden and became Christian*

Then they took their spears and ran each at other with all the might they had, and smote each other through their shields into their shoulders, wherefore anon they pulled out their swords, and smote great strokes that the fire sprang out of their helms. Then Sir Gawain was all abashed, and with Galatine his good sword he smote through shield and thick hauberk made of thick mails, and all to-rushed and brake the precious stones, and made him a large wound, that men might see both liver and lung. Then groaned that knight, and addressed him to Sir Gawain, and with an awke stroke gave him a great wound and cut a vein, which grieved Gawain sore, and he bled sore.

Then the knight said to Sir Gawain, 'Bind thy wound or thy blee change, for thou be-bleedest all thy horse and thy fair arms, for all the barbers of Brittany shall not can staunch thy blood, for whosomever is hurt with this blade he shall never be staunched of bleeding.'

Then answered Gawain, 'It grieveth me but little, thy

fewtered his spear: fixed his spear in its rest. *grame*: harm.
to-rushed: smashed. *awke*: back-handed. *blee*: complexion.
can staunch: be able to staunch.

great words shall not fear me ne less my courage, but thou shalt suffer tene and sorrow or we depart, but tell me in haste who may staunch my bleeding.'

'That may I do,' said the knight, 'if I will, and so will I if thou wilt succour and aid me, that I may be christened and believe on God, and thereof I require thee of thy manhood, and it shall be great merit for thy soul.'

'I grant,' said Sir Gawain, 'so God help me, to accomplish all thy desire, but first tell me what thou soughtest here thus alone, and of what land and liegiance thou art of.'

'Sir,' he said, 'my name is Priamus, and a great prince is my father, and he hath been rebel unto Rome and overriden many of their lands. My father is lineally descended of Alexander and of Hector by right line. And Duke Joshua and Maccabæus were of our lineage. I am right inheritor of Alexandria and Africa, and all the out isles, yet will I believe on thy Lord that thou believest on; and for thy labour I shall give thee treasure enough. I was so elate and hautain in my heart that I thought no man my peer, ne to me semblable. I was sent into this war with seven score knights, and now I have encountered with thee, which hast given to me of fighting my fill, wherefore sir knight, I pray thee to tell me what thou art.'

'I am no knight,' said Gawain, 'I have been brought up in the guardrobe with the noble King Arthur many years, for to take heed to his armour and his other array, and to point his paltocks that longen to himself. At Yule last he made me yeoman, and gave to me horse and harness, and an hundred pound in money; and if fortune be my friend, I doubt not but to be well advanced and holpen by my liege lord.'

'Ah,' said Priamus, 'if his knaves be so keen and fierce, his knights be passing good. Now for the King's love of Heaven, whether thou be a knave or a knight, tell thou me thy name.'

'By God,' said Sir Gawain, 'now will I say thee sooth, my name is Sir Gawain, and known I am in his court and in his

semblable: comparable. *hautain*: haughty. *guardrobe*: wardrobe. *point*: lace. *paltocks*: doublets.

chamber, and one of the knights of the Round Table, he dubbed me a duke with his own hand. Therefore grudge not if this grace is to me fortuned, it is the goodness of God that lent to me my strength.'

'Now am I better pleased,' said Priamus, 'than thou hadst given to me all the Provence and Paris the rich. I had lever to have been torn with wild horses, than any varlet had won such loos, or any page or priker should have had prize on me. But now sir knight I warn thee that hereby is a Duke of Lorraine with his army, and the noblest men of Dauphiné, and lords of Lombardy, with the garnison of Gotthard, and Saracens of Southland, numbered sixty thousand of good men of arms; wherefore but if we hie us hence, it will harm us both, for we be sore hurt, never like to recover; but take heed to my page, that he no horn blow, for if he do, there be hoving here fast by an hundred knights awaiting on my person, and if they take thee, there shall no ransom of gold ne silver acquit thee.'

Then Sir Gawain rode over a water for to save him, and the knight followed him, and so rode forth till they came to his fellows which were in the meadow, where they had been all the night. Anon as Sir Wisshard was ware of Sir Gawain and saw that he was hurt, he ran to him sorrowfully weeping, and demanded of him who had so hurt him; and Gawain told how he had foughten with that man, and each of them had hurt other, and how he had salves to heal them; 'but I can tell you other tidings, that soon we shall have ado with many enemies.'

Then Sir Priamus and Sir Gawain alighted, and let their horses graze in the meadow, and unarmed them, and then the blood ran freshly from their wounds. And Priamus took from his page a vial full of the four waters that came out of Paradise, and with certain balm anointed their wounds, and washed them with that water, and within an hour after they were both as whole as ever they were.

And then with a trumpet were they all assembled to

loos: renown. *garnison*: garrison.

council, and there Priamus told unto them what lords and knights had sworn to rescue him, and that without fail they should be assailed with many thousands, wherefore he counselled them to withdraw them.

Then Sir Gawain said it were great shame to them to avoid without any strokes; 'wherefore I advise to take our arms and to make us ready to meet with these Saracens and misbelieving men, and with the help of God we shall overthrow them and have a fair day on them. And Sir Florence shall abide still in this field to keep the stale as a noble knight, and we shall not forsake yonder fellows.'

'Now,' said Priamus, 'cease your words, for I warn you ye shall find in yonder woods many perilous knights; they will put forth beasts to call you on, they be out of number, and ye are not past seven hundred, which be over few to fight with so many.'

'Nevertheless,' said Sir Gawain, 'we shall once encounter them, and see what they can do, and the best shall have the victory.'

CHAPTER 11: *How the Saracens came out of a wood for to rescue their beasts, and of a great battle*

Then Sir Florence called to him Sir Floridas, with an hundred knights, and drove forth the herd of beasts. Then followed him seven hundred men of arms; and Sir Ferant of Spain on a fair steed came springing out of the woods, and came to Sir Florence and asked him why he fled. Then Sir Florence took his spear and rode against him, and smote him in the forehead and brake his neck bone. Then all the other were moved, and thought to avenge the death of Sir Ferant, and smote in among them, and there was great fight, and many slain and laid down to ground, and Sir Florence with his hundred knights alway kept the stale, and fought manly.

Then when Priamus the good knight perceived the great

stale: position.

fight, he went to Sir Gawain, and bad him that he should go and succour his fellowship, which were sore bestad with their enemies.

'Sir, grieve you not,' said Sir Gawain, 'for their gree shall be theirs. I shall not once move my horse to them ward, but if I see more than there be; for they be strong enough to match them.'

And with that he saw an earl called Sir Ethelwold and the duke of Dutchmen came leaping out of a wood with many thousands, and Priamus' knights, and came straight unto the battle. Then Sir Gawain comforted his knights, and bad them not to be abashed, 'for all shall be ours.'

Then they began to wallop and met with their enemies, there were men slain and overthrown on every side. Then thrusted in among them the knights of the Table Round, and smote down to the earth all them that withstood them, in so much that they made them to recoil and flee.

'By God,' said Sir Gawain, 'this gladdeth my heart, for now be they less in number by twenty thousand.'

Then entered into the battle Jubance a giant, and fought and slew downright, and distressed many of our knights, among whom was slain Sir Gherard, a knight of Wales. Then our knights took heart to them, and slew many Saracens. And then came in Sir Priamus with his pennon, and rode with the knights of the Round Table, and fought so manfully that many of their enemies lost their lives. And there Sir Priamus slew the Marquis of Moyses land, and Sir Gawain with his fellows so quit them that they had the field, but in that stour was Sir Chestelaine, a child and ward of Sir Gawain, slain, wherefore was much sorrow made, and his death was soon avenged. Thus was the battle ended, and many lords of Lombardy and Saracens left dead in the field.

Then Sir Florence and Sir Gawain harboured surely their people, and tooken great plenty of bestial, of gold and silver, and great treasure and riches, and returned unto King Arthur, which lay still at the siege. And when they came to

gree: victory. *stour*: battle.

the king they presented their prisoners and recounted their adventures, and how they had vanquished their enemies.

CHAPTER 12: *How Sir Gawain returned to King Arthur with his prisoners, and how the king won a city, and how he was crowned emperor*

'Now thanked be God,' said the noble King Arthur. 'But what manner man is he that standeth by himself, him seemed no prisoner?'

'Sir,' said Gawain, 'this is a good man of arms, he hath matched me, but he is yielden unto God, and to me, for to become Christian; had not he have been we should never have returned, wherefore I pray you that he may be baptised, for there liveth not a nobler man ne better knight of his hands.'

Then the king let him anon be christened, and did do call his first name Priamus, and made him a duke and knight of the Table Round.

And then anon the king let do cry assault to the city, and there was rearing of ladders, breaking of walls, and the ditch filled, that men with little pain might enter into the city.

Then came out a duchess, and Clarisin the countess, with many ladies and damosels, and kneeling before King Arthur, required him for the love of God to receive the city, and not to take it by assault, for then should many guiltless be slain.

Then the king avaled his visor with a meek and noble countenance, and said, 'Madam, there shall none of my subjects misdo you ne your maidens, ne to none that to you longen, but the duke shall abide my judgement.'

Then anon the king commanded to leave the assault, and anon the duke's oldest son brought out the keys, and kneel-

avaled: lowered.

ing delivered them to the king, and besought him of grace. And the king seized the town by assent of his lords, and took the duke and sent him to Dover, there for to abide prisoner term of his life, and assigned certain rents for the dower of the duchess and for her children.

Then he made lords to rule those lands, and laws as a lord ought to do in his own country. And after he took his journey toward Rome, and sent Sir Florence and Sir Floridas tofore, with five hundred men of arms, and they came to the city of Urbino and laid there a bushment, thereas them seemed most best for them, and rode tofore the town, where anon issued out much people and skirmished with the fore-riders. Then brake out the bushment and won the bridge, and after the town, and set upon the walls the king's banner. Then came the king upon an hill, and saw the city and his banner on the walls, by which he knew that the city was won. And anon he sent and commanded that none of his liege men should defoul ne lie by no lady, wife, ne maid; and when he came into the city, he passed to the castle, and comforted them that were in sorrow, and ordained there a captain, a knight of his own country.

And when they of Milan heard that thilk city was won, they sent to King Arthur great sums of money, and besought him as their lord to have pity of them, promising to be his subjects for ever, and yield to him homage and fealty for the lands of Pleasance and Pavia, Petersaint, and the Port of Tremble,[1] and to give him yearly a million of gold all his lifetime.

Then he rideth into Tuscany, and winneth towns and castles, and wasted all in his way that to him will not obey, and so to Spoleto and Viterbo, and from thence he rode into the Vale of Vicecount among the vines.

And from thence he sent to the senators, to wit whether they would know him for their lord. But soon after on a Saturday came unto King Arthur all the senators that were left alive, and the noblest cardinals that then dwelt in Rome,

thilk: that.

and prayed him of peace, and proferred him full large, and besought him as governor to give licence for six weeks for to assemble all the Romans, and then to crown him emperor with cream as it belongeth to so high estate.

'I assent,' said the king, 'like as ye have devised, and at Christmas there to be crowned, and to hold my Round Table with my knights as me liketh.'

And then the senators made ready for his enthronization. And at the day appointed, as the romance telleth, he came into Rome, and was crowned emperor by the Pope's hand, with all the royalty that could be made, and sojourned there a time, and established all his lands from Rome into France, and gave lands and realms unto his servants and knights, to every each after his desert, in such wise that none complained, rich ne poor. And he gave to Sir Priamus the duchy of Lorraine; and he thanked him, and said he would serve him the days of his life; and after made dukes and earls, and made every man rich.

Then after this all his knights and lords assembled them afore him, and said, 'Blessed be God, your war is finished and your conquest achieved, in so much that we know none so great ne mighty that dare make war against you; wherefore we beseech you to return homeward, and give us licence to go home to our wives, from whom we have been long, and to rest us, for your journey is finished with honour and worship.'

Then said the king, 'Ye say truth, and for to tempt God it is no wisdom, and therefore make you ready and return we into England.'

Then there was trussing of harness and baggage and great carriage. And after licence given, he returned and commanded that no man in pain of death should not rob ne take victual, ne other thing by the way but that he should pay therefore. And thus he came over the sea and landed at Sandwich, against whom Queen Guenever his wife came and met him, and he was nobly received of all his commons in every

cream: chrism.

city and burgh, and great gifts presented to him at his homecoming to welcome him with.

Thus endeth the fifth book of the conquest that King Arthur had against Lucius the Emperor of Rome, and here followeth the sixth book, which is of Sir Launcelot du Lake

burgh: town.

Book VI

CHAPTER 1 : *How Sir Launcelot and Sir Lionel departed from the court for to seek adventures, and how Sir Lionel left him sleeping and was taken*

Soon after that King Arthur was come from Rome into England, then all the knights of the Table Round resorted unto the king, and made many jousts and tournaments. And some there were that were but knights, which increased so in arms and worship that they passed all their fellows in prowess and noble deeds, and that was well proved on many; but in especial it was proved on Sir Launcelot du Lake, for in all tournaments and jousts and deeds of arms, both for life and death, he passed all other knights, and at no time he was never overcome but if it were by treason or enchantment, so Sir Launcelot increased so marvellously in worship, and in honour, therefore is he the first knight that the French book maketh mention of after King Arthur came from Rome. Wherefore Queen Guenever had him in great favour above all knights, and in certain he loved the queen again above all other ladies damosels of his life, and for her he did many deeds of arms, and saved her from the fire through his noble chivalry.

Thus Sir Launcelot rested him long with play and game. And then he thought himself to prove himself in strange adventures, then he bad his nephew, Sir Lionel, for to make him ready, 'for we two will seek adventures.'

So they mounted on their horses, armed at all rights, and rode into a deep forest and so into a deep plain. And then the weather was hot about noon, and Sir Launcelot had great lust to sleep. Then Sir Lionel espied a great apple tree that stood by an hedge, and said, 'Brother, yonder is a fair shadow, there may we rest us on our horses.'

'It is well said, fair brother,' said Sir Launcelot, 'for this seven year I was not so sleepy as I am now.'

And so they there alighted and tied their horses unto sundry trees, and so Sir Launcelot laid him down under an apple tree, and his helm he laid under his head. And Sir Lionel waked while he slept. So Sir Launcelot was asleep passing fast.

And in the meanwhile there came three knights riding, as fast fleeing as ever they might ride. And there followed them three but one knight. And when Sir Lionel saw him, him thought he saw never so great a knight, nor so well faring a man, neither so well apparelled unto all rights.

So within a while this strong knight had overtaken one of these knights, and there he smote him to the cold earth that he lay still. And then he rode unto the second knight, and smote him so that man and horse fell down. And then straight to the third knight he rode, and smote him behind his horse's arse a spear length. And then he alit down and reined his horse on the bridle, and bound all the three knights fast with the reins of their own bridles.

When Sir Lionel saw him do thus, he thought to assay him, and made him ready, and stilly and privily he took his horse, and thought not for to awake Sir Launcelot. And when he was mounted upon his horse, he overtook this strong knight, and bad him turn, and the other smote Sir Lionel so hard that horse and man he bare to the earth, and so he alit down and bound him fast, and threw him overthwart his own horse, and so he served them all four, and rode with them away to his own castle.

And when he came there he gart unarm them, and beat them with thorns all naked, and after put them in a deep prison where were many more knights that made great dolour.

CHAPTER 2: *How Sir Ector followed for to seek Sir Launcelot, and how he was taken by Sir Turquin*

When Sir Ector de Maris wist that Sir Launcelot was passed out of the court to seek adventures, he was wroth with himself, and made him ready to seek Sir Launcelot, and as he had ridden long in a great forest he met with a man was like a forester. 'Fair fellow,' said Sir Ector, 'knowest thou in this county any adventures that be here nigh hand?'

'Sir,' said the forester, 'this country know I well, and hereby, within this mile, is a strong manor, and well dyked, and by that manor, on the left hand, there is a fair ford for horses to drink of, and over that ford there groweth a fair tree, and thereon hangen many fair shields that wielded sometime good knights, and at the hole of the tree hangeth a basin of copper and laton, and strike upon that basin with the butt of thy spear thrice, and soon after thou shalt hear new tidings, and else hast thou the fairest grace that many a year had ever knight that passed through this forest.'

'Gramercy,' said Sir Ector, and departed and came to the tree, and saw many fair shields.

And among them he saw his brother's shield, Sir Lionel, and many more that he knew that were his fellows of the Round Table, the which grieved his heart, and promised to revenge his brother. Then anon Sir Ector beat on the basin as he were wood, and then he gave his horse drink at the ford, and there came a knight behind him and bad him come out of the water and make him ready; and Sir Ector anon turned him shortly, and in fewter cast his spear, and smote the other knight a great buffet that his horse turned twice about.

'This was well done,' said the strong knight, 'and knightly thou hast stricken me;' and therewith he rushed his horse on Sir Ector and cleyght him under his right arm, and bare him clean out of the saddle, and rode with him away into his own

fewter: rest for a spear. *cleyght*: seized.

hall, and threw him down in midst of the floor. The name of this knight was Sir Turquin.

Then he said unto Sir Ector, 'For thou hast done this day more unto me than any knight did these twelve years, now will I grant thee thy life so thou wilt be sworn to be my prisoner all thy life days.'

'Nay,' said Sir Ector, 'that will I never promise thee, but that I will do mine advantage.'

'That me repenteth,' said Sir Turquin.

And then he gart to unarm him, and beat him with thorns all naked, and sithen put him down in a deep dungeon, where he knew many of his fellows. But when Sir Ector saw Sir Lionel, then made he great sorrow.

'Alas, brother,' said Sir Ector, 'where is my brother, Sir Launcelot?'

'Fair brother, I left him asleep when that I from him yode, under an apple tree; and what is become of him I cannot tell you.'

'Alas,' said the knights, 'but Sir Launcelot help us we may never be delivered, for we know now no knight that is able to match our master Turquin.'

CHAPTER 3: *How four queens found Launcelot sleeping, and how by enchantment he was taken and led into a castle*

Now leave we these knights prisoners, and speak we of Sir Launcelot du Lake that lieth under the apple tree sleeping. Even about the noon there come by him four queens of great estate; and, for the heat should not nigh them, there rode four knights about them, and bare a cloth of green silk on four spears, betwixt them and the sun, and the queens rode on four white mules.

Thus as they rode they heard by them a great horse grimly neigh, then were they ware of a sleeping knight, that lay all armed under an apple tree; anon as these queens looked on his face, they knew it was Sir Launcelot. Then they began for to strive for that knight, every each one said they would have him to her love.

'We shall not strive,' said Morgan le Fay, that was King Arthur's sister, 'I shall put an enchantment upon him that he shall not awake in six hours, and then I will lead him away unto my castle, and when he is surely within my hold, I shall take the enchantment from him, and then let him choose which of us he will have unto paramour.'

So this enchantment was cast upon Sir Launcelot, and then they laid him upon his shield, and bare him so on horseback betwixt two knights, and brought him unto the castle Chariot, and there they laid him in a chamber cold, and at night they sent unto him a fair damosel with his supper ready dight. By that the enchantment was past, and when she came she saluted him, and asked him what cheer.

'I cannot say, fair damosel,' said Sir Launcelot, 'for I wot not how I came into this castle but it be by an enchantment.'

'Sir,' said she, 'ye must make good cheer, and if ye be such a knight as it is said ye be, I shall tell you more to-morn by prime of the day.'

'Gramercy, fair damosel,' said Sir Launcelot, 'of your good will I require you.'

And so she departed. And there he lay all that night without comfort of anybody. And on the morn early came these four queens, passingly well beseen, all they bidding him good morn, and he them again.

'Sir knight,' the four queens said, 'thou must understand thou art our prisoner, and we here know thee well that thou art Sir Launcelot du Lake, King Ban's son, and because we understand your worthiness, that thou art the noblest knight living, and as we know well there can no lady have thy love but one, and that is Queen Guenever, and now thou shalt lose her for ever, and she thee, and therefore thee behoveth now to choose one of us four.'

'I am the Queen Morgan le Fay, queen of the land of Gore, and here is the Queen of Northgales, and the Queen of Eastland, and the Queen of the Out Isles; now choose one of us which thou wilt have to thy paramour, for thou mayest not choose or else in this prison to die.'

'This is an hard case,' said Sir Launcelot, 'that either I must die or else choose one of you, yet had I lever to die in this prison with worship, than to have one of you to my paramour maugre my head. And therefore ye be answered, I will none of you, for ye be false enchantresses, and as for my lady, Dame Guenever, were I at my liberty as I was, I would prove it on you or on yours, that she is the truest lady unto her lord living.'

'Well,' said the queens, 'is this your answer, that ye will refuse us?'

'Yea, on my life,' said Sir Launcelot, 'refused ye be of me.'

So they departed and left him there alone that made great sorrow.

CHAPTER 4: *How Sir Launcelot was delivered by the mean of a damosel*

Right so at the noon came the damosel unto him with his dinner, and asked him what cheer.

'Truly, fair damosel,' said Sir Launcelot, 'in my life days never so ill.'

'Sir,' she said, 'that me repentest, but and ye will be ruled by me, I shall help you out of this distress, and ye shall have no shame nor villainy, so that ye hold me a promise.'

'Fair damosel, I will grant you, and sore I am of these queens sorceresses afeared, for they have destroyed many a good knight.'

'Sir,' said she, 'that is sooth, and for the renown and bounty that they hear of you they would have your love, and sir, they say, your name is Sir Launcelot du Lake, the flower of knights, and they be passing wroth with you that ye have refused them. But sir, and ye would promise me to help my father on Tuesday next coming, that hath made a tournament betwixt him and the King of Northgales, for the last

Tuesday past my father lost the field through three knights of Arthur's court, and ye will be there on Tuesday next coming, and help my father, to-morn or prime, by the grace of God, I shall deliver you clean.'

'Fair maiden,' said Sir Launcelot, 'tell me what is your father's name, and then shall I give you an answer.'

'Sir knight,' she said, 'my father is King Bagdemagus, that was foul rebuked at the last tournament.'

'I know your father well,' said Sir Launcelot, 'for a noble king and a good knight, and by the faith of my body, ye shall have my body ready to do your father and you service at that day.'

'Sir,' she said, 'gramercy, and to-morn await ye be ready betimes, and I shall be she that shall deliver you, and take you your armour and your horse, shield and spear, and hereby, within this ten mile, is an abbey of white monks,[1] there I pray you that ye me abide, and thither shall I bring my father unto you.'

'All this shall be done,' said Sir Launcelot, 'as I am true knight.'

And so she departed, and came on the morn early, and found him ready; then she brought him out of twelve locks, and brought him unto his armour, and when he was clean armed, she brought him until his own horse, and lightly he saddled him and took a great spear in his hand, and so rode forth, and said, 'Fair damosel, I shall not fail you by the grace of God.'

And so he rode into a great forest all that day, and never could find no highway, and so the night fell on him, and then was he ware in a slade, of a pavilion of red sendal.

'By my faith,' said Sir Launcelot, 'in that pavilion will I lodge all this night,' and so there he alit down, and tied his horse to the pavilion, and there he unarmed him, and there he found a bed, and laid him therein and fell asleep sadly.

slade: valley. *sadly*: soundly.

CHAPTER 5: *How a knight found Sir Launcelot lying in his leman's bed, and how Sir Launcelot fought with the knight*

Then within an hour there came the knight to whom the pavilion ought, and he weened that his leman had lain in that bed, and so he laid him down beside Sir Launcelot, and took him in his arms and began to kiss him.

And when Sir Launcelot felt a rough beard kissing him, he start out of the bed lightly, and the other knight after him, and either of them gat their swords in their hands, and out at the pavilion door went the knight of the pavilion, and Sir Launcelot followed him, and there by a little slake Sir Launcelot wounded him sore, nigh unto the death. And then he yielded him unto Sir Launcelot, and so he granted him, so that he would tell him why he came in to the bed.

'Sir,' said the knight, 'the pavilion is mine own, and there this night I had assigned my lady to have slept with me, and now I am likely to die of this wound.'

'That me repenteth,' said Launcelot, 'of your hurt, but I was adread of treason, for I was late beguiled, and therefore come on your way into your pavilion and take your rest, and as I suppose I shall staunch your blood.'

And so they went both into the pavilion, and anon Sir Launcelot staunched his blood. Therewithal came the knight's lady, that was a passing fair lady, and when she espied that her lord Belleus was sore wounded, she cried out on Sir Launcelot, and made great dole out of measure.

'Peace, my lady and my love,' said Belleus, 'for this knight is a good man, and a knight adventurous,' and there he told her all the cause how he was wounded; 'And when that I yielded me unto him, he left me goodly and hath staunched my blood.'

'Sir,' said the lady, 'I require thee tell me what knight ye be, and what is your name?'

ought: belonged. *slake*: ravine.

'Fair lady,' he said, 'my name is Sir Launcelot du Lake.'

'So me thought ever by your speech,' said the lady, 'for I have seen you oft or this, and I know you better than ye ween. But now and ye would promise me of your courtesy, for the harms that ye have done to me and to my lord Belleus, that when he cometh unto Arthur's court for to cause him to be made knight of the Round Table, for he is a passing good man of arms, and a mighty lord of lands of many out isles.'

'Fair lady,' said Sir Launcelot, 'let him come unto the court the next high feast, and look that ye come with him, and I shall do my power, and ye prove you doughty of your hands, that ye shall have your desire.'

So thus within a while as they thus talked the night passed, and the day shone, and then Sir Launcelot armed him, and took his horse, and they taught him to the abbey, and thither he rode within the space of two hours.

CHAPTER 6: *How Sir Launcelot was received of King Bagdemagus' daughter, and he made his complaint to her father*

And soon as Sir Launcelot came within the abbey yard, the daughter of King Bagdemagus heard a great horse go on the pavement. And she then arose and yede unto a window, and there she saw Sir Launcelot, and anon she made men fast to take his horse from him and let lead him into a stable, and himself was led into a fair chamber, and unarmed him, and the lady sent him a long gown, and anon she came herself. And then she made Launcelot passing good cheer, and she said he was the knight in the world was most welcome to her.

Then in all haste she sent for her father Bagdemagus that was within twelve mile of that abbey, and afore even he came with a fair fellowship of knights with him. And when the king was alit off his horse he yode straight unto Sir Launcelot's chamber and there he found his daughter, and then the king embraced Sir Launcelot in his arms and either made other good cheer.

Anon Sir Launcelot made his complaint unto the king how he was betrayed, and how his brother Sir Lionel was departed from him he nist not where, and how his daughter had delivered him out of prison. 'Therefore while I live I shall do her service and all her kindred.'

'Then am I sure of your help,' said the king, 'on Tuesday next coming?'

'Yea, sir,' said Sir Launcelot, 'I shall not fail you, for so I have promised my lady your daughter. But sir, what knights be they of my lord Arthur's that were with the King of Northgales?'

And the king said, 'It was Sir Mador de la Porte, and Sir Mordred and Sir Gahalantine that all for-fared my knights, for against them three I nor my knights might bear no strength.'

'Sir,' said Sir Launcelot, 'as I hear say that the tournament shall be here within this three mile of this abbey, ye shall send unto me three knights of yours, such as ye trust, and look that the three knights have all white shields, and I also, and no painture on the shields, and we four will come out of a little wood in midst of both parties, and we shall fall in the front of our enemies and grieve them that we may; and thus shall I not be known what knight I am.'

So they took their rest that night, and this was on the Sunday, and so the king departed, and sent unto Sir Launcelot three knights with the four white shields. And on the Tuesday they lodged them in a little leaved wood beside there the tournament should be. And there were scaffolds and holes that lords and ladies might behold and to give the prize.

Then came into the field the King of Northgales with eight score helms. And then the three knights of Arthur's stood by themself. Then came into the field King Bagdemagus with four score of helms. And then they fewtered their

nist: did not know. *holes*: i.e. windows.

spears, and came together with a great dash, and there were slain of knights at the first recounter twelve of King Badgemagus' party, and six of the King of Northgales' party, and King Bagdemagus' party was far set aback.

CHAPTER 7: *How Sir Launcelot behaved him in a tournament, and how he met with Sir Turquin leading Sir Gaheris*

With that came Sir Launcelot du Lake, and he thrust in with his spear in the thickest of the press, and there he smote down with one spear five knights, and of four of them he brake their backs. And in that throng he smote down the King of Northgales, and brake his thigh in that fall. All this doing of Sir Launcelot saw the three knights of Arthur's.

'Yonder is a shrewd guest,' said Sir Mador de la Porte, 'therefore have here once at him.'

So they encountered, and Sir Launcelot bare him down horse and man, so that his shoulder went out of lith.

'Now befalleth it to me to joust,' said Mordred, 'for Sir Mador hath a sore fall.'

Sir Launcelot was ware of him, and gat a great spear in his hand, and met him, and Sir Mordred brake a spear upon him, and Sir Launcelot gave him such a buffet that the arson of his saddle brake, and so he flew over his horse's tail, that his helm butted into the earth a foot and more, that nigh his neck was broken; and there he lay long in a swoon.

Then came in Sir Gahalantine with a great spear and Launcelot against him, with all their strength that they might drive, that both their spears to-brast even to their hands, and then they flung out with their swords and gave many a grim stroke. Then was Sir Launcelot wroth out of measure, and then he smote Sir Gahalantine on the helm that his nose brast out on blood, and ears and mouth both, and therewith his head hung low. And therewith his horse ran away with him, and he fell down to the earth.

shrewd: mischievous. *arson*: saddle-bow.

Anon therewithal Sir Launcelot gat a great spear in his hand, and or ever that great spear brake, he bare down to the earth sixteen knights, some horse and man, and some the man and not the horse, and there was none but that he hit surely, he bare none arms that day. And then he gat another great spear, and smote down twelve knights, and the most part of them never throve after.

And then the knights of the King of Northgales would joust no more. And there the gree was given to King Bagdemagus.

So either party departed unto his own place, and Sir Launcelot rode forth with King Bagdemagus unto his castle, and there he had passing good cheer both with the king and with his daughter, and they proffered him great gifts. And on the morn he took his leave, and told the king that he would go and seek his brother Sir Lionel, that went from him when that he slept, so he took his horse, and betaught them all to God.

And there he said unto the king's daughter, 'If ye have need any time of my service I pray you let me have knowledge, and I shall not fail you as I am true knight.'

And so Sir Launcelot departed, and by adventure he came into the same forest there he was take sleeping. And in the midst of an highway he met a damosel riding on a white palfrey, and there either saluted other.

'Fair damosel,' said Sir Launcelot, 'know ye in this country any adventures?'

'Sir knight,' said that damosel, 'here are adventures near hand, and thou durst prove them.'

'Why should I not prove adventures?' said Sir Launcelot. 'For that cause come I hither.'

'Well,' said she, 'thou seemest well to be a good knight, and if thou dare meet with a good knight, I shall bring thee where is the best knight, and the mightiest that ever thou found, so thou wilt tell me what is thy name, and what knight thou art.'

betaught: commended.

'Damosel, as for to tell thee my name I take no great force, truly my name is Sir Launcelot du Lake.'

'Sir, thou beseemest well; here be adventures by that fallen for thee, for hereby dwelleth a knight that will not be overmatched for no man I know but ye overmatch him, and his name is Sir Turquin. And, as I understand, he hath in his prison, of Arthur's court, good knights three score and four, that he hath won with his own hands. But when ye have done that journey ye shall promise me as ye are a true knight for to go with me, and to help me and other damosels that are distressed daily with a false knight.'

'All your intent, damosel, and desire I will fulfil, so ye will bring me unto this knight.'

'Now, fair knight, come on your way;' and so she brought him unto the ford and the tree where hung the basin.

So Sir Launcelot let his horse drink, and sithen he beat on the basin with the butt of his spear so hard with all his might till the bottom fell out, and long he did so but he saw nothing.

Then he rode endlong the gates of that manor nigh half-an-hour. And then was he ware of a great knight that drove an horse afore him, and overthwart the horse there lay an armed knight bounden. And ever as they came near and near, Sir Launcelot thought he should know him. Then Sir Launcelot was ware that it was Sir Gaheris, Gawain's brother, a knight of the Table Round.

'Now, fair damosel,' said Sir Launcelot, 'I see yonder cometh a knight fast bounden that is a fellow of mine, and brother he is unto Sir Gawain. And at the first beginning I promise you, by the leave of God, to rescue that knight; but if his master sit better in the saddle I shall deliver all the prisoners that he hath out of danger, for I am sure he hath two brethren of mine prisoners with him.'

By that time that either had seen other, they gripped their spears unto them.

'Now, fair knight,' said Sir Launcelot, 'put that wounded

beseemest: appear. *endlong*: along.

knight off the horse, and let him rest awhile, and let us two prove our strengths; for as it is informed me, thou doest and hast done great despite and shame unto knights of the Round Table, and therefore now defend thee.'

'And thou be of the Table Round,' said Turquin, 'I defy thee and all thy fellowship.'

'That is overmuch said,' said Sir Launcelot.

CHAPTER 8: *How Sir Launcelot and Sir Turquin fought together*

And then they put their spears in the rests, and came together with their horses as fast as they might run, and either smote other in midst of their shields that both their horses' backs brast under them and the knights were both astonied, and as soon as they might avoid their horses they took their shields afore them, and drew out their swords, and came together eagerly, and either gave other many strong strokes, for there might neither shields nor harness hold their strokes. And so within a while they had both grimly wounds, and bled passing grievously. Thus they fared two hours or more tracing and rasing either other where they might hit any bare place. Then at the last they were breathless both, and stood leaning on their swords.

'Now fellow,' said Sir Turquin, 'hold thy hand a while, and tell me what I shall ask thee.'

'Say on.'

Then Turquin said, 'Thou art the biggest man that ever I met withal, and the best breathed, and like one knight that I hate above all other knights; so be it that thou be not he I will lightly accord with thee, and for thy love I will deliver all the prisoners that I have, that is three score and four, so thou wilt tell me thy name. And thou and I we will be fellows together, and never to fail the while that I live.'

'It is well said,' said Sir Launcelot, 'but sithen it is so that

tracing: pursuing. *rasing*: slashing.

I may have thy friendship, what knight is he that thou so hatest above all other?'

'Faithfully,' said Sir Turquin, 'his name is Sir Launcelot du Lake, for he slew my brother, Sir Carados, at the Dolorous Tower, that was one of the best knights alive; and therefore him I except of all knights, for may I once meet with him, the one of us shall make an end of other, I make mine avow. And for Sir Launcelot's sake I have slain an hundred good knights, and as many I have maimed all utterly that they might never after help themself, and many have died in prison, and yet have I three score and four, and all shall be delivered so thou wilt tell me thy name, so be it that thou be not Sir Launcelot.'

'Now, see I well,' said Sir Launcelot, 'that such a man I might be, I might have peace, and such a man I might be, that there should be war mortal betwixt us. And now, sir knight, at thy request I will that thou wit and know that I am Launcelot du Lake, King Ban's son of Benwick, and very knight of the Table Round. And now I defy thee, and do thy best.'

'Ah,' said Turquin, 'Launcelot, thou art unto me most welcome that ever was knight, for we shall never depart till the one of us be dead.'

Then they hurtled together as two wild bulls rashing and lashing with their shields and swords, that sometime they fell both over their noses. Thus they fought still two hours and more, and never would have rest, and Sir Turquin gave Sir Launcelot many wounds that all the ground thereas they fought was all bespeckled with blood.

CHAPTER 9: *How Sir Turquin was slain, and how Sir Launcelot bad Sir Gaheris deliver all the prisoners*

Then at the last Sir Turquin waxed faint, and gave somewhat aback, and bare his shield low for weariness. That espied Sir Launcelot, and leapt upon him fiercely and gat him by the

rashing: dashing.

beaver of his helmet, and plucked him down on his knees, and anon he rased off his helm, and smote his neck in sunder.

And when Sir Launcelot had done this, he yode unto the damosel and said, 'Damosel, I am ready to go with you where ye will have me, but I have no horse.'

'Fair sir,' said she, 'take this wounded knight's horse and send him into this manor, and command him to deliver all the prisoners.'

So Sir Launcelot went unto Gaheris, and prayed him not to be aggrieved for to lend him his horse.

'Nay, fair lord,' said Gaheris, 'I will that ye take my horse at your own commandment, for ye have both saved me and my horse, and this day I say ye are the best knight in the world, for ye have slain this day in my sight the mightiest man and the best knight except you that ever I saw, and, fair sir,' said Gaheris, 'I pray you tell me your name.'

'Sir, my name is Sir Launcelot du Lake, that ought to help you of right for King Arthur's sake, and in especial for my lord Sir Gawain's sake, your own dear brother. And when that ye come within yonder manor, I am sure ye shall find there many knights of the Round Table, for I have seen many of their shields that I know on yonder tree. There is Kay's shield, and Sir Brandiles' shield, and Sir Marhaus' shield, and Sir Galihud's shield, and Sir Brian de Listonoise's shield, and Sir Aliduke's shield, with many more that I am not now advised of, and also my two brethren's shields, Sir Ector de Maris and Sir Lionel. Wherefore I pray you greet them all from me, and say that I bid them take such stuff there as they find, and that in any wise my brethren go unto the court and abide me there till that I come, for by the feast of Pentecost I cast me to be there, for as at this time I must ride with this damosel for to save my promise.'

And so he departed from Gaheris, and Gaheris yede into the manor, and there he found a yeoman porter keeping there many keys. Anon withal Sir Gaheris threw the porter unto the ground and took the keys from him, and hastily he opened the prison door, and there he let out all the prisoners, and every man loosed other of their bonds. And when they saw Sir Gaheris, all they thanked him, for they weened that he was wounded.

'Not so,' said Gaheris, 'it was Launcelot that slew him worshipfully with his own hands. I saw it with mine own eyen. And he greeteth you all well, and prayeth you to haste you to the court; and as unto Sir Lionel and Ector de Maris he prayeth you to abide him at the court.'

'That shall we not do,' said his brethren, 'we will find him and we may live.'

'So shall I,' said Sir Kay, 'find him or I come at the court as I am true knight.'

Then all those knights sought the house thereas the armour was, and then they armed them, and every knight found his own horse, and all that ever longed unto him. And when this was done, there came a forester with four horses lade with fat venison.

Anon, Sir Kay said, 'Here is good meat for us for one meal, for we had not many a day no good repast.'

And so that venison was roasted, baken, and sodden, and so after supper some abode there all that night, but Sir Lionel and Ector de Maris and Sir Kay rode after Sir Launcelot to find him if they might.

CHAPTER 10: *How Sir Launcelot rode with the damosel and slew a knight that distressed all ladies and also a villain that kept a bridge*

Now turn we unto Sir Launcelot, that rode with the damosel in a fair highway.

'Sir,' said the damosel, 'here by this way haunteth a knight that distressed all ladies and gentlewomen, and at the least he robbeth them or lieth by them.'

'What,' said Sir Launcelot, 'is he a thief and a knight and a ravisher of women? He doth shame unto the order of

sodden: boiled.

knighthood, and contrary unto his oath; it is pity that he liveth. But, fair damosel, ye shall ride on afore, yourself, and I will keep myself in covert, and if that he trouble you or distress you I shall be your rescue and learn him to be ruled as a knight.'

So the maid rode on by the way a soft ambling pace. And within a while came out that knight on horseback out of the wood, and his page with him, and there he put the damosel from her horse, and then she cried.

With that came Launcelot as fast as he might till he came to that knight, saying, 'O thou false knight and traitor unto knighthood, who did learn thee to distress ladies and gentlewomen?'

When the knight saw Sir Launcelot thus rebuking him he answered not, but drew his sword and rode unto Sir Launcelot, and Sir Launcelot threw his spear from him, and drew out his sword, and struck him such a buffet on the helmet that he clave his head and neck unto the throat.

'Now hast thou thy payment that long thou hast deserved.'

'That is truth,' said the damosel. 'For like as Sir Turquin watched to destroy knights, so did this knight attend to destroy and distress ladies, damosels, and gentlewomen, and his name was Sir Peris de Forest Savage.'

'Now, damosel,' said Sir Launcelot, 'will ye any more service of me?'

'Nay, sir,' she said, 'at this time, but Almighty Jesu preserve you wheresomever ye ride or go, for the courteoust knight thou art, and meekest, unto all ladies and gentlewomen that now liveth. But one thing, sir knight, methinketh ye lack, ye that are a knight wifeless, that ye will not love some maiden or gentlewoman, for I could never hear say that ever ye loved any of no manner degree, and that is greater pity; but it is noised that ye love Queen Guenever, and that she hath ordained by enchantment that ye shall never love none other but her, ne none other damosel ne lady shall rejoice you; wherefore many in this land of high estate and low make great sorrow.'

'Fair damosel,' said Sir Launcelot, 'I may not warn people to speak of me what it pleaseth them; but for to be a wedded man, I think it not; for then I must couch with her, and leave arms and tournaments, battles, and adventures; and as for to say for to take my pleasance with paramours, that will I refuse in principle for dread of God; for knights that be adventurous or lecherous[1] shall not be happy ne fortunate unto the wars, for either they shall be overcome with a simpler knight than they be themself, other else they shall by unhap and their cursedness slay better men than they be themself. And so who that useth paramours shall be unhappy, and all thing is unhappy that is about them.'

And so Sir Launcelot and she departed. And then he rode in a deep forest two days and more, and had strait lodging. So on the third day he rode over a long bridge, and there start upon him suddenly a passing foul churl, and he smote his horse on the nose that he turned about, and asked him why he rode over that bridge without his licence.

'Why should I not ride this way?' said Sir Launcelot, 'I may not ride beside.'

'Thou shalt not choose,' said the churl, and lashed at him with a great club shod with iron.

Then Sir Launcelot drew his sword and put the stroke aback, and clave his head unto the paps.

At the end of the bridge was a fair village, and all the people, men and women, cried on Sir Launcelot, and said, 'A worse deed didst thou never for thyself, for thou hast slain the chief porter of our castle.'

Sir Launcelot let them say what they would, and straight he went into the castle; and when he came into the castle he alit, and tied his horse to a ring on the wall, and there he saw a fair green court, and thither he dressed him, for there him thought was a fair place to fight in. So he looked about, and saw much people in doors and windows that said, 'Fair knight, thou art unhappy.'

warn: prevent. *strait*: confined.

CHAPTER 11: *How Sir Launcelot slew two giants, and made a castle free*

Anon withal came there upon him two great giants, well armed all save the heads, with two horrible clubs in their hands. Sir Launcelot put his shield afore him and put the stroke away of the one giant, and with his sword he clave his head asunder. When his fellow saw that, he ran away as he were wood, for fear of the horrible strokes, and Launcelot after him with all his might, and smote him on the shoulder, and clave him to the navel.

Then Sir Launcelot went into the hall, and there came afore him three score ladies and damosels, and all kneeled unto him, and thanked God and him of their deliverance. 'For sir,' said they, 'the most part of us have been here this seven year their prisoners, and we have worked all manner of silk works for our meat, and we are all great gentlewomen born. And blessed be the time, knight, that ever thou be born; for thou hast done the most worship that ever did knight in this world, that will we bear record, and we all pray you to tell us your name, that we may tell our friends who delivered us out of prison.'

'Fair damosel,' he said, 'my name is Sir Launcelot du Lake.'

'Ah, sir,' said they all, 'well mayest thou be he, for else save yourself, as we deemed, there might never knight have the better of these two giants; for many fair knights have assayed it, and here have ended, and many times have we wished after you, and these two giants dread never knight but you.'

'Now may ye say,' said Sir Launcelot, 'unto your friends how and who hath delivered you, and greet them all from me, and if that I come in any of your marches, show me such cheer as ye have cause, and what treasure that there in this castle is I give it you for a reward for your grievance. And the lord that is owner of this castle I would he received it as is right.'

'Fair sir,' said they, 'the name of this castle is Tintagel, and a duke ought it sometime that had wedded fair Igraine and after wedded her Uther Pendragon, and gat on her Arthur.'

'Well,' said Sir Launcelot, 'I understand to whom this castle belongeth;' and so he departed from them, and betaught them unto God.

And then he mounted upon his horse, and rode into many strange and wild countries, and through many waters and valleys, and evil was he lodged. And at the last by fortune him happened, against a night, to come to a fair courtelage, and therein he found an old gentlewoman that lodged him with good will, and there he had good cheer for him and his horse. And when time was, his host brought him into a fair garret, over the gate, to his bed. There Sir Launcelot unarmed him, and set his harness by him, and went to bed, and anon he fell asleep.

So, soon after, there came one on horseback, and knocked at the gate in great haste, and when Sir Launcelot heard this, he arose up and looked out at the window, and saw by the moonlight three knights came riding after that one man, and all three lashed on him at once with swords, and that one knight turned on them knightly again, and defended him.

'Truly,' said Sir Launcelot, 'yonder one knight shall I help, for it were shame for me to see three knights on one. And if he be slain I am partner of his death,' and therewith he took his harness, and went out at a window by a sheet down to the four knights, and then Sir Launcelot said on high, 'Turn you knights unto me, and leave your fighting with that knight.'

And then they all three left Sir Kay, and turned unto Sir Launcelot, and there began great battle, for they alit all three, and struck many great strokes at Sir Launcelot, and assailed him on every side. Then Sir Kay dressed him for to have holpen Sir Launcelot.

'Nay, sir,' said he, 'I will none of your help; therefore as ye will have my help, let me alone with them.'

Sir Kay, for the pleasure of the knight, suffered him for to do his will, and so stood aside. And then anon within six strokes, Sir Launcelot had stricken them to the earth. And then they all three cried, 'Sir knight, we yield us unto you as man of might, makeless.'

'As to that,' said Sir Launcelot, 'I will not take your yielding unto me. But so that ye will yield you unto Sir Kay the Seneschal, on that covenant I will save your lives, and else not.'

'Fair knight,' said they, 'that were we loth to do; for as for Sir Kay, we chased him hither, and had overcome him had not ye been, therefore to yield us unto him it were no reason.'

'Well, as to that,' said Launcelot, 'advise you well, for ye may choose whether ye will die or live, for and ye be yielden it shall be unto Sir Kay.'

'Fair knight,' then they said, 'in saving of our lives we will do as thou commandest us.'

'Then shall ye,' said Sir Launcelot, 'on Whitsunday next coming, go unto the court of King Arthur and there shall ye yield you unto Queen Guenever, and put you all three in her grace and mercy, and say that Sir Kay sent you thither to be her prisoners.'

'Sir,' they said, 'it shall be done by the faith of our bodies, and we be living,' and there they swore every knight upon his sword.

And so Sir Launcelot suffered them so to depart. And then Sir Launcelot knocked at the gate with the pommel of his sword, and with that came his host, and in they entered Sir Kay and he.

'Sir,' said his host, 'I weened ye had been in your bed.'

'So I was,' said Sir Launcelot, 'but I arose and leapt out at my window for to help an old fellow of mine.'

And so when they came nigh the light, Sir Kay knew well that it was Sir Launcelot, and therewith he kneeled down

makeless: matchless.

and thanked him of all his kindness that he had holpen him twice from the death.

'Sir,' he said, 'I have nothing done but that me ought for to do, and ye are welcome, and here shall ye repose you and take your rest.'

So when Sir Kay was unarmed, he asked after meat; so there was meat fetched him, and he ate strongly. And when he had supped they went to their beds and were lodged together in one bed.

On the morn Sir Launcelot arose early, and left Sir Kay sleeping, and Sir Launcelot took Sir Kay's armour and his shield, and armed him, and so he went to the stable, and took his horse, and took his leave of his host, and so he departed. Then soon after arose Sir Kay and missed Sir Launcelot. And then he espied that he had his armour and his horse.

'Now by my faith I know well that he will grieve some of the court of King Arthur; for on him knights will be bold, and deem that it is I, and that will beguile them. And because of his armour and shield I am sure I shall ride in peace.'

And then soon after departed Sir Kay and thanked his host.

CHAPTER 12: *How Sir Launcelot rode disguised in Sir Kay's harness, and how he smote down a knight*

Now turn we unto Sir Launcelot that had ridden long in a great forest, and at the last he came into a low country, full of fair rivers and meadows. And afore him he saw a long bridge, and three pavilions stood thereon, of silk and sendal of divers hue. And without the pavilion hung three white shields on truncheons of spears, and great long spears stood upright by the pavilions, and at every pavilion's door stood three fresh squires. And so Sir Launcelot passed by them and spake no word.

When he was passed the three knights saiden him that it was the proud Kay: 'He weeneth no knight so good as he, and the contrary is ofttime proved.'

'By my faith,' said one of the knights, his name was Sir Gauter, 'I will ride after him and assay him for all his pride, and ye may behold how that I speed.'

So this knight, Sir Gauter, armed him, and hung his shield upon his shoulder, and mounted upon a great horse, and gat his spear in his hand, and walloped after Sir Launcelot. And when he came nigh him, he cried, 'Abide, thou proud knight Sir Kay, for thou shalt not pass quit.'

So Sir Launcelot turned him, and either fewtered their spears, and came together with all their mights, and Sir Gauter's spear brake, but Sir Launcelot smote him down horse and man.

And when Sir Gauter was at the earth his brethren said each one to other, 'Yonder knight is not Sir Kay, for he is bigger than he.'

'I dare lay my head,' said Sir Gilmere, 'yonder knight hath slain Sir Kay and hath taken his horse and his harness.'

'Whether it be so or no,' said Sir Arnold, the third brother, 'let us now go mount upon our horses and rescue our brother Sir Gauter, upon pain of death. We all shall have work enough to match that knight, for ever meseemeth by his person it is Sir Launcelot, or Sir Tristram, or Sir Pelleas, the good knight.'

Then anon they took their horses and overtook Sir Launcelot, and Sir Gilmere put forth his spear, and ran to Sir Launcelot, and Sir Launcelot smote him down that he lay in a swoon.

'Sir knight,' said Sir Arnold, 'thou art a strong man, and as I suppose thou hast slain my two brethren, for the which riseth my heart sore against thee. And if I might with my worship I would not have ado with you, but needs I must take part as they do, and therefore, knight,' he said, 'keep thyself.'

And so they hurtled together with all their mights, and all to-shivered both their spears. And then they drew their swords and lashed together eagerly.

Anon therewith arose Sir Gauter, and came unto his brother Sir Gilmere, and bad him, 'Arise, and help we our brother Sir Arnold, that yonder marvellously matched yonder good knight.'

Therewithal, they leapt on their horses and hurtled unto Sir Launcelot. And when he saw them come he smote a sore stroke unto Sir Arnold, that he fell off his horse to the ground, and then he struck to the other two brethren, and at two strokes he strake them down to the earth.

With that Sir Arnold began to start up with his head all bloody, and came straight unto Sir Launcelot.

'Now let be,' said Sir Launcelot, 'I was not far from thee when thou were made knight, Sir Arnold, and also I know thou art a good knight, and loth I were to slay thee.'

'Gramercy,' said Sir Arnold, 'as for your goodness; and I dare say as for me and my brethren, we will not be loth to yield us unto you, with that we knew your name, for well we know ye are not Sir Kay.'

'As for that be it as it be may, for ye shall yield you unto Dame Guenever, and look that ye be with her on Whitsunday, and yield you unto her as prisoners, and say that Sir Kay sent you unto her.'

Then they swore it should be done, and so passed forth Sir Launcelot, and each one of the brethren halp other as well as they might.

CHAPTER 13: *How Sir Launcelot jousted against four knights of the Round Table and overthrew them*

So Sir Launcelot rode into a deep forest, and thereby in a slade, he saw four knights hoving under an oak, and they were of Arthur's court: one was Sir Sagramore le Desirous, and Ector de Maris, and Sir Gawain, and Sir Uwain. Anon as these four knights had espied Sir Launcelot, they weened by his arms it had been Sir Kay.

'Now by my faith,' said Sir Sagramore, 'I will prove Sir

Kay's might,' and gat his spear in his hand, and came toward Sir Launcelot.

Therewith Sir Launcelot was ware and knew him well, and fewtered his spear against him, and smote Sir Sagramore so sore that horse and man fell both to the earth.

'Lo, my fellows,' said he, 'yonder ye may see what a buffet he hath; that knight is much bigger than ever was Sir Kay. Now shall ye see what I may do to him.'

So Sir Ector gat his spear in his hand and walloped toward Sir Launcelot, and Sir Launcelot smote him through the shield and shoulder, that man and horse went to the earth, and ever his spear held.

'By my faith,' said Sir Uwain, 'yonder is a strong knight, and I am sure he hath slain Sir Kay; and I see by his great strength it will be hard to match him.'

And therewithal, Sir Uwain gat his spear in his hand and rode toward Sir Launcelot, and Sir Launcelot knew him well, and so he met him on the plain, and gave him such a buffet that he was astonied, that long he wist not where he was.

'Now see I well,' said Sir Gawain, 'I must encounter with that knight.'

Then he dressed his[1] shield and gat a good spear in his hand, and Sir Launcelot knew him well; and then they let run their horses with all their mights, and either knight smote other in midst of the shield. But Sir Gawain's spear to-brast, and Sir Launcelot charged so sore upon him that his horse reversed up-so-down.

And much sorrow had Sir Gawain to avoid his horse, and so Sir Launcelot passed on a pace and smiled, and said, 'God give him joy that this spear made, for there came never a better in my hand.'

Then the four knights went each one to other and comforted each other.

'What say ye by this guest?' said Sir Gawain, 'that one spear hath felled us all four.'

'We commend him unto the devil,' they said all, 'for he is a man of great might.'

'Ye may well say it,' said Sir Gawain, 'that he is a man of might, for I dare lay my head it is Sir Launcelot, I know it by his riding. Let him go,' said Sir Gawain, 'for when we come to the court then shall we wit.'

And then had they much sorrow to get their horses again.

CHAPTER 14: *How Sir Launcelot followed a brachet into a castle, where he found a dead knight, and how he after was required of a damosel to heal her brother*

Now leave we there and speak of Sir Launcelot that rode a great while in a deep forest, where he saw a black brachet, seeking in manner as it had been in the feute of an hurt deer. And therewith he rode after the brachet, and he saw lie on the ground a large feute of blood. And then Sir Launcelot rode after. And ever the brachet looked behind her, and so she went through a great marsh, and ever Sir Launcelot followed.

And then was he ware of an old manor, and thither ran the brachet, and so over the bridge. So Sir Launcelot rode over that bridge that was old and feeble; and when he came in midst of a great hall, there he saw lie a dead knight that was a seemly man, and that brachet licked his wounds.

And therewithal came out a lady weeping and wringing her hands; and then she said, 'O knight, too much sorrow hast thou brought me.'

'Why say ye so?' said Sir Launcelot, 'I did never this knight no harm, for hither by feute of blood this brachet brought me; and therefore, fair lady, be not displeased with me, for I am full sore aggrieved of your grievance.'

'Truly, sir,' she said, 'I trow it be not ye that hath slain my husband, for he that did that deed is sore wounded, and he is never likely to recover, that shall I ensure him.'

'What was your husband's name?' said Sir Launcelot.

feute: track.

'Sir,' said she, 'his name was called Sir Gilbert the Bastard, one of the best knights of the world, and he that hath slain him I know not his name.'

'Now God send you better comfort,' said Sir Launcelot.

And so he departed and went into the forest again, and there he met with a damosel, the which knew him well, and she said aloud, 'Well be ye found, my lord; and now I require thee, on thy knighthood, help my brother that is sore wounded, and never stinteth bleeding; for this day he fought with Sir Gilbert the Bastard and slew him in plain battle, and there was my brother sore wounded. And there is a lady, a sorceress, that dwelleth in a castle here beside, and this day she told me my brother's wounds should never be whole till I could find a knight would go into the Chapel Perilous, and there he should find a sword and a bloody cloth that the wounded knight was lapped in, and a piece of that cloth and sword should heal my brother's wounds, so that his wounds were searched with the sword and the cloth.'

'This is a marvellous thing,' said Sir Launcelot, 'but what is your brother's name?'

'Sir,' she said, 'his name was Sir Meliot de Logris.'

'That me repenteth,' said Sir Launcelot, 'for he is a fellow of the Table Round, and to his help I will do my power.'

'Then, sir,' said she, 'follow even this highway, and it will bring you unto the Chapel Perilous; and here I shall abide till God send you here again, and, but you speed, I know no knight living that may achieve that adventure.'

CHAPTER 15: *How Sir Launcelot came into the Chapel Perilous and gat there of a dead corpse a piece of the cloth and a sword*

Right so Sir Launcelot departed, and when he came unto the Chapel Perilous he alit down, and tied his horse unto a little gate. And as soon as he was within the churchyard he

plain: open.

saw on the front of the chapel many fair rich shields turned up-so-down, and many of the shields Sir Launcelot had seen knights bear beforehand. With that he saw by him there stand a thirty great knights, more by a yard than any man that ever he had seen, and all those grinned and gnashed at Sir Launcelot.

And when he saw their countenance he dread him sore, and so put his shield afore him, and took his sword ready in his hand ready unto battle, and they were all armed in black harness ready with their shields and their swords drawn. And when Sir Launcelot would have gone throughout them, they scattered on every side of him, and gave him the way, and therewith he waxed all bold, and entered into the chapel, and then he saw no light but a dim lamp burning, and then was he ware of a corpse hilled with a cloth of silk.

Then Sir Launcelot stooped down, and cut a piece away of that cloth, and then it fared under him as the earth had quaked a little; therewithal he feared. And then he saw a fair sword lie by the dead knight, and that he gat in his hand and hied him out of the chapel. Anon as ever he was in the chapel yard all the knights spake to him with a grimly voice, and said, 'Knight Sir Launcelot, lay that sword from thee or else thou shalt die.'

'Whether that I live or die,' said Sir Launcelot, 'with no great word get ye it again, therefore fight for it and ye list.'

Then right so he passed throughout them, and beyond the chapel yard there met him a fair damosel, and said, 'Sir Launcelot, leave that sword behind thee, or thou will die for it.'

'I leave it not,' said Sir Launcelot, 'for no treaties.'

'No,' said she, 'and thou didst leave that sword, Queen Guenever should thou never see.'

'Then were I a fool and I would leave this sword,' said Launcelot.

'Now, gentle knight,' said the damosel, 'I require thee to kiss me but once.'

hilled: covered. *grinned*: grimaced.

'Nay,' said Sir Launcelot, 'that God me forbid.'

'Well, sir,' said she, 'and thou hadst kissed me thy life days had been done, but now, alas,' she said, 'I have lost all my labour, for I ordained this chapel for thy sake, and for Sir Gawain. And once I had Sir Gawain within me, and at that time he fought with that knight that lieth there dead in yonder chapel, Sir Gilbert the Bastard; and at that time he smote the left hand off of Sir Gilbert the Bastard. And, Sir Launcelot, now I tell thee, I have loved thee this seven year, but there may no woman have thy love but Queen Guenever. But sithen I may not rejoice thee to have thy body alive, I had kept no more joy in this world but to have thy body dead. Then would I have balmed it and served it, and so have kept it my life days, and daily I should have clipped thee, and kissed thee, in despite of Queen Guenever.'

'Ye say well,' said Sir Launcelot. 'Jesu preserve me from your subtle crafts.'

And therewithal he took his horse and so departed from her. And as the book saith, when Sir Launcelot was departed she took such sorrow that she died within a fourteen night, and her name was Hellawes the sorceress, Lady of the Castle Nigramous.

Anon Sir Launcelot met with the damosel, Sir Meliot's sister. And when she saw him she clapped her hands, and wept for joy. And then they rode unto a castle thereby where lay Sir Meliot. And anon as Sir Launcelot saw him he knew him, but he was passing pale as the earth for bleeding.

When Sir Meliot saw Sir Launcelot he kneeled upon his knees and cried on high, 'O lord Sir Launcelot, help me!'

Anon Sir Launcelot leapt unto him and touched his wounds with Sir Gilbert's sword. And then he wiped his wounds with a part of the bloody cloth that Sir Gilbert was wrapped in, and anon an wholer man in his life was he never.

And then there was great joy between them, and they made Sir Launcelot all the cheer that they might, and so on the morn Sir Launcelot took his leave, and bad Sir Meliot hie him 'to the court of my lord Arthur, for it draweth nigh to the feast of Pentecost, and there by the grace of God ye shall find me.' And therewith they departed.

CHAPTER 16: *How Sir Launcelot at the request of a lady recovered a falcon, by which he was deceived*

And so Sir Launcelot rode through many strange countries, over marsh and valleys, till by fortune he came to a fair castle, and as he passed beyond the castle him thought he heard two bells ring.

And then was he ware of a falcon came flying over his head towards an high elm, and long lunes about her feet, and she flew unto the elm to take her perch. The lunes overcast about a bough, and when she would have taken her flight she hung by the legs fast; and Sir Launcelot saw how she hung, and beheld the fair falcon perigot, and he was sorry for her.

The meanwhile came a lady out of the castle and cried on high, 'O Launcelot, Launcelot, as thou art flower of all knights, help me to get my hawk, for and my hawk be lost my lord will destroy me; for I kept the hawk and she slipped from me, and if my lord my husband wit it he is so hasty that he will slay me.'

'What is your lord's name?' said Sir Launcelot.

'Sir,' she said, 'his name is Sir Phelot, a knight that longeth unto the King of Northgales.'

'Well, fair lady, since that ye know my name, and require me of knighthood to help you, I will do what I may to get your hawk, and yet God knoweth I am an ill climber, and the tree is passing high, and few boughs to help me withal.'

And therewith Sir Launcelot alit, and tied his horse to the same tree, and prayed the lady to unarm him. And so when

lunes: leashes.

he was unarmed, he put off all his clothes unto his shirt and breech, and with might and force he clomb up to the falcon, and tied the lunes to a great rotten bush, and threw the hawk down and it withal.

Anon the lady gat the hawk in her hand; and therewithal came out Sir Phelot out of the groves suddenly, that was her husband, all armed and with his naked sword in his hand, and said: 'O knight Launcelot, now have I found thee as I would,' and stood at the bole of the tree to slay him.

'Ah, lady,' said Sir Launcelot, 'why have ye betrayed me?'

'She hath done,' said Sir Phelot, 'but as I commanded her, and therefore there nis none other boot but thine hour is come that thou must die.'

'That were shame unto thee,' said Sir Launcelot, 'thou an armed knight to slay a naked man by treason.'

'Thou gettest none other grace,' said Sir Phelot, 'and therefore help thyself and thou canst.'

'Truly,' said Sir Launcelot, 'that shall be thy shame, but since thou wilt do none other, take mine harness with thee, and hang my sword upon a bough that I may get it, and then do thy best to slay me and thou canst.'

'Nay, nay,' said Sir Phelot, 'for I know thee better than thou weenest, therefore thou gettest no weapon and I may keep you therefrom.'

'Alas,' said Sir Launcelot, 'that ever a knight should die weaponless.'

And therewith he waited above him and under him, and over his head he saw a rownsepyk,[1] a big bough leafless, and therewith he brake it off by the body. And then he came lower and awaited how his own horse stood, and suddenly he leapt on the further side of the horse, froward the knight.

And then Sir Phelot lashed at him eagerly, weening to have slain him. But Sir Launcelot put away the stroke with the rownsepyk, and therewith he smote him on the one side of the head, that he fell down in a swoon to the ground. So

boot: remedy.

then Sir Launcelot took his sword out of his hand, and struck his neck from the body.

Then cried the lady, 'Alas! why hast thou slain my husband?'

'I am not causer,' said Sir Launcelot, 'for with falsehood ye would have slain me with treason, and now it is fallen on you both.'

And then she swooned as though she would die. And therewithal Sir Launcelot gat all his armour as well as he might, and put it upon him for dread of more resort, for he dread that the knight's castle was so nigh. And so as soon as he might he took his horse and departed, and thanked God that he had escaped that adventure.

CHAPTER 17: *How Sir Launcelot overtook a knight which chased his wife to have slain her, and how he said to him*

So Sir Launcelot rode many wild ways, throughout marsh and many wild ways. And as he rode in a valley he saw a knight chasing a lady, with a naked sword, to have slain her. And by fortune as this knight should have slain this lady, she cried on Sir Launcelot and prayed him to rescue her.

When Sir Launcelot saw that mischief, he took his horse and rode between them, saying, 'Knight, fie for shame, why wilt thou slay this lady? Thou dost shame unto thee and all knights.'

'What hast thou to do betwixt me and my wife?' said the knight. 'I will slay her maugre thy head.'

'That shall ye not,' said Sir Launcelot, 'for rather we two will have ado together.'

'Sir Launcelot,' said the knight, 'thou dost not thy part, for this lady hath betrayed me.'

'It is not so,' said the lady, 'truly he saith wrong on me. And for because I love and cherish my cousin germain, he is jealous betwixt him and me; and as I shall answer to God there was never sin betwixt us. But, sir,' said the lady, 'as thou art called the worshipfullest knight of the world, I require thee of true knighthood, keep me and save me. For whatsomever ye say he will slay me, for he is without mercy.'

'Have ye no doubt,' said Launcelot, 'it shall not lie in his power.'

'Sir,' said the knight, 'in your sight I will be ruled as ye will have me.'

And so Sir Launcelot rode on the one side and she on the other. He had not ridden but a while, but the knight bad Sir Launcelot turn him and look behind him, and said, 'Sir, yonder come men of arms after us riding.'

And so Sir Launcelot turned him and thought no treason, and therewith was the knight and the lady on one side, and suddenly he swapped off his lady's head.

And when Sir Launcelot had espied him what he had done, he said, and called him, 'Traitor, thou has shamed me for ever.' And suddenly Sir Launcelot alit off his horse, and pulled out his sword to slay him, and therewithal he fell flat to the earth, and gripped Sir Launcelot by the thighs, and cried mercy.

'Fie on thee,' said Sir Launcelot, 'thou shameful knight, thou mayest have no mercy, and therefore arise and fight with me.'

'Nay,' said the knight, 'I will never arise till ye grant me mercy.'

'Now will I proffer thee fair,' said Launcelot, 'I will unarm me unto my shirt, and I will have nothing upon me but my shirt, and my sword and my hand. And if thou canst slay me, quit be thou for ever.'

'Nay, sir,' said Pedivere, 'that will I never.'

'Well,' said Sir Launcelot, 'take this lady and the head, and bear it upon thee, and here shalt thou swear upon my sword,

swapped: struck.

to bear it always upon thy back, and never to rest till thou come to Queen Guenever.'

'Sir,' said he, 'that will I do, by the faith of my body.'

'Now,' said Launcelot, 'tell me what is your name?'

'Sir, my name is Pedivere.'

'In a shameful hour were thou born,' said Launcelot.

So Pedivere departed with the dead lady and the head, and found the queen with King Arthur at Winchester, and there he told all the truth.

'Sir knight,' said the queen, 'this is an horrible deed and a shameful, and a great rebuke unto Sir Launcelot; but notwithstanding his worship is not known in many divers countries. But this shall I give you in penance, make ye as good shift as ye can, ye shall bear this lady with you on horseback unto the Pope of Rome, and of him receive your penance for your foul deeds; and ye shall never rest one night thereas ye do another, and ye go to any bed the dead body shall lie with you.'

This oath there he made, and so departed. And as it telleth in the French book, when he came to Rome, the Pope bad him go again unto Queen Guenever, and in Rome was his lady buried by the Pope's commandment. And after this Sir Pedivere fell to great goodness, and was an holy man and an hermit.

CHAPTER 18: *How Sir Launcelot came to King Arthur's court, and how there were recounted all his noble feats and acts*

Now turn we unto Sir Launcelot du Lake, that came home two days afore the feast of Pentecost; and the king and all the court were passing fain of his coming. And when Sir Gawain, Sir Uwain, Sir Sagramore, Sir Ector de Maris, saw Sir Launcelot in Kay's armour, then they wist well it was he that smote them down all with one spear. Then there was laughing and smiling among them. And ever now and now came all the knights home that Sir Turquin had prisoners, and they all honoured and worshipped Sir Launcelot.

When Sir Gaheris heard them speak, he said, 'I saw all the battle from the beginning to the ending,' and there he told King Arthur all how it was, and how Sir Turquin was the strongest knight that ever he saw except Sir Launcelot; there were many knights bare him record, nigh three score.

Then Sir Kay told the king how Sir Launcelot had rescued him when he should have been slain, and how 'he made the knights yield them to me, and not to him.' And there they were all three, and bare record. 'And by Jesu,' said Sir Kay, 'because Sir Launcelot took my harness and left me his I rode in good peace, and no man would have ado with me.'

Anon therewithal there came the three knights that fought with Sir Launcelot at the long bridge. And there they yielded them unto Sir Kay, and Sir Kay forsook them and said he fought never with them. 'But I shall ease your heart,' said Sir Kay, 'yonder is Sir Launcelot that overcame you.' When they wist that they were glad.

And then Sir Meliot de Logris came home, and told the king how Sir Launcelot had saved him from the death.

And all his deeds were known, how four queens, sorceresses, had him in prison, and how he was delivered by King Bagdemagus' daughter. Also there were told all the great deeds of arms that Sir Launcelot did betwixt the two kings, that is for to say the King of Northgales and King Bagdemagus. All the truth Sir Gahalantine did tell, and Sir Mador de la Porte and Sir Mordred, for they were at that same tournament.

Then came in the lady that knew Sir Launcelot when that he wounded Sir Belleus at the pavilion. And there, at request of Sir Launcelot, Sir Belleus was made knight of the Round Table.

And so at that time Sir Launcelot had the greatest name

of any knight of the world, and most he was honoured of high and low.

Explicit the noble tale of Sir Launcelot du Lake, which is the vi. book. Here followeth the tale of Sir Gareth of Orkney that was called Beaumains by Sir Kay, and is the seventh book

Book VII

CHAPTER 1: *How Beaumains came to King Arthur's court and demanded three petitions of King Arthur*

When Arthur held his Round Table most plenour, it fortuned that he commanded that the high feast of Pentecost should be holden at a city and a castle, the which in those days was called Kinkenadon, upon the sands that marched nigh Wales. So ever the king had a custom that at the feast of Pentecost in especial, afore other feasts in the year, he would not go that day to meat until he had heard or seen of a great marvel. And for that custom all manner of strange adventures came before Arthur as at that feast before all other feasts.

And so Sir Gawain, a little tofore noon of the day of Pentecost, espied at a window three men upon horseback, and a dwarf on foot, and so the three men alit, and the dwarf kept their horses, and one of the three men was higher than the other twain by a foot and an half.

Then Sir Gawain went unto the king and said, 'Sir, go to your meat, for here at the hand comen strange adventures.'

So Arthur went unto his meat with many other kings. And there were all the knights of the Round Table only those that were prisoners or slain at a recounter. Then at the high feast evermore they should be fulfilled the whole number of an hundred and fifty, for then was the Round Table fully complished.

Right so came into the hall two men well beseen and richly, and upon their shoulders there leaned the goodliest young man and the fairest that ever they all saw, and he was large and long and broad in the shoulders, and well visaged,

plenour: with the full number. *complished*: filled.

and the fairest and the largest handed that ever man saw, but he fared as though he might not go nor bear himself but if he leaned upon their shoulders. Anon as Arthur saw him there was made peace and room, and right so they yede with him unto the high dais, without saying of any words.

Then this much young man pulled him aback, and easily stretched up straight, saying, 'King Arthur, God you bless and all your fair fellowship, and in especial the fellowship of the Table Round. And for this cause I am come hither, to pray you and require you to give me three gifts, and they shall not be unreasonably asked, but that ye may worshipfully and honourably grant them me, and to you no great hurt nor loss. And the first done and gift I will ask now, and the other two gifts I will ask this day twelvemonth, wheresomever ye hold your high feast.'

'Now ask,' said Arthur, 'and ye shall have your asking.'

'Now, sir, this is my petition for this feast, that ye will give me meat and drink sufficiently for this twelvemonth, and at that day I will ask mine other two gifts.'

'My fair son,' said Arthur, 'ask better, I counsel thee, for this is but a simple asking; for my heart giveth me to thee greatly, that thou art come of men of worship, and greatly my conceit faileth me but thou shalt prove a man of right great worship.'

'Sir,' he said, 'thereof be as it be may, I have asked that I will ask.'

'Well,' said the king, 'ye shall have meat and drink enough; I never defended that none, neither my friend ne my foe. But what is thy name I would wit?'

'I cannot tell you,' said he.

'That is marvel,' said the king, 'that thou knowest not thy name, and thou art the goodliest young man one that ever I saw.'

Then the king betook him to Sir Kay the steward, and charged him that he should give him of all manner of meats

defended: refused.

and drinks of the best, and also that he had all manner of finding as though he were a lord's son.

'That shall little need,' said Sir Kay, 'to do such cost upon him; for I dare undertake he is a villain born, and never will make man, for and he had come of gentlemen he would have asked of you horse and armour, but such as he is, so he asketh. And sithen he hath no name, I shall give him a name that shall be Beaumains, that is Fair-hands. And into the kitchen I shall bring him, and there he shall have fat brose every day, that he shall be as fat by the twelvemonths' end as a pork hog.'

Right so the two men departed and beleft him to Sir Kay, that scorned him and mocked him.

CHAPTER 2: *How Sir Launcelot and Sir Gawain were wroth because Sir Kay mocked Beaumains, and of a damosel which desired a knight to fight for a lady*

Thereat was Sir Gawain wroth, and in especial Sir Launcelot bad Sir Kay leave his mocking, 'for I dare lay my head he shall prove a man of great worship.'

'Let be,' said Sir Kay, 'it may not be by no reason, for as he is, so he hath asked.'

'Beware,' said Sir Launcelot, 'so ye gave the good knight Breunor, Sir Dinadan's brother, a name, and ye called him La Cote Male Taile,[1] and that turned you to anger afterward.'

'As for that,' said Sir Kay, 'this shall never prove none such. For Sir Breunor desired ever worship, and this desireth bread and drink and broth; upon pain of my life he was fostered up in some abbey, and, howsomever it was, they failed meat and drink, and so hither he is come for his sustenance.'

And so Sir Kay bad get him a place, and sit down to meat; so Beaumains went to the hall door, and set him down among boys and lads, and there he ate sadly. And then Sir Launcelot after meat bad him come to his chamber, and there he should

brose: broth.

have meat and drink enough. And so did Sir Gawain; but he refused them all; he would do none other but as Sir Kay commanded him, for no proffer.

But as touching Sir Gawain, he had reason to proffer him lodging, meat, and drink, for that proffer came of his blood, for he was nearer kin to him than he wist. But that as Sir Launcelot did was of his great gentleness and courtesy.

So thus he was put into the kitchen, and lay nightly as the boys of the kitchen did. And so he endured all that twelvemonth, and never displeased man nor child, but always he was meek and mild. But ever when that he saw any jousting of knights, that would he see and he might. And ever Sir Launcelot would give him gold to spend, and clothes, and so did Sir Gawain, and where there were any masteries done, thereat would he be, and there might none cast bar nor stone to him by two yards. Then would Sir Kay say, 'How liketh you my boy of the kitchen?'

So it passed on till the feast of Whitsuntide. And at that time the king held it at Caerleon in the most royallest wise that might be, like as he did yearly. But the king would no meat eat upon the Whitsunday, until he heard some adventures.

Then came there a squire to the king and said, 'Sir, ye may go to your meat, for here cometh a damosel with some strange adventures.'

Then was the king glad and sat him down. Right so there came a damosel into the hall and saluted the king, and prayed him of succour.

'For whom?' said the king, 'What is the adventure?'

'Sir,' she said, 'I have a lady of great worship and renown, and she is besieged with a tyrant, so that she may not out of her castle; and because here are called the noblest knights of the world, I come to you to pray you of succour.'

'What heteth your lady, and where dwelleth she, and who is he, and what is his name that hath besieged her?'

'Sir King,' she said, 'as for my lady's name that shall not

heteth: is called.

ye know for me as at this time, but I let you wit she is lady of great worship and of great lands; and as for the tyrant that besiegeth her and destroyeth her lands, he is called the Red Knight of the Red Launds.'

'I know him not,' said the king.

'Sir,' said Sir Gawain, 'I know him well, for he is one of the perilous knights of the world; men say that he hath seven men's strength, and from him I escaped once full hard with my life.'

'Fair damosel,' said the king, 'there be knights here would do their power for to rescue your lady, but because ye will not tell her name, nor where she dwelleth, therefore none of my knights that here be now shall go with you by my will.'

'Then must I speak further,' said the damosel.

CHAPTER 3: *How Beaumains desired the battle, and how it was granted to him, and how he desired to be made knight of Sir Launcelot*

With these words came before the king Beaumains, while the damosel was there, and thus he said: 'Sir king, God thank you I have been this twelvemonth in your kitchen, and have had my full sustenance, and now I will ask my two gifts that be behind.'

'Ask, upon my peril,' said the king.

'Sir, this shall be my two gifts, first that ye will grant me to have this adventure of the damosel, for it belongeth unto me.'

'Thou shalt have it,' said the king, 'I grant it thee.'

'Then, sir, this is the other gift, that ye shall bid Launcelot du Lake to make me knight, for of him I will be made knight and else of none. And when I am passed I pray you let him ride after me, and make me knight when I require him.'

'All this shall be done,' said the king.

'Fie on thee,' said the damosel, 'shall I have none but one that is your kitchen page?'

Then was she wroth, and took her horse and departed.

And with that there came one to Beaumains and told him his horse and armour was come for him; and there was the dwarf come with all thing that him needed, in the richest manner; thereat all the court had much marvel from whence came all that gear. So when he was armed there was none but few so goodly a man as he was; and right so as he came into the hall and took his leave of King Arthur, and Sir Gawain, and Sir Launcelot, and prayed that he would hie after him, and so departed and rode after the damosel.

CHAPTER 4: *How Beaumains departed, and how he gat of Sir Kay a spear and a shield, and how he jousted and fought with Sir Launcelot*

But there went many after to behold how well he was horsed and trapped in cloth of gold, but he had neither shield nor spear.

Then Sir Kay said all open in the hall, 'I will ride after my boy in the kitchen, to wit whether he will know me for his better.'

Said Sir Launcelot and Sir Gawain, 'Yet abide at home.'

So Sir Kay made him ready and took his horse and his spear, and rode after him. And right as Beaumains overtook the damosel, right so came Sir Kay and said, 'Beaumains, what, sir, know ye not me?'

Then he turned his horse, and knew it was Sir Kay, that had done him all the despite as ye have heard afore.

'Yea,' said Beaumains, 'I know you for an ungentle knight of the court, and therefore beware of me.'

Therewith Sir Kay put his spear in the rest, and ran straight upon him; and Beaumains came as fast upon him with his sword in his hand, and so he put away his spear with his sword, and with a foin thrusted him through the

foin: thrust.

side, that Sir Kay fell down as he had been dead; and he alit down and took Sir Kay's shield and his spear, and start upon his own horse and rode his way.

All that saw Sir Launcelot, and so did the damosel. And then he bad his dwarf start upon Sir Kay's horse, and so he did. By that Sir Launcelot was come, then he proffered Sir Launcelot to joust; and either made them ready, and they came together so fiercely that either bare down other to the earth, and sore were they bruised. Then Sir Launcelot arose and halp him from his horse. And then Beaumains threw his shield from him, and proffered to fight with Sir Launcelot on foot: and so they rashed together like boars, tracing, rasing, and foining to the mountenance of an hour; and Sir Launcelot felt him so big that he marvelled of his strength, for he fought more liker a giant than a knight, and that his fighting was durable and passing perilous. For Sir Launcelot had so much ado with him that he dread himself to be shamed, and said, 'Beaumains, fight not so sore, your quarrel and mine is not so great but we may leave off.'

'Truly that is truth,' said Beaumains, 'but it doth me good to feel your might, and yet, my lord, I showed not the utterance.'

CHAPTER 5: *How Beaumains told to Sir Launcelot his name, and how he was dubbed knight of Sir Launcelot, and after overtook the damosel*

'In God's name,' said Sir Launcelot, 'for I promise you, by the faith of my body, I had as much to do as I might to save myself from you unshamed, and therefore have ye no doubt of none earthly knight.'

'Hope ye so that I may any while stand a proved knight?' said Beaumains.

'Yea,' said Launcelot, 'do as ye have done, and I shall be your warrant.'

mountenance: duration.

'Then, I pray you,' said Beaumains, 'give me the order of knighthood.'

'Then must ye tell me your name,' said Launcelot, 'and of what kin ye be born.'

'Sir, so that ye will not discover me I shall,' said Beaumains.

'Nay,' said Sir Launcelot, 'and that I promise you by the faith of my body until it be openly known.'

'Then, sir,' he said, 'my name is Gareth, and brother unto Sir Gawain of father and mother.'

'Ah, sir,' said Sir Launcelot, 'I am more gladder of you than I was; for ever me thought ye should be of great blood, and that ye came not to the court neither for meat ne for drink.'

And then Sir Launcelot gave him the order of knighthood, and then Sir Gareth prayed him for to depart and let him go.

So Sir Launcelot departed from him and came to Sir Kay, and made him to be borne home upon his shield, and so he was healed hard with the life; and all men scorned Sir Kay, and in especial Sir Gawain and Sir Launcelot said it was not his part to rebuke no young man, for full little knew he 'of what birth he is comen, and for what cause he came to this court!' and so we leave Sir Kay and turn we unto Beaumains.

When he had overtaken the damosel, anón she said, 'What dost thou here? Thou stinkest all of the kitchen, thy clothes be bawdy of the grease and tallow that thou gainest in King Arthur's kitchen; weenest thou,' said she, 'that I allow thee, for yonder knight that thou killest? Nay truly, for thou slewest him unhappily and cowardly; therefore turn again, bawdy kitchen page, I know thee well, for Sir Kay named thee Beaumains. What art thou but a lusk and a turner of broches and a ladle-washer?'

'Damosel,' said Beaumains, 'say to me what ye will, I will not go from you whatsomever ye say, for I have undertake to King Arthur for to achieve your adventure, and so shall I finish it to the end, either I shall die therefore.'

bawdy: dirty. *lusk*: idle lout.

'Fie on thee, kitchen knave, wilt thou finish mine adventure? Thou shalt anon be met withal, that thou wouldest not for all the broth that ever thou suppest once look him in the face.'

'I shall assay,' said Beaumains.

So thus as they rode in the wood, there came a man fleeing all that ever he might.

'Whither wilt thou?' said Beaumains.

'O lord,' he said, 'help me, for here by in a slade are six thieves that have taken my lord and bound him, so I am afeared lest they will slay him.'

'Bring me thither,' said Beaumains.

And so they rode together until they came thereas was the knight bounden; and then he rode unto them, and struck one unto the death, and then another, and at the third stroke he slew a third thief, and then the other three fled. And he rode after them, and he overtook them; and then those three thieves turned again and assailed Beaumains hard, but at the last he slew them, and returned and unbound the knight. And the knight thanked him, and prayed him to ride with him to his castle there a little beside, and he should worshipfully reward him for his good deeds.

'Sir,' said Beaumains, 'I will no reward have. I was this day made knight of noble Sir Launcelot, and therefore I will no reward have, but God reward me. And also I must follow this damosel.'

And when he came nigh her she bad him ride from her, 'For thou smellest all of the kitchen. Weenest thou that I have joy of thee? For all this deed that thou hast done is but mishappen thee; but thou shalt see a sight shall make thee turn again, and that lightly.'

Then the same knight which was rescued of the thieves rode after that damosel, and prayed her to lodge with him all that night. And because it was near night the damosel rode with him to his castle, and there they had great cheer, and at supper the knight sat Sir Beaumains afore the damosel.

'Fie, fie,' said she, 'Sir knight, ye are uncourteous to set a kitchen page afore me; him beseemeth better to stick a swine than to sit afore a damosel of high parage.'

Then the knight was ashamed at her words, and took him up, and set him at a sideboard, and set himself afore him, and so all that night they had good cheer and merry rest.

CHAPTER 6: *How Beaumains fought and slew two knights at a passage*

And on the morn the damosel and he took their leave and thanked the knight, and so departed, and rode on their way until they came to a great forest. And there was a great river and but one passage, and there were ready two knights on the farther side to let them the passage.

'What sayest thou,' said the damosel, 'wilt thou match yonder knights or turn again?'

'Nay,' said Sir Beaumains, 'I will not turn again and they were six more.'

And therewithal he rashed into the water, and in midst of the water either brake their spears upon other to their hands, and then they drew their swords, and smote eagerly at other. And at the last Sir Beaumains smote the other upon the helm that his head stonied, and therewithal he fell down in the water, and there was he drowned. And then he spurred his horse upon the land, where the other knight fell upon him, and brake his spear, and so they drew their swords and fought long together. At the last Sir Beaumains clave his helm and his head down to the shoulders; and so he rode unto the damosel and bad her ride forth on her way.

'Alas,' she said, 'that ever a kitchen page should have that fortune to destroy such two doughty knights. Thou weenest thou hast done doughtily, that is not so; for the first knight his horse stumbled, and there he was drowned in the water, and never it was by thy force, nor by thy might. And the last

parage: lineage.

knight by mishap thou camest behind him and mishaply thou slew him.'

'Damosel,' said Beaumains, 'ye may say what ye will, but with whomsoever I have ado withal, I trust to God to serve him or he depart. And therefore I reck not what ye say, so that I may win your lady.'

'Fie fie, foul kitchen knave, thou shalt see knights that shall abate thy boast.'

'Fair damosel, give me goodly language, and then my care is past, for what knights somever they be, I care not, ne I doubt them not.'

'Also,' said she, 'I say it for thine avail, yet mayest thou turn again with thy worship; for and thou follow me, thou art but slain, for I see all that ever thou dost is but by misadventure, and not by prowess of thy hands.'

'Well, damosel, ye may say what ye will, but wheresomever ye go I will follow you.'

So this Beaumains rode with that lady till evensong time, and ever she chid him, and would not rest. And they came to a black laund; and there was a black hawthorn, and thereon hung a black banner, and on the other side there hung a black shield, and by it stood a black spear great and long, and a great black horse covered with silk, and a black stone fast by.

CHAPTER 7: *How Beaumains fought with the Knight of the Black Launds, and fought with him till he fell down and died*

There sat [a] knight all armed in black harness, and his name was the Knight of the Black Launds. Then the damosel, when she saw that knight, she bad him flee down that valley, for his horse was not saddled.

'Gramercy,' said Beaumains, 'for always ye would have me a coward.'

mishaply: by misfortune. *reck*: care.

With that the Black Knight, when she came nigh him, spake and said, 'Damosel, have ye brought this knight of King Arthur to be your champion?'

'Nay, fair knight,' said she, 'this is but a kitchen knave that was fed in King Arthur's kitchen for alms.'

'Why cometh he,' said the knight, 'in such array? It is shame that he beareth you company.'

'Sir, I cannot be delivered of him,' said she, 'for with me he rideth maugre mine head. God would that ye should put him from me, other to slay him and ye may, for he is an unhappy knave, and unhappily he hath done this day: through mishap I saw him slay two knights at the passage of the water; and other deeds he did before right marvellous and through unhappiness.'

'That marvelleth[1] me,' said the Black Knight, 'that any man that is of worship will have ado with him.'

'They know him not,' said the damosel, 'and for because he rideth with me, they ween that he be some man of worship born.'

'That may be,' said the Black Knight; 'howbeit as ye say that he be no man of worship, he is a full likely person, and full like to be a strong man. But thus much shall I grant you,' said the Black Knight; 'I shall put him down upon one foot, and his horse and his harness he shall leave with me, for it were shame to me to do him any more harm.'

When Sir Beaumains heard him say thus, he said, 'Sir knight, thou art full large of my horse and my harness; I let thee wit it cost thee nought, and whether it liketh thee or not, this laund will I pass maugre thine head. And horse ne harness gettest thou none of mine, but if thou win them with thy hands; and therefore let see what thou canst do.'

'Sayest thou that?' said the Black Knight, 'Now yield thy lady from thee, for it beseemeth never a kitchen page to ride with such a lady.'

'Thou liest,' said Beaumains, 'I am a gentleman born, and of more high lineage than thou, and that will I prove on thy body.'

Then in great wrath they departed with their horses, and came together as it had been the thunder, and the Black Knight's spear brake, and Beaumains thrust him through both his sides, and therewith his spear brake, and the truncheon left still in his side. But nevertheless the Black Knight drew his sword, and smote many eager strokes, and of great might, and hurt Beaumains full sore. But at the last the Black Knight, within an hour and an half, he fell down off his horse in swoon, and there he died.

And then Beaumains saw him so well horsed and armed, then he alit down and armed him in his armour, and so took his horse and rode after the damosel.

When she saw him come nigh, she said, 'Away, kitchen knave, out of the wind, for the smell of thy bawdy clothes grieveth me. Alas,' she said, 'that ever such a knave should by mishap slay so good a knight as thou hast done, but all this is thine unhappiness. But here by is one shall pay thee all thy payment, and therefore yet I counsel thee flee.'

'It may happen me,' said Beaumains, 'to be beaten or slain, but I warn you, fair damosel, I will not flee away, nor leave your company, for all that ye can say; for ever ye say that they will kill me or beat me, but howsomever it happeneth I escape, and they lie on the ground. And therefore it were as good for you to hold you still thus all day rebuking me, for away will I not till I see the uttermost of this journey, or else I will be slain, other truly beaten; therefore ride on your way, for follow you I will whatsomever happen.'

CHAPTER 8: *How the brother of the knight that was slain met with Beaumains, and fought with Beaumains till he was yielden*

Thus as they rode together, they saw a knight come driving by them all in green, both his horse and his harness; and when he came nigh the damosel, he asked her, 'Is that my brother the Black Knight that ye have brought with you?'

'Nay, nay,' she said, 'this unhappy kitchen knave hath slain your brother through unhappiness.'

'Alas,' said the Green Knight, 'that is great pity, that so noble a knight as he was should so unhaply be slain, and, namely of a knave's hand, as ye say that he is. Ah! traitor,' said the Green Knight, 'thou shalt die for slaying of my brother; he was a full noble knight, and his name was Sir Percard.'

'I defy thee,' said Beaumains, 'for I let thee wit I slew him knightly and not shamefully.'

Therewithal the Green Knight rode unto an horn that was green, and it hung upon a thorn, and there he blew three deadly motes, and there came two damosels and armed him lightly. And then he took a great horse, and a green shield and a green spear.

And then they ran together with all their mights, and brake their spears unto their hands. And then they drew their swords, and gave many sad strokes, and either of them wounded other full ill. And at the last at an overthwart Beaumains with his horse struck the Green Knight's horse upon the side, that he fell to the earth. And then the Green Knight avoided his horse lightly, and dressed him upon foot. That saw Beaumains, and therewithal he alit, and they rashed together like two mighty kemps a long while, and sore they bled both.

With that came the damosel, and said, 'My lord the Green Knight, why for shame stand ye so long fighting with the kitchen knave? Alas, it is shame that ever ye were made knight, to see such a lad to match such a knight, as the weed overgrew the corn.'

Therewith the Green Knight was ashamed, and therewithal he gave a great stroke of might, and clave his shield through. When Beaumains saw his shield cloven asunder he was a little ashamed of that stroke and of her language; and then he gave him such a buffet upon the helm that he fell on his knees. And so suddenly Beaumains pulled him upon the

motes: notes. *kemps*: warriors.

ground grovelling. And then the Green Knight cried him mercy, and yielded him unto Sir Beaumains, and prayed him to slay him not.

'All is in vain,' said Beaumains, 'for thou shalt die but if this damosel that came with me pray me to save thy life.' And therewithal he unlaced his helm like as he would slay him.

'Fie upon thee, false kitchen page, I will never pray thee to save his life, for I will never be so much in thy danger.'

'Then shall he die,' said Beaumains.

'Not so hardy, thou bawdy knave,' said the damosel, 'that thou slay him.'

'Alas,' said the Green Knight, 'suffer me not to die for a fair word may save me. Fair knight,' said the Green Knight, 'save my life, and I will forgive thee the death of my brother, and for ever to become thy man, and thirty knights that hold of me for ever shall do you service.'

'In the devil's name,' said the damosel, 'that such a bawdy kitchen knave should have thee and thirty knights' service.'

'Sir knight,' said Beaumains, 'all this availeth thee not, but if my damosel speak with me for thy life.' And therewithal he made a semblant to slay him.

'Let be,' said the damosel, 'thou bawdy knave; slay him not, for and thou do thou shalt repent it.'

'Damosel,' said Beaumains, 'your charge is to me a pleasure, and at your commandment his life shall be saved, and else not.' Then he said, 'Sir knight with the green arms, I release thee quit at this damosel's request, for I will not make her wroth, I will fulfil all that she chargeth me.'

And then the Green Knight kneeled down, and did him homage with his sword.

Then said the damosel, 'Me repenteth, Green Knight, of your damage and of your brother's death, the Black Knight, for of your help I had great mister, for I dread me sore to pass this forest.'

'Nay, dread you not,' said the Green Knight, 'for ye shall

in thy danger: under an obligation to you.

lodge with me this night, and to-morn I shall help you through this forest.'

So they took their horses and rode to his manor, which was fast there beside.

CHAPTER 9: *How the damosel ever rebuked Beaumains, and would not suffer him to sit at her table, but called him kitchen boy*

And ever she rebuked Beaumains, and would not suffer him to sit at her table, but as the Green Knight took him and sat him at a side table.

'Marvel methinketh,' said the Green Knight to the damosel, 'why ye rebuke this noble knight as ye do, for I warn you, damosel, he is a full noble knight, and I know no knight is able to match him; therefore ye do great wrong to rebuke him, for he shall do you right good service, for whatsomever he maketh himself, ye shall prove at the end that he is come of a noble blood and of king's lineage.'

'Fie, fie,' said the damosel, 'it is shame for you to say of him such worship.'

'Truly,' said the Green Knight, 'it were shame for me to say of him any disworship, for he hath proved himself a better knight than I am, yet have I met with many knights in my days, and never or this time have I found no knight his match.'

And so that night they yede unto rest, and all that night the Green Knight commanded thirty knights privily to watch Beaumains, for to keep him from all treason.

And so on the morn they all arose, and heard their mass and brake their fast; and then they took their horses and rode on their way, and the Green Knight conveyed them through the forest; and there the Green Knight said, 'My lord Beaumains, I and these thirty knights shall be alway at your summons, both early and late, at your calling and whither that ever ye will send us.'

'It is well said,' said Beaumains; 'when that I call upon you, ye must yield you unto King Arthur, and all your knights.'

'If that ye so command us, we shall be ready at all times,' said the Green Knight.

'Fie, fie upon thee, in the devil's name,' said the damosel, 'that any good knights should be obedient unto a kitchen knave.'

So then departed the Green Knight and the damosel. And then she said unto Beaumains,

'Why followest thou me, thou kitchen boy? Cast away thy shield and thy spear, and flee away; yet I counsel thee betimes or thou shalt say right soon, alas; for were thou as wight as ever was Wade or Launcelot, Tristram,[1] or the good knight Sir Lamorak, thou shalt not pass a pass here that is called the Pass Perilous.'

'Damosel,' said Beaumains, 'who is afeared let him flee, for it were shame to turn again sithen I have ridden so long with you.'

'Well,' said the damosel, 'ye shall soon, whether ye will or not.'

CHAPTER 10: *How the third brother, called the Red Knight, jousted and fought against Beaumains, and how Beaumains overcame him*

So within a while they saw a tower as white as any snow, well matchecold all about, and double dyked. And over the tower gate there hung a fifty shields of divers colours, and under that tower there was a fair meadow. And therein were many knights and squires to behold, scaffolds and pavilions; for there upon the morn should be a great tournament. And the lord of the tower was in his castle and looked out at a window, and saw a damosel, a dwarf, and a knight armed at all points.

wight: stalwart. *matchecold*: machicolated.

'So God help me,' said the lord, 'with that knight will I joust, for I see that he is a knight errant.'

And so he armed him and horsed him hastily. And when he was on horseback with his shield and his spear, it was all red both his horse and his harness, and all that to him longeth. And when that he came nigh him he weened it had been his brother the Black Knight; and then he cried aloud, 'Brother what do ye in these marches?'

'Nay, nay,' said the damosel, 'it is not he; this is but a kitchen knave that was brought up for alms in King Arthur's court.'

'Nevertheless,' said the Red Knight, 'I will speak with him or he depart.'

'Ah,' said the damosel, 'this knave hath killed thy brother, and Sir Kay named him Beaumains, and this horse and this harness was thy brother's, the Black Knight. Also I saw thy brother the Green Knight overcome of his hands. Now may ye be revenged upon him, for I may never be quit of him.'

With this either knights departed in sunder, and they came together with all their might, and either of their horses fell to the earth, and they avoided their horses, and put their shields afore them and drew their swords, and either gave other sad strokes, now here, now there, rasing, tracing, foining, and hurling like two boars, the space of two hours.

And then she cried on high to the Red Knight, 'Alas, thou noble Red Knight, think what worship hath followed thee, let never a kitchen knave endure thee so long as he doth.'

Then the Red Knight waxed wroth and doubled his strokes, and hurt Beaumains wonderly sore, that the blood ran down to the ground, that it was wonder to see that strong battle. Yet at the last Sir Beaumains struck him to the earth, and as he would have slain the Red Knight, he cried mercy, saying, 'Noble knight, slay me not, and I shall yield me to thee with fifty knights with me that be at my commandment. And I forgive thee all the despite that thou hast done to me, and the death of my brother the Black Knight.'

'All this availeth not,' said Beaumains, 'but if my damosel pray me to save thy life.' And therewith he made semblant to strike off his head.

'Let be, thou Beaumains, slay him not, for he is a noble knight, and not so hardy upon thine head, but thou save him.'

Then Beaumains bad the Red Knight, 'Stand up, and thank the damosel now of thy life.'

Then the Red Knight prayed him to see his castle, and to be there all night. So the damosel then granted him, and there they had merry cheer. But always the damosel spake many foul words unto Beaumains, whereof the Red Knight had great marved; and all that night the Red Knight made three score knights to watch Beaumains, that he should have no shame nor villainy.

And upon the morn they heard mass and dined, and the Red Knight came before Beaumains with his three score knights, and there he proffered him his homage and fealty at all times, he and his knights to do him service.

'I thank you,' said Beaumains, 'but this ye shall grant me: when I call upon you, to come afore my lord King Arthur, and yield you unto him to be his knights.'

'Sir,' said the Red Knight, 'I will be ready and my fellowship at your summons.'

So Sir Beaumains departed and the damosel, and ever she rode chiding him in the foulest manner.

CHAPTER 11: *How Sir Beaumains suffered great rebukes of the damosel, and he suffered it patiently*

'Damosel,' said Beaumains, 'ye are uncourteous so to rebuke me as ye do, for meseemeth I have done you good service, and ever ye threat me I shall be beaten with knights that we meet, but ever for all your boast they lie in the dust or in the mire, and therefore I pray you rebuke me no more; and when ye see me beaten or yielden as recreant, then may ye bid me go from you shamefully; but first I let you wit I will not depart from you, for I were worse than a fool and I would depart from you all the while that I win worship.'

'Well,' said she, 'right soon there shall meet a knight shall pay thee all thy wages, for he is the most man of worship of the world, except King Arthur.'

'I will well,' said Beaumains, 'the more he is of worship, the more shall be my worship to have ado with him.'

Then anon they were ware where was afore them a city rich and fair. And betwixt them and the city a mile and an half there was a fair meadow that seemed new mown, and therein were many pavilions fair to behold.

'Lo,' said the damosel, 'yonder is a lord that oweth yonder city, and his custom is when the weather is fair to lie in this meadow to joust and tourney. And ever there be about him five hundred knights and gentlemen of arms, and there be all manner of games that any gentleman can devise.'

'That goodly lord,' said Beaumains, 'would I fain see.'

'Thou shalt see him time enough,' said the damosel, and so as she rode near she espied the pavilion where he was. 'Lo,' said she, 'seest thou yonder pavilion that is all of the colour of Inde?' And all manner of thing that there is about, men and women, and horses trapped, shields and spears were all of the colour of Inde, 'And his name is Sir Persant of Inde, the most lordliest knight that ever thou lookedst on.'

'It may well be,' said Beaumains, 'but be he never so stout a knight, in this field I shall abide till that I see him under his shield.'

'Ah, fool,' said she, 'thou were better flee betimes.'

'Why?' said Beaumains, 'and he be such a knight as ye make him, he will not set upon me with all his men, or with his five hundred knights. For and there come no more but one at once, I shall him not fail whilst my life lasteth.'

'Fie, fie,' said the damosel, 'that ever such a stinking knave should blow such a boast.'

'Damosel,' he said, 'ye are to blame so to rebuke me, for I

had lever do five battles than so to be rebuked, let him come and then let him do his worst.'

'Sir,' she said, 'I marvel what thou art and of what kin thou art come; boldly thou speakest, and boldly thou hast done, that have I seen; therefore I pray thee save thyself and thou mayest, for thy horse and thou have had great travail, and I dread we dwell over long from the siege, for it is but hence seven mile, and all perilous passages we are passed save all only this passage; and here I dread me sore lest ye shall catch some hurt, therefore I would ye were hence, that ye were not bruised nor hurt with this strong knight. But I let you wit this Sir Persant of Inde is nothing of might nor strength unto the knight that laid the siege about my lady.'

'As for that,' said Sir Beaumains, 'be it as it be may. For sithen I am come so nigh this knight I will prove his might or I depart from him, and else I shall be shamed and I now withdraw me from him. And therefore, damosel, have ye no doubt by the grace of God I shall so deal with this knight that within two hours after noon I shall deliver him. And then shall we come to the siege by daylight.'

'O Jesu, marvel have I,' said the damosel, 'what manner a man ye be, for it may never be otherwise but that ye be comen of a noble blood, for so foul ne shamefully did never woman rule a knight as I have done you, and ever courteously ye have suffered me, and that came never but of a gentle blood.'

'Damosel,' said Beaumains, 'a knight may little do that may not suffer a damosel, for whatsomever ye said unto me I took none heed to your words, for the more ye said the more ye angered me, and my wrath I wreaked upon them that I had ado withal. And therefore all the missaying that ye missaid me furthered me in my battle, and caused me to think to show and prove myself at the end what I was; for peradventure though I had meat in King Arthur's kitchen, yet I might have had meat enough in other places, but all that I did it for to prove and assay my friends, and that shall be known another day; and whether that I be a gentleman born or none, I let you wit, fair damosel, I have done you gentleman's service, and peradventure better service yet will I do or I depart from you.'

'Alas,' she said, 'fair Beaumains, forgive me all that I have missaid or done against thee.'

'With all my heart,' said he, 'I forgive it you, for ye did nothing but as ye should do, for all your evil words pleased me; and damosel,' said Beaumains, 'since it liketh you to say thus fair unto me, wit ye well it gladdeth my heart greatly, and now meseemeth there is no knight living but I am able enough for him.'

CHAPTER 12: *How Beaumains fought with Sir Persant of Inde, and made him to be yielden*

With this Sir Persant of Inde had espied them as they hoved in the field, and knightly he sent to them whether he came in war or in peace.

'Say to thy lord,' said Beaumains, 'I take no force, but whether as him list himself.'

So the messenger went again unto Sir Persant and told him all his answer.

'Well then will I have ado with him to the utterance,' and so he purveyed him and rode against him.

And Beaumains saw him and made him ready, and there they met with all that ever their horses might run, and brast their spears either in three pieces, and their horses rashed so together that both their horses fell dead to the earth; and lightly they avoided their horses and put their shields afore them, and drew their swords, and gave many great strokes that sometime they hurtled together that they fell grovelling on the ground. Thus they fought two hours and more, that their shields and their hauberks were all forhewn, and in many steads they were wounded.

So at the last Sir Beaumains smote him through the cost of

the body, and then he retrayed him here and there, and knightly maintained his battle long time. And at the last, though him loth were, Beaumains smote Sir Persant above upon the helm, that he fell grovelling to the earth; and then he leapt upon him overthwart and unlaced his helm to have slain him. Then Sir Persant yielded him and asked him mercy. With that came the damosel and prayed to save his life.

'I will well, for it were pity this noble knight should die.'

'Gramercy,' said Persant, 'gentle knight and damosel. For certainly now I wot well it was ye that slew my brother the Black Knight at the black thorn; he was a full noble knight, his name was Sir Percard. Also I am sure that ye are he that won mine other brother the Green Knight, his name was Sir Pertolepe. Also ye won my brother the Red Knight, Sir Perimones. And now since ye have won these, this shall I do for to please you: ye shall have homage and fealty of me, and an hundred knights to be always at your commandment, to go and ride where ye will command us.'

And so they went unto Sir Persant's pavilion and drank the wine, and ate spices, and afterward Sir Persant made him to rest upon a bed until supper time, and after supper to bed again. When Beaumains was abed, Sir Persant had a lady, a fair daughter of eighteen year of age, and there he called her unto him, and charged her and commanded her upon his blessing to go unto the knight's bed, 'and lie down by his side, and make him no strange cheer, but good cheer, and take him in thine arms and kiss him, and look that this be done, I charge you, as ye will have my love and my good will.'

So Sir Persant's daughter did as her father bad her, and so she went unto Sir Beaumains' bed, and privily she dispoiled her, and laid her down by him, and then he awoke and saw her, and asked her what she was.

'Sir,' she said, 'I am Sir Persant's daughter, that by the commandment of my father am come hither.'

retrayed him: drew back. *dispoiled her*: undressed.

'Be ye a maid or a wife?' said he.

'Sir,' she said, 'I am a clean maiden.'

'God defend,' said he, 'that I should defile you to do Sir Persant such a shame; therefore, fair damosel, arise out of this bed or else I will.'

'Sir,' she said, 'I came not to you by mine own will, but as I was commanded.'

'Alas,' said Sir Beaumains, 'I were a shameful knight and I would do your father any disworship;' and so he kissed her, and so she departed and came unto Sir Persant her father, and told him all how she had sped.

'Truly,' said Sir Persant, 'whatsomever he be, he is comen of a noble blood.'

And so we leave them there till on the morn.

CHAPTER 13: *Of the goodly communication between Sir Persant and Beaumains, and how he told him that his name was Sir Gareth*

And so on the morn the damosel and Sir Beaumains heard mass and brake their fast, and so took their leave.

'Fair damosel,' said Persant, 'whitherward are ye way-leading this knight?'

'Sir,' she said, 'this knight is going to the siege that besiegeth my sister in the Castle Dangerous.'

'Ah, ah,' said Persant, 'that is the Knight of the Red Launds, the which is the most perilous knight that I know now living, and a man that is withouten mercy, and men sayen that he hath seven men's strength. God save you,' said he to Beaumains, 'from that knight, for he doth great wrong to that lady, and that is great pity, for she is one of the fairest ladies of the world, and meseemeth that your damosel is her sister: is not your name Lynet?' said he.

'Yea, sir,' said she, 'and my lady my sister's name is Dame Lyonesse.'

'Now shall I tell you,' said Sir Persant, 'this Red Knight of the Red Launds hath lain long at the siege, well-nigh this two years, and many times he might have had her and he had would, but he prolongeth the time to this intent, for to have Sir Launcelot du Lake to do battle with him, or Sir Tristram, or Sir Lamorak de Gales, or Sir Gawain, and this is his tarrying so long at the siege.'

'Now my lord Sir Persant of Inde,' said the damosel Lynet, 'I require you that ye will make this gentleman knight or ever he fight with the Red Knight.'

'I will with all my heart,' said Sir Persant, 'and it please him to take the order of knighthood of so simple a man as I am.'

'Sir,' said Beaumains, 'I thank you for your good will, for I am better sped, for certainly the noble knight Sir Launcelot made me knight.'

'Ah,' said Sir Persant, 'of a more renowned knight might ye not be made knight; for of all knights he may be called chief of knighthood; and so all the world saith, that betwixt three knights is departed clearly knighthood, that is Launcelot du Lake, Sir Tristram de Liones, and Sir Lamorak de Gales: these bear now the renown. There be many other knights, as Sir Palomides the Saracen and Sir Safer his brother; also Sir Bleoberis and Sir Blamor de Ganis his brother; also Sir Bors de Ganis and Sir Ector de Maris and Sir Percival de Gales; these and many more be noble knights, but there be none that pass the three above said; therefore God speed you well,' said Sir Persant, 'for and ye may match the Red Knight ye shall be called the fourth of the world.'

'Sir,' said Beaumains, 'I would fain be of good fame and of knighthood. And I let you wit I came of good men, for I dare say my father was a noble man, and so that ye will keep it in close, and this damosel, I will tell you of what kin I am.'

'We will not discover you,' said they both, 'till ye command us, by the faith we owe unto God.'

'Truly then,' said he, 'my name is Gareth of Orkney, and King Lot was my father, and my mother is King Arthur's

and he had would: if he had wished.

sister, her name is Dame Margawse, and Sir Gawain is my brother, and Sir Agravain and Sir Gaheris, and I am the youngest of them all. And yet wot not King Arthur nor Sir Gawain what I am.'

CHAPTER 14: *How the lady that was besieged had word from her sister how she had brought a knight to fight for her, and what battles he had achieved*

So the book saith that the lady that was besieged had word of her sister's coming by the dwarf, and a knight with her, and how he had passed all the perilous passages.

'What manner a man is he?' said the lady.

'He is a noble knight truly, madam,' said the dwarf, 'and but a young man, but he is as likely a man as ever ye saw any.'

'What is he?' said the damosel, 'and of what kin is he comen, and of whom was he made knight?'

'Madam,' said the dwarf, 'he is the King's son of Orkney, but his name I will not tell you as at this time; but wit ye well, of Sir Launcelot was he made knight, for of none other would he be made knight, and Sir Kay named him Beaumains.'

'How escaped he,' said the lady, 'from the brethren of Persant?'

'Madam,' he said, 'as a noble knight should. First, he slew two brethren at a passage of a water.'

'Ah!' said she, 'they were good knights, but they were murderers, the one hight Garard de Breuse, and the other knight hight Sir Arnold de Breuse.'

'Then, madam, he recountered with the Black Knight, and slew him in plain battle, and so he took his horse and his armour and fought with the Green Knight and won him in plain battle, and in like wise he served the Red Knight, and after in the same wise he served the Blue Knight and won him in plain battle.'

'Then,' said the lady, 'he hath overcome Sir Persant of Inde, one of the noblest knights of the world.'

And the dwarf said, 'He hath won all the four brethren and slain the Black Knight, and yet he did more tofore: he overthrew Sir Kay and left him nigh dead upon the ground; also he did a great battle with Sir Launcelot, and there they departed on even hands: and then Sir Launcelot made him knight.'

'Dwarf,' said the lady, 'I am glad of these tidings, therefore go thou in an hermitage of mine hereby, and there shalt thou bear with thee of my wine in two flagons of silver, they are of two gallons, and also two cast of bread with fat venison baked, and dainty fowls; and a cup of gold here I deliver thee, that is rich and precious; and bear all this to mine hermitage, and put it in the hermit's hands. And sithen go thou unto my sister and greet her well, and commend me unto that gentle knight, and pray him to eat and to drink and make him strong, and say ye him I thank him of his courtesy and goodness, that he would take upon him such labour for me that never did him bounty nor courtesy. Also pray him that he be of good heart and courage, for he shall meet with a full noble knight, but he is neither of bounty, courtesy, nor gentleness; for he attendeth unto nothing but to murder, and that is the cause I cannot praise him nor love him.'

So this dwarf departed, and came to Sir Persant, where he found the damosel Lynet and Sir Beaumains, and there he told them all as ye have heard; and then they took their leave, but Sir Persant took an ambling hackney and conveyed them on their ways, and then beleft them to God; and so within a little while they came to that hermitage, and there they drank the wine, and ate the venison and the fowls baken.

And so when they had repasted them well, the dwarf returned again with his vessel unto the castle again; and there met with him the Red Knight of the Red Launds, and asked

on even hands: with honours even.

him from whence that he came, and where he had been.

'Sir,' said the dwarf, 'I have been with my lady's sister of this castle and she hath been at King Arthur's court, and brought a knight with her.'

'Then I account her travail but lost; for though she had brought with her Sir Launcelot, Sir Tristram, Sir Lamorak, or Sir Gawain, I would think myself good enough for them all.'

'It may well be,' said the dwarf, 'but this knight hath passed all the perilous passages, and slain the Black Knight and other two more, and won the Green Knight, the Red Knight, and the Blue Knight.'

'Then is he one of these four that I have afore rehearsed.'

'He is none of those,' said the dwarf, 'but he is a king's son.'

'What is his name?' said the Red Knight of the Red Launds.

'That will I not tell you,' said the dwarf, 'but Sir Kay upon scorn named him Beaumains.'

'I care not,' said the knight, 'what knight so ever he be, for I shall soon deliver him. And if I ever match him he shall have a shameful death as many other have had.'

'That were pity,' said the dwarf, 'and it is marvel that ye make such shameful war upon noble knights.'

CHAPTER 15: *How the damosel and Beaumains came to the siege, and came to a sycamore tree, and there Beaumains blew an horn, and then the Knight of the Red Launds came to fight with him*

Now leave we the knight and the dwarf, and speak we of Beaumains, that all night lay in the hermitage; and upon the morn he and the damosel Lynet heard their mass and brake their fast. And then they took their horses and rode throughout a fair forest; and then they came to a plain, and saw where were many pavilions and tents, and a fair castle, and there was much smoke and great noise. And when they came near the siege Sir Beaumains espied upon great trees, as he rode, how there hung full goodly armed knights by the neck, and their shields about their necks with their swords, and gilt spurs upon their heels, and so there hung nigh a forty knights shamefully with full rich arms. Then Sir Beaumains abated his countenance and said, 'What meaneth this?'

'Fair sir,' said the damosel, 'abate not your cheer for all this sight, for ye must courage yourself, or else ye be all shent, for all these knights came hither to this siege to rescue my sister Dame Lyonesse, and when the Red Knight of the Red Launds had overcome them, he put them to this shameful death without mercy and pity. And in the same wise he will serve you but if ye quit you the better.'

'Now Jesu defend me,' said Beaumains, 'from such a villainous death and shenship of arms. For rather than I should so be faren withal, I would rather be slain manly in plain battle.'

'So were ye better,' said the damosel; 'for trust not, in him is no courtesy, but all goeth to the death or shameful murder, and that is pity, for he is a full likely man, well made of body, and a full noble knight of prowess, and a lord of great lands and possessions.'

'Truly,' said Beaumains, 'he may well be a good knight, but he useth shameful customs, and it is marvel that he endureth so long that none of the noble knights of my lord Arthur's have not dealt with him.'

And then they rode to the dykes, and saw them double dyked with full warly walls; and there were lodged many great lords nigh the walls; and there was great noise of minstrelsy; and the sea beated upon the one side of the walls, where were many ships and mariners' noise with 'hale and how.' And also there was fast by a sycamore tree, and there hung an horn, the greatest that ever they saw, of an elephant's bone; and this Knight of the Red Launds had hanged

shent: disgraced. *shenship*: disgrace. *warly*: warlike.

it up there, that if there came any errant knight, he must blow that horn, and then will he make him ready and come to him to do battle.

'But, sir, I pray you,' said the damosel Lynet, 'blow ye not the horn till it be high noon, for now it is about prime, and now increaseth[1] his might, that as men say he hath seven men's strength.'

'Ah, fie for shame, fair damosel, say ye never so more to me; for and he were as good a knight as ever was, I shall never fail him in his most might, for either I will win worship worshipfully, or die knightly in the field.'

And therewith he spurred his horse straight to the sycamore tree, and blew so the horn eagerly that all the siege and the castle rang thereof. And then there leapt out knights out of their tents and pavilions, and they within the castle looked over the walls and out at windows.

Then the Red Knight of the Red Launds armed him hastily, and two barons set on his spurs upon his heels, and all was blood red, his armour, spear and shield. And an earl buckled his helm upon his head, and then they brought him a red spear and a red steed, and so he rode into a little vale under the castle, that all that were in the castle and at the siege might behold the battle.

CHAPTER 16: *How the two knights met together, and of their talking, and how they began their battle*

'Sir,' said the damosel Lynet unto Sir Beaumains, 'look ye be glad and light, for yonder is your deadly enemy, and at yonder window is my lady, my sister, Dame Lyonesse.'

'Where?' said Beaumains.

'Yonder,' said the damosel, and pointed with her finger.

'That is truth,' said Beaumains. 'She beseemeth afar the fairest lady that ever I looked upon; and truly,' he said, 'I ask no better quarrel than now for to do battle, for truly she shall be my lady, and for her I will fight.'

And ever he looked up to the window with glad countenance. And the Lady Lyonesse made curtsey to him down to the earth, with holding up both their hands.

With that the Red Knight of the Red Launds called to Sir Beaumains, 'Leave, sir knight, thy looking, and behold me, I counsel thee; for I warn thee well she is my lady, and for her I have done many strong battles.'

'If thou have so done,' said Beaumains, 'meseemeth it was but waste labour, for she loveth none of thy fellowship, and thou to love that loveth not thee is but great folly. For and I understand that she were not glad of my coming, I would be advised or I did battle for her. But I understand by the sieging of this castle she may forbear thy fellowship. And therefore wit thou well, thou Red Knight of the Red Launds, I love her, and will rescue her, or else to die.'

'Sayest thou that?' said the Red Knight, 'meseemeth thou ought of reason to be ware by yonder knights that thou sawest hang upon yonder trees.'

'Fie for shame,' said Beaumains, 'that ever thou shouldest say or do so evil, for in that thou shamest thyself and knighthood, and thou mayest be sure there will no lady love thee that knoweth thy wicked customs. And now thou weenest that the sight of these hanged knights should fear me. Nay truly, not so; that shameful sight causeth me to have courage and hardiness against thee, more than I would have had against thee and thou were a well-ruled knight.'

'Make thee ready,' said the Red Knight of the Red Launds, 'and talk no longer with me.'

Then Sir Beaumains bad the damosel go from him; and then they put their spears in their rests, and came together with all their might that they had both, and either smote other in midst of their shields that the paytrels, surcingles, and cruppers brast, and fell to the earth both, and the reins of their bridles in their hands; and so they lay a great while sore stonied, that all that were in the castle and in the siege weened their necks had been broken.

paytrels: breast armour for a horse. *surcingles*: girths for a horse.

And then many a stranger and other said the strange knight was a big man, and a noble jouster, 'for or now we saw never no knight match the Red Knight of the Red Launds'. Thus they said both within the castle and without.

Then lightly they avoided their horses and put their shields afore them, and drew their swords and ran together like two fierce lions, and either gave other such buffets upon their helms that they reeled backward both two strides; and then they recovered both, and hew great pieces off their harness and their shields that a great part fell into the fields.

CHAPTER 17: *How after long fighting Beaumains overcame the knight and would have slain him, but at the request of the lords he saved his life, and made him to yield him to the lady*

And then thus they fought till it was past noon, and never would stint, till at the last they lacked wind both; and then they stood wagging and scattering, panting, blowing and bleeding, that all that beheld them for the most part wept for pity. So when they had rested them a while they yede to battle again, tracing, rasing, foining as two boars. And at some time they took their run as it had been two rams, and hurtled together that sometime they fell grovelling to the earth; and at sometime they were so amazed that either took other's sword instead of his own. Thus they endured till evensong time, that there was none that beheld them might know whether was like to win the battle; and their armour was so forhewen that men might see their naked sides; and in other places they were naked, but ever the naked places they did defend. And the Red Knight was a wily knight of war, and his wily fighting taught Sir Beaumains to be wise; but he abought it full sore or he did espy his fighting.

And thus by assent of them both they granted either other to rest; and so they set them down upon two mole-hills there

wagging: tottering.

besides the fighting place, and either of them unlaced his helm, and took the cold wind; for either of their pages was fast by them, to come when they called to unlace their harness and to set them on again at their commandment.

And then when Sir Beaumains' helm was off, he looked up to the window, and there he saw the fair lady Dame Lyonesse, and she made him such countenance that his heart waxed light and jolly; and therewith he bad the Red Knight of the Red Launds make him ready, 'and let us do the battle to the utterance.'

'I will well,' said the knight.

And then they laced up their helms, and their pages avoided, and they stepped together and fought freshly; but the Red Knight of the Red Launds awaited him, and at an overthwart smote him within the hand, that his sword fell out of his hand; and yet he gave him another buffet upon the helm that he fell grovelling to the earth, and the Red Knight fell over him, for to hold him down.

Then cried the maiden Lynet on high, 'O Sir Beaumains, where is thy courage become? Alas, my lady my sister beholdeth thee, and she sobbeth and weepeth, that maketh mine heart heavy.'

When Sir Beaumains heard her say so, he abrayed up with a great might and gat him upon his feet, and lightly he leapt to his sword and gripped it in his hand, and doubled his pace unto the Red Knight, and there they fought a new battle together. But Sir Beaumains then doubled his strokes, and smote so thick that he smote the sword out of his hand, and then he smote him upon the helm that he fell to the earth, and Sir Beaumains fell upon him, and unlaced his helm to have slain him; and then he yielded him and asked mercy, and said with a loud voice, 'O noble knight, I yield me to thy mercy.'

Then Sir Beaumains bethought him upon the knights that he had made to be hanged shamefully, and then he said, 'I may not with my worship save thy life, for the shameful

abrayed: started.

deaths that thou hast caused many full good knights to die.'

'Sir,' said the Red Knight of the Red Launds, 'hold your hand and ye shall know the causes why I put them to so shameful a death.'

'Say on,' said Sir Beaumains.

'Sir, I loved once a lady, a fair damosel, and she had her brother slain; and she said it was Sir Launcelot du Lake, or else Sir Gawain; and she prayed me as that I loved her heartily, that I would make her a promise by the faith of my knighthood, for to labour daily in arms unto I met with one of them; and all that I might overcome I should put them unto a villainous death; and this is the cause that I have put all these knights to death, and so I ensured her to do all the villainy unto King Arthur's knights, and that I should take vengeance upon all these knights. And, sir, now I will thee tell that every day my strength increaseth till noon, and all this time have I seven men's strength.'

CHAPTER 18: *How the knight yielded him, and how Beaumains made him to go unto King Arthur's court, and to cry Sir Launcelot mercy*

Then came there many earls, and barons, and noble knights, and prayed that knight to save his life, 'and take him to your prisoner.' And all they fell upon their knees, and prayed him of mercy, and that he would save his life; 'and, sir,' they all said, 'it were fairer of him to take homage and fealty, and let him hold his lands of you than for to slay him; by his death ye shall have none advantage, and his misdeeds that be done may not be undone; and therefore he shall make amends to all parties, and we all will become your men and do you homage and fealty.'

'Fair lords,' said Beaumains, 'wit you well I am full loth to slay this knight, nevertheless he hath done passing ill and shamefully; but insomuch all that he did was at a lady's request I blame him the less; and so for your sake I will release him that he shall have his life upon this covenant, that he go within the castle, and yield him there to the lady, and if she will forgive and quit him, I will well; with this he make her amends of all the trespass he hath done against her and her lands. And also, when that is done, that ye go unto the court of King Arthur, and there that ye ask Sir Launcelot mercy, and Sir Gawain, for the evil will ye have had against them.'

'Sir,' said the Red Knight of the Red Launds, 'all this will I do as ye command, and siker assurance and borows ye shall have.'

And so then when the assurance was made, he made his homage and fealty, and all those earls and barons with him.

And then the maiden Lynet came to Sir Beaumains, and unarmed him and searched his wounds, and stinted his blood, and in likewise she did to the Red Knight of the Red Launds. And there they sojourned ten days in their tents; and the Red Knight made his lords and servants to do all the pleasure that they might unto Sir Beaumains.

And so within a while the Red Knight of the Red Launds yede unto the castle, and put him in her grace. And so she received him upon sufficient surety, so all her hurts were well restored of all that she could complain. And then he departed unto the court of King Arthur, and there openly the Red Knight of the Red Launds put him in the mercy of Sir Launcelot and Sir Gawain, and there he told openly how he was overcome and by whom, and also he told all the battles from the beginning unto the ending.

'Jesu mercy,' said King Arthur and Sir Gawain, 'we marvel much of what blood he is come, for he is a noble knight.'

'Have ye no marvel,' said Sir Launcelot, 'for ye shall right well wit that he is comen of a full noble blood; and as for his might and hardiness, there be but few now living that is so mighty as he is, and so noble of prowess.'

'It seemeth by you,' said King Arthur, 'that ye know his name, and from whence he is come, and of what blood he is.'

siker: sure. *borows*: pledges.

'I suppose I do so,' said Launcelot, 'or else I would not have given him the order of knighthood; but he gave me such charge at that time that I should never discover him until he required me, or else it be known openly by some other.'

CHAPTER 19: *How Beaumains came to the lady, and when he came to the castle the gates were closed against him, and of the words that the lady said to him*

Now turn we unto Sir Beaumains that desired of Lynet that he might see her sister, his lady.

'Sir,' she said, 'I would fain ye saw her.'

Then Sir Beaumains all armed him, and took his horse and his spear, and rode straight unto the castle. And when he came to the gate he found there many men armed, and pulled up the drawbridge and drew the port close. Then marvelled he why they would not suffer him to enter.

And then he looked up to the window; and there he saw the fair Lyonesse that said on high, 'Go thy way, Sir Beaumains, for as yet thou shalt not have wholly my love, unto the time that thou be called one of the number of the worthy knights. And therefore go labour in worship this twelvemonth, and then thou shalt hear new tidings.'

'Alas, fair lady,' said Beaumains, 'I have not deserved that ye should show me this strangeness, and I had weened that I should have right good cheer with you, and unto my power I have deserved thank, and well I am sure I have bought your love with part of the best blood within my body.'

'Fair courteous knight,' said Dame Lyonesse, 'be not displeased nor over-hasty; for wit you well your great travail nor good love shall not be lost, for I consider your great travail and labour, your bounty and your goodness as me ought to do. And therefore go on your way, and look that ye be of good comfort, for all shall be for your worship and for the best, and perdy a twelvemonth will soon be done, and trust me, fair knight, I shall be true to you, and never to betray you, but to my death I shall love you and none other.'

And therewithal she turned her from the window, and Sir Beaumains rode awayward from the castle, making great dole, and so he rode here and there and wist not ne where he rode, till it was dark night. And then it happened him to come to a poor man's house, and there he was harboured all that night. But Sir Beaumains had no rest, but wallowed and writhed for the love of the lady of the castle.

And so upon the morrow he took his horse and rode until undern, and then he came to a broad water, and thereby was a great lodge, and there he alit to sleep and laid his head upon the shield, and betook his horse to the dwarf, and commanded him to watch all night.

Now turn we to the lady of the same castle, that thought much upon Beaumains, and then she called unto her Sir Gringamore her brother, and prayed him in all manner, as he loved her heartily, that he would ride after Sir Beaumains: 'And ever have ye wait upon him till ye may find him sleeping, for I am sure in his heaviness he will alight down in some place, and lie him down to sleep; and therefore have ye your wait upon him, and in the priviest manner ye can, take his dwarf, and go ye your way with him as fast as ever ye may or Sir Beaumains awake. For my sister Lynet telleth me that he can tell of what kindred he is come, and what is his right name. And the meanwhile I and my sister will ride unto your castle to await when ye bring with you the dwarf. And then when ye have brought him unto your castle, I will have him in examination myself. Unto the time that I know what is his right name, and of what kindred he is come, shall I never be merry at my heart.'

'Sister,' said Sir Gringamore, 'all this shall be done after your intent.'

And so he rode all the other day and the night till that he found Sir Beaumains lying by a water, and his head upon

perdy: indeed. *undern*: about 9 a.m. or later.

his shield, for to sleep. And then when he saw Sir Beaumains fast asleep, he came stilly stalking behind the dwarf, and plucked him fast under his arm, and so he rode away with him as fast as ever he might unto his own castle. And this Sir Gringamore's arms were all black, and that to him longeth. But ever as he rode with the dwarf toward his castle, he cried unto his lord and prayed him of help. And therewith awoke Sir Beaumains, and up he leapt lightly, and saw where Sir Gringamore rode his way with the dwarf, and so Sir Gringamore rode out of his sight.

CHAPTER 20: *How Sir Beaumains rode after to rescue his dwarf, and came into the castle where he was*

Then Sir Beaumains put on his helm anon, and buckled his shield, and took his horse, and rode after him all that ever he might ride through marsh, and fields, and great dales, that many times his horse and he plunged over the head in deep mires, for he knew not the way, but took the gainest way in that woodness, that many times he was like to perish. And at the last him happened to come to a fair green way, and there he met with a poor man of the country, whom he saluted and asked him whether he met not with a knight upon a black horse and all black harness, a little dwarf sitting behind him with heavy cheer.

'Sir,' said this poor man, 'here by me came Sir Gringamore the knight, with such a dwarf mourning as ye say; and therefore I rede you not follow him, for he is one of the periloust knights of the world, and his castle is here nigh hand but two mile; therefore we advise you ride not after Sir Gringamore, but if ye owe him good will.'

So leave we Sir Beaumains riding towards the castle, and speak we of Sir Gringamore and the dwarf. Anon as the dwarf was come to the castle, Dame Lyonesse and Dame Lynet her sister, asked the dwarf where was his master born,

gainest: quickest.

and of what lineage he was come. 'And but if thou tell me,' said Dame Lyonesse, 'thou shalt never escape this castle, but ever here to be prisoner.'

'As for that,' said the dwarf, 'I fear not greatly to tell his name and of what kin he is come. Wit ye well he is a king's son, and his mother is sister to King Arthur, and he is brother to the good knight Sir Gawain,[1] and his name is Sir Gareth of Orkney. And now I have told you his right name, I pray you, fair lady, let me go to my lord again, for he will never out of this country until that he have me again. And if he be angry he will do much harm or that he be stint, and work you wrack in this country.'

'As for that threating,' said Sir Gringamore, 'be it as it be may, we will go to dinner.'

And so they washed and went to meat, and made them merry and well at ease; because the Lady Lyonesse of the castle was there, they made great joy.

'Truly, madam,' said Lynet unto her sister, 'well may he be a king's son, for he hath many good tatches on him, for he is courteous and mild, and the most suffering man that ever I met withal. For I dare say there was never gentlewoman reviled man in so foul a manner as I have rebuked him; and at all times he gave me goodly and meek answers again.'

And as they sat thus talking, there came Sir Gareth in at the gate with an angry countenance, and his sword drawn in his hand, and cried aloud that all the castle might hear it, saying, 'Thou traitor, Sir Gringamore, deliver me my dwarf again, or by the faith that I owe to the order of knighthood, I shall do thee all the harm that I can.'

Then Sir Gringamore looked out at a window and said, 'Sir Gareth of Orkney, leave thy boasting words, for thou gettest not thy dwarf again.'

'Thou coward knight,' said Sir Gareth, 'bring him with thee, and come and do battle with me, and win him and take him.'

wrack: strife.

'So will I do,' said Sir Gringamore, 'and me list, but for all thy great words thou gettest him not.'

'Ah! fair brother,' said Dame Lyonesse, 'I would he had his dwarf again, for I would he were not wroth, for now he hath told me all my desire I keep no more of the dwarf. And also, brother, he hath done much for me, and delivered me from the Red Knight of the Red Launds, and therefore, brother, I owe him my service afore all knights living. And wit ye well that I love him before all other, and full fain I would speak with him. But in nowise I would that he wist what I were, but that I were another strange lady.'

'Well,' said Sir Gringamore, 'sithen I know now your will, I will obey now unto him.'

And right therewithal he went down unto Sir Gareth, and said, 'Sir, I cry you mercy, and all that I have misdone I will amend it at your will. And therefore I pray you that ye would alight, and take such cheer as I can make you in this castle.'

'Shall I have my dwarf?' said Sir Gareth.

'Yea, sir, and all the pleasance that I can make you, for as soon as your dwarf told me what ye were and of what blood ye are come, and what noble deeds ye have done in these marches, then I repented of my deeds.'

And then Sir Gareth alit, and there came his dwarf and took his horse.

'O my fellow,' said Sir Gareth, 'I have had many adventures for thy sake.'

And so Sir Gringamore took him by the hand and led him into the hall where his own wife was.

CHAPTER 21: *How Sir Gareth, otherwise called Beaumains, came to the presence of his lady, and how they took acquaintance, and of their love*

And then came forth Dame Lyonesse arrayed like a princess, and there she made him passing good cheer, and he her again;

and they had goodly language and lovely countenance together.

And Sir Gareth thought many times, 'Jesu, would that the lady of the Castle Perilous were so fair as she was.'

There were all manner of games and plays, of dancing and singing. And ever the more Sir Gareth beheld that lady, the more he loved her; and so he burned in love that he was past himself in his reason; and forth toward night they yede unto supper, and Sir Gareth might not eat, for his love was so hot that he wist not where he was.

All these looks espied Sir Gringamore, and then at after-supper he called his sister Dame Lyonesse unto a chamber, and said, 'Fair sister, I have well espied your countenance betwixt you and this knight, and I will, sister, that ye wit he is a full noble knight, and if ye can make him to abide here I will do him all the pleasure that I can, for and ye were better than ye are, ye were well bewared upon him.'

'Fair brother,' said Dame Lyonesse, 'I understand well that the knight is good, and come he is of a noble house. Notwithstanding, I will assay him better, howbeit I am most beholding to him of any earthly man; for he hath had great labour for my love, and passed many a dangerous passage.'

Right so Sir Gringamore went unto Sir Gareth, and said, 'Sir, make ye good cheer, for ye shall have none other cause, for this lady, my sister, is yours at all times, her worship saved, for wit ye well she loveth you as well as ye do her, and better if better may be.'

'And I wist that,' said Sir Gareth, 'there lived not a gladder man than I would be.'

'Upon my worship,' said Sir Gringamore, 'trust unto my promise; and as long as it liketh you ye shall sojourn with me, and this lady shall be with us daily and nightly to make you all the cheer that she can.'

'I will well,' said Sir Gareth, 'for I have promised to be nigh this country this twelvemonth. And well I am sure King Arthur and other noble knights will find me where

bewared: bestowed.

that I am within this twelvemonth. For I shall be sought and founden, if that I be alive.'

And then the noble knight Sir Gareth went unto the Dame Lyonesse, which he then much loved, and kissed her many times, and either made great joy of other. And there she promised him her love certainly, to love him and none other the days of her life. Then this lady, Dame Lyonesse, by the assent of her brother, told Sir Gareth all the truth what she was, and how she was the same lady that he did battle for, and how she was lady of the Castle Perilous, and there she told him how she caused her brother to take away his dwarf.

CHAPTER 22: *How at night came an armed knight, and fought with Sir Gareth, and he, sore hurt in the thigh, smote off the knight's head*

'For this cause, to know the certainty what was your name, and of what kin ye were come.'

And then she let fetch tofore him Lynet, the damosel that had ridden with him many wildsome ways. Then was Sir Gareth more gladder than he was tofore.

And then they troth-plight each other to love, and never to fail whiles their life lasteth. And so they burnt both in love, that they were accorded to abate their lusts secretly. And there Dame Lyonesse counselled Sir Gareth to sleep in none other place but in the hall. And there she promised him to come to his bed a little afore midnight.

This counsel was not so privily kept but it was understand; for they were but young both, and tender of age, and had not used none such crafts tofore. Wherefore the damosel Lynet was a little displeased, and she thought her sister Dame Lyonesse was a little over-hasty, that she might not abide the time of her marriage; and for saving their worship she thought to abate their hot lusts. And so she let ordain by her subtle crafts that they had not their intents neither with other, as in their delights, until they were married.

And so it passed on. At after-supper was made clean avoidance, that every lord and lady should go unto his rest. But Sir Gareth said plainly he would go no farther than the hall, for in such places, he said, was convenient for an errant knight to take his rest in; and so there were ordained great couches, and thereon feather beds, and there laid him down to sleep; and within a while came Dame Lyonesse, wrapped in a mantle furred with ermine, and laid her down besides Sir Gareth. And therewithal he began to kiss her.

And then he looked afore him, and there he apperceived and saw come an armed knight, with many lights about him; and this knight had a long gisarme in his hand, and made grim countenance to smite him. When Sir Gareth saw him come in that wise, he leapt out of his bed, and gat in his hand his sword, and leapt straight toward that knight. And when the knight saw Sir Gareth come so fiercely upon him, he smote him with a foin through the thick of the thigh that the wound was a shaftmon broad and had cut a-two many veins and sinews. And therewithal Sir Gareth smote him upon the helm such a buffet that he fell grovelling; and then he leapt over him and unlaced his helm, and smote off his head from the body. And then he bled so fast that he might not stand, but so he laid him down upon his bed, and there he swooned and lay as he had been dead.

Then Dame Lyonesse cried aloud, that her brother Sir Gringamore heard, and came down. And when he saw Sir Gareth so shamefully wounded he was sore displeased, and said, 'I am ashamed that this noble knight is thus honoured. Sister,'[1] said Sir Gringamore, 'how may this be, that ye be here, and this noble knight wounded?'

'Brother,' she said, 'I can not tell you, for it was not done by me, nor by mine assent. For he is my lord and I am his, and he must be mine husband; therefore, my brother, I will that ye wit I shame me not to be with him, nor to do him all the pleasure that I can.'

'Sister,' said Sir Gringamore, 'and I will that ye wit it, and

shaftmon: hand-breadth.

Sir Gareth both, that it was never done by me, nor by my assent that this unhappy deed was done.'

And there they staunched his bleeding as well as they might, and great sorrow made Sir Gringamore and Dame Lyonesse.

And forthwithal came Dame Lynet, and took up the head in the sight of them all, and anointed it with an ointment thereas it was smitten off; and in the same wise she did to the other part thereas the head stuck, and then she set it together, and it stuck as fast as ever it did. And the knight arose lightly up, and the damosel Lynet put him in her chamber. All this saw Sir Gringamore and Dame Lyonesse, and so did Sir Gareth; and well he espied that it was the damosel Lynet, that rode with him through the perilous passages.

'Ah well, damosel,' said Sir Gareth, 'I weened [ye] would not have done as ye have done.'

'My lord Gareth,' said Lynet, 'all that I have done I will avow, and all that I have done shall be for your honour and worship, and to us all.'

And so within a while Sir Gareth was nigh whole, and waxed light and jocund, and sang, danced, and gamed; and he and Dame Lyonesse were so hot in burning love that they made their covenant at the tenth night after, that she should come to his bed. And because he was wounded afore, he laid his armour and his sword nigh his bed's side.

CHAPTER 23: *How the said knight came again the next night and was beheaded again, and how at the feast of Pentecost all the knights that Sir Gareth had overcome came and yielded them to King Arthur*

Right as she promised she came; and she was not so soon in his bed but she espied an armed knight coming toward the bed: therewithal she warned Sir Gareth, and lightly through the good help of Dame Lyonesse he was armed; and they hurtled together with great ire and malice all about the hall; and there was great light as it had been the number of twenty torches both before and behind, so that Sir Gareth strained him, so that his old wound brast again on bleeding; but he was hot and courageous and took no keep, but with his great force he struck down that knight, and voided his helm, and struck off his head. Then he hew the head in an hundred pieces. And when he had done so he took up all those pieces, and threw them out at a window into the ditches of the castle; and by this done he was so faint that unnethes he might stand for bleeding.

And by then he was almost unarmed he fell in a deadly swoon on the floor; and then Dame Lyonesse cried so that Sir Gringamore heard; and when he came and found Sir Gareth in that plight he made great sorrow; and there he awaked Sir Gareth, and gave him a drink that relieved him wonderly well; but the sorrow that Dame Lyonesse made there may no tongue tell, for she so fared with herself as she would have died.

Right so came this damosel Lynet before them all, and she had fetched all the gobbets of the head that Sir Gareth had thrown out at a window, and there she anointed them as she had done tofore, and set them together again.

'Well, damosel Lynet,' said Sir Gareth, 'I have not deserved all this despite that ye do unto me.'

'Sir knight,' she said, 'I have nothing done but I will avow, and all that I have done shall be to your worship, and to us all.'

And then was Sir Gareth staunched of his bleeding. But the leeches said that there was no man that bare the life should heal him throughout of his wound but if they healed him that caused that stroke by enchantment.

So leave we Sir Gareth there with Sir Gringamore and his sisters, and turn we unto King Arthur, that at the next feast of Pentecost held his feast; and there came the Green Knight with fifty knights, and yielded them all unto King Arthur. And so there came the Red Knight his brother, and yielded him to King Arthur, and three score knights with him. Also there came the Blue Knight, brother to them, with an hundred knights, and yielded them unto King Arthur; and the Green Knight's name was Pertolepe, and the Red Knight's name was Perimones, and the Blue Knight's name was Sir Persant of Inde. These three brethren told King Arthur how they were overcome by a knight that a damosel had with her, and called him Beaumains.

'Jesu,' said the king, 'I marvel what knight he is, and of what lineage he is come. He was with me a twelvemonth, and poorly and shamefully he was fostered, and Sir Kay in scorn named him Beaumains.'

So right as the king stood so talking with these three brethren, there came Sir Launcelot du Lake, and told the king that there was come a goodly lord with six hundred knights with him. Then the king went out of Caerleon, for there was the feast, and there came to him this lord, and saluted the king in a goodly manner.

'What will ye,' said King Arthur, 'and what is your errand?'

'Sir,' he said, 'my name is the Red Knight of the Red Launds, but my name is Sir Ironside; and sir, wit ye well, here I am sent to you of a knight that is called Beaumains, for he won me in plain battle hand for hand, and so did never no knight but he, that ever had the better of me this thirty winter; the which commanded to yield me to you at your will.'

'Ye are welcome,' said the king, 'for ye have been long a great foe to me and my court, and now I trust to God I shall so entreat you that ye shall be my friend.'

'Sir, both I and these five hundred knights shall always be at your summons to do you service as may lie in our powers.'

'Jesu mercy,' said King Arthur, 'I am much beholding unto that knight that hath put so his body in devoir to worship me and my court. And as to thee, Ironside, that are called

devoir: endeavour.

the Red Knight of the Red Launds, thou art called a perilous knight; and if thou wilt hold of me I shall worship thee and make thee knight of the Table Round; but then thou must be no more a murderer.'

'Sir, as to that, I have promised unto Sir Beaumains never more to use such customs, for all the shameful customs that I used I did at the request of a lady that I loved; and therefore I must go unto Sir Launcelot, and unto Sir Gawain, and ask them forgiveness of the evil will I had unto them; for all that I put to death was all only for the love of Sir Launcelot and of Sir Gawain.'

'They be here now,' said the king, 'afore thee, now may ye say to them what ye will.'

And then he kneeled down unto Sir Launcelot, and to Sir Gawain, and prayed them of forgiveness of his enmity that ever he had against them.

CHAPTER 24: *How King Arthur pardoned them, and demanded of them where Sir Gareth was*

Then goodly they said all at once, 'God forgive you, and we do, and pray you that ye will tell us where we may find Sir Beaumains.'

'Fair lords,' said Sir Ironside, 'I cannot tell you, for it is full hard to find him; for such young knights as he is one, when they be in their adventures be never abiding in no place.'

But to say the worship that the Red Knight of the Red Launds, and Sir Persant and his brother said of Beaumains, it was marvel to hear.

'Well, my fair lords,' said King Arthur, 'wit you well I shall do you honour for the love of Sir Beaumains, and as soon as ever I meet with him I shall make you all upon one day knights of the Table Round. And as to thee, Sir Persant of Inde, thou hast been ever called a full noble knight, and so have ever been thy three brethren called. But I marvel,' said the king, 'that I hear not of the Black Knight your brother, he was a full noble knight.'

'Sir,' said Pertolepe, the Green Knight, 'Sir Beaumains slew him in a recounter with his spear, his name was Sir Percard.'

'That was great pity,' said the king, and so said many knights. For these four brethren were full well known in the court of King Arthur for noble knights, for long time they had holden war against the knights of the Round Table.

Then said Pertolepe, the Green Knight, to the king, 'At a passage of the water of Mortaise there encountered Sir Beaumains with two brethren that ever for the most part kept that passage, and they were two deadly knights, and there he slew the eldest brother in the water, and smote him upon the head such a buffet that he fell down in the water, and there he was drowned, and his name was Sir Garard le Breuse; and after he slew the other brother upon the land, his name was Sir Arnold le Breuse.'

CHAPTER 25: *How the Queen of Orkney came to this feast of Pentecost, and Sir Gawain and his brethren came to ask her blessing*

So then the king and they went to meat, and were served in the best manner. And as they sat at the meat, there came in the Queen of Orkney, with ladies and knights a great number. And then Sir Gawain, Sir Agravain, and Gaheris arose, and went to her and saluted her upon their knees, and asked her blessing; for in fifteen year they had not seen her. Then she spake on high to her brother King Arthur:

'Where have ye done my young son Sir Gareth? He was here amongst you a twelvemonth, and ye made a kitchen knave of him, the which is shame to you all. Alas, where have ye done my dear son that was my joy and bliss?'

'O dear mother,' said Sir Gawain, 'I knew him not.'

'Nor I,' said the king, 'that now me repenteth, but thanked

be God he is proved a worshipful knight as any is now living of his years, and I shall never be glad till I may find him.'

'Ah, brother,' said the queen unto King Arthur, and unto Sir Gawain, and to all her sons, 'ye did yourself great shame when ye amongst you kept my son in the kitchen and fed him like a poor hog.'

'Fair sister,' said King Arthur, 'ye shall right well wit I knew him not, nor no more did Sir Gawain, nor his brethren; but sithen it is so,' said the king, 'that he is thus gone from us all, we must shape a remedy to find him. Also, sister, meseemeth ye might have done me to wit of his coming, and then and I had not done well to him ye might have blamed me. For when he came to this court he came leaning upon two men's shoulders, as though he might not have gone. And then he asked me three gifts; and one he asked the same day, that was that I would give him meat enough that twelvemonth; and the other two gifts he asked that day a twelvemonth, and that was that he might have the adventure of the damosel Lynet, and the third was that Sir Launcelot should make him knight when he desired him. And so I granted him all his desire, and many in this court marvelled that he desired his sustenance for a twelvemonth. And thereby, we deemed, many of us, that he was not come of a noble house.'

'Sir,' said the Queen of Orkney unto King Arthur her brother, 'wit ye well that I sent him unto you right well armed and horsed, and worshipfully beseen of his body, and gold and silver plenty to spend.'

'It may be,' said the King, 'but thereof saw we none, save that same day as he departed from us, knights told me that there came a dwarf hither suddenly, and brought him armour and a good horse full well and richly beseen; and thereat we all had marvel from whence that riches came, that we deemed all that he was come of men of worship.'

'Brother,' said the queen, 'all that ye say I believe, for ever sithen he was grown he was marvellously witted, and ever he was faithful and true of his promise. But I marvel,' said she, 'that Sir Kay did mock him and scorn him, and gave him that name Beaumains; yet, Sir Kay,' said the queen, 'named him more righteously than he weened; for I dare say and he be alive, he is as fair an handed man and well disposed as any is living.'

'Sister,' said Arthur, 'let this language be still, and by the grace of God he shall be found and he be within this seven realms, and let all this pass and be merry, for he is proved to be a man of worship, and that is my joy.'

CHAPTER 26: *How King Arthur sent for the Lady Lyonesse, and how she let cry a tourney at her castle, whereas came many knights*

Then said Sir Gawain and his brethren unto Arthur, 'Sir, and ye will give us leave, we will go and seek our brother.'

'Nay,' said Sir Launcelot, 'that shall ye not need!' and so said Sir Baudwin of Britain: 'for as by our advice the king shall send unto Dame Lyonesse a messenger, and pray her that she will come to the court in all the haste that she may, and doubt ye not she will come; and then she may give you best counsel where ye shall find him.'

'This is well said of you,' said the king.

So then goodly letters were made, and the messenger sent forth, that night and day he went till he came unto the Castle Perilous. And then the lady Dame Lyonesse was sent for thereas she was with Sir Gringamore her brother and Sir Gareth. And when she understood this message, she bad him ride on his way unto King Arthur, and she would come after in all goodly haste.

Then when she came to Sir Gringamore and to Sir Gareth, she told them all how King Athur had sent for her.

'That is because of me,' said Sir Gareth.

'Now advise me,' said Dame Lyonesse, 'what shall I say, and in what manner I shall rule me.'

'My lady and my love,' said Sir Gareth, 'I pray you in no wise be ye aknown where I am. But well I wot my mother is there and all my brethren, and they will take upon them to seek me, I wot well that they do. But this, madam, I would ye said and advised the king when he questioned with you of me. Then may ye say, this is your advice that, and it like his good grace, ye will do make a cry against the feast of the Assumption of Our Lady, that what knight there proveth him best he shall wield you and all your land. And if so be that he be a wedded man, that his wife shall the degree, and a coronal of gold beset with stones of virtue to the value of a thousand pound,[1] and a white gerfalcon.'

So Dame Lyonesse departed and came to King Arthur, where she was nobly received, and there she was sore questioned of the king and of the Queen of Orkney. And she answered, where Sir Gareth was she could not tell. But thus much she said unto Arthur:

'Sir, I will let cry a tournament that shall be done before my castle at the Assumption of Our Lady, and the cry shall be this: that you, my lord Arthur, shall be there, and your knights, and I will purvey that my knights shall be against yours; and then I am sure ye shall hear of Sir Gareth.'

'This is well advised,' said King Arthur.

And so she departed. And the king and she made great provision to that tournament.

When Dame Lyonesse was come to the Isle of Avilion, that was the same isle thereas her brother Sir Gringamore dwelt, then she told them all how she had done, and what promise she had made to King Arthur.

'Alas,' said Sir Gareth, 'I have been so wounded with unhappiness sithen I came into this castle that I shall not be able to do at that tournament like a knight; for I was never thoroughly whole since I was hurt.'

'Be ye of good cheer,' said the damosel Lynet, 'for I undertake within these fifteen days to make ye whole, and as lusty as ever ye were.'

aknown: aware. *wield*: possess.

And then she laid an ointment and a salve to him as it pleased to her, that he was never so fresh nor so lusty.

Then said the damosel Lynet, 'Send you unto Sir Persant of Inde, and assummon him and his knights to be here with you as they have promised. Also, that ye send unto Sir Ironside, that is the Red Knight of the Red Launds, and charge him that he be ready with you with his whole sum of knights, and then shall ye be able to match with King Arthur and his knights.'

So this was done, and all knights were sent for unto the Castle Perilous; and then the Red Knight answered and said unto Dame Lyonesse, and to Sir Gareth,

'Madam, and my lord Sir Gareth, ye shall understand that I have been at the court of King Arthur, and Sir Persant of Inde and his brethren, and there we have done our homage as ye commanded us. Also,' Sir Ironside said, 'I have taken upon me with Sir Persant of Inde and his brethen to hold part against my lord Sir Launcelot and the knights of that court. And this have I done for the love of my lady Dame Lyonesse, and you my lord Sir Gareth.'

'Ye have well done,' said Sir Gareth; 'but wit you well ye shall be full sore matched with the most noble knights of the world; therefore we must purvey us of good knights, where we may get them.'

'That is well said,' said Sir Persant, 'and worshipfully.'

And so the cry was made in England, Wales, and Scotland, Ireland, Cornwall, and in all the Out Isles, and in Brittany and in many countries, that at the feast of Our Lady the Assumption next coming, men should come to the Castle Perilous beside the Isle of Avilion; and there all the knights that there came should have the choice whether them list to be on the one party with the knights of the castle, or on the other party with King Arthur. And two months was to the day that the tournament should be.

And so there came many good knights that were at their large, and held them for the most part against King Arthur and his knights of the Round Table, came in the side of them of the castle. For Sir Epinogrus was the first, and he was the King's son of Northumberland, and Sir Palomides the Saracen was another, and Sir Safer his brother, and Sir Segwarides his brother, but they were christened, and Sir Malgrin another, and Sir Brian de les Isles, a noble knight, and Sir Grummor Grummorson, a good knight of Scotland, and Sir Carados of the Dolorous Tower, a noble knight, and Sir Turquin his brother, and Sir Arnold and Sir Gauter, two brethren, good knights of Cornwall. There came Sir Tristram de Liones, and with him Sir Dinas, the Seneschal, and Sir Sadok; but this Sir Tristram was not at that time knight of the Table Round, but he was one of the best knights of the world.

And so all these noble knights accompanied them with the lady of the castle, and with the Red Knight of the Red Launds; but as for Sir Gareth, he would not take upon him more but as other mean knights.

CHAPTER 27: *How King Arthur went to the tournament with his knights, and how the lady received him worshipfully, and how the knights encountered*

And then there came with King Arthur Sir Gawain, Agravain, Gaheris, his brethren. And then his nephews Sir Uwain le Blanchemains, and Sir Agloval, Sir Tor, Sir Percival de Gales, and Sir Lamorak de Gales.

Then came Sir Launcelot du Lake with his brethren, nephews, and cousins, as Sir Lionel, Sir Ector de Maris, Sir Bors de Ganis, and Sir Galihodin, Sir Galihud, and many more of Sir Launcelot's blood, and Sir Dinadan, Sir La Cote Male Taile, his brother, a good knight, and Sir Sagramore, a good knight; and all the most part of the Round Table.

Also there came with King Arthur these knights: the King of Ireland, King Agwisance, and the King of Scotland, King Carados and King Uriens of the land of Gore, and King Bagdemagus and his son Sir Meliagaunt, and Sir Galahaut the noble prince. All these kings, princes, and earls, barons, and other noble knights, as Sir Brandiles, Sir Uwain les Avoutres, and Sir Kay, Sir Bedevere, Sir Meliot de Logris, Sir Petipace of Winchelsea, Sir Godelake: all these came with King Arthur, and more that cannot be rehearsed.

Now leave we of these kings and knights, and let us speak of the great array that was made within the castle and about the castle for both parties. The lady Dame Lyonesse ordained great array upon her part for her noble knights, for all manner of lodging and victual that came by land and by water, that there lacked nothing for her party, nor for the other, but there was plenty to be had for gold and silver for King Arthur and his knights. And then there came the harbingers from King Arthur for to harbour him, and his kings, dukes, earls, barons, and knights.

And then Sir Gareth prayed Dame Lyonesse and the Red Knight of the Red Launds, and Sir Persant and his brother, and Sir Gringamore, that in no wise there should none of them tell not his name, and make no more of him than of the least knight that there was, 'for,' he said, 'I will not be known of neither more ne less, neither at the beginning neither at the ending.'

Then Dame Lyonesse said unto Sir Gareth, 'Sir, I will lend you a ring, but I would pray you as you love me heartily let me have it again when the tournament is done, for that ring increaseeth my beauty much more than it is of himself.[1] And the virtue of my ring is that, that is green it will turn to red, and that is red it will turn in likeness to green, and that is blue it will turn to likeness of white, and that is white it will turn in likeness to blue, and so it will do of all manner of colours. Also who that beareth my ring shall lose no blood, and for great love I will give you this ring.'

'Gramercy,' said Sir Gareth, 'mine own lady, for this ring is passing meet for me, for it will turn all manner of likeness that I am in, and that shall cause me that I shall not be known.'

Then Sir Gringamore gave Sir Gareth a bay courser that was a passing good horse; also he gave him good armour and sure, and a noble sword that sometime Sir Gringamore's father won upon an heathen tyrant. And so thus every knight made him ready to that tournament.

And King Arthur was comen two days tofore the Assumption of Our Lady. And there was all manner of royalty of all minstrelsy that might be found. Also there came Queen Guenever and the Queen of Orkney, Sir Gareth's mother. And upon the Assumption Day, when mass and matins were done, there were heralds with trumpets commanded to blow to the field.

And so there came out Sir Epinogrus, the King's son of Northumberland, from the castle, and there encountered with him Sir Sagramore le Desirous, and either of them brake their spears to their hands. And then came in Sir Palomides out of the castle, and there encountered with him Gawain, and either of them smote other so hard that both the good knights and their horses fell to the earth. And then knights of either party rescued their knights. And then came in Sir Safer and Sir Segwarides, brethren to Sir Palomides; and there encountered Sir Agravain with Sir Safer and Sir Gaheris encountered with Sir Segwarides. So Sir Safer smote down Agravain, Sir Gawain's brother; and Sir Segwarides, Sir Safer's brother. And Sir Malgrin, a knight of the castle, encountered with Sir Uwain le Blanchemains, and there Sir Uwain gave Sir Malgrin a fall, that he had almost broke his neck.

CHAPTER 28: *How the knights bare them in the battle*

Then Sir Brian de les Isles and Grummor Grummorson, knights of the castle, encountered[1] with Sir Agloval, and Sir Tor smote down Sir Grummor Grummorson to the earth.

Then came in Sir Carados of the Dolorous Tower, and Sir Turquin, knights of the castle; and there encountered with them Sir Percival de Gales and Sir Lamorak[2] de Gales, that were two brethren. And there encountered Sir Percival with Sir Carados, and either brake their spears unto their hands, and then Sir Turquin with Sir Lamorak, and either of them smote down other's horse and all to the earth, and either parties rescued other, and horsed them again.

And Sir Arnold and Sir Gauter, knights of the castle, encountered with Sir Brandiles and Sir Kay, and these four knights encountered mightily, and brake their spears to their hands.

Then came in Sir Tristram, Sir Sadok, and Sir Dinas, knights of the castle, and there encountered Sir Tristram with Sir Bedevere, and there Sir Bedevere was smitten to the earth both horse and man. And Sir Sadok encountered with Sir Petipace, and there Sir Sadok was overthrown. And there Uwain les Avoutres smote down Sir Dinas, the Seneschal.

Then came in Sir Persant of Inde, a knight of the castle, and there encountered with him Sir Launcelot du Lake, and there he smote Sir Persant, horse and man, to the earth. Then came Sir Pertolepe from the castle, and there encountered with him Sir Lionel, and there Sir Pertolepe, the Green Knight, smote down Sir Lionel, brother to Sir Launcelot.

All this was marked by noble heralds, who bare him best, and their names.

And then came into the field Sir Perimones, the Red[3] Knight, Sir Persant's brother, that was a knight of the castle, and he encountered with Sir Ector de Maris, and either smote other so hard that both their horses and they fell to the earth.

And then came in the Red Knight of the Red Launds, and Sir Gareth, from the castle, and there encountered with them Sir Bors de Ganis and Sir Bleoberis, and there the Red Knight and Sir Bors smote other so hard that their spears brast, and their horses fell grovelling to the earth. Then Sir Blamor brake his spear upon Sir Gareth, but of that stroke Sir Blamor fell to the earth.

When Sir Galihodin saw that, he bad Sir Gareth keep him, and Sir Gareth smote him to the earth. Then Sir Galihud gat a spear to avenge his brother, and in the same wise Sir Gareth served him, and Sir Dindan and his brother, La Cote Male

Taile, and Sir Sagramore le Desirous, and Sir Dodinas le Savage. All these he bare down with one spear.

When King Agwisance of Ireland saw Sir Gareth fare so, he marvelled what he might be that one time seemed green, and another time, at his again coming, he seemed blue. And thus at every course that he rode to and fro he changed his colour, so that there might neither king nor knight have ready cognisance of him. Then Sir Agwisance, the King of Ireland, encountered with Sir Gareth, and there Sir Gareth smote him from his horse, saddle and all. And then came King Carados of Scotland, and Sir Gareth smote him down horse and man. And in the same wise he served King Uriens of the land of Gore. And then came in Sir Bagdemagus, and Sir Gareth smote him down, horse and man, to the earth. And Bagdemagus' son, Meliagaunt, brake a spear upon Sir Gareth mightily and knightly.

And then Sir Galahaut, the noble prince, cried on high, 'Knight with the many colours, well hast thou jousted; now make thee ready that I may joust with thee.'

Sir Gareth heard him, and he gat a great spear, and so they encountered together, and there the prince brake his spear; but Sir Gareth smote him upon the left side of the helm that he reeled here and there, and he had fall down had not his men recovered him.

'So God me help,' said King Arthur, 'that same knight with the many colours is a good knight.'

Wherefore the king called unto him Sir Launcelot, and prayed him to encounter with that knight.

'Sir,' said Launcelot, 'I may well find in my heart for to forbear him as at this time, for he hath had travail enough this day; and when a good knight doth so well upon some day, it is no good knight's part to let him of his worship, and namely, when he seeth a knight hath done so great labour; for peradventure,' said Sir Launcelot, 'his quarrel is here this day, and peradventure he is best beloved with this lady of all that be here; for I see well he paineth him and enforceth him to do great deeds, and therefore,' said Sir Launcelot, 'as for me, this day he shall have the honour; though it lay in my power to put him from it I would not.'

CHAPTER 29: *Yet of the said tournament*

Then when this was done there was drawing of swords, and then there began a sore tournament. And there did Sir Lamorak marvellous deeds of arms; and betwixt Sir Lamorak and Sir Ironside that was the Red Knight of the Red Launds, there was strong battle; and betwixt Sir Palomides and Bleoberis there was a strong battle; and Sir Gawain and Sir Tristram met, and there Sir Gawain had the worse, for he pulled Sir Gawain from his horse, and there he was long upon foot, and defiled.

Then came in Sir Launcelot, and he smote Sir Turquin, and he him; and then came Sir Carados his brother, and both at once they assailed him, and he as the most noblest knight of the world worshipfully fought with them both, that all men wondered of the noblesse of Sir Launcelot.

And then came in Sir Gareth, and knew that it was Sir Launcelot that fought with those two perilous knights. And then Sir Gareth came with his good horse and hurtled them in-sunder, and no stroke would he smite to Sir Launcelot. That espied Sir Launcelot, and deemed it should be the good knight Sir Gareth; and then Sir Gareth rode here and there, and smote on the right hand and on the left hand, that all the folk might well espy where that he rode. And by fortune he met with his brother Sir Gawain, and there he put Sir Gawain to the worse, for he put off his helm, and so he served five or six knights of the Round Table, that all men said he put him in the most pain, and best he did his devoir.

For when Sir Tristram beheld him how he first jousted and after fought so well with a sword, then he rode unto Sir Ironside and to Sir Persant of Inde, and asked them, by their faith, 'What manner a knight is yonder knight that

defiled: put to shame.

seemeth in so many divers colours? Truly, meseemeth,' said Tristram, 'that he putteth himself in great pain, for he never ceaseth.'

'Wot ye not what he is?' said Sir Ironside.

'No,' said Sir Tristram.

'Then shall ye know that this is he that loveth the lady of the castle, and she him again; and this is he that won me when I besieged the lady of this castle, and this is he that won Sir Persant of Inde, and his three brethren.'

'What is his name,' said Sir Tristram, 'and of what blood is he come?'

'He was called in the court of King Arthur, Beaumains, but his right name is Sir Gareth of Orkney, brother to Sir Gawain.'

'By my head,' said Sir Tristram, 'he is a good knight, and a big man of arms, and if he be young he shall prove a full noble knight.'

'He is but a child,' they all said, 'and of Sir Launcelot he was made knight.'

'Therefore he is mickle the better,' said Tristram.

And then Sir Tristram, Sir Ironside, Sir Persant, and his brother, rode together for to help Sir Gareth; and then there were given many strong strokes.

And then Sir Gareth rode out on the one side to amend his helm; and then said his dwarf, 'Take me your ring, that ye lose it not while that ye drink.'

And so when he had drunken he gat on his helm, and eagerly took his horse and rode into the field, and left his ring with his dwarf; and the dwarf was glad the ring was from him, for then he wist well he should be known.

And then when Sir Gareth was in the field all folks saw him well and plainly that he was in yellow colours; and there he rased off helms and pulled down knights, that King Arthur had marvel what knight he was, for the king saw by his hair that it was the same knight.

CHAPTER 30: *How Sir Gareth was espied by the heralds, and how he escaped out of the field*

'But before he was in so many colours, and now he is but in one colour; that is yellow. Now go,' said King Arthur unto divers heralds, 'and ride about him, and espy what manner knight he is, for I have spered of many knights this day that be upon his party, and all say they know him not.'

And so an herald rode nigh Gareth as he could; and there he saw written about his helm in gold, THIS HELM IS SIR GARETH OF ORKNEY.

Then the herald cried as he were wood, and many heralds with him: 'This is Sir Gareth of Orkney in the yellow arms;' that by all kings and knights of Arthur's beheld him and awaited; and then they pressed all to behold him, and ever the heralds cried: 'This is Sir Gareth of Orkney, King Lot's son.'

And when Sir Gareth espied that he was discovered, then he doubled his strokes and smote down Sir Sagramore, and his brother Sir Gawain.

'O brother,' said Sir Gawain, 'I weened ye would not have stricken me.'

So when he heard him say so he thrang here and there, and so with great pain he gat out of the press, and there he met with his dwarf.

'Oh boy,' said Sir Gareth, 'thou hast beguiled me foul this day that thou kept my ring; give it me anon again, that I may hide my body withal;' and so he took it him.

And then they all wist not where he was become; and Sir Gawain had in manner espied where Sir Gareth rode, and then he rode after with all his might. That espied Sir Gareth, and rode lightly into the forest, that Sir Gawain wist not where he was become. And when Sir Gareth wist that Sir Gawain was passed, he asked the dwarf of best counsel.

spered: asked. *thrang*: thrust.

'Sir,' said the dwarf, 'meseemeth it were best, now that ye are escaped from spying, that ye send my lady Dame Lyonesse her ring.'

'It is well advised,' said Sir Gareth; 'now have it here and bear it to her, and say that I recommend me unto her good grace, and say her I will come when I may, and I pray her to be true and faithful to me as I will be to her.'

'Sir,' said the dwarf, 'it shall be done as ye command;' and so he rode his way, and did his errand unto the lady.

Then she said, 'Where is my knight, Sir Gareth?'

'Madam,' said the dwarf, 'he bad me say that he would not be long from you.'

And so lightly the dwarf came again unto Sir Gareth, that would full fain have had a lodging, for he had need to be reposed. And then fell there a thunder and a rain, as heaven and earth should go together. And Sir Gareth was not a little weary, for of all that day he had but little rest, neither his horse nor he. So this Sir Gareth rode so long in that forest until the night came. And ever it lightened and thundered, as it had been wood. At the last by fortune he came to a castle, and there he heard the waits upon the walls.

CHAPTER 31: *How Sir Gareth came to a castle where he was well lodged, and he jousted with a knight and slew him*

Then Sir Gareth rode unto the barbican of the castle, and prayed the porter fair to let him into the castle.

The porter answered ungoodly again, and said, 'Thou gettest no lodging here.'

'Fair sir, say not so, for I am a knight of King Arthur's, and pray the lord or the lady of this castle to give me harbour for the love of King Arthur.'

Then the porter went unto the duchess, and told her how there was a knight of King Arthur's would have harbour.

waits: watchmen.

'Let him in,' said the duchess, 'for I will see that knight, and for King Arthur's sake he shall not be harbourless.'

Then she yode up into a tower over the gate, with great torch-light. When Sir Gareth saw that torch-light he cried on high,

'Whether thou be lord or lady, giant or champion I take no force so that I may have harbour this night; and if it so be that I must needs fight, spare me not to-morn when I have rested me, for both I and mine horse be weary.'

'Sir knight,' said the lady, 'thou speakest knightly and boldly; but wit thou well the lord of this castle loveth not King Arthur, nor none of his court, for my lord hath ever been against him; and therefore thou were better not to come within this castle; for and thou come in this night, thou must come in under such form, that wheresomever thou meet my lord, by stigh or by street, thou must yield thee to him as prisoner.'

'Madam,' said Sir Gareth, 'what is your lord, and what is his name?'

'Sir, my lord's name is the Duke de la Rowse.'

'Well madam,' said Sir Gareth, 'I shall promise you in what place I meet your lord I shall yield me unto him and to his good grace, with that I understand he will do me no harm; and if I understand that he will, I will release myself, and I can, with my spear and my sword.'

'Ye say well,' said the duchess.

And then she let the drawbridge down, and so he rode into the hall, and there he alit, and his horse was led into a stable; and in the hall he unarmed him and said, 'Madam, I will not out of this hall this night; and when it is daylight, let see who will have ado with me, he shall find me ready.'

Then was he set unto supper, and had many good dishes. Then Sir Gareth list well to eat, and knightly he ate his meat, and eagerly; there was many a fair lady by him, and some said they never saw a goodlier man nor so well of eating. Then they made him passing good cheer, and shortly when

stigh: path.

he had supped his bed was made there; so he rested him all night.

And on the morn he heard mass, and brake his fast and took his leave at the duchess, and at them all; and thanked her goodly of her lodging, and of his good cheer; and then she asked him his name.

'Madam,' he said, 'truly my name is Gareth of Orkney, and some men call me Beaumains.'

Then knew she well it was the same knight that fought for Dame Lyonesse.

So Sir Gareth departed and rode up into a mountain, and there met him a knight, his name was Sir Bendelaine, and said to Sir Gareth, 'Thou shalt not pass this way, for either thou shalt joust with me, or else be my prisoner.'

'Then will I joust,' said Sir Gareth.

And so they let their horses run, and there Sir Gareth smote him throughout the body; and Sir Bendelaine rode forth to his castle there beside, and there died. So Sir Gareth would have rested him, and he came riding to Bendelaine's castle.

Then his knights and servants espied that it was he that had slain their lord. Then they armed twenty good men, and came out and assailed Sir Gareth; and so he had no spear, but his sword, and put his shield afore him; and there they brake their spears upon him, and they assailed him passingly sore. But ever Sir Gareth defended him as a knight.

CHAPTER 32: *How Sir Gareth fought with a knight that held within his castle thirty ladies, and how he slew him*

So when they saw that they might not overcome him, they rode from him, and took their counsel to slay his horse; and so they came in upon Sir Gareth, and with spears they slew his horse, and then they assailed him hard. But when he was on foot, there was none that he raught but he gave him

raught: reached.

such a buffet that he did never recover. So he slew them by one and one till they were but four, and there they fled; and Sir Gareth took a good horse that was one of theirs, and rode his way. Then he rode a great pace till that he came to a castle, and there he heard much mourning of ladies and gentlewomen. So there came by him a page.

'What noise is this,' said Sir Gareth, 'that I hear within this castle?'

'Sir knight,' said the page, 'here be within this castle thirty ladies, and all they be widows; for here is a knight that waiteth daily upon this castle, and his name is the Brown Knight without Pity,[1] and he is the periloust knight that now liveth; and therefore sir,' said the page, 'I rede you flee.'

'Nay,' said Sir Gareth, 'I will not flee though thou be afeared of him.'

And then the page saw where came the Brown Knight. 'Lo,' said the page, 'yonder he cometh.'

'Let me deal with him,' said Sir Gareth.

And when either of other had a sight they let their horses run, and the Brown Knight brake his spear, and Sir Gareth smote him throughout the body, that he overthrew him to the ground stark dead. So Sir Gareth rode into the castle, and prayed the ladies that he might repose him.

'Alas,' said the ladies, 'ye may not be lodged here.'

'Make him good cheer,' said the page, 'for this knight hath slain your enemy.'

Then they all made him good cheer as lay in their power. But wit ye well they made him good cheer for they might none otherwise do, for they were but poor.

And so on the morn he went to mass, and there he saw the thirty ladies kneel, and lay grovelling upon divers tombs, making great dole and sorrow. Then Sir Gareth wist well that in the tombs lay their lords.

'Fair ladies,' said Sir Gareth, 'ye must at the next feast of Pentecost be at the court of King Arthur, and say that I, Sir Gareth, sent you thither.'

'We shall do this,' said the ladies.

So he departed, and by fortune he came to a mountain, and there he found a goodly knight that bad him, 'Abide sir knight, and joust with me.'

'What are ye?' said Sir Gareth.

'My name is,' said he, 'the Duke de la Rowse.'

'Ah sir, ye are the same knight that I lodged once in your castle; and there I made promise unto your lady that I should yield me unto you.'

'Ah,' said the duke, 'art thou that proud knight that profferest to fight with my knights? Therefore make thee ready, for I will have ado with you.'

So they let their horses run, and there Sir Gareth smote the duke down from his horse. But the duke lightly avoided his horse, and dressed his shield and drew his sword, and bad Sir Gareth alight and fight with him. So he did alight, and they did great battle together more than an hour, and either hurt other full sore. At the last Sir Gareth gat the duke to the earth, and would have slain him, and then he yielded him to him.

'Then must ye go,' said Sir Gareth, 'unto Sir Arthur my lord at the next feast, and say that I, Sir Gareth of Orkney, sent you unto him.'

'It shall be done,' said the duke, 'and I will do to you homage and fealty with an hundred knights with me; and all the days of my life to do you service where ye will command me.'

CHAPTER 33: *How Sir Gawain and Sir Gareth fought each against other, and how they knew each other by the damosel Lynet*

So the duke departed, and Sir Gareth stood there alone; and there he saw an armed knight coming toward him. Then Sir Gareth took the duke's shield, and mounted upon horseback, and so without bidding they ran together as it had been the thunder. And there that knight hurt Sir Gareth under the side with his spear. And then they alit and drew their swords, and gave great strokes that the blood trailed to the ground. And so they fought two hours.

At last there came the damosel Lynet, that some men call the Damosel Savage, and she came riding upon an ambling mule; and there she cried all on high, 'Sir Gawain, Sir Gawain, leave thy fighting with thy brother Sir Gareth.'

And when he heard her say so he threw away his shield and his sword, and ran to Sir Gareth, and took him in his arms, and sithen kneeled down and asked him mercy.

'What are ye,' said Sir Gareth, 'that right now were so strong and so mighty, and now so suddenly yield you to me?'

'O Gareth, I am your brother Sir Gawain, that for your sake have had great sorrow and labour.'

Then Sir Gareth unlaced his helm, and kneeled down to him, and asked him mercy. Then they rose both, and embraced either other in their arms, and wept a great while or they might speak, and either of them gave other the prize of the battle. And there were many kind words between them. 'Alas, my fair brother,' said Sir Gawain, 'perdy I owe of right to worship you and ye were not my brother, for ye have worshipped King Arthur and all his court, for ye have sent me more worshipful knights this twelvemonth than six the best of the Round Table have done, except Sir Launcelot.'

Then came the Damosel Savage that was the Lady Lynet, that rode with Sir Gareth so long and there she did staunch Sir Gareth's wounds and Sir Gawain's.

'Now what will ye do?' said the Damosel Savage, 'Meseemeth that it were well done that Arthur had witting of you both, for your horses are so bruised that they may not bear.'

'Now, fair damosel,' said Sir Gawain, 'I pray you ride unto my lord mine uncle, King Arthur, and tell him what adventure is to me betid here, and I suppose he will not tarry long.'

Then she took her mule and lightly she came to King Arthur that was but two mile thence. And when she had told him tidings the king bad get him a palfrey. And when he was upon his back he bad the lords and ladies come after, who that would; and there was saddling and bridling of queens' horses and princes' horses, and well was him that soonest might be ready.

So when the king came thereas they were, he saw Sir Gawain and Sir Gareth sit upon a little hill-side, and then the king avoided his horse. And when he came nigh Sir Gareth he would have spoken but he might not; and therewith he sank down in a swoon for gladness. And so they start unto their uncle, and required him of his good grace to be of good comfort. Wit ye well the king made great joy, and many a piteous complaint he made to Sir Gareth, and ever he wept as he had been a child.

With that came his mother, the Queen of Orkney, Dame Margawse, and when she saw Sir Gareth readily in the visage she might not weep, but suddenly fell down in a swoon, and lay there a great while like as she had been dead. And then Sir Gareth recomforted his mother in such wise that she recovered and made good cheer.

Then the king commanded that all manner of knights that were under his obeissance should make their lodging right there for the love of his nephews. And so it was done, and all manner of purveyance purveyed, that there lacked nothing that might be gotten of tame nor wild for gold or silver. And then by the means of the Damosel Savage Sir Gawain and Sir Gareth were healed of their wounds; and there they sojourned eight days.

Then said King Arthur unto the Damosel Savage, 'I marvel that your sister, Dame Lyonesse, cometh not here to me, and in especial that she cometh not to visit her knight, my nephew Sir Gareth, that hath had so much travail for her love.'

'My lord,' said the damosel Lynet, 'ye must of your good grace hold her excused, for she knoweth not that my lord, Sir Gareth, is here.'

'Go then for her,' said King Arthur, 'that we may be

appointed what is best to done, according to the pleasure of my nephew.'

'Sir,' said the damosel, 'that shall be done,' and so she rode unto her sister.

And, as lightly as she might, made her ready; and she came on the morn with her brother Sir Gringamore, and with her forty knights. And so when she was come she had all the cheer that might be done, both of the king, and of many other kings and queens.

CHAPTER 34: *How Sir Gareth acknowledged that they loved each other to King Arthur, and of the appointment of their wedding*

And among all these ladies she was named the fairest, and peerless. Then when Sir Gawain saw her[1] there was many a goodly look and goodly words, that all men of worship had joy to behold them.

Then came King Arthur and many other kings, and Dame Guenever, and the Queen of Orkney. And there the king asked his nephew, Sir Gareth, whether he would have that lady as paramour, or to have her to his wife.

'My lord, wit you well that I love her above all ladies living.'

'Now, fair lady,' said King Arthur, 'what say ye?'

'Most noble king,' said Dame Lyonesse, 'wit you well that my lord, Sir Gareth, is to me more lever to have and wield as my husband, than any king or prince that is christened; and if I may not have him I promise you I will never have none. For, my lord Arthur,' said Dame Lyonesse, 'wit ye well he is my first love, and he shall be the last; and if ye will suffer him to have his will and free choice I dare say he will have me.'

'That is truth,' said Sir Gareth; 'and I have not you and wield not you as my wife, there shall never lady ne gentlewoman rejoice me.'

'What, nephew,' said the king, 'is the wind in that door? For wit ye well I would not for the stint of my crown to be causer to withdraw your hearts; and wit ye well ye cannot love so well but I shall rather increase it than distress it. And also ye shall have my love and my lordship in the uttermost wise that may lie in my power.' And in the same wise said Sir Gareth's mother.

Then there was made a provision for the day of marriage; and by the king's advice it was provided that it should be at Michaelmas following, at Kinkenadon by the seaside, for there is a plentiful country And so it was cried in all the places through the realm. And then Sir Gareth sent his summons to all these knights and ladies that he had won in battle tofore, that they should be at his day of marriage at Kinkenadon by the sands.

And then Dame Lyonesse and the damosel Lynet with Sir Gringamore, rode to their castle; and a goodly and a rich ring she gave to Sir Gareth and he gave her another. And King Arthur gave her a rich bee of gold; and so she departed.

And King Arthur and his fellowship rode toward Kinkenadon, and Sir Gareth brought his lady on the way, and so came to the king again and rode with him.

Lord! the great cheer that Sir Launcelot made of Sir Gareth and he of him, for there was never no knight that Sir Gareth loved so well as he did Sir Launcelot; and ever for the most part he would be in Sir Launcelot's company; for after Sir Gareth had espied Sir Gawain's conditions, he withdrew himself from his brother Sir Gawain's fellowship, for he was vengeable, and where he hated he would be avenged with murder, and that hated Sir Gareth.

bee: bracelet.

CHAPTER 35: *Of the great royalty, and what officers were made at the feast of the wedding, and of the jousts at the feast*

So it drew fast to Michaelmas; and thither came Dame Lyonesse, the lady of the Castle Perilous, and her sister, Dame Lynet, with Sir Gringamore, her brother, with them, for he had the conduct of these ladies. And there they were lodged at the device of King Arthur. And upon Michaelmas Day the Bishop of Canterbury made the wedding betwixt Sir Gareth and the Lady Lyonesse with great solemnity.

And King Arthur made Gaheris to wed the Damosel Savage, that was Dame Lynet; and King Arthur made Sir Agravain to wed Dame Lyonesse's niece, a fair lady, her name was Dame Laurel.

And so when this solemnation was done, then came in the Green Knight, Sir Pertolepe, with thirty knights, and there he did homage and fealty to Sir Gareth, and these knights to hold of him for evermore. Also Sir Pertolepe said, 'I pray you that at this feast I may be your chamberlain.'

'With a good will,' said Sir Gareth, 'sith it liketh you to take so simple an office.'

Then came in the Red Knight, with three score knights with him, and did to Sir Gareth homage and fealty, and all those knights to hold of him for evermore. And then this Sir Perimones prayed Sir Gareth to grant him to be his chief butler at that high feast.

'I will well,' said Sir Gareth, 'that ye have this office, and it were better.'

Then came in Sir Persant of Inde, with an hundred knights with him, and there he did homage and fealty, and all his knights should do him service, and hold their lands of him for ever; and there he prayed Sir Gareth to make him his sewer-chief at the feast.

device: arrangement. *sewer-chief*: chief serving man.

'I will well,' said Sir Gareth, 'that ye have it, and it were better.'

Then came the Duke de la Rowse, with an hundred knights with him, and there he did homage and fealty to Sir Gareth, and so to hold their lands of him for ever. And he required Sir Gareth that he might serve him of the wine that day at that feast.

'I will well,' said Sir Gareth, 'and it were better.'

Then came in the Red Knight of the Red Launds, that was Sir Ironside, and he brought with him three hundred knights, and there he did homage and fealty, and all these knights to hold their lands of him for ever. And then he asked Sir Gareth to be his carver.

'I will well,' said Sir Gareth, 'and it please you.'

Then came into the court thirty ladies, and all they seemed widows, and those thirty ladies brought with them many fair gentlewomen. And all they kneeled down at once unto King Arthur and unto Sir Gareth, and there all those ladies told the king how Sir Gareth delivered them from the Dolorous Tower, and slew the Brown Knight without Pity: 'And therefore we, and our heirs for evermore, will do homage unto Sir Gareth of Orkney.'

So then the kings and queens, princes and earls, barons and many bold knights, went unto meat; and well may ye wit there were all manner of meat plenteously, all manner revels and games, with all manner of minstrelsy that was used in those days. Also there was great jousts three days. But the king would not suffer Sir Gareth to joust, because of his new bride; for, as the French book sayeth, that Dame Lyonesse desired of the king that none that were wedded should joust at that feast.

So the first day there jousted Sir Lamorak de Gales, for he overthrew thirty knights, and did passing marvellously deeds of arms; and then King Arthur made Sir Persant and his two brethren knights of the Round Table to their lives' end, and gave them great lands.

Also the second day there jousted Tristram best, and he

overthrew forty knights, and did there marvellous deeds of arms. And there King Arthur made Ironside, that was the Red Knight of the Red Launds, a knight of the Table Round to his life's end, and gave him great lands.

The third day there jousted Sir Launcelot du Lake, and he overthrew fifty knights, and did many marvellous deeds of arms, that all men wondered on him. And there King Arthur made the Duke de la Rowse a knight of the Round Table to his life's end, and gave him great lands to spend.

But when these jousts were done, Sir Lamorak and Sir Tristram departed suddenly, and would not be known, for the which King Arthur and all the court were sore displeased. And so they held the court forty days with great solemnity. And this Sir Gareth was a noble knight, and a well-ruled, and fair-languaged.

Thus endeth this tale of Sir Gareth of Orkney that wedded Dame Lyonesse of the Castle Perilous. And also Sir Gaheris wedded her sister, Dame Lynet, that was called the Damosel Savage. And Sir Agravain wedded Dame Laurel, a fair lady, and great and mighty lands with great riches gave with them King Arthur, that royally they might live till their lives' end.

Here followeth the viii. book, the which is the first book of Sir Tristram de Liones, and who was his father and his mother, and how he was born and fostered, and how he was made knight

Book VIII

CHAPTER 1: *How Sir Tristram de Liones was born, and how his mother died at his birth, wherefore she named him Tristram*

It was a king that hight Meliodas, and he was lord and king of the country of Liones, and this Meliodas was a likely knight as any was that time living. And by fortune he wedded King Mark's sister of Cornwall, and she was called Elizabeth, that was called both good and fair.

And at that time King Arthur reigned, and he was whole king of England, Wales, and Scotland, and of many other realms: howbeit there were many kings that were lords of many countries, but all they held their lands of King Arthur; for in Wales were two kings, and in the north were many kings; and in Cornwall and in the west were two kings; also in Ireland were two or three kings, and all were under the obeissance of King Arthur. So was the King of France, and the King of Brittany, and all the lordships unto Rome.

So when this Meliodas had been with his wife, within a while she waxed great with child, and she was a full meek lady, and well she loved her lord, and he her again, so there was great joy betwixt them.

Then there was a lady in that country that had loved King Meliodas long, and by no mean she never could get his love; therefore she let ordain upon a day, as King Meliodas rode on hunting, for he was a great chaser, and there by an enchantment she made him chase an hart by himself alone till that he came to an old castle, and there anon he was taken prisoner by the lady that him loved.

When Elizabeth, King Meliodas' wife,[1] missed her lord, and she was nigh out of her wit, and also, as great with child as she was, she took a gentlewoman with her, and ran into the forest to seek her lord. And when she was far in the forest she might no farther, for she began to travail fast of her child. And she had many grimly throes; her gentlewoman halp her all that she might, and so by miracle of Our Lady of Heaven she was delivered with great pains. But she had taken such cold for the default of help that deep draughts of death took her, that needs she must die and depart out of this world, there was none other boot.

And when this Queen Elizabeth saw that there was none other boot, then she made great dole, and said unto her gentlewoman, 'When ye see my lord, King Meliodas, recommend me unto him, and tell him what pains I endure here for his love and how I must die here for his sake for default of good help; and let him wit that I am full sorry to depart out of this world from him, therefore pray him to be friend to my soul. Now let me see my little child, for whom I have had all this sorrow.'

And when she saw him she said thus: 'Ah, my little son, thou hast murdered thy mother, and therefore I suppose, thou that art a murderer so young, thou art full likely to be a manly man in thine age. And because I shall die of the birth of thee, I charge thee, gentlewoman, that thou pray my lord, King Meliodas, that when he is christened let call him Tristram, that is as much to say as a sorrowful birth.'

And therewith this queen gave up the ghost and died. Then the gentlewoman laid her under an umbre of a great tree, and then she lapped the child as well as she might for cold.

Right so there came the barons, following after the queen, and when they saw that she was dead, and understood none other but the king was destroyed.

umbre: shadow

CHAPTER 2: *How the stepmother of Sir Tristram had ordained poison for to have poisoned Sir Tristram*

Then certain of them would have slain the child, because they would have been lords of the country of Liones. But then through the fair speech of the gentlewoman, and by the means that she made, the most part of the barons would not assent thereto. And then they let carry home the dead queen, and much dole was made for her.

Then this meanwhile Merlin delivered King Meliodas out of prison on the morn after his queen was dead. And so when the king was come home the most part of the barons made great joy. But the sorrow that the king made for his queen that might no tongue tell. So then the king let inter her richly, and after he let christen his child as his wife had commanded afore her death. And then he let call him Tristram, the sorrowful born child.

Then the King Meliodas endured seven years without a wife, and all this time Tristram was nourished well. Then it befell that King Meliodas wedded King Howel's daughter of Brittany, and anon she had children of King Meliodas; then was she heavy and wroth that her children should not rejoice the country of Liones, wherefore this queen ordained for to poison young Tristram.

So she let poison be put in a piece of silver in the chamber whereas Tristram and her children were together, unto that intent that when Tristram were thirsty he should drink that drink. And so it fell upon a day, the queen's son, as he was in that chamber, espied the piece with poison, and he weened it had been good drink, and because the child was thirsty he took the piece with poison and drank freely; and therewithal suddenly the child brast and was dead.

When the queen [of] Meliodas wist of the death of her son, wit ye well that she was heavy. But yet the king understood nothing of her treason. Notwithstanding the queen would not leave this, but eft she let ordain more poison, and put it in a piece.

And by fortune King Meliodas, her husband, found the piece with wine where was the poison, and he that was much thirsty took the piece for to drink thereout. And as he would have drunken thereof the queen espied him, and then she ran unto him, and pulled the piece from him suddenly. The king marvelled why she did so, and remembered him how her son was suddenly slain with poison. And then he took her by the hand, and said,

'Thou false traitress, thou shalt tell me what manner of drink this is, or else I shall slay thee.' And therewith he pulled out his sword, and sware a great oath that he should slay her but if she told him truth.

'Ah! mercy, my lord,' said she, 'and I shall tell you all.' And then she told him why she would have slain Tristram, because her children should rejoice his land.

'Well,' said King Meliodas, 'and therefore shall ye have the law.'

And so she was damned by the assent of the barons to be burnt; and then was there made a great fire, and right as she was at the fire to take her execution, young Tristram kneeled afore King Meliodas, and besought him to give him a boon.

'I will well,' said the king again.

Then said young Tristram, 'Give me the life of thy queen, my stepmother.'

'That is unrightfully asked,' said King Meliodas, 'for thou ought of right to hate her, for she would have slain thee with that poison and she might have had her will; and for thy sake most is my cause that she should die.'

'Sir,' said Tristram, 'as for that, I beseech you of your mercy that ye will forgive it her, and as for my part, God forgive it her, and I do; and so much it liked your highness to grant me my boon, for God's love I require you hold your promise.'

eft: afterwards.

'Sithen it is so,' said the king, 'I will that ye have her life. Then,' said the king, 'I give her to you, and go ye to the fire and take her, and do with her what ye will.'

So Sir Tristram went to the fire, and by the commandment of the king delivered her from the death. But after that King Meliodas would never have ado with her as at bed and board. But by the good means of young Tristram he made the king and her accorded. But then the king would not suffer young Tristram to abide no longer in his court.

CHAPTER 3: *How Sir Tristram was sent into France, and had one to govern him named Gouvernail, and how he learned to harp, hawk, and hunt*

And then he let ordain a gentleman that was well learned and taught, his name was Gouvernail; and then he sent young Tristram with Gouvernail into France to learn the language, and nurture, and deeds of arms. And there was Tristram more than seven years. And then when he well could speak the language, and had learned all that he might learn in that countries, then he came home to his father, King Meliodas, again.

And so Tristram learned to be an harper passing all other, that there was none such called in no country, and so in harping and on instruments of music he applied him in his youth for to learn. And after, as he growed in might and strength, he laboured ever in hunting and in hawking, so that never gentleman more, that ever we heard read of. And as the book saith, he began good measures of blowing of beasts of venery, and beasts of chase, and all manner of vermins, and all these terms we have yet of hawking and hunting. And therefore the book of venery, of hawking, and hunting, is called the book of Sir Tristram.

Wherefore, as meseemeth, all gentlemen that bearen old arms ought of right to honour Sir Tristram for the goodly terms that gentlemen have and use, and shall to the day of doom, that thereby in a manner all men of worship may dissever a gentleman from a yeoman, and from a yeoman a villain. For he that gentle is will draw him unto gentle tatches, and to follow the customs of noble gentlemen.

Thus Sir Tristram endured in Cornwall until he was big and strong, of the age of eighteen years. And then the King Meliodas had great joy of Sir Tristram, and so had the queen, his wife. For ever after in her life, because Sir Tristram saved her from the fire, and she did never hate him more after, but loved him ever after, and gave Tristram many great gifts; for every estate loved him, where that he went.

CHAPTER 4: *How Sir Marhaus came out of Ireland for to ask truage of Cornwall, or else he would fight therefore*

Then it befell that King Agwisance of Ireland sent unto King Mark of Cornwall for his truage, that Cornwall had paid many winters. And all that time King Mark was behind of the truage for seven years.

And King Mark and his barons gave unto the messenger of Ireland these words and answer, that they would none pay; and bad the messenger go unto his king Agwisance, 'And tell him we will pay him no truage, but tell your lord, and he will always have truage of us of Cornwall, bid him send a trusty knight of his land, that will fight for his right, and we shall find another for to defend our right.'

With this answer the messengers departed into Ireland. And when King Agwisance understood the answer of the messengers he was wonderly wroth. And then he called unto him Sir Marhaus, the good knight, that was nobly proved, and a knight of the Table Round. And this Marhaus was brother unto the Queen of Ireland. Then the king said thus: 'Fair brother, Sir Marhaus, I pray you go into Cornwall for

dissever: distinguish.

my sake, and do battle for our truage that of right we ought to have; and whatsomever ye spend ye shall have sufficiently more than ye shall need.'

'Sir,' said Marhaus, 'wit ye well that I shall not be loth to do battle in the right of you and your land with the best knight of the Table Round; for I know them, for the most part, what be their deeds; and for to advance my deeds and to increase my worship I will right gladly go unto this journey for our right.'

So in all haste there was made purveyance for Sir Marhaus, and he had all thing that to him needed; and so he departed out of Ireland, and arrived up in Cornwall even fast by the Castle of Tintagel. And when King Mark understood that he was there arrived to fight for Ireland, then made King Mark great sorrow when he understood that the good and noble knight Sir Marhaus was come. For they knew no knight that durst have ado with him. For at that time Sir Marhaus was called one of the famousest and renowned knights of the world.

And thus Sir Marhaus abode in the sea, and every day he sent unto King Mark for to pay the truage that was behind of seven year, other-else to find a knight to fight with him for the truage. This manner of message Sir Marhaus sent daily unto King Mark.

Then they of Cornwall let make cries in every place, that what knight would fight for to save the truage of Cornwall, he should be rewarded so that he should fare the better the term of his life.

Then some of the barons said to King Mark, and counselled him to send to the court of King Arthur for to seek Sir Launcelot du Luke, that was that time named for the marvelloust knight of all the world. Then there were some other barons that counselled the king not to do so, and said that it was labour in vain, because Sir Marhaus was a knight of the Round Table, 'therefore any of them will be loth to have ado with other, but if it were any knight at his own request would fight disguised and unknown.' So the king and all his barons assented that it was no boot to seek any knight of the Round Table.

This meanwhile came the language and the noise unto King Meliodas, how that Sir Marhaus abode battle fast by Tintagel, and how King Mark could find no manner knight to fight for him. When young Tristram heard of this he was wroth, and sore ashamed that there durst no knight in Cornwall have ado with Sir Marhaus of Ireland.

CHAPTER 5: *How Tristram enterprized the battle to fight for the truage of Cornwall, and how he was made knight*

Therewithal Tristram went unto his father, King Meliodas, and asked him counsel what was best to do for to recover Cornwall from truage. 'For, as meseemeth,' said Sir Tristram, 'it were shame that Sir Marhaus, the Queen's brother of Ireland, should go away unless that he were foughten withal.'

'As for that,' said King Meliodas, 'wit you well, son Tristram, that Sir Marhaus is called one of the best knights of the world, and knight of the Table Round; and therefore I know no knight in this country that is able to match with him.'

'Alas,' said Sir Tristram, 'that I am not made knight. And if Sir Marhaus should thus depart into Ireland, God let me never have worship; and I were made knight I should match him. And sir,' said Tristram, 'I pray you give me leave to ride to King Mark; and so ye be not displeased, of King Mark will I be made knight.'

'I will well,' said King Meliodas, 'that ye be ruled as your courage will rule you.'

Then Sir Tristram thanked his father much. And then he made him ready to ride into Cornwall.

In the meanwhile there came a messenger with letters of love from King Faramon of France's daughter unto Sir Tristram, that were full piteous letters, and in them were written many complaints of love; but Sir Tristram had no joy of her letters not regard unto her. Also she sent him a little brachet that was passing fair. But when the king's daughter understood that Sir Tristram would not love her, as the book saith, she died for sorrow. And then the same squire that brought the letter and the brachet came again unto Sir Tristram, as after ye shall hear in the tale.

So this young Sir Tristram rode unto his eme King Mark of Cornwall. And when he came there he heard say that there would no knight fight with Sir Marhaus.

Then yede Sir Tristram unto his eme and said, 'Sir, if ye will give me the order of knighthood, I will do battle with Sir Marhaus.'

'What are ye,' said the king, 'and from whence be ye comen?'

'Sir,' said Tristram, 'I come from King Meliodas that wedded your sister, and a gentleman wit ye well I am.'

King Mark beheld Sir Tristram and saw that he was but a young man of age, but he was passingly well made and big.

'Fair sir,' said the king, 'what is your name, and where were ye born?'

'Sir,' said he again, 'my name is Tristram, and in the country of Liones was I born.'

'Ye say well,' said the king; 'and if ye will do this battle I shall make you knight.'

'Therefore I come to you,' said Sir Tristram, 'and for none other cause.'

But then King Mark made him knight. And therewithal, anon as he had made him knight, he sent a messenger unto Sir Marhaus with letters that said that he had found a young knight ready for to take the battle to the uttermost.

'It may well be,' said Sir Marhaus; 'but tell King Mark I will not fight with no knight but he be of blood royal, that is to say, other king's son, other queen's son, born of a prince or princess.'

When King Mark understood that, he sent for Sir Tristram de Liones and told him what was the answer of Sir Marhaus.

eme: uncle.

Then said Sir Tristram. 'Sithen that he sayeth so, let him wit that I am comen of father side and mother side of as noble blood as he is: for, sir, now shall ye know that I am King Meliodas' son, born of your own sister, Dame Elizabeth, that died in the forest in the birth of me.'

'O Jesu,' said King Mark, 'ye are welcome fair nephew to me.'

Then in all the haste the king let horse Sir Tristram, and arm him in the best manner that might be had or gotten for gold or silver. And then King Mark sent unto Sir Marhaus, and did him to wit that a better born man than he was himself should fight with him, 'and his name is Sir Tristram de Liones, gotten of King Meliodas, and born of King Mark's sister.' Then was Sir Marhaus glad and blithe that he should fight with such a gentleman.

And so by the assent of King Mark and of Sir Marhaus they let ordain that they should fight within an island nigh Sir Marhaus' ships; and so was Sir Tristram put into a vessel both his horse and he, and all that to him longed both for his body and for his horse. Sir Tristram lacked nothing. And when King Mark and his barons of Cornwall beheld how young Sir Tristram departed with such a carriage to fight for the right of Cornwall, there was neither man ne woman of worship but they wept to see and understand so young a knight to jeopard himself for their right.

CHAPTER 6: *How Sir Tristram arrived into the island for to furnish the battle with Sir Marhaus*

So to shorten this tale, when Sir Tristram was arrived within the island he looked to the farther side, and there he saw at an anchor six ships nigh to the land; and under the shadow of the ships upon the land, there hoved the noble knight, Sir Marhaus of Ireland. Then Sir Tristram commanded his servant Gouvernail to bring his horse to the land, and dress his harness at all manner of rights.

And then when he had so done he mounted upon his horse; and when he was in his saddle well apparelled, and his shield dressed upon his shoulder, Tristram asked Gouvernail, 'Where is this knight that I shall have ado withal?'

'Sir,' said Gouvernail, 'see ye him not? I weened ye had seen him; yonder he hoveth under the umbre of his ships on horseback, with his spear in his hand and his shield upon his shoulder.'

'That is truth,' said the noble knight, Sir Tristram, 'now I see him well enough.'

Then he commanded his servant Gouvernail to go to his vessel again. 'And commend me unto mine eme King Mark, and pray him if that I be slain in this battle for to inter my body as him seemed best; and as for me, let him wit that I will never yield me for cowardice; and if I be slain and flee not, then they have lost no truage for me; and if so be that I flee or yield me as recreant, bid mine eme never bury me in Christian burials. And upon thy life,' said Sir Tristram to Gouvernail, 'come thou not nigh this island till that thou see me overcomen or slain, or else that I win yonder knight.'

So either departed from other sore weeping.

CHAPTER 7: *How Sir Tristram fought against Sir Marhaus and achieved his battle, and how Sir Marhaus fled to his ship*

And then Sir Marhaus advised Sir Tristram, and said thus: 'Young knight, Sir Tristram, what dost thou here? Me sore repenteth of thy courage, for wit thou well I have been assayed, and the best knights of this land have been assayed of my hand; and also I have matched with the best knights of the world, and therefore by my counsel return again unto thy vessel.'

'And fair knight, and well-proved knight,' said Sir Tristram, 'thou shalt well wit I may not forsake thee in this quarrel, for I am for thy sake made knight. And thou shalt well wit that I am a king's son born, and gotten upon a queen; and such promise I have made at my nephew's request and mine own seeking, that I shall fight with thee unto the uttermost, and deliver Cornwall from the old truage. And also wit thou well, Sir Marhaus, that this is the greatest cause that thou couragest me to have ado with thee, for thou art called one of the most renowned knights of the world, and because of that noise and fame that thou hast thou givest me courage to have ado with thee, for never yet was I proved with good knight; and sithen I took the order of knighthood this day, I am well pleased that I may have ado with so good a knight as thou art. And now wit thou well, Sir Marhaus, that I cast me to get worship on thy body; and if that I be not proved, I trust to God that I shall be worshipfully proved upon thy body, and to deliver the country of Cornwall for ever from all manner of truage from Ireland for ever.'

When Sir Marhaus had heard him say what he would, he said then thus again: 'Fair knight, sithen it is so that thou castest to win worship of me, I let thee wit worship may thou none lose by me if thou mayest stand me three strokes; for I let thee wit for my noble deeds, proved and seen, King Arthur made me knight of the Table Round.'

Then they began to fewter their spears, and they met so fiercely together that they smote either other down, both horse and all. But Sir Marhaus smote Sir Tristram a great wound in the side with his spear, and then they avoided their horses, and pulled out their swords, and threw their shields afore them. And then they lashed together as men that were wild and courageous. And when they had stricken so together long, then they left their strokes, and foined at their breaths and visors; and when they saw that that might not prevail them, then they hurtled together like rams to bear either other down.

Thus they fought still more than half a day, and either were wounded passing sore, that the blood ran down freshly from them upon the ground. By then Sir Tristram waxed

cast: intend.

more fresher than Sir Marhaus, and better winded and bigger; and with a mighty stroke he smote Sir Marhaus upon the helm such a buffet that it went through his helm, and through the coif of steel, and through the brain-pan, and the sword stuck so fast in the helm and in his brain-pan that Sir Tristram pulled thrice at his sword or ever he might pull it out from his head; and there Marhaus fell down on his knees, the edge of Tristram's sword left in his brain-pan. And suddenly Sir Marhaus rose grovelling, and threw his sword and his shield from him, and so ran to his ships and fled his way, and Sir Tristram had ever his shield and his sword.

And when Sir Tristram saw Sir Marhaus withdraw him, he said, 'Ah ! sir knight of the Round Table, why withdrawest thou thee? Thou dost thyself and thy kin great shame, for I am but a young knight, or now I was never proved, and rather than I should withdraw me from thee, I had rather be hew in [an] hundred pieces.'

Sir Marhaus answered no word but yede his way sore groaning.

'Well, sir knight,' said Sir Tristram, 'I promise thee thy sword and thy shield shall be mine; and thy shield shall I wear in all places where I ride on mine adventures, and in the sight of King Arthur and all the Round Table.'

CHAPTER 8: *How Sir Marhaus after that he was arrived in Ireland died of the stroke that Sir Tristram had given to him, and how Tristram was hurt*

Anon Sir Marhaus and his fellowship departed into Ireland. And as soon as he came to the king, his brother, he let search his wounds. And when his head was searched a piece of Sir Tristram's sword was founden therein, and might never be had out of his head for no surgeons, and so he died of Sir Tristram's sword; and that piece of the sword the queen, his

coif: close fitting cap. *brain-pan*: skull.

sister, kept it for ever with her, for she thought to be revenged and she might.

Now turn we again unto Sir Tristram, that was sore wounded, and full sore bled that he might not within a little while, when he had taken cold, unnethe stir him of his limbs. And then he set him down softly upon a little hill, and bled fast. Then anon came Gouvernail, his man, with his vessel; and the king and his barons came with procession against him.

And when he was come unto the land, King Mark took him in his arms, and the king and Sir Dinas, the Seneschal, led Sir Tristram into the Castle of Tintagel. And then was he searched in the best manner, and laid in his bed. And when King Mark saw his wounds he wept heartily and so did all his lords.

'So God me help,' said King Mark, 'I would not for all my lands that my nephew died.'

So Sir Tristram lay there a month and more, and ever he was like to die of that stroke that Sir Marhaus smote him first with the spear. For, as the French book saith, the spear's head was envenomed, that Sir Tristram might not be whole. Then was King Mark and all his barons passing heavy, for they deemed none other but that Sir Tristram should not recover. Then the king let send after all manner of leeches and surgeons, both unto men and women, and there was none that would behote him the life.

Then came there a lady that was a right wise lady, and she said plainly unto King Mark, and to Sir Tristram, and to all his barons, that he should never be whole but if Sir Tristram went in the same country that the venom came from, and in that country should he be holpen or else never. Thus said the lady unto the king. When King Mark understood that, he let purvey for Sir Tristram a fair vessel, well victualled, and therein was put Sir Tristram, and Gouvernail with him, and Sir Tristram took his harp with him, and so he was put into the sea to sail into Ireland.

And so by good fortune he arrived up in Ireland, even fast

by a castle where the king and the queen was; and at his arrival he sat and harped in his bed a merry lay, such one heard they never none in Ireland afore that time. And when it was told the king and the queen of such a knight that was such an harper, anon the king sent for him, and let search his wounds, and then asked him his name.

Then he answered, 'I am of the country of Liones, and my name is Tramtrist, that thus was wounded in a battle as I fought for a lady's right.'

'So God me help,' said King Agwisance, 'ye shall have all the help in this land that ye may have here. But I let you wit, in Cornwall I had a great loss as ever had king, for there I lost the best knight of the world; his name was Marhaus, a full noble knight, and knight of the Table Round;' and there he told Sir Tristram wherefore Sir Marhaus was slain. Sir Tristram made semblant as he had been sorry, and better knew he how it was than the king.

CHAPTER 9: *How Sir Tristram was put to the keeping of La Beale Isoud first for to be healed of his wound*

Then the king for great favour made Tramtrist to be put in his daughter's ward and keeping, because she was a noble surgeon. And when she had searched him she found in the bottom of his wound that therein was poison, and so she healed him within a while; and therefore Tramtrist cast great love to La Beale Isoud, for she was at that time the fairest maid and lady of the world. And there Tramtrist learned her to harp, and she began to have a great fantasy unto him. And at that time Sir Palomides, the Saracen, was in that country, and well cherished with the king and the queen And every day Sir Palomides drew unto La Beale Isoud and proffered her many gifts, for he loved her passingly well. All that espied Tramtrist, and full well knew he Sir Palomides for a noble knight and a mighty man. And wit ye well Sir Tramtrist had great despite at Sir Palomides, for La Beale

Isoud told Tramtrist that Palomides was in will to be chrisened for her sake. Thus was there great envy betwixt Tramtrist and Sir Palomides.

Then it befell that King Agwisance let cry a great jousts and a great tournament for a lady that was called the Lady of the Launds, and she was nigh cousin unto the king. And what man won her, three days after he should wed her and have all her lands. This cry was made in England, Wales, Scotland, and also in France and in Brittany.

It befell upon a day La Beale Isoud came unto Sir Tramtrist, and told him of this tournament.

He answered and said, 'Fair lady, I am but a feeble knight, and but late I had been dead had not your good ladyship been. Now, fair lady, what would ye I should do in this matter? Well ye wot, my lady, that I may not joust.'

'Ah, Tramtrist,' said La Beale Isoud, 'why will ye not have ado at that tournament? Well I wot Sir Palomides shall be there, and to do what he may; and therefore Tramtrist, I pray you for to be there, for else Sir Palomides is like to win the degree.'

'Madam,' said Tramtrist, 'as for that, it may be so, for he is a proved knight, and I am but a young knight and late made; and the first battle that I did it mishapped me to be sore wounded as ye see. But and I wist ye would be my better lady, at that tournament I will be, so that ye will keep my counsel and let no creature have knowledge that I shall joust but yourself, and such as ye will to keep your counsel, my poor person shall I jeopard there for your sake, that, peradventure, Sir Palomides shall know when that I come.'

'Thereto,' said La Beale Isoud, 'do your best, and as I can,' said La Beale Isoud, 'I shall purvey horse and armour for you at my device.'

'As ye will so be it,' said Sir Tramtrist, 'I will be at your commandment.'

So at the day of jousts there came Sir Palomides with a black shield, and he overthrew many knights, that all the people had marvel of him. For he put to the worse Sir

Gawain, Gaheris, Agravain, Bagdemagus, Kay, Dodinas le Savage, Sagramore le Desirous, Gumret le Petit, and Griflet le Fise de Dieu. All these the first day Sir Palomides struck down to the earth. And then all manner of knights were adread of Sir Palomides, and many called him the Knight with the Black Shield. So that day Sir Palomides had great worship.

Then came King Agwisance unto Tramtrist, and asked him why he would not joust.

'Sir,' he said, 'I was but late hurt, and as yet I dare not adventure me.'

Then came there the same squire that was sent from the king's daughter of France unto Sir Tristram. And when he had espied Sir Tristram he fell flat to his feet. All that espied La Beale Isoud, what courtesy the squire made unto Sir Tristram. And therewithal suddenly Sir Tristram ran unto his squire, whose name was Hebes le Renoumes, and prayed him heartily in no wise to tell his name.

'Sir,' said Hebes, 'I will not discover your name but if ye command me.'

CHAPTER 10: *How Sir Tristram won the degree at a tournament in Ireland, and there made Palomides to bear no harness in a year*

Then Sir Tristram asked him what he did in those countries.

'Sir,' he said, 'I came hither with Sir Gawain for to be made knight, and if it please you, of your hands that I may be made knight.'

'Await upon me as tomorn secretly, and in the field I shall make you a knight.'

Then had La Beale Isoud great suspicion unto Tramtrist, that he was some man of worship proved, and therewith she comforted herself, and cast more love unto him than she had done tofore.

And so on the morn Sir Palomides made him ready to

come into the field as he did the first day. And there he smote down the King with the Hundred Knights, and the King of Scots. Then had La Beale Isoud ordained and well arrayed Sir Tristram in white horse and harness. And right so she let put him out at a privy postern, and so he came into the field as it had been a bright angel. And anon Sir Palomides espied him, and therewith he fewtered a spear unto Sir Tramtrist, and he again unto him. And there Sir Tristram smote down Sir Palomides unto the earth.

And then there was a great noise of people: some said Sir Palomides had a fall, some said the Knight with the Black Shield had a fall. And wit you well La Beale Isoud was passing glad. And then Sir Gawain and his fellows nine had marvel what knight it might be that had smitten down Sir Palomides. Then would there none joust with Tramtrist, but all that there were forsook him, most and least.

Then Sir Tristram made Hebes a knight, and caused him to put himself forth, and did right well that day. So after Sir Hebes held him with Sir Tristram.

And when Sir Palomides had received this fall, wit ye well that he was sore ashamed, and as privily as he might he withdrew him out of the field. All that espied Sir Tristram, and lightly he rode after Sir Palomides and overtook him, and bad him turn, for better he would assay him or ever he departed. Then Sir Palomides turned him, and either lashed at other with their swords. But at the first stroke Sir Tristram smote down Palomides, and gave him such a stroke upon the head that he fell to the earth. So then Tristram bad yield him, and do his commandment, or else he would slay him. When Sir Palomides beheld his countenance, he dread his buffets so, that he granted all his askings.

'Well said,' said Sir Tristram, 'this shall be your charge: First, upon pain of your life that ye forsake my lady La Beale Isoud, and in no manner wise that ye draw not to her. Also this twelvemonth and a day that ye bear none armour nor none harness of war. Now promise me this, or here shalt thou die.'

'Alas,' said Palomides, 'for ever I am ashamed.'

Then he sware as Sir Tristram had commanded him. Then for despite and anger Sir Palomides cut off his harness, and threw them away.

And so Sir Tristram turned again to the castle where was La Beale Isoud; and by the way he met with a damosel that asked after Sir Launcelot, that won the Dolorous Guard worshipfully; and this damosel asked Sir Tristram what he was. For it was told her that it was he that smote down Sir Palomides, by whom the ten knights of King Arthur's were smitten down. Then the damosel prayed Sir Tristram to tell her what he was, and whether that he were Sir Launcelot du Lake, for she deemed that there was no knight in the world might do such deeds of arms but it were Launcelot.

'Fair damosel,' said Sir Tristram, 'wit ye well that I am not Sir Launcelot, for I was never of such prowess, but in God is all that He may make me as good a knight as the good knight Sir Launcelot.'

'Now, gentle knight,' said she, 'put up thy visor;' and when she beheld his visage she thought she saw never a better man's visage, nor a better faring knight. And then when the damosel knew certainly that he was not Sir Launcelot, then she took her leave, and departed from him.

And then Sir Tristram rode privily unto the postern, where kept him La Beale Isoud, and there she made him good cheer, and thanked God of his good speed. So anon, within a while the king and the queen understood that it was Tramtrist that smote down Sir Palomides; then was he much made of, more than he was before.

CHAPTER 11: *How the queen espied that Sir Tristram had slain her brother Sir Marhaus by his sword, and in what jeopardy he was*

Thus was Sir Tramtrist long there well cherished with the king and the queen, and namely with La Beale Isoud.

So upon a day the queen and La Beale Isoud made a bain for Sir Tramtrist. And when he was in his bain the queen and Isoud, her daughter, roamed up and down in the chamber; and therewhiles Gouvernail and Hebes attended upon Tramtrist, and the queen beheld his sword there as it lay upon his bed. And then by unhap the queen drew out his sword and beheld it a long while, and both they thought it a passing fair sword; but within a foot and an half of the point there was a great piece thereof out broken of the edge. And when the queen espied that gap in the sword, she remembered her of a piece of a sword that was found in the brain-pan of Sir Marhaus, the good knight that was her brother.

'Alas then,' said she unto her daughter, La Beale Isoud, 'this is the same traitor knight that slew my brother, thine eme.'

When Isoud heard her say so she was passing sore abashed, for passing well she loved Tramtrist, and full well she knew the cruelness of her mother the queen.

Anon therewithal the queen went unto her own chamber, and sought her coffer, and there she took out the piece of the sword that was pulled out of Sir Marhaus' head after that he was dead. And then she ran with that piece of iron to the sword that lay upon the bed. And when she put that piece of steel and iron unto the sword, it was as meet as it might be when it was new broken.

And then the queen gripped that sword in her hand fiercely, and with all her might she ran straight upon Tramtrist where he sat in his bain, and there she had rived him through had not Sir Hebes gotten her in his arms, and pulled the sword from her, and else she had thrust him through.

Then when she was letted of her evil will she ran to the King Agwisance, her husband, and said on her knees, 'O my lord, here have ye in your house that traitor knight that slew my brother and your servant, that noble knight, Sir Marhaus.'

bain: bath.

'Who is that,' said King Agwisance, 'and where is he?'

'Sir,' she said, 'it is Sir Tramtrist, the same knight that my daughter healed.'

'Alas,' said the king, 'therefore am I right heavy, for he is a full noble knight as ever I saw in field. But I charge you,' said the king to the queen, 'that ye have not ado with that knight, but let me deal with him.'

Then the king went into the chamber unto Sir Tramtrist, and then was he gone unto his chamber, and the king found him all ready armed to mount upon his horse. When the king saw him all ready armed to go unto horseback, the king said,

'Nay, Tramtrist, it will not avail to compare thee against me; but thus much I shall do for my worship and for thy love; in so much as thou art within my court it were no worship for me to slay thee; therefore upon this condition I will give thee leave for to depart from this court in safety, so thou wilt tell me who was thy father, and what is thy name, and if thou slew Sir Marhaus, my brother.'

CHAPTER 12: *How Sir Tristram departed from the king and La Beale Isoud out of Ireland for to come into Cornwall*

'Sir,' said Tristram, 'now I shall tell you all the truth: my father's name is Sir Meliodas, King of Liones, and my mother hight Elizabeth, that was sister unto King Mark of Cornwall; and my mother died of me in the forest, and because thereof she commanded or she died that when I were christened they should christen me Tristram; and because I would not be known in this country I turned my name and let me call Tramtrist; and for the truage of Cornwall I fought for my eme's sake, and for the right of Cornwall that ye had posseded many years. And wit ye well,' said Tristram unto the king, 'I did the battle for the love of mine uncle, King Mark, and for the love of the country of Cornwall, and for to increase mine honour; for that same day that I fought with Sir Marhaus I was made knight, and never or then did I battle with no knight, and from me he went alive, and left his shield and his sword behind.'

'So God me help,' said the king, 'I may not say but ye did as a knight should, and it was your part to do for your quarrel, and to increase your worship as a knight should; howbeit I may not maintain you in this country with my worship, unless that I should displease my barons, and my wife and her kin.'

'Sir,' said Tristram, 'I thank you of your good lordship that I have had with you here, and the great goodness my lady, your daughter, hath showed me, and therefore,' said Sir Tristram, 'it may so happen that ye shall win more by my life than by my death, for in the parts of England it may happen I may do you service at some season, that ye shall be glad that ever ye showed me your good lordship. With more I promise you as I am true knight, that in all places I shall be my lady, your daughter's, servant and knight in right and in wrong, and I shall never fail her to do as much as a knight may do. Also I beseech your good grace that I may take my leave at my lady, your daughter, and at all the barons and knights.'

'I will well,' said the king.

Then Sir Tristram went unto La Beale Isoud and took his leave of her. And then he told her all, what he was, and how he had changed his name because he would not be known, and how a lady told him that he[1] should never be whole till he came into this country where the poison was made, 'wherethrough I was near my death had not your ladyship been.'

'O gentle knight,' said La Beale Isoud, 'full woe am I of thy departing, for I saw never man that I ought so good will to.' And therewithal she wept heartily.

'Madam,' said Sir Tristram, 'ye shall understand that my name is Sir Tristram de Liones, gotten of King Meliodas, and born of his queen. And I promise you faithfully that I shall be all the days of my life your knight.'

'Gramercy,' said La Beale Isoud, 'and I promise you there-against that I shall not be married this seven years but by your assent; and to whom that ye will I shall be married to, him will I have, and he will have me if ye will consent.'

And then Sir Tristram gave her a ring, and she gave him another; and therewith he departed from her, leaving her making great dole and lamentation.

And he straight went unto the court among all the barons, and there he took his leave at most and least, and openly he said among them all, 'Fair lords, now it is so that I must depart. If there be any man here that I have offended unto, or that any man be with me grieved, let complain him here afore me or that ever I depart, and I shall amend it unto my power. And if there be any that will proffer me wrong, or say of me wrong or shame behind my back, say it now or never, and here is my body to make it good, body against body.'

And all they stood still, there was not one that would say one word; yet were there some knights that were of the queen's blood, and of Sir Marhaus' blood, but they would not meddle with him.

CHAPTER 13: *How Sir Tristram and King Mark hurted each other for the love of a knight's wife*

So Sir Tristram departed, and took the sea, and with good wind he arrived up at Tintagel in Cornwall. And when King Mark was whole in his prosperity there came tidings that Sir Tristram was arrived, and whole of his wounds: thereof was King Mark passing glad, and so were all the barons. And when he saw his time he rode unto his father, King Meliodas, and there he had all the cheer that the king and the queen could make him. And then largely King Meliodas and his queen departed of their lands and goods to Sir Tristram.

Then by the license of King Meliodas, his father, he returned again unto the court of King Mark, and there he lived

at most and least: of everyone.

in great joy long time, until at the last there befell a jealousy and an unkindness betwixt King Mark and Sir Tristram, for they loved both one lady. And she was an earl's wife that hight Sir Segwarides. And this lady loved Sir Tristram passingly well. And he loved her again, for she was a passing fair lady, and that espied Sir Tristram well. Then King Mark understood that and was jealous, for King Mark loved her passingly well.

So it fell upon a day this lady sent a dwarf unto Sir Tristram, and bad him, as he loved her, that he would be with her the night next following. 'Also she charged you that ye come not to her but if ye be well armed, for her lord was called a good knight.'

Sir Tristram answered to the dwarf, 'Recommend me unto my lady, and tell her I will not fail but I will be with her the term that she hath set me.'

And with this answer the dwarf departed. And King Mark espied that the dwarf was with Sir Tristram upon message from Segwarides' wife; then King Mark sent for the dwarf, and when he was comen he made the dwarf by force to tell him all, why and wherefore that he came on message from Sir Tristram.

'Now,' said King Mark, 'go where thou wilt, and upon pain of death that thou say no word that thou spakest with me.'

So the dwarf departed from the king. And that same night that the steven was set betwixt Segwarides' wife and Sir Tristram, King Mark armed him, and made him ready, and took two knights of his council with him; and so he rode afore for to abide by the way, for to await upon Sir Tristram.

And as Sir Tristram came riding upon his way with his spear in his hand, King Mark came hurtling upon him with his two knights suddenly. And all three smote him with their spears, and King Mark hurt Sir Tristram on the breast right sore. And then Sir Tristram fewtered his spear, and smote his uncle, King Mark, so sore, that he rashed him to

steven: assignation. *rashed*: dragged.

the earth, and bruised him that he lay still in a swoon, and long it was or ever he might wield himself. And then he ran to the one knight, and eft to the other, and smote them to the cold earth, that they lay still.

And therewithal Sir Tristram rode forth sore wounded to the lady, and found her abiding him at a postern.

CHAPTER 14: *How Sir Tristram lay with the lady, and how her husband fought with Sir Tristram*

And there she welcomed him fair, and either halsed other in arms, and so she let put up his horse in the best wise, and then she unarmed him. And so they supped lightly, and went to bed with great joy and pleasance; and so in his raging he took no keep of his green wound that King Mark had given him. And so Sir Tristram be-bled both the over sheet and the nether, and pillows, and head sheet.

And within a while there came one afore, that warned her that her lord was near hand within a bow draught. So she made Sir Tristram to arise, and so he armed him, and took his horse, and so departed. By then was come Segwarides, her lord, and when he found her bed troubled and broken, and went near and beheld it by candle light, then he saw that there had lain a wounded knight.

'Ah, false traitress,' then he said, 'why hast thou betrayed me?' And therewithal he swung out a sword, and said, 'But if thou tell me who hath been here, here thou shalt die.'

'Ah, my lord, mercy,' said the lady, and held up her hands, saying, 'Slay me not, and I shall tell you all who hath been here.'

'Tell anon' said Segwarides, 'to me all the truth.'

Anon for dread she said, 'Here was Sir Tristram with me, and by the way as he came to meward, he was sore wounded.'

'Ah, false traitress,' said Segwarides, 'where is he become?'

'Sir,' she said, 'he is armed, and departed on horseback, not yet hence half a mile.'

'Ye say well,' said Segwarides.

Then he armed him lightly, and gat his horse, and rode after Sir Tristram that rode straightway unto Tintagel. And within a while he overtook Sir Tristram, and then he bad him, 'Turn, false traitor-knight.'

And Sir Tristram anon turned him against him. And therewithal Segwarides smote Sir Tristram with a spear that it all to-brast; and then he swung out his sword and smote fast at Sir Tristram.

'Sir knight,' said Sir Tristram, 'I counsel you that ye smite no more, howbeit for the wrongs that I have done you I will forbear you as long as I may.'

'Nay,' said Segwarides, 'that shall not be, for either thou shalt die or I.'

Then Sir Tristram drew out his sword, and hurtled his horse unto him fiercely, and through the waist of the body he smote Sir Segwarides that he fell to the earth in a swoon.

And so Sir Tristram departed and left him there. And so he rode unto Tintagel and took his lodging secretly, for he would not be known that he was hurt. Also Sir Segwarides' men rode after their master, whom they found lying in the field sore wounded, and brought him home on his shield, and there he lay long or that he were whole, but at the last he recovered.

Also King Mark would not be aknown of that Sir Tristram and he had met that night. And as for Sir Tristram, he knew not that King Mark had met with him. And so the king's assistance came to Sir Tristram, to comfort him as he lay sick in his bed. But as long as King Mark lived he loved never Sir Tristram after that; though there was fair speech, love was there none.

And thus it passed many weeks and days, and all was forgiven and forgotten; for Sir Segwarides durst not have ado with Sir Tristram, because of his noble prowess, and also because he was nephew unto King Mark; therefore he let it overslip: for he that hath a privy hurt is loth to have a shame outward.

CHAPTER 15: *How Sir Bleoberis demanded the fairest lady in King Mark's court, whom he took away, and how he was foughten with*

Then it befell upon a day that the good knight Bleoberis de Ganis, brother to Blamor de Ganis, and nigh cousin unto the good knight Sir Launcelot du Lake, this Bleoberis came unto the court of King Mark, and there he asked of King Mark a boon, to give him what gift that he would ask in his court. When the king heard him ask so, he marvelled of his asking, but because he was a knight of the Round Table, and of a great renown, King Mark granted him his whole asking.

'Then,' said Sir Bleoberis, 'I will have the fairest lady in your court that me list to choose.'

'I may not say nay,' said King Mark; 'now choose at your adventure.'

And so Sir Bleoberis did choose Sir Segwarides' wife, and took her by the hand, and so went his way with her; and so he took his horse and gart set her behind his squire, and rode upon his way.

When Sir Segwarides heard tell that his lady was gone with a knight of King Arthur's court, then he armed him and rode after that knight for to rescue his lady. So when Bleoberis was gone with this lady, King Mark and all the court was wroth that she was away.

Then there were certain ladies that knew that there was great love between Sir Tristram and her, and also that lady loved Sir Tristram above all other knights. Then there was one lady that rebuked Sir Tristram in the horriblest wise, and called him coward knight, that he would for shame of his knighthood see a lady so shamefully be taken away from his uncle's court. But she meant that either of them had loved other with entire heart. But Sir Tristram answered her thus:

'Fair lady, it is not my part to have ado in such matters while her lord and husband is present here; and if it had been that her lord had not been here in this court, then for the worship of this court peradventure I would have been her champion, and if so be Sir Segwarides speed not well, it may happen that I will speak with that good knight or ever he pass from this country.'

Then within a while came one of Sir Segwarides' squires, and told in the court that Sir Segwarides was beaten sore and wounded to the point of death; 'as he would have rescued his lady, Sir Bleoberis overthrew him and sore hath wounded him.'

Then was King Mark heavy thereof, and all the court. When Sir Tristram heard of this he was ashamed and sore grieved; and then was he soon armed and on horseback, and Gouvernail, his servant, bare his shield and spear.

And so as Sir Tristram rode fast he met with Sir Andred his cousin, that by the commandment of King Mark was sent to bring forth, and ever it lay in his power, two knights of Arthur's court, that rode by the country to seek their adventures. When Sir Tristram saw Sir Andred he asked him what tidings.

'So God me help,' said Sir Andred, 'there was never worse with me, for here by the commandment of King Mark I was sent to fetch two knights of King Arthur's court, and that one beat me and wounded me, and set nought by my message.'

'Fair cousin,' said Sir Tristram, 'ride on your way, and if I may meet them it may happen I shall revenge you.'

So Sir Andred rode into Cornwall, and Sir Tristram rode after the two knights, the which one hight Sagramore le Desirous, and the other hight Dodinas le Savage.

CHAPTER 16: *How Sir Tristram fought with two knights of the Round Table*

Then within a while Sir Tristram saw them afore him, two likely knights.

'Sir,' said Gouvernail unto his master, 'Sir, I would counsel you not to have ado with them, for they be two proved knights of Arthur's court.'

'As for that,' said Sir Tristran, 'have ye no doubt but I will have ado with them to increase my worship, for it is many day sithen I did any deeds of arms.'

'Do as ye list,' said Gouvernail.

And therewithal anon Sir Tristram asked them from whence they came, and whither they would, and what they did in those marches.

Sir Sagramore looked upon Sir Tristram, and had scorn of his words, and asked him again, 'Fair knight, be ye a knight of Cornwall?'

'Whereby ask ye it?' said Sir Tristram.

'For it is seldom seen,' said Sir Sagramore, 'that ye Cornish knights be valiant men of arms; for which these two hours there met us one of you Cornish knights, and great words he spake, and anon with little might he was laid to the earth. And, as I trow,' said Sir Sagramore, 'ye shall have the same handsel that he had.'

'Fair lords,' said Sir Tristram, 'it may so happen that I may better withstand than he did, and whether ye will or nill I will have ado with you, because he was my cousin that ye beat. And therefore here do your best, and wit ye well but if ye quit you the better here upon this ground, one knight of Cornwall shall beat you both.'

When Sir Dodinas le Savage heard him say so he gat a spear in his hand, and said, 'Sir knight, keep[1] thyself.'

And then they departed and came together as it had been thunder. And Sir Dodinas' spear brast in sunder, but Sir Tristram smote him with a more might, that he smote him clean over the horse's croup, that nigh he had broken his neck.

When Sir Sagramore saw his fellow have such a fall he marvelled what knight he might be. And he dresseth his spear with all his might, and Sir Tristram against him, and they came together as the thunder, and there Sir Tristram

handsel: gift.

smote Sir Sagramore a strong buffet, that he bare his horse and him to the earth, and in the falling he brake his thigh.

When this was done Sir Tristram asked them, 'Fair knights, will ye any more? Be there no bigger knights in the court of King Arthur? It is to you shame to say of us knights of Cornwall dishonour, for it may happen a Cornish knight may match you.'

'That is truth,' said Sir Sagramore, 'that have we well proved; but I require thee,' said Sir Sagramore, 'tell us your right name, by the faith and troth that ye owe to the high order of knighthood.'

'Ye charge me with a great thing,' said Sir Tristram, 'and sithen ye list to wit it, ye shall know and understand that my name is Sir Tristram de Liones, King Meliodas' son, and nephew unto King Mark.'

Then were they two knights fain that they had met with Tristram, and so they prayed him to abide in their fellowship.

'Nay,' said Sir Tristram, 'for I must have ado with one of your fellows, his name is Sir Bleoberis de Ganis.'

'God speed you well,' said Sir Sagramore and Dodinas.

Sir Tristram departed and rode onward on his way. And then was he ware before him in a valley where rode Sir Bleoberis with Sir Segwarides' lady that rode behind his squire upon a palfrey.

CHAPTER 17: *How Sir Tristram fought with Sir Bleoberis for a lady, and how the lady was put to choice to whom she would go*

Then Sir Tristram rode more than a pace until that he had overtaken him. Then spake Sir Tristram:

'Abide,' he said, 'knight of Arthur's court, bring again that lady, or deliver her to me.'

'I will do neither,' said Bleoberis, 'for I dread no Cornish knight so sore that me list to deliver her.'

'Why,' said Sir Tristram, 'may not a Cornish knight do as well as another knight? This same day two knights of your court within this three mile met with me, and or ever we departed they found a Cornish knight good enough for them both.'

'What were their names?' said Bleoberis.

'They told me,' said Sir Tristram, 'that the one of them hight Sir Sagramore le Desirous, and the other hight Dodinas le Savage.'

'Ah,' said Sir Bleoberis, 'have ye met with them? So God me help, they were two good knights and men of great worship, and if ye have beat them both ye must needs be a good knight; but if it so be ye have beat them both, yet shall ye not fear me, but ye shall beat me or ever ye have this lady.'

'Then defend you,' said Sir Tristram.

So they departed and came together like thunder, and either bare other down, horse and all, to the earth. Then they avoided their horses, and lashed together eagerly with swords, and mightily, now tracing and traversing on the right hand and on the left hand more than two hours. And sometime they rashed together with such a might that they lay both grovelling on the ground. Then Sir Bleoberis de Ganis start aback, and said thus:

'Now, gentle good knight, a while hold your hands, and let us speak together.'

'Say what ye will,' said Tristram, 'and I will answer you.'

'Sir,' said Bleoberis, 'I would wit of whence ye be, and of whom ye be come, and what is your name?'

'So God me help,' said Sir Tristram, 'I fear not to tell you my name. Wit ye well I am King Meliodas' son, and my mother is King Mark's sister, and my name is Sir Tristram de Liones, and King Mark is mine uncle.'

'Truly,' said Bleoberis, 'I am right glad of you, for ye are he that slew Marhaus the knight, hand for hand in an island, for the truage of Cornwall; also ye overcame Sir Palomides the good knight, at a tournament in an island, where he beat[1] Sir Gawain and his nine fellows.'

'So God me help,' said Sir Tristram, 'wit ye well that I am the same knight; now I have told you my name, tell me yours with good will.'

'Wit ye well that my name is Sir Bleoberis de Ganis, and my brother hight Sir Blamor de Ganis, that is called a good knight, and we be sister's children unto my lord Sir Launcelot du Lake, that we call one of the best knights of the world.'

'That is truth,' said Sir Tristram, 'Sir Launcelot is called peerless of courtesy and of knighthood; and for his sake,' said Sir Tristram, 'I will not with my good will fight no more with you, for the great love I have to Sir Launcelot du Lake.'

'In good faith,' said Bleoberis, 'as for me I will be loth to fight with you; but sithen ye follow me here to have this lady, I shall proffer you kindness, courtesy, and gentleness right here upon this ground. This lady shall be betwixt us both, and to whom that she will go, let him have her in peace.'

'I will well,' said Tristram, 'for, as I deem, she will leave you and come to me.'

'Ye shall prove it anon,' said Bleoberis.

CHAPTER 18: *How the lady forsook Sir Tristram and abode with Sir Bleoberis, and how she desired to go to her husband*

So when she was set betwixt them both she said these words unto Sir Tristram:

'Wit ye well, Sir Tristram de Liones, that but late thou was the man in the world that I most loved and trusted, and I weened thou hadst loved me again above all ladies; but when thou sawest this knight lead me away thou madest no cheer to rescue me, but suffered my lord Segwarides ride after me; but until that time I weened thou haddest loved me, and therefore now I will leave thee, and never love thee more.'

And therewithal she went unto Sir Bleoberis. When Sir Tristram saw her do so he was wonderly wroth with that lady, and ashamed to come to the court.

'Sir Tristram,' said Sir Bleoberis, 'ye are in the default for I hear by these lady's words she before this day trusted you above all earthly knights, and, as she sayeth, ye have deceived her, therefore wit ye well, there may no man hold that will away; and rather than ye should be heartily displeased with me I would ye had her, and she would abide with you.'

'Nay,' said the lady, 'so God me help I will never go with him; for he that I loved most I weened he had loved me. And therefore, Sir Tristram,' she said, 'ride as thou came, for though thou haddest overcome this knight, as ye was likely, with thee never would I have gone. And I shall pray this knight so fair of his knighthood, that or ever he pass this country that he will lead me to the abbey there my lord Sir Segwarides lieth.'

'So God me help,' said Bleoberis, 'I let you wit, good knight Sir Tristram, because King Mark gave me the choice of a gift in this court, and so this lady liked me best, notwithstanding she is wedded and hath a lord, and I have fulfilled my quest, she shall be sent unto her husband again, and in especial most for your sake, Sir Tristram; and if she would go with you I would ye had her.'

'I thank you,' said Sir Tristram, 'but for her love I shall beware what manner a lady I shall love or trust; for had her lord, Sir Segwarides been away from the court, I should have been the first that should have followed you; but sithen ye have refused me, as I am true knight I shall her know passingly well that I shall love or trust.'

And so they took their leave one from the other and departed. And so Sir Tristram rode unto Tintagel, and Sir Bleoberis rode unto the abbey where Sir Segwarides lay sore wounded, and there he delivered his lady, and departed as a noble knight. And when Sir Segwarides saw his lady, he was greatly comforted; and then she told him that Sir Tristram had done great battle with Sir Bleoberis, and caused him to bring her again. These words pleased Sir Segwarides right well, that Sir Tristram would do so much; and so that lady told all the battle unto King Mark betwixt Sir Tristram and Sir Bleoberis.

CHAPTER 19: *How King Mark sent Sir Tristram for La Beale Isoud toward Ireland, and how by fortune he arrived into England*

Then when this was done King Mark cast always in his heart how he might destroy Sir Tristram. And then he imagined in himself to send Sir Tristram into Ireland for La Beale Isoud. For Sir Tristram had so praised her beauty and her goodness that King Mark said he would wed her, whereupon he prayed Sir Tristram to take his way into Ireland for him on message. And all this was done to the intent to slay Sir Tristram. Notwithstanding, Sir Tristram would not refuse the message for no danger nor peril that might fall, for the pleasure of his uncle, but to go he made him ready in the most goodliest wise that might be devised. For Sir Tristram took with him the most goodliest knights that he might find in the court; and they were arrayed, after the guise that was then used, in the goodliest manner. So Sir Tristram departed and took the sea with all his fellowship.

And anon, as he was in the broad sea tempest took him and his fellowship, and drove them back into the coast of England; and there they arrived fast by Camelot, and full fain they were to take the land. And when they were landed Sir Tristram set up his pavilion upon the land of Camelot, and there he let hang his shield upon the pavilion.

And that same day came two knights of King Arthur's, that one was Sir Ector de Maris, and Sir Morganor. And they touched the shield, and bad him come out of the pavilion for to joust and he would joust.

'Ye shall be answered,' said Sir Tristram, 'and ye will tarry a little while.'

So he made him ready, and first he smote down Sir Ector de Maris, and after he smote down Sir Morganor, all with one spear, and sore bruised them. And when they lay upon the earth they asked Sir Tristram what he was, and of what country he was knight.

'Fair lords,' said Sir Tristram, 'wit ye well that I am of Cornwall.'

'Alas,' said Sir Ector, 'now am I ashamed that ever any Cornish knight should overcome me.'

And then for despite Sir Ector put off his armour from him, and went on foot, and would not ride.

CHAPTER 20: *How King Agwisance of Ireland was summoned to come to King Arthur's court for treason*

Then it fell that Sir Bleoberis and Sir Blamor de Ganis, that were brethren, they had assummoned the King Agwisance of Ireland for to come to Arthur's court upon pain of forfeiture of King Arthur's good grace. And if the King of Ireland came not in at the day assigned and set, the king should lose his lands.

So by it happened that at the day assigned, King Arthur neither Sir Launcelot might not be there for to give the judgement, for King Arthur was with Sir Launcelot at the Castle Joyous Gard. And so King Arthur assigned King Carados and the King of Scots to be there that day as judges.

So when the kings were at Camelot King Agwisance of Ireland was come to know his accusers. Then was there Blamor de Ganis, and appeled the King of Ireland of treason, that he had slain a cousin of his in his court in Ireland by treason.

The king was sore abashed of his accusation, for why he was come at the summons of King Arthur, and or that he came at Camelot he wist not wherefore he was sent after. And when the king heard Sir Blamor say his will, he under-

appeled: accused.

stood well there was none other remedy but to answer him knightly, for the custom was such in those days, that and any man were appeled of any treason or murder he should fight body for body, or else to find another knight for him. And all manner of murderers in those days were called treason. So when King Agwisance understood his accusing he was passing heavy, for he knew Sir Blamor de Ganis that he was a noble knight, and of noble knights comen. Then the King of Ireland was simply purveyed of his answer; therefore the judges gave him respite by the third day to give his answer. So the king departed unto his lodging.

The meanwhile there came a lady by Sir Tristram's pavilion making great dole.

'What aileth you,' said Sir Tristram, 'that ye make such dole?'

'Ah, fair knight,' said the lady, 'I am ashamed unless that some good knight help me; for a great lady of worship sent by me a fair shield and a rich, unto Sir Launcelot du Lake, and hereby there met with me a knight, and threw me down from my palfrey, and took away the shield from me.'

'Well, my lady,' said Sir Tristram, 'and for my lord Sir Launcelot's sake I shall get you that shield again, or else I shall be beaten for it.'

And so Sir Tristram took his horse, and asked the lady which way the knight rode; and then she told him. And he rode after him, and within a while he overtook that knight. And then Sir Tristram bad him turn and give again the shield.

CHAPTER 21: *How Sir Tristram rescued a shield from a knight, and how Gouvernail told him of King Agwisance*

The knight turned his horse and he made him ready to fight. And then Sir Tristram smote him with a sword such a buffet that he tumbled to the earth. And then he yielded him unto Sir Tristram.

'Then come thy way,' said Sir Tristram, 'and bring the shield to the lady again.'

So he took his horse weakly and rode with Sir Tristram; and then by the way Sir Tristram asked him his name.

Then he said, 'My name is Breunis Saunce Pité.'

So when he had delivered that shield to the lady, he said, 'Sir, as in this the shield is well remedied.'

Then Sir Tristram let him go again that sore repented him after, for he was a great foe unto many good knights of King Arthur's court.

Then when Sir Tristram was in his pavilion, Gouvernail, his man, came and told him how that King Agwisance of Ireland was come thither, and he was put in great distress; and there Gouvernail told Sir Tristram how King Agwisance was summoned and appeled of murder.

'So God me help,' said Sir Tristram, 'these be the best tidings that ever came to me this seven year, for now shall the King of Ireland have need of my help; for I daresay there is no knight in this country that is not of Arthur's court dare do battle with Sir Blamor de Ganis; and for to win the love of the King of Ireland I will take the battle upon me; and therefore Gouvernail bring me, I charge thee, to the king.'

Then Gouvernail went unto King Agwisance of Ireland, and saluted him fair. The king welcomed him and asked him what he would.

'Sir,' said Gouvernail, 'here is a knight near hand that desireth to speak with you: he bad me say he would do you service.'

'What knight is he?' said the king.

'Sir,' he said, 'it is Sir Tristram de Liones, that for your good grace that ye showed him in your lands will reward you in these countries.'

'Come on, fellow,' said the king, 'with me anon and show me unto Sir Tristram.'

So the king took a little hackney and but few fellowship with him, until he came unto Sir Tristram's pavilion. And

hackney: ambling horse.

when Sir Tristram saw the king he ran unto him and would have holden his stirrup. But the king leapt from his horse lightly, and either halsed other in arms.

'My gracious lord,' said Sir Tristram, 'gramercy of your great goodnesses showed unto me in your marches and lands: and at that time I promised you to do my service and ever it lay in my power.'

'And, gentle knight,' said the king unto Sir Tristram, 'now have I great need of you, never had I so great need of no knight's help.'

'How so, my good lord?' said Sir Tristram.

'I shall tell you,' said the king: 'I am assummoned and appeled from my country for the death of a knight that was kin unto the good knight Sir Launcelot; wherefore Sir Blamor de Ganis, brother to Sir Bleoberis hath appeled me to fight with him, other to find a knight in my stead. And well I wot,' said the king, 'these that are come of King Ban's blood, as Sir Launcelot and these other, are passing good knights, and hard men for to win in battle as any that I know now living.'

'Sir,' said Sir Tristram, 'for the good lordship ye showed me in Ireland, and for my lady your daughter's sake, La Beale Isoud, I will take the battle for you upon this condition that ye shall grant me two things: that one is that ye shall swear to me that ye are in the right, that ye were never consenting to the knight's death. Sir, then,' said Sir Tristram, 'when that I have done this battle, if God give me grace that I speed, that ye shall give me a reward, what thing reasonable that I will ask of you.'

'So God me help,' said the king, 'ye shall have whatsomever ye will ask.'

'It is well said,' said Sir Tristram.

CHAPTER 22: *How Sir Tristram fought for Sir Agwisance and overcame his adversary, and how his adversary would never yield him*

'Now make your answer that your champion is ready, for I shall die in your quarrel rather than to be recreant.'

'I have no doubt of you,' said the king, 'that and ye should have ado with Sir Launcelot du Lake.'

'Sir,' said Sir Tristram, 'as for Sir Launcelot, he is called the noblest knight of the world, and wit ye well that the knights of his blood are noble men, and dread shame; and as for Bleoberis, brother to Sir Blamor, I have done battle with him, therefore upon my head it is no shame to call him a good knight.'

'It is noised,' said the king, 'that Blamor is the hardier knight.'

'Sir, as for that let him be, he shall never be refused, and as he were the best knight that now beareth shield or spear.'

So King Agwisance departed unto King Carados and the kings that were that time as judges, and told them that he had found his champion ready. Then by the commandments of the kings Sir Blamor de Ganis and Sir Tristram were sent for to hear the charge. And when they were come before the judges there were many kings and knights beheld Sir Tristram, and much speech they had of him because he slew Sir Marhaus, the good knight, and because he forjousted Sir Palomides the good knight. So when they had taken their charge they withdrew them to make them ready to do battle.

Then said Sir Bleoberis unto his brother, Sir Blamor, 'Fair dear brother, remember of what kin we be come of, and what a man is Sir Launcelot du Lake, neither farther nor nearer but brother's children, and there was never none of our kin that ever was shamed in battle; and rather suffer death, brother, than to be shamed.'

'Brother,' said Blamor, 'have ye no doubt of me, for I shall never shame none of my blood; howbeit I am sure that yonder knight is called a passing good knight as of his time one of the world, yet shall I never yield me, nor say the loth word. Well may he happen to smite me down with his great might of chivalry, but rather shall he slay me than I shall yield me as recreant.'

'God speed you well,' said Sir Bleoberis, 'for ye shall find him the mightiest knight that ever ye had ado withal, for I know him, for I have had ado with him'

'God me speed,' said Sir Blamor de Ganis; and therewith he took his horse at the one end of the lists, and Sir Tristram at the other end of the lists, and so they fewtered their spears and came together as it had been thunder; and there Sir Tristram through great might smote down Sir Blamor and his horse to the earth.

Then anon Sir Blamor avoided his horse and pulled out his sword and threw his shield afore him, and bad Sir Tristram alight, 'For though an horse hath failed me, I trust to God the earth will not fail me.'

And then Sir Tristram alit, and dressed him unto battle; and there they lashed together strongly as rasing and tracing, foining and dashing, many sad strokes, that the kings and knights had great wonder that they might stand; for ever they fought like wood men, so that there were never knights seen fight more fiercely than they did; for Sir Blamor was so hasty he would have no rest, that all men wondered that they had breath to stand on their feet; and all the place was bloody that they fought in. And at the last, Sir Tristram smote Sir Blamor such a buffet upon the helm that he there fell down upon his side, and Sir Tristram stood and beheld him.

CHAPTER 23: *How Sir Blamor desired Tristram to slay him, and how Sir Tristram spared him, and how they took appointment*

Then when Sir Blamor might speak, he said thus:

'Sir Tristram de Liones, I require thee, as thou art a noble knight, and the best knight that ever I found, that thou wilt slay me out, for I would not live to be made lord of all the earth, for I have lever die with worship than live with shame; and needs, Sir Tristram, thou must slay me, or else thou shalt never win the field, for I will never say the loth word. And therefore if thou dare slay me, slay me, I require thee.'

When Sir Tristram heard him say so knightly, he wist not what to do with him, he remembering him of both parts, of what blood he was comen, and for Sir Launcelot's sake he would be loth to slay him; and in the other part in no wise he might not choose, but that he must make him to say the loth word, or else to slay him.

Then Sir Tristram start aback, and went to the kings that were judges, and there he kneeled down tofore them, and besought them for their worships, and for King Arthur's and Sir Launcelot's sake, that they would take this matter in their hands. 'For, my fair lords,' said Sir Tristram, 'it were shame and pity that this noble knight that yonder lieth should be slain; for ye hear well, shamed will he not be, and I pray to God that he never be slain nor shamed for me. And as for the king for whom I fight for, I shall require him, as I am his true champion and true knight in this field, that he will have mercy upon this knight.'

'So God me help,' said King Agwisance, 'I will for your sake, Sir Tristram, be ruled as ye will have me, for I know you for my true knight; and therefore I will heartily pray the kings that be here as judges to take it in their hands.'

And the kings that were judges called Sir Bleoberis to them, and asked him his advice.

'My lords,' said Bleoberis, 'though my brother be beaten,

and hath the worse through might of arms, I dare say, though Sir Tristram hath beaten his body he hath not beaten his heart, and I thank God he is not shamed this day; and rather than he should be shamed I require you,' said Bleoberis, 'let Sir Tristram slay him out.'

'It shall not be so,' said the kings, 'for his party adversary, both the king and the champion, have pity of Sir Blamor's knighthood.'

'My lords,' said Bleoberis, 'I will right well as ye will.'

Then the kings called the King of Ireland, and found him goodly and treatable. And then, by all their advices, Sir Tristram and Sir Bleoberis took up Sir Blamor, and the two brethren were accorded with King Agwisance, and kissed and made friends for ever. And then Sir Blamor and Sir Tristram kissed together, and there they made their oaths that they would never none of them two brethren fight with Sir Tristram, and Sir Tristram made the same oath. And for that gentle battle all the blood of Sir Launcelot loved Sir Tristram for ever.

Then King Agwisance and Sir Tristram took their leave, and sailed into Ireland with great noblesse and joy. So when they were in Ireland the king let make it known throughout all the land how and in what manner Sir Tristram had done for him. Then the queen and all that there were made the most of him that they might. But the joy that La Beale Isoud made of Sir Tristram there might no tongue tell, for of all men earthly she loved him most.

CHAPTER 24: *How Sir Tristram demanded La Beale Isoud for King Mark, and how Sir Tristram and Isoud drank the love drink*

Then upon a day King Agwisance asked Sir Tristram why he asked not his boon, for whatsomever he had promised him he should have it without fail.

'Sir,' said Sir Tristram, 'now is it time; this is all that I will desire, that ye will give me La Beale Isoud, your daughter, not for myself, but for mine uncle, King Mark, that shall have her to wife, for so have I promised him.'

'Alas,' said the king, 'I had lever than all the land that I have ye would wed her yourself.'

'Sir, and I did then I were shamed for ever in this world, and false of my promise. Therefore,' said Sir Tristram, 'I pray you hold your promise that ye promised me; for this is my desire, that ye will give me La Beale Isoud to go with me unto Cornwall for to be wedded to King Mark, mine uncle.'

'As for that,' said King Agwisance, 'ye shall have her with you to do with her what it please you; that is for to say if that ye list to wed her yourself, that is me levest, and if ye will give her unto King Mark, your uncle, that is in your choice.'

So to make short conclusion, La Beale Isoud was made ready to go with Sir Tristram, and Dame Bragwaine went with her for her chief gentlewoman, with many other.

Then the queen, Isoud's mother, gave to her and Dame Bragwaine, her daughter's gentlewoman, and unto Gouvernail, a drink,[1] and charged them that what day King Mark should wed, that same day they should give him that drink, so that King Mark should drink to La Beale Isoud, 'and then,' said the queen, 'I undertake either shall love other the days of their life.' So this drink was given unto Dame Bragwaine, and unto Gouvernail.

And then anon Sir Tristram took the sea, and La Beale Isoud; and when they were in their cabin, it happed so that they were thirsty, and they saw a little flacket of gold stand by them, and it seemed by the colour and the taste that it was noble wine.

Then Sir Tristram took the flacket in his hand, and said, 'Madam Isoud, here is the best drink that ever ye drank, that Dame Bragwaine, your maiden, and Gouvernail, my servant, have kept for themself.'

Then they laughed and made good cheer, and either drank

flacket: flask.

to other freely, and they thought never drink that ever they drank to other was so sweet nor so good. But by that their drink was in their bodies, they loved either other so well that never their love departed for weal neither for woe. And thus it happed the love first betwixt Sir Tristram and La Beale Isoud, the which love never departed the days of their life.

So then they sailed till by fortune, they came nigh a castle that hight Pluere, and thereby arrived for to repose them, weening to them to have had good harbour. But anon as Sir Tristram was within the castle they were taken prisoners; for the custom of the castle was such, who that rode by that castle and brought any lady, he must needs fight with the lord, that high Breunor. And if it were so that Breunor won the field, then should the knight stranger and his lady be put to death, what that ever they were; and if it were so that the strange knight won the field of Sir Breunor, then should he die and his lady both. This custom was used many winters, for it was called the Castle Pluere, that is to say the Weeping Castle.

CHAPTER 25: *How Sir Tristram and Isoud were in prison, and how he fought for her beauty, and smote off another lady's head*

Thus as Sir Tristram and La Beale Isoud were in prison, it happed a knight and a lady came unto them where they were, to cheer them.

'I have marvel,' said Tristram unto the knight and the lady, 'what is the cause the lord of this castle holdeth us in prison. It was never the custom of no place of worship that ever I came in, when a knight and a lady asked harbour, and they to receive them, and after to destroy them that be his guests.'

'Sir,' said the knight, 'this is the old custom of this castle, that when a knight cometh here he must needs fight with our lord, and he that is the weaker must lose his head. And when that is done, if his lady that he bringeth be fouler than our lord's wife, she must lose her head, and if she be fairer proved than is our lady, then shall the lady of this castle lose her head.'

'So God help me,' said Sir Tristram, 'this is a foul custom and a shameful. But one advantage have I,' said Sir Tristram, 'I have a lady is fair enough, fairer saw I never in all my life days, and I doubt not for lack of beauty she shall not lose her head; and rather than I should lose my head I will fight for it on a fair field. Wherefore, sir knight, I pray you tell your lord that I will be ready as tomorn with my lady, and myself to do battle, if it be so I may have my horse and mine armour.'

'Sir,' said that knight, 'I undertake that your desire shall be sped right well.' And then he said, 'Take your rest, and look that ye be up betimes and make you ready and your lady, for ye shall want no thing that you behoveth.'

And therewith he departed, and on the morn betimes that same knight came to Sir Tristram, and fetched him out and his lady, and brought him horse and armour that was his own, and bad him make him ready to the field, for all the estates and commons of that lordship were there ready to behold that battle and judgement.

Then came Sir Breunor, the lord of that castle, with his lady in his hand, muffled, and asked Sir Tristram where was his lady: 'For and thy lady be fairer than mine, with thy sword smite off my lady's head; and if my lady be fairer than thine,[1] with my sword I must strike off her head. And if I may win thee, yet shall thy lady be mine, and thou shalt lose thy head.'

'Sir,' said Tristram, 'this is a foul custom and horrible; and rather than my lady should lose her head, yet had I lever lose my head.'

'Nay, nay,' said Sir Breunor, 'the ladies shall be first showed together, and the one shall have her judgement.'

'Nay, I will not so,' said Sir Tristram, 'for here is none that

behoveth: is necessary.

will give righteous judgement. But I doubt not,' said Sir Tristram, 'my lady is fairer than thine, and that will I prove and make good with my hand. And whosomever he be that will say the contrary I will prove it on his head.'

And therewith Sir Tristram showed La Beale Isoud, and turned her thrice about with his naked sword in his hand. And when Sir Brenuor saw that, he did the same wise turn his lady. But when Sir Breunor beheld La Beale Isoud, him thought he saw never a fairer lady, and then he dread his lady's head should be off. And so all the people that were there present gave judgement that La Beale Isoud was the fairer lady and the better made.

'How now?' said Sir Tristram, 'Mesceemeth it were pity that my lady should lose her head, but because thou and she of long time have used this wicked custom, and by you both have many good knights and ladies been destroyed, for that cause it were no loss to destroy you both.'

'So God me help,' said Sir Breunor, 'for to say the sooth, thy lady is fairer than mine, and that me sore repenteth. And so I hear the people privily say, for of all women I saw none so fair; and therefore, and thou wilt slay my lady, I doubt not but I shall slay thee and have thy lady.'

'Thou shalt win her,' said Sir Tristram, 'as dear as ever knight won lady. And because of thine own judgement, as thou wouldst have done to my lady if that she had been fouler, and because of the evil custom, give me thy lady,' said Sir Tristram.

And therewithal Sir Tristram strode unto him and took his lady from him, and with an awke stroke he smote off her head clean.

'Well, knight,' said Sir Breunor, 'now hast thou done me a despite.'

CHAPTER 26: *How Sir Tristram fought with Sir Breunor, and at the last smote off his head*

'Now take thine horse: sithen I am ladyless I will win thy lady and I may.'

Then they took their horses and came together as it had been the thunder; and Sir Tristram smote Sir Breunor clean from his horse, and lightly he rose up; and as Sir Tristram came again by him he thrust his horse throughout both the shoulders, that his horse hurled here and there and fell dead to the ground. And ever Sir Breunor ran after to have slain Sir Tristram, but Sir Tristram was light and nimble, and voided his horse lightly. And or ever Sir Tristram might dress his shield and his sword the other gave him three or four sad strokes. Then they rashed together like two boars, tracing and traversing mightily and wisely as two noble knights. For this Sir Breunor was a proved knight, and had been or then the death of many good knights, that it was pity that he had so long endured. Thus they fought, hurling here and there nigh two hours, and either were wounded sore.

Then at the last Sir Breunor rushed upon Sir Tristram and took him in his arms, for he trusted much in his strength. Then was Sir Tristram called the strongest and the highest knight of the world; for he was called bigger than Sir Launcelot, but Sir Launcelot was better breathed. So anon Sir Tristram thrust Sir Breunor down grovelling, and then he unlaced his helm and struck off his head.

And then all they that longed to the castle came to him, and did him homage and fealty, praying him that he would abide there still a little while to fordo that foul custom. Sir Tristram granted thereto. The meanwhile one of the knights of the castle rode unto Sir Galahaut, the Haut Prince, the which was Sir Breunor's son, which was a noble knight, and told him what misadventure his father had and his mother.

CHAPTER 27: *How Sir Galahaut fought with Sir Tristram, and how Sir Tristram yielded him and promised to fellowship with Launcelot*

Then came Sir Galahaut, and the King with the Hundred Knights with him; and this Sir Galahaut proffered to fight with Sir Tristram hand for hand. And so they made them ready to go unto battle on horseback with great courage.

Then Sir Galahaut and Sir Tristram met together so hard that either bare other down, horse and all, to the earth. And then they avoided their horses as noble knights, and dressed their shields, and drew their swords with ire and rancour, and they lashed together many sad strokes, and one while striking, another while foining, tracing and traversing as noble knights: thus they fought long, near half a day, and either were sore wounded.

At the last Sir Tristram waxed light and big, and doubled his strokes, and drove Sir Galahaut aback on the one side and on the other, so that he was like to have been slain. With that came the King with the Hundred Knights, and all that fellowship went fiercely upon Sir Tristram. When Sir Tristram saw them coming upon him, then he wist well he might not endure. Then as a wise knight of war, he said to Sir Galahaut, the Haut Prince,

'Sir, ye show to me no knighthood, for to suffer all your men to have ado with me all at once; and as meesemeth ye be a noble knight of your hands it is great shame to you.'

'So God me help,' said Sir Galahaut, 'there is none other way but thou must yield thee to me, other else to die,' said Sir Galahaut to Sir Tristram.

'I will rather yield me to you than die, for that is more for the might of your men than of your hands.' And therewithal Sir Tristram took his own sword by the point, and put the pommel in the hand of Sir Galahaut.

Therewithal came the King with the Hundred Knights, and hard began to assail Sir Tristram.

'Let be,' said Sir Galahaut, 'be ye not so hardy to touch him, for I have given this knight his life.'

'That is your shame,' said the King with the Hundred Knights; 'hath he not slain your father and your mother?'

'As for that,' said Sir Galahaut, 'I may not wit him greatly, for my father had him in prison, and inforced him to do battle with him; and my father had such a custom that was a shameful custom, that what knight came there to ask harbour his lady must needs die but if she were fairer than my mother; and if my father overcame that knight he must needs die. This was a shameful custom and usage, a knight for his harbour asking to have such harbourage. And for this custom I would never draw about him.'

'So God me help,' said the king, 'this was a shameful custom.'

'Truly,' said Sir Galahaut, 'so seemed me; and meseemed it had been great pity that this knight should have been slain, for I dare say he is the noblest man that beareth life, but if it were Sir Launcelot du Lake. Now, fair knight,' said Sir Galahaut, 'I require thee tell me thy name, and of whence thou art, and whither thou wilt.'

'Sir,' he said, 'my name is Tristram de Liones, and from King Mark of Cornwall I was sent on message unto King Agwisance of Ireland, for to fetch his daughter to be his wife, and here she is ready to go with me into Cornwall, and her name is La Beale Isoud.'

'And, Sir Tristram,' said Sir Galahaut, the Haut Prince, 'well be ye found in these marches, and so ye will promise me to go unto Sir Launcelot du Lake, and accompany with him, ye shall go where ye will, and your fair lady with you; and I shall promise you never in all my days shall such customs be used in this castle as have been used.'

'Sir,' said Sir Tristram, 'now I let you wit, so God me help, I weened ye had been Sir Launcelot du Lake when I saw you first, and therefore I dread you the more; and sir, I promise you,' said Sir Tristram, 'as soon as I may I will see Sir

Launcelot and infellowship me with him; for of all the knights of the world I most desire his fellowship.'

CHAPTER 28: *How Sir Launcelot met with Sir Carados bearing away Sir Gawain, and of the rescues of Sir Gawain*

And then Sir Tristram took his leave when he saw his time and took the sea.

And in the meanwhile word came unto Sir Launcelot and to Sir Tristram that Sir Carados, the mighty king, that was made like a giant, fought with Sir Gawain,[1] and gave him such strokes that he swooned in his saddle, and after that he took him by the collar and pulled him out of his saddle, and fast bound him to the saddle-bow, and so rode his way with him towards his castle. And as he rode, by fortune Sir Launcelot met with Sir Carados, and anon he knew Sir Gawain that lay bound after him.

'Ah', said Sir Launcelot unto Sir Gawain, 'how stand[s] it with you?'

'Never so hard,' said Sir Gawain, 'unless that ye help me, for so God me help, without ye rescue me I know no knight that may, but other you or Sir Tristram.'

Wherefore Sir Launcelot was heavy of Sir Gawain's words. And then Sir Launcelot bad Sir Carados: 'Lay down that knight and fight with me.'

'Thou art but a fool,' said Carados, 'for I will serve you in the same wise.'

'As for that,' said Sir Launcelot, 'spare me not, for I warn thee I will not spare thee.'

And then he bound Sir Gawain hand and foot, and so threw him to the ground. And then he gat his spear of his squire, and departed from Sir Launcelot to fetch his course. And so either met with other, and brake their spears to their hands; and then they pulled out swords, and hurtled together on horseback more than an hour. And at the last Sir Launcelot smote Sir Carados such a buffet upon the helm that it pierced his brain pan. So then Sir Launcelot took Sir Carados by the collar and pulled him under his horse's feet, and then he alit and pulled off his helm and struck off his head. And then Sir Launcelot unbound Sir Gawain.

So this same tale was told to Sir Galahad and to Sir Tristram: – here may ye hear the nobleness that followeth Sir Launcelot.

'Alas,' said Sir Tristram, 'and I had not this message in hand with this fair lady, truly I would never stint or I had found Sir Launcelot.'

Then Sir Tristram and La Beale Isoud went to the sea and came into Cornwall, and there all the barons met them.

CHAPTER 29: *Of the wedding of King Mark to La Beale Isoud, and of Bragwaine her maid, and of Palomides*

And anon they were richly wedded with great nobley. But ever, as the French book saith, Sir Tristram and La Beale Isoud loved ever together. Then was there great jousts and great tourneying, and many lords and ladies were at that feast, and Sir Tristram was most praised of all other.

Thus dured the feast long, and after the feast was done, within a little while after, by the assent of two ladies that were with Queen Isoud, they ordained for hate and envy for to destroy Dame Bragwaine, that was maiden and lady unto La Beale Isoud; and she was sent into the forest for to fetch herbs, and there she was met, and bound feet and hand to a tree, and so she was bounden three days. And by fortune, Sir Palomides found Dame Bragwaine, and there he delivered her from the death, and brought her to a nunnery there beside, for to be recovered.

When Isoud the queen missed her maiden, wit ye well she was right heavy as ever was any queen, for of all earthly women she loved her best: the cause was for she came with her out of her country. And so upon a day Queen Isoud

nobley: pomp.

walked into the forest to put away her thoughts, and there she went herself unto a well and made great moan.

And suddenly there came Palomides to her, and had heard all her complaint, and said, 'Madam Isoud, and ye will grant me my boon, I shall bring to you Dame Bragwaine safe and sound.'

And the queen was so glad of his proffer that suddenly unadvised she granted all his asking.

'Well, madam,' said Palomides, 'I trust to your promise, and if ye will abide here half an hour I shall bring her to you.'

'I shall abide you,' said La Beale Isoud.

And Sir Palomides rode forth his way to that nunnery, and lightly he came again with Dame Bragwaine; but by her good will she would not have comen again, because for love of the queen she stood in adventure of her life. Notwithstanding, half against her will, she went with Sir Palomides unto the queen. And when the queen saw her she was passing glad.

'Now, madam,' said Palomides, 'remember upon your promise, for I have fulfilled my promise.'

'Sir Palomides,' said the queen, 'I wot not what is your desire, but I will that ye wit, howbeit I promised you largely, I thought none evil, nor I warn you none ill will I do.'

'Madam,' said Sir Palomides, 'as at this time, ye shall not know my desire, but before my lord your husband there shall ye know that I will have my desire that ye have promised me.'

And therewith the queen departed, and rode home to the king, and Sir Palomides rode after her.

And when Sir Palomides came before the king, he said, 'Sir King, I require you as ye be a righteous king, that ye will judge me the right.'

'Tell me your cause,' said the king, 'and ye shall have right.'

unadvised: rashly.

CHAPTER 30: *How Palomides demanded Queen Isoud, and how Lambegus rode after to rescue her, and of the escape of Isoud*

'Sir,' said Palomides, 'I promised your Queen Isoud to bring again Dame Bragwaine that she had lost, upon this covenant, that she should grant me a boon that I would ask, and without grudging, other advisement, she granted me.'

'What say ye, my lady?' said the king.

'It is as he saith, so God help me,' said the queen; 'to say thee sooth I promised him his asking for love and joy that I had to see her.'

'Well, madam,' said the king, 'and if ye were hasty to grant him what boon he would ask, I will well that ye perform your promise.'

'Then,' said Palomides, 'I will that ye wit that I will have your queen to lead her and govern her whereas me list.'

Therewith the king stood still, and bethought him of Sir Tristram, and deemed that he would rescue her. And then hastily the king answered, 'Take her with the adventures that shall fall of it, for as I suppose thou wilt not enjoy her no while.'

'As for that,' said Palomides, 'I dare right well abide the adventure.'

And so, to make short tale, Sir Palomides took her by the hand and said, 'Madam, grudge not to go with me, for I desire nothing but your own promise.'

'As for that,' said the queen, 'I fear not greatly to go with thee, howbeit thou hast me at advantage upon my promise, for I doubt not I shall be worshipfully rescued from thee.'

'As for that,' said Sir Palomides, 'be it as it be may.'

So Queen Isoud was set behind Palomides, and rode his way.

Anon the king sent after Sir Tristram, but in no wise he could be found, for he was in the forest an-hunting; for that was always his custom, but if he used arms, to chase and to hunt in the forests.

'Alas,' said the king, 'now I am shamed for ever, that by mine own assent my lady and my queen shall be devoured.'

Then came forth a knight, his name was Lambegus, and he was a knight of Sir Tristram.

'My lord,' said this knight, 'sith ye have trust in my lord, Sir Tristram, wit ye well for his sake I will ride after your queen and rescue her, or else I shall be beaten.'

'Gramercy,' said the king, 'and I live, Sir Lambegus, I shall deserve it.'

And then Sir Lambegus armed him, and rode after as fast as he might. And then within a while he overtook Sir Palomides. And then Sir Palomides left the queen.

'What art thou?' said Palomides, 'Art thou Tristram?'

'Nay,' he said, 'I am his servant, and my name is Sir Lambegus.'

'That me repenteth,' said Palomides. 'I had lever thou haddest been Sir Tristram.'

'I believe you well,' said Lambegus, 'but when thou meetest with Sir Tristram thou shalt have thy hands full.'

And then they hurtled together and all to-brast their spears, and then they pulled out their swords, and hewed on helms and hauberks. At the last Sir Palomides gave Sir Lambegus such a wound that he fell down like a dead knight to the earth. Then he looked after La Beale Isoud, and then she was gone he nist where. Wit ye well Sir Palomides was never so heavy.

So the queen ran into the forest, and there she found a well, and therein she had thought to have drowned herself. And as good fortune would, there came a knight to her that had a castle thereby, his name was Sir Adtherp. And when he found the queen in that mischief he rescued her, and brought her to his castle.

And when he wist what she was he armed him, and took his horse, and said he would be avenged upon Palomides. And so he rode on till he met with him, and there Sir Palomides wounded him sore, and by force he made him to tell him the cause why he did battle with him, and how he had led the queen unto his castle.

'Now bring me there,' said Palomides, 'or thou shalt die of my hands.'

'Sir,' said Sir Adtherp, 'I am so wounded I may not follow, but ride you this way and it shall bring you into my castle, and there within is the queen.'

Then Sir Palomides rode still till he came to the castle. And at a window La Beale Isoud saw Sir Palomides; then she made the gates to be shut strongly. And when he saw he might not come within the castle, he put off his bridle and his saddle, and put his horse to pasture, and set himself down at the gate like a man that was out of his wit that recked not of himself.

CHAPTER 31: *How Sir Tristram rode after Palomides, and how he found him and fought with him, and by the mean of Isoud the battle ceased*

Now turn we unto Sir Tristram, that when he was come home and wist La Beale Isoud was gone with Sir Palomides, wit ye well he was wroth out of measure.

'Alas,' said Sir Tristram, 'I am this day shamed.' Then he cried to Gouvernail his man, 'Haste thee that I were armed and on horseback, for well I wot Lambegus hath no might nor strength to withstand Sir Palomides; alas that I have not been in his stead!'

So anon as he was armed and horsed Sir Tristram and Gouvernail rode after into the forest, and within a while he found his knight Lambegus almost wounded to the death; and Sir Tristram bare him to a forester, and charged him to keep him well.

And then he rode forth, and there he found Sir Adtherp sore wounded, and he told him how the queen would have drowned herself had he not been, and how for her sake and love he had taken upon him to do battle with Sir Palomides.

'Where is my lady?' said Sir Tristram.

'Sir,' said the knight, 'she is sure enough within my castle, and she can hold her within it.'

'Gramercy,' said Sir Tristram, 'of thy great goodness.'

And so he rode till he came nigh to that castle; and then Sir Tristram saw where Sir Palomides sat at the gate sleeping, and his horse pastured fast afore him.

'Now go thou, Gouvernail,' said Sir Tristram, 'and bid him awake, and make him ready.'

So Gouvernail rode unto him and said, 'Sir Palomides, arise, and take to thee thine harness.'

But he was in such a study he heard not what Gouvernail said. So Gouvernail came again and told Sir Tristram he slept, or else he was mad.

'Go thou again,' said Sir Tristram, 'and bid him arise, and tell him that I am here, his mortal foe.'

So Gouvernail rode again and put upon him the butt of his spear, and said, 'Sir Palomides, make thee ready, for wit ye well Sir Tristram hoveth yonder, and sendeth thee word he is thy mortal foe.'

And therewithal Sir Palomides arose stilly, without words, and gat his horse, and saddled him and bridled him, and lightly he leapt upon, and gat his spear in his hand, and either fewtered their spears and hurtled fast together; and there Tristram smote down Sir Palomides over his horse's tail. Then lightly Sir Palomides put his shield afore him and drew his sword.

And there began strong battle on both parts, for both they fought for the love of one lady, and ever she lay on the walls and beheld them how they fought out of measure, and either were wounded passing sore, but Palomides was much sorer wounded. Thus they fought tracing and traversing more than two hours, that well-nigh for dole and sorrow La Beale Isoud swooned.

'Alas,' she said 'that one I loved and yet do, and the other I love not, yet it were great pity that I should see Sir Palomides slain; for well I know by that time the end be done Sir Palomides is but a dead knight; because he is not christened I would be loth that he should die a Saracen.'

And therewithal she came down and besought Sir Tristram to fight no more.

'Ah, madam,' said he, 'what mean you, will ye have me shamed? Well ye know I will be ruled by you.'

'I will not your dishonour,' said La Beale Isoud, 'but I would that ye would for my sake spare this unhappy Saracen, Palomides.'

'Madam,' said Sir Tristram, 'I will leave fighting at this time for your sake.'

Then she said to Sir Palomides, 'This shall be your charge, that thou shalt go out of this country while I am therein.'

'I will obey your commandment,' said Sir Palomides, 'the which is sore against my will.'

'Then take thy way,' said La Beale Isoud, 'unto the court of King Arthur, and there recommend me unto Queen Guenever, and tell her that I send her word that there be within this land but four lovers, that is, Sir Launcelot du Lake and Queen Guenever, and Sir Tristram de Liones and Queen Isoud.'

CHAPTER 32: *How Sir Tristram brought Queen Isoud home, and of the debate of King Mark and Sir Tristram*

And so Sir Palomides departed with great heaviness. And Sir Tristram took the queen and brought her again to King Mark, and then was there made great joy of her homecoming. Who was cherished but Sir Tristram!

Then Sir Tristram let fetch Sir Lambegus, his knight, from the forester's house, and it was long or he was whole, but at last he was well recovered. Thus they lived with joy and play a long while. But ever Sir Andred, that was nigh cousin to Sir Tristram, lay in a watch to wait betwixt Sir Tristram and La Beale Isoud, for to take them and slander them.

So upon a day Sir Tristram talked with La Beale Isoud in a window, and that espied Sir Andred, and told it to the king. Then King Mark took a sword in his hand and came to Sir Tristram, and called him false traitor, and would have stricken him. But Sir Tristram was nigh him, and ran under his sword, and took it out of his hand.

And then the king cried, 'Where are my knights and my men? I charge you slay this traitor.'

But at that time there was not one would move for his words.

When Sir Tristram saw that there was not one would be against him, he shook the sword to the king, and made countenance as though he would have striken him. And then King Mark fled, and Sir Tristram followed him, and smote upon him five or six strokes flatling on the neck, that he made him to fall upon the nose.

And then Sir Tristram yede his way and armed him, and took his horse and his men, and so he rode into that forest. And there upon a day Sir Tristram met with two brethren that were knights with King Mark, and there he struck off the head of the one, and wounded the other to the death; and he made him to bear his brother's head in his helm unto the king, and thirty more there he wounded. And when that knight came before the king to say his message, he there died afore the king and the queen. Then King Mark called his council unto him, and asked advice of his barons what was best to do with Sir Tristram.

'Sir,' said the barons, in especial Sir Dinas, the Seneschal, 'Sir, we will give you counsel for to send for Sir Tristram, for we will that ye wit many men will hold with Sir Tristram and he were hard bestad.'

'And sir,' said Sir Dinas, 'ye shall understand that Sir Tristram is called peerless and makeless of any Christian knight, and of his might and hardiness we knew none so good a knight, but if it be Sir Launcelot du Lake. And if he depart from your court and go to King Arthur's court, wit ye well he will get him such friends there that he will not set by your malice. And therefore, sir, I counsel you to take him to your grace.'

'I will well,' said the king, 'that he be sent for, that we may be friends.'

Then the barons sent for Sir Tristram under a safe conduct. And so when Sir Tristram came to the king he was welcome, and no rehearsal was made, and there was game and play. And then the king and queen went on hunting, and Sir Tristram.

CHAPTER 33: *How Sir Lamorak jousted with thirty knights, and Sir Tristram at the request of King Mark smote his horse down*

The king and the queen made their pavilions and their tents in that forest beside a river, and there was daily hunting and jousting, for there were ever thirty knights ready to joust unto all them that came in at that time. And there by fortune came Sir Lamorak de Gales and Sir Driant; and there Sir Driant jousted right well, but at the last he had a fall. Then Sir Lamorak proffered to joust. And when he began he fared so with the thirty knights that there was not one of them but that he gave him a fall, and some of them were sore hurt.

'I marvel,' said King Mark, 'what knight he is that doth such deeds of arms.'

'Sir,' said Sir Tristram, 'I know him well for a noble knight as few now be living, and his name is Sir Lamorak de Gales.'

'It were great shame,' said the king, 'that he should go thus away, unless that some of you meet with him better.'

'Sir,' said Sir Tristram, 'meseemeth it were no worship for a noble man to have ado with him; and for because at this time he hath done over much for any mean knight living, therefore, as meseemeth, it were great shame and villainy to tempt him any more at this time, insomuch as he and his horse are weary both; for the deeds of arms that he hath

any mean knight: any ordinary knight.

done this day, and they be well considered, it were enough for Sir Launcelot du Lake.'

'As for that,' said King Mark, 'I require you, as ye love me and my lady the queen, La Beale Isoud, take your arms and joust with Sir Lamorak de Gales.'

'Sir,' said Sir Tristram, 'ye bid me do a thing that is against knighthood, and well I can deem that I shall give him a fall, for it is no mastery, for my horse and I be fresh both, and so is not his horse and he; and wit ye well that he will take it for great unkindness, for ever one good is loth to take another at disadvantage; but because I will not displease you, as ye require me so will I do, and obey your commandment.'

And so Sir Tristram armed him and took his horse, and put him forth, and there Sir Lamorak met him mightily, and what with the might of his own spear, and of Sir Tristram's spear, Sir Lamorak's horse fell to the earth, and he sitting in the saddle. Then anon as lightly as he might he avoided the saddle and his horse, and put his shield afore him and drew his sword.

And then he bad Sir Tristram: 'Alight, thou knight, and thou darst.'

'Nay,' said Sir Tristram, 'I will no more have ado with thee, for I have done to thee over much unto my dishonour and to thy worship.'

'As for that,' said Sir Lamorak, 'I can thee no thank; since thou hast for-jousted me on horseback I require thee and I beseech thee, and thou be Sir Tristram, fight with me on foot.'

'I will not so,' said Sir Tristram; 'and wit ye well my name is Sir Tristram de Liones, and well I know ye be Sir Lamorak de Gales, and this that I have done to you was against my will, but I was required thereto. But to say that I will do at your request as at this time, I will have no more ado with you, for me shameth of that I have done.'

'As for the shame,' said Sir Lamorak, 'on thy part or on mine, bear thou it and thou wilt, for though a mare's son hath failed me, now a queen's son shall not fail thee; and therefore, and thou be such a knight as men call thee, I require thee, alight, and fight with me.'

'Sir Lamorak,' said Sir Tristram, 'I understand your heart is great, and cause why ye have, to say thee sooth; for it would grieve me and any knight should keep him fresh and then to strike down a weary knight, for that knight nor horse was never formed that alway might stand or endure. And therefore,' said Sir Tristram, 'I will not have ado with you, for me forthinketh of that I have done.'

'As for that,' said Sir Lamorak, 'I shall quit you and ever I see my time.'

CHAPTER 34: *How Sir Lamorak sent an horn to King Mark in despite of Sir Tristram, and how Sir Tristram was driven into a chapel*

So he departed from him with Sir Driant, and by the way they met with a knight that was sent from Morgan le Fay unto King Arthur; and this knight had a fair horn harnessed with gold, and the horn had such a virtue that there might no lady ne gentlewoman drink of that horn but if she were true to her husband, and if she were false she should spill all the drink, and if she were true to her lord she might drink peaceable. And because of the Queen Guenever, and in the despite of Sir Launcelot, this horn was sent unto King Arthur; and by force Sir Lamorak made that knight to tell all the cause why he bare that horn.

'Now shalt thou bear this horn,' said Lamorak, 'unto King Mark, or else choose thou to die for it; for I tell thee plainly, in despite and reproof of Sir Tristram thou shalt bear that horn unto King Mark, his uncle, and say thou to him that I sent it him for to assay his lady, and if she be true to him he shall prove her.'

So the knight went his way unto King Mark, and brought him that rich horn, and said that Sir Lamorak sent it him, and thereto he told him the virtue of that horn. Then the king made Queen Isoud to drink thereof, and an hundred ladies, and there were but four ladies of all those that drank clean.

'Alas,' said King Mark, 'this is a great despite,' and sware a great oath that she should be burnt and the other ladies.

Then the barons gathered them together, and said plainly they would not have those ladies burnt for an horn made by sorcery, that came from as false a sorceress and witch as then was living. For that horn did never good, but caused strife and debate, and always in her days she had been an enemy to all true lovers. So there were many knights made their avow and ever they met with Morgan le Fay that they would show her short courtesy. Also Sir Tristram was passing wroth that Sir Lamorak sent that horn unto King Mark, for well he knew that it was done in the despite of him. And therefore he thought to quit Sir Lamorak.

Then Sir Tristram used daily and nightly to go to Queen Isoud when he might, and ever Sir Andred his cousin watched him night and day for to take him with La Beale Isoud.

And so upon a night Sir Andred espied the hour and the time when Sir Tristram went to his lady. Then Sir Andred gat unto him twelve knights, and at midnight he set upon Sir Tristram secretly and suddenly, and there Sir Tristram was take naked abed with La Beale Isoud, and then was he bound hand and foot, and so was he kept until day.

And then by the assent of King Mark, and of Sir Andred, and of some of the barons, Sir Tristram was led unto a chapel that stood upon the sea rocks, there for to take his judgement: and so he was led bounden with forty knights. And when Sir Tristram saw that there was none other boot but needs that he must die, then said he,

'Fair lords, remember what I have done for the country of Cornwall, and in what jeopardy I have been in for the weal of you all; for when I fought for the truage of Cornwall with Sir Marhaus, the good knight, I was promised for to be better rewarded, when ye all refused to take the battle; therefore, as ye be good gentle knights, see me not thus shamefully to die, for it is shame to all knighthood thus to see me die; for I daresay,' said Sir Tristram, 'that I never met with no knight but I was as good as he, or better.'

'Fie upon thee,' said Sir Andred, 'false traitor that thou art, with thine avaunting; for all thy boast thou shalt die this day.'

'O Andred, Andred,' said Sir Tristram, 'thou shouldst be my kinsman, and now thou art to me full unfriendly, but and there were no more but thou and I, thou wouldst not put me to death.'

'No,' said Sir Andred, and therewith he drew his sword, and would have slain him.

When Sir Tristram saw him make such countenance he looked upon both his hands that were fast bounden unto two knights, and suddenly he pulled them both to him, and unwrast his hands, and then he leapt unto his cousin, Sir Andred, and wrothe his sword out of his hands; then he smote Sir Andred that he fell to the earth, and so Sir Tristram fought till that he had killed ten knights. So then Sir Tristram gat the chapel and kept it mightily.

Then the cry was great, and the people drew fast unto Sir Andred, more than an hundred. When Sir Tristram saw the people draw unto him, he remembered he was naked, and sparred fast the chapel door, and brake the bars of a window, and so he leapt out and fell upon the crags in the sea. And so at that time Sir Andred nor none of his fellows might get to him at that time.

CHAPTER 35: *How Sir Tristram was holpen by his men, and of Queen Isoud which was put in a lazar-cote, and how Tristram was hurt*

So when they were departed, Gouvernail, and Sir Lambegus, and Sir Sentraille de Lushon, that were Sir Tristram's men,

unwrast: wrenched free. *wrothe*: twisted.

sought their master. When they heard he was escaped then they were passing glad; and on the rocks they found him, and with towels they pulled him up. And then Sir Tristram asked them where was La Beale Isoud, for he weened she had been had away of Andred's people.

'Sir,' said Gouvernail, 'she is put in a lazar-cote.'

'Alas,' said Sir Tristram, 'this is a full ungoodly place for such a fair lady, and if I may she shall not be long there.'

And so he took his men and went thereas was La Beale Isoud, and fetched her away, and brought her into a forest to a fair manor, and Sir Tristram there abode with her.

So the good knight bad his men go from him: 'For at this time I may not help you.' So they departed all save Gouvernail.

And so upon a day Sir Tristram yede into the forest for to disport him, and then it happened that there he fell asleep; and there came a man that Sir Tristram aforehand had slain his brother, and when this man had found him he shot him through the shoulder with an arrow, and Sir Tristram leapt up and killed that man.

And in the meantime it was told King Mark how Sir Tristram and La Beale Isoud were in that same manor, and as soon as ever he might thither he came with many knights to slay Sir Tristram. And when he came there he found him gone; and there he took La Beale Isoud home with him, and kept her strait that by no mean never she might wit nor send unto Tristram, nor he unto her.

And then when Sir Tristram came toward the old manor he found the track of many horses, and thereby he wist his lady was gone. And then Sir Tristram took great sorrow, and endured with great pain long time, for the arrow that he was hurt withal was envenomed.

Then by the mean of La Beale Isoud she told a lady that was cousin unto Dame Bragwaine, and she came to Sir Tristram, and told him that he might not be whole by no means: 'For thy lady, La Beale Isoud, may not help thee, therefore

lazar-cote: hut for lepers.

she biddeth you haste into Brittany to King Howel, and there ye shall find his daughter, Isoud la Blanche Mains, and she shall help thee.'

Then Sir Tristram and Gouvernail gat them shipping, and so sailed into Brittany. And when King Howel wist that it was Sir Tristram he was full glad of him.

'Sir,' he said, 'I am comen into this country to have help of your daughter, for it is told me that there is none other may heal me but she.

And so within a while she healed him.

CHAPTER 36: *How Sir Tristram served in war the King Howel of Brittany, and slew his adversary in the field*

There was an earl that hight Grip, and this earl made great war upon the king, and put the king to the worse, and besieged him. And on a time Sir Kehydius, that was son to King Howel, as he issued out he was sore wounded nigh to the death.

Then Gouvernail went to the king and said, 'Sir, I counsel you to desire my lord, Sir Tristram, as in your need to help you.'

'I will do by your counsel,' said the king.

And so he yede unto Sir Tristram, and prayed him in his wars to help him: 'For my son, Sir Kehydius, may not go into the field.'

'Sir,' said Sir Tristram, 'I will go to the field and do what I may.'

Then Sir Tristram issued out of the town with such fellowship as he might make, and did such deeds that all Brittany spake of him. And then, at the last, by great might and force, he slew the Earl Grip with his own hands, and more than an hundred knights he slew that day.

And then Sir Tristram was received worshipfully with procession. Then King Howel embraced him in his arms, and said, 'Sir Tristram, all my kingdom I will resign to thee.'

'God defend,' said Sir Tristram, 'for I am beholden unto you for your daughter's sake to do for you.'

Then by the great means of King Howel and Kehydius his son, by great proffers, there grew great love betwixt Isoud and Sir Tristram for that lady was both good and fair, and a woman of noble blood and fame. And for because Sir Tristram had such cheer and riches, and all other pleasance that he had, almost he had forsaken La Beale Isoud.

And so upon a time Sir Tristram agreed to wed Isoud la Blanche Mains. And at the last they were wedded, and solemnly held their marriage.

And so when they were abed both, Sir Tristram remembered him of his old lady La Beale Isoud. And then he took such a thought suddenly that he was all dismayed, and other cheer made he none but with clipping and kissing; as for other fleshly lusts Sir Tristram never thought nor had ado with her: such mention maketh the French book; also it maketh mention that the lady weened there had been no pleasure but kissing and clipping.

And in the meantime there was a knight in Brittany, his name was Suppinabiles, and he came over the sea into England, and then he came into the court of King Arthur, and there he met with Sir Launcelot du Lake, and told him of the marriage of Sir Tristram.

Then said Sir Launcelot, 'Fie upon him, untrue knight to his lady that so noble a knight as Sir Tristram is should be found to his first lady false, La Beale Isoud, Queen of Cornwall; but say ye him this,' said Sir Launcelot, 'that of all knights in the world I loved him most, and had most joy of him, and all was for his noble deeds; and let him wit the love between him and me is done for ever, and that I give him warning from this day forth as his mortal enemy.'

CHAPTER 37: *How Sir Suppinabiles told Sir Tristram how he was defamed in the court of King Arthur, and of Sir Lamorak*

Then departed Sir Suppinabiles unto Brittany again, and there he found Sir Tristram, and told him that he had been in King Arthur's court.

Then said Sir Tristram, 'Heard ye anything of me?'

'So God me help,' said Sir Suppinabiles, 'there I heard Sir Launcelot speak of you great shame, and that ye be a false knight to your lady, and he bad me do you to wit that he will be your mortal enemy in every place where he may meet you.'

'That me repenteth,' said Tristram, 'for of all knights I loved to be in his fellowship.' So Sir Tristram made great moan and was ashamed that noble knights should defame him for the sake of his lady.

And in this meanwhile La Beale Isoud made a letter unto Queen Guenever, complaining her of the untruth of Sir Tristram, and how he had wedded the king's daughter of Brittany.

Queen Guenever sent her another letter, and bad her be of good cheer, for she should have joy after sorrow, for Sir Tristram was so noble a knight called, that by crafts of sorcery, ladies would make such noble men to wed them. 'But in the end,' Queen Guenever said, 'it shall be thus, that he shall hate her, and love you better than ever he did tofore.'

So leave we Sir Tristram in Brittany, and speak we of Sir Lamorak de Gales, that as he sailed his ship fell on a rock and perished all, save Sir Lamorak and his squire. And there he swam mightily, and fishers of the Isle of Servage took him up, and his squire was drowned, and the shipmen had great labour to save Sir Lamorak's life for all the comfort that they could do.

And the lord of that isle hight Sir Nabon le Noire, a great mighty giant. And this Sir Nabon hated all the knights of

King Arthur's, and in no wise he would do them favour. And these fishers told Sir Lamorak all the guise of Sir Nabon, how there came never knight of King Arthur's but he destroyed him. And at the last battle that he did was slain Sir Nanowne le Petite, the which he put to a shameful death in despite of King Arthur, for he was drawn limb-meal.

'That forthinketh me,' said Sir Lamorak, 'for that knight's death, for he was my cousin; and if I were at mine ease as well as ever I was, I would revenge his death.'

'Peace,' said the fishers, 'and make here no words, for or ever ye depart from hence Sir Nabon must know that ye have been here, or else we should die for your sake.'

'So that I be whole,' said Lamorak, 'of my disease that I have taken in the sea, I will that ye tell him that I am a knight of King Arthur's, for I was never afeared to reney my lord.'

CHAPTER 38: *How Sir Tristram and his wife arrived in Wales, and how he met there with Sir Lamorak*

Now turn we unto Sir Tristram, that upon a day he took a little barget, and his wife Isoud la Blanche Mains, with Sir Kehydius her brother, to play them in the coasts. And when they were from the land, there was a wind drove them in to the coast of Wales upon this Isle of Servage, whereas was Sir Lamorak, and there the barget all to-rove; and there Dame Isoud was hurt. And as well as they might they gat into the forest, and there by a well he saw Segwarides and a damosel. And then either saluted other.

'Sir,' said Segwarides, 'I know you for Sir Tristram de Liones, the man in the world that I have most cause to hate, because ye departed the love between me and my wife; but as for that,' said Segwarides, 'I will never hate a noble knight for a light lady; and therefore, I pray you, be my friend, and I will be yours unto my power; for wit ye well ye are hard

limb-meal: limb from limb. *reney*: deny.

bestad in this valley, and we shall have enough to do either of us to succour other.'

And then Sir Segwarides brought Sir Tristram to a lady there by that was born in Cornwall, and she told him all the perils of that valley, and how there came never knight there but he were taken prisoner or slain.

'Wit you well, fair lady,' said Sir Tristram, 'that I slew Sir Marhaus and delivered Cornwall from the truage of Ireland, and I am he that delivered the King of Ireland from Sir Blamor de Ganis, and I am he that beat Sir Palomides; and wit ye well I am Sir Tristram de Liones, that by the grace of God shall deliver this woful Isle of Servage.'

So Sir Tristram was well eased. Then one told him there was a knight of King Arthur's that had wrecked on the rocks.

'What is his name?' said Sir Tristram.

'We wot not,' said the fishers, 'but he keepeth it no counsel but that he is a knight of King Arthur, and by the mighty lord of this isle he setteth nought by.'

'I pray you,' said Sir Tristram, 'and ye may, bring him hither that I may see him, and if he be any of the knights of Arthur's I shall know him.'

Then the lady prayed the fishers to bring him to her place. So on the morrow they brought him thither in a fisher's raiment; and as soon as Sir Tristram saw him he smiled upon him and knew him well, but he knew not Sir Tristram.

'Fair sir,' said Sir Tristram, 'meseemeth by your cheer ye have been diseased but late and also methinketh I should know you heretofore.'

'I will well,' said Sir Lamorak, 'that ye have seen me and met with me.'

'Fair sir,' said Sir Tristram, 'tell me your name.'

'Upon a covenant I will tell you,' said Sir Lamorak, 'that is, that ye will tell me whether ye be lord of this island or no, that is called Nabon le Noire.'

'Forsooth,' said Sir Tristram, 'I am not he, nor I hold not

of him; I am his foe as well as ye be, and so shall I be found or I depart out of this isle.'

'Well,' said Sir Lamorak, 'since ye have said so largely unto me, my name is Sir Lamorak de Gales, son unto King Pellinor.'

'Forsooth, I trow well,' said Sir Tristram, 'for and ye said other I know the contrary.'

'What are ye,' said Sir Lamorak, 'that knoweth me?'

'I am Sir Tristram de Liones.'

'Ah, sir, remember ye not of the fall ye did give me once, and after ye refused me to fight on foot.'

'That was not for fear I had of you,' said Sir Tristram, 'but me shamed at that time to have more ado with you, for meseemed ye had enough; but, Sir Lamorak, for my kindness many ladies ye put to a reproof when ye sent the horn from Morgan le Fay to King Mark, whereas ye did this in despite of me.'

'Well,' said he, 'and it were to do again, so would I do, for I had lever strife and debate fell in King Mark's court rather than Arthur's court, for the honour of both courts be not alike.'

'As to that,' said Sir Tristram, 'I know well; but that that was done it was for despite of me, but all your malice, I thank God, hurt not greatly. Therefore,' said Sir Tristram, 'ye shall leave all your malice, and so will I, and let us assay how we may win worship between you and me upon this giant, Sir Nabon le Noire that is lord of this island, to destroy him.'

'Sir,' said Sir Lamorak, 'now I understand your knighthood, it may not be false that all men say, for of your bounty, noblesse, and worship, of all knights ye are peerless, and for your courtesy and gentleness I showed you ungentleness, and that now me repenteth.'

CHAPTER 39: *How Sir Tristram fought with Sir Nabon, and overcame him, and made Sir Segwarides lord of the isle*

In the meantime there came word that Sir Nabon had made a cry that all the people of that isle should be at his castle the fifth day after. And the same day the son of Nabon should be made knight, and all the knights of that valley and thereabout should be there to joust, and all those of the realm of Logris should be there to joust with them of North Wales: and thither came five hundred knights, and they of the country brought thither Sir Lamorak, and Sir Tristram, and Sir Kehydius, and Sir Segwarides, for they durst none otherwise do.

And then Sir Nabon lent Sir Lamorak horse and armour at Sir Lamorak's desire, and Sir Lamorak jousted and did such deeds of arms that Nabon and all the people said there was never knight that ever they saw do such deeds of arms; for, as the French book saith, he forjousted all that were there for the most part of five hundred knights, that none abode him in his saddle.

Then Sir Nabon proffered to play with him his play: 'For I saw never no knight do so much upon a day.'

'I will well,' said Sir Lamorak, 'play as I may, but I am weary and sore bruised.'

And there either gat a spear, but Nabon would not encounter with Sir Lamorak, but smote his horse in the forehead, and so slew him; and then Sir Lamorak yede on foot, and turned his shield and drew his sword, but there began strong battle on foot. But Sir Lamorak was so sore bruised and short breathed, that he traced and traversed somewhat aback.

'Fair fellow,' said Sir Nabon, 'hold thy hand and I shall show thee more courtesy than ever I showed knight, because I have seen this day thy noble knighthood, and therefore stand thou by, and I will wit whether any of thy fellows will have ado with me.'

Then when Sir Tristram heard that, he stepped forth and said, 'Nabon, lend me horse and sure armour, and I will have ado with thee.'

'Well, fellow,' said Sir Nabon, 'go thou to yonder pavilion, and arm thee of the best thou findest there, and I shall play a marvellous play with thee.'

Then said Sir Tristram, 'Look ye play well, or else peradventure, I shall learn you a new play.'

'That is well said, fellow,' said Sir Nabon.

So when Sir Tristram was armed as him liked best, and well shielded and sworded, he dressed to him on foot; for well he knew Sir Nabon would not abide a stroke with a spear, therefore he would slay all knights' horses.

'Now, fair fellow,' said Sir Nabon, 'let us play.'

So then they fought long on foot, tracing and traversing, smiting and foining long without any rest.

At the last Sir Nabon prayed him to tell him his name.

'Sir Nabon, I tell thee my name is Sir Tristram de Liones, a knight of Cornwall under King Mark.'

'Thou art welcome,' said Sir Nabon, 'for of all knights I have most desired to fight with thee or with Sir Launcelot.'

So then they went eagerly together, and Sir Tristam slew Sir Nabon, and so forthwith he leapt to his son, and struck off his head. And then all the country said they would hold of Sir Tristram.

'Nay,' said Sir Tristram, 'I will not so; here is a worshipful knight, Sir Lamorak de Gales, that for me he shall be lord of this country, for he hath done here great deeds of arms.'

'Nay,' said Sir Lamorak, 'I will not be lord of this country, for I have not deserved it as well as ye, therefore give ye it where ye will, for I will none have.'

'Well,' said Sir Tristram, 'since ye nor I will not have it, let us give it to him that hath not so well deserved it.'

'Do as ye list,' said Segwarides, 'for the gift is yours, for I will none have and I had deserved it.'

So was it given to Segwarides, whereof he thanked them;

and so was he lord, and worshipfully he did govern it. And then Sir Segwarides delivered all prisoners, and set good governance in that valley; and so he turned into Cornwall, and told King Mark and La Beale Isoud how Sir Tristram had advanced him to the Isle of Servage, and there he proclaimed in all Cornwall of all the adventures of these two knights, so was it openly known.

But full woe was La Beale Isoud when she heard tell that Sir Tristram was wedded to Isoud la Blanche Mains.

CHAPTER 40: *How Sir Lamorak departed from Sir Tristram, and how he met with Sir Froll, and after with Sir Launcelot*

So turn we unto Sir Lamorak, that rode toward Arthur's court. (And Sir Tristram's wife and Kehydius took a vessel and sailed into Brittany, unto King Howel, where he was welcome. And when he heard of these adventures they marvelled of his noble deeds.) Now turn we unto Sir Lamorak, that when he was departed from Sir Tristram he rode out of the forest, till he came to an hermitage. When the hermit saw him, he asked him from whence he came.

'Sir,' said Sir Lamorak, 'I come from this valley.'

'Sir,' said the hermit, 'thereof I marvel. For this twenty winter I saw never no knight pass this country but he was other slain or villainously wounded, or pass as a poor prisoner.'

'Those ill customs,' said Sir Lamorak, 'are fordone, for Sir Tristram slew your lord, Sir Nabon, and his son.'

Then was the hermit glad, and all his brethren, for he said there was never such a tyrant among christian men. 'And therefore,' said the hermit, 'this valley and franchise we will hold of Sir Tristram.'

So on the morrow Sir Lamorak departed; and as he rode he saw four knights fight against one, and that one knight defended him well, but at the last the four knights had him down. And then Sir Lamorak went betwixt them, and asked them why they would slay that one knight, and said it was shame, four against one.

'Thou shalt well wit,' said the four knights, 'that he is false.'

'That is your tale,' said Sir Lamorak, 'and when I hear him also speak, I will say as ye say.' Then said Lamorak, 'Ah, knight, can ye not excuse you, but that ye are a false knight.'

'Sir,' said he, 'yet can I excuse me both with my word and with my hands, that I will make good upon one of the best of them, my body to his body.'

Then spake they all at once: 'We will not jeopardy our bodies as for thee. But wit thou well,' they said, 'and King Arthur were here himself, it should not lie in his power to save his life.'

'That is too much said,' said Sir Lamorak, 'but many speak behind a man more than they will say to his face; and because of your words ye shall understand that I am one of the simplest of King Arthur's court; in the worship of my lord now do your best, and in despite of you I shall rescue him.'

And then they lashed all at once to Sir Lamorak, but anon at two strokes Sir Lamorak had slain two of them, and then the other two fled. So then Sir Lamorak turned again to that knight, and asked him his name.

'Sir,' he said, 'my name is Sir Froll of the Out Isles.'

Then he rode with Sir Lamorak and bare him company. And as they rode by the way they saw a seemly knight riding against them, and all in white.

'Ah,' said Froll, 'yonder knight jousted late with me and smote me down, therefore I will joust with him.'

'Ye shall not do so,' said Sir Lamorak, 'by my counsel, and ye will tell me your quarrel, whether ye jousted at his request, or he at yours.'

'Nay,' said Sir Froll, 'I jousted with him at my request.'

'Sir,' said Lamorak, 'then will I counsel you deal no more with him, for meseemeth by his countenance he should be a noble knight, and no japer; for methinketh he should be of the Table Round.'

'Therefore I will not spare,' said Sir Froll. And then he cried and said, 'Sir knight, make thee ready to joust.'

'That needeth not,' said the White Knight, 'for I have no lust to joust with thee.'

But yet they fewtered their spears, and the White Knight overthrew Sir Froll, and then he rode his way a soft pace. Then Sir Lamorak rode after him, and prayed him to tell him his name: 'For meseemeth ye should be of the fellowship of the Round Table.'

'Upon a covenant,' said he, 'I will tell you my name, so that ye will not discover my name, and also that ye will tell me yours.'

'Then' said he, 'my name is Sir Lamorak de Gales.'

'And my name is Sir Launcelot du Lake.'

Then they put up their swords, and kissed heartily together, and either made great joy of other.

'Sir,' said Sir Lamorak, 'and it please you I will do you service.'

'God defend,' said Launcelot, 'that any of so noble a blood as ye be should do me service.' Then he said, 'More, I am in a quest that I must do myself alone.'

'Now God speed you,' said Sir Lamorak, and so they departed.

Then Sir Lamorak came to Sir Froll and horsed him again.

'What knight is that?' said Sir Froll.

'Sir,' he said, 'it is not for you to know, nor it is no point of my charge.'

'Ye are the more uncourteous,' said Sir Froll, 'and therefore I will depart from you.'

'Ye may do as ye list,' said Sir Lamorak, 'and yet by my company ye have saved the fairest flower of your garland.' So they departed.

CHAPTER 41 : *How Sir Lamorak slew Sir Froll, and of the courteous fighting with Sir Belliance his brother*

Then within two or three days Sir Lamorak found a knight at a well sleeping, and his lady sat with him and waked. Right so came Sir Gawain and took the knight's lady, and set her up behind his squire.

So Sir Lamorak rode after Sir Gawain, and said, 'Sir Gawain, turn again.'

And then said Sir Gawain, 'What will ye do with me? For I am nephew unto King Arthur.'

'Sir,' said he, 'for that cause I will spare you, else that lady should abide with me, or else ye should joust with me.'

Then Sir Gawain turned him and ran to him that ought the lady, with his spear, but the knight with pure might smote down Sir Gawain, and took his lady with him.

All this Sir Lamorak saw, and said to himself, 'But I revenge my fellow he will say of me dishonour in King Arthur's court.' Then Sir Lamorak returned and proffered that knight to joust.

'Sir,' said he, 'I am ready.'

And there they came together with all their might, and there Sir Lamorak smote the knight through both sides that he fell to the earth dead.

Then that lady rode to that knight's brother that hight Belliance le Orgulus, that dwelt fast thereby, and then she told him how his brother was slain.

'Alas,' said he, 'I will be revenged.'

And so he horsed him, and armed him, and within a while he overtook Sir Lamorak, and bad him : 'Turn and leave that lady, for thou and I must play a new play; for thou hast slain my brother Sir Froll, that was a better knight than ever were thou.'

'It might well be,' said Sir Lamorak, 'but this day in the field I was found the better.'

So they rode together, and unhorsed other, and turned

their shields, and drew their swords, and fought mightily as noble knights proved, by the space of two hours. So then Sir Belliance prayed him to tell him his name.

'Sir,' said he, 'my name is Sir Lamorak de Gales.'

'Ah,' said Sir Belliance, 'thou art the man in the world that I most hate, for I slew my sons for thy sake, where I saved thy life, and now thou hast slain my brother Sir Froll. Alas, how should I be accorded with thee; therefore defend thee, for thou shalt die, there is none other remedy.'

'Alas,' said Sir Lamorak, 'full well me ought to know you, for ye are the man that most have done for me.' And therewithal Sir Lamorak kneeled down and besought him of grace.

'Arise,' said Sir Belliance, 'or else thereas thou kneelest I shall slay thee.'

'That shall not need,' said Sir Lamorak, 'for I will yield me unto you, not for fear of you, nor for your strength, but your goodness maketh me full loth to have ado with you; wherefore I require you for God's sake, and for the honour of knighthood, forgive me all that I have offended unto you.'

'Alas,' said Belliance, 'leave thy kneeling, or else I shall slay thee without mercy.'

Then they yede again unto battle, and either wounded other, that all the ground was bloody there as they fought. And at the last Belliance withdrew him aback and set him down softly upon a little hill, for he was so faint for bleeding that he might not stand. Then Sir Lamorak threw his shield upon his back, and asked him what cheer.

'Well,' said Sir Belliance.

'Ah, sir, yet shall I show you favour in your mal-ease.'

'Ah, knight,' Sir Belliance said, 'Sir Lamorak, thou art a fool, for and I had had thee at such advantage as thou hast done me, I should slay thee; but thy gentleness is so good and so large, that I must needs forgive thee mine evil will.'

And then Sir Lamorak kneeled down, and unlaced first his umberere, and then his own, and then either kissed other

umberere: visor.

with weeping tears. Then Sir Lamorak led Sir Belliance to an abbey fast by, and there Sir Lamorak would not depart from Belliance till he was whole. And then they sware together that none of them should never fight against other.

So Sir Lamorak departed and went to the court of King Arthur.

Here leave we of Sir Lamorak and of Sir Tristram. And here beginneth the history of La Cote Male Taile.

Book IX

CHAPTER 1: *How a young man came into the court of King Arthur, and how Sir Kay called him in scorn La Cote Male Taile*

At the court of King Arthur there came a young man and bigly made, and he was richly beseen, and he desired to be made knight of the king; but his over-garment sat overthwartly, howbeit it was rich cloth of gold.

'What is your name?' said King Arthur.

'Sir,' said he, 'my name is Breunor le Noire, and within short space ye shall know that I am of good kin.'

'It may well be,' said Sir Kay, the Seneschal, 'but in mockage ye shall be called La Cote Male Taile, that is as much to say, the evil-shapen coat.'

'It is a great thing that thou askest,' said the king. 'And for what cause wearest thou that rich coat? Tell me, for I can well think for some cause it is.'

'Sir,' he answered, 'I had a father, a noble knight, and as he rode on hunting, upon a day it happed him to lay him down to sleep; and there came a knight that had been long his enemy, and when he saw he was fast asleep he all to-hew him; and this same coat had my father on the same time; and that maketh this coat to sit so evil upon me, for the strokes be on it as I found it, and never shall be amended for me. Thus to have my father's death in remembrance I wear this coat till I be revenged; and because ye are called the most noblest king of the world I come to you that ye should make me knight.'

'Sir,' said Sir Lamorak and Sir Gaheris, 'it were well done to make him knight; for him beseemeth well of person and of countenance, that he shall prove a good man, and a good knight, and a mighty; for, sir, and ye be remembered, even such one was Sir Launcelot du Lake when he came first into this court, and full few of us knew from whence he came; and now is he proved the man of most worship in the world, and all your court and all your Round Table is by Sir Launcelot worshipped and amended more than by any knight now living.'

'That is truth,' said the king, 'and tomorrow at your request I shall make him knight.'

So on the morrow there was an hart founden, and thither rode King Arthur with a company of his knights to slay the hart. And this young man that Sir Kay named La Cote Male Taile was there left behind with Queen Guenever; and by sudden adventure there was an horrible lion kept in a strong tower of stone, and it happened that he at that time brake loose, and came hurling afore the queen and her knights. And when the queen saw the lion she cried and fled, and prayed her knights to rescue her. And there was none of them all but twelve that abode, and all the other fled.

Then said La Cote Male Taile, 'Now I see well that all coward knights be not dead;' and therewithal he drew his sword and dressed him afore the lion.

And that lion gaped wide and came upon him ramping to have slain him. And he then smote him in the midst of the head such a mighty stroke that it clave his head in sunder, and dashed to the earth.

Then was it told the queen how the young man that Sir Kay named by scorn La Cote Male Taile had slain the lion.

With that the king came home, and when the queen told him of that adventure, he was well pleased, and said, 'Upon pain of mine head he shall prove a noble man and a faithful knight, and true of his promise.' Then the king forthwithal made him knight.

'Now sir,' said this young knight, 'I require you and all the knights of your court, that ye call me by none other name but La Cote Male Taile: in so much that Sir Kay hath so named me so will I be called.'

'I assent me well thereto,' said the king.

CHAPTER 2: *How a damosel came into the court and desired a knight to take on him an enquest, which La Cote Male Taile enprised*

Then that same day there came a damosel into the court, and she brought with her a great black shield, with a white hand in the midst holding a sword. Other picture was there none in that shield. When King Arthur saw her he asked her from whence she came and what she would.

'Sir,' she said, 'I have ridden long and many a day with this shield many ways, and for this cause I am come to your court: there was a good knight that ought this shield, and this knight had undertaken a great deed of arms to achieve it; and so it misfortuned him another strong knight met with him by sudden adventure, and there they fought long, and either wounded other passing sore; and they were so weary that they left that battle even hand. So this knight that ought this shield saw none other way but he must die; and then he commanded me to bear this shield to the court of King Arthur, he requiring and praying some good knight to take this shield, and that he would fulfil the quest that he was in.'

'Now what say ye to this quest?' said King Arthur. 'Is there any of you here that will take upon him to wield this shield?'

Then was there not one that would speak one word. Then Sir Kay took the shield in his hands.

'Sir knight,' said the damosel, 'what is your name?'

'Wit ye well,' said he, 'my name is Sir Kay, the Seneschal, that wide-where is known.'

'Sir,' said that damosel, 'lay down that shield, for wit ye well it falleth not for you, for he must be a better knight than ye that shall wield this shield.'

'Damosel,' said Sir Kay, 'wit ye well I took this shield in my hands by your leave for to behold it, not to that intent; but go wheresomever thou wilt, for I will not go with you.'

wide-where: far and wide.

Then the damosel stood still a great while and beheld many of those knights. Then spake the knight, La Cote Male Taile:

'Fair damosel, I will take the shield and that adventure upon me, so I wist I should know whitherward my journey might be; for because I was this day made knight I would take this adventure upon me.'

'What is your name, fair young man?' said the damosel.

'My name is,' said he, 'La Cote Male Taile.'

'Well mayest thou be called so,' said the damosel, '"the knight with the evil-shapen coat"; but and thou be so hardy to take upon thee to bear that shield and to follow me, wit thou well thy skin shall be as well hewn as thy coat.'

'As for that,' said La Cote Male Taile, 'when I am so hewn I will ask you no salve to heal me withal.'

And forthwithal there came into the court two squires and brought him great horses, and his armour, and his spears, and anon he was armed and took his leave.

'I would not by my will,' said the king, 'that ye took upon you that hard adventure.'

'Sir,' said he, 'this adventure is mine, and the first that ever I took upon me, and that will I follow whatsomever come of me.'

Then that damosel departed, and La Cote Male Taile fast followed after. And within a while he overtook the damosel, and anon she missaid him in the foulest manner.

CHAPTER 3: *How La Cote Male Taile overthrew Sir Dagonet the king's fool, and of the rebuke that he had of the damosel*

Then Sir Kay ordained Sir Dagonet, King Arthur's fool, to follow after La Cote Male Taile; and there Sir Kay ordained that Sir Dagonet was horsed and armed, and bad him follow La Cote Male Taile and proffer him to joust, and so he did.

And when he saw La Cote Male Taile, he cried and bad him make him ready to joust. So Sir La Cote Male Taile smote Sir Dagonet over his horse's croup.

Then the damosel mocked La Cote Male Taile, and said, 'Fie for shame! Now art thou shamed in Arthur's court, when they send a fool to have ado with thee, and specially at thy first jousts;' thus she rode long, and chid.

And within a while there came Sir Bleoberis, the good knight, and there he jousted with La Cote Male Taile, and there Sir Bleoberis smote him so sore, that horse and all fell to the earth. Then La Cote Male Taile arose up lightly, and dressed his shield, and drew his sword, and would have done battle to the utterance, for he was wood wroth.

'Not so,' said Sir Bleoberis de Ganis, 'as at this time I will not fight upon foot.'

Then the Damosel Maledisant rebuked him in the foulest manner, and bad him: 'Turn again, coward.'

'Ah, damosel,' he said, 'I pray you of mercy to missay me no more, my grief is enough though ye give me no more; I call myself never the worse knight when a mare's son faileth me, and also I count me never the worse knight for a fall of Sir Bleoberis.'

So thus he rode with her two days; and by fortune there came Sir Palomides and encountered with him, and he in the same wise served him as did Bleoberis tofore hand.

'What dost thou here in my fellowship?' said the Damosel Maledisant, 'Thou canst not sit no knight, nor withstand him one buffet, but if it were Sir Dagonet.'

'Ah, fair damosel, I am not the worse to take a fall of Sir Palomides, and yet great disworship have I none, for neither Bleoberis nor yet Palomides would not fight with me on foot.'

'As for that,' said the damosel, 'wit thou well they have disdain and scorn to light off their horses to fight with such a lewd knight as thou art.'

So in the meanwhile there came Sir Mordred, Sir Gawain's brother, and so he fell in the fellowship with the Damosel Maledisant.

And then they came afore the Castle Orgulous, and there was such a custom that there might no knight come by that castle but other he must joust or be prisoner, or at the least to lose his horse and his harness.

And there came out two knights against them, and Sir Mordred jousted with the foremost, and that knight of the castle smote Sir Mordred down off his horse. And then La Cote Male Taile jousted with the other, and either of them smote other down, horse and all, to the earth. And when they avoided their horses, then either of them took other's horses.

And then La Cote Male Taile rode unto that knight that smote down Sir Mordred, and jousted with him. And there Sir La Cote Male Taile hurt and wounded him passing sore, and put him from his horse as he had been dead. So he turned unto him that met him afore, and he took the flight toward the castle, and Sir La Cote Male Taile rode after him into the Castle Orgulous, and there La Cote Male Taile slew him.

CHAPTER 4: *How La Cote Male Taile fought against an hundred knights, and how he escaped by the mean of a lady*

And anon there came an hundred knights about him and assailed him; and when he saw his horse should be slain he alit and voided his horse, and put the bridle under his feet, and so put him out of the gate. And when he had so done he hurled in among them, and dressed his back unto a lady's chamber-wall, thinking himself that he had lever die there with worship than to abide the rebukes of the Damosel Maledisant.

And in the meantime as he stood and fought, that lady whose was the chamber went out slily at her postern, and without the gates she found La Cote Male Taile's horse, and lightly she gat him by the bridle, and tied him to the postern.

And then she went unto her chamber slily again for to behold how that one knight fought against an hundred knights. And when she had beheld him long she went to a window behind his back, and said,

'Thou knight, thou fightest wonderly well, but for all that at the last thou must needs die, but and thou canst through thy mighty prowess win unto yonder postern, for there have I fastened thy horse to abide thee: but wit thou well thou must think on thy worship, and think not to die, for thou mayst not win unto that postern without thou do nobly and mightily.'

When La Cote Male Taile heard her say so he gripped his sword in his hands, and put his shield fair afore him, and through the thickest press he thrulled through them. And when he came to the postern he found there ready four knights, and at two the first strokes he slew two of the knights, and the other fled; and so he won his horse and rode from them. And all as it was it was rehearsed in King Arthur's court, how he slew twelve knights within the Castle Orgulous; and so he rode on his way.

And in the meanwhile the damosel said to Sir Mordred, 'I ween my foolish knight be other slain or taken prisoner.'

Then were they ware where he came riding. And when he was come unto them he told all how he had sped and escaped in despite of them all: 'And some of the best of them will tell no tales.'

'Thou liest ſalsely,' said the damosel, 'that dare I make good, but as a fool and a dastard to all knighthood they have let thee pass.'

'That may ye prove,' said La Cote Male Taile.

With that she sent a courier of hers that rode alway with her for to know the truth of this deed; and so he rode thither lightly, and asked how and in what manner that La Cote Male Taile was escaped out of the castle. Then all the knights cursed him, and said that he was a fiend and no man: 'for he hath slain here twelve of our best knights, and we weened

thrulled: pierced.

unto this day that it had been too much for Sir Launcelot du Lake or for Sir Tristram de Liones. And in despite of us all he is departed from us and maugre our heads.'

With this answer the courier departed and came to Maledisant his lady, and told her all how Sir La Cote Male Taile had sped at the Castle Orgulous. Then she smote down her head, and said little.

'By my head,' said Sir Mordred to the damosel, 'ye are greatly to blame so to rebuke him, for I warn you plainly he is a good knight, and I doubt not but he shall prove a noble knight; but as yet he may not yet sit sure on horseback, for he that shall be a good horseman it must come of usage and exercise. But when he cometh to the strokes of his sword he is then noble and mighty, and that saw Sir Bleoberis and Sir Palomides, for wit ye well they are wily men of arms, and anon they know when they see a young knight by his riding, how they are sure to give him a fall from his horse or a great buffet. But for the most part they will not light on foot with young knights, for they are wight and strongly armed. For in likewise Sir Launcelot du Lake, when he was first made knight, he was often put to the worse upon horseback, but ever upon foot he recovered his renown, and slew and defiled many knights of the Round Table. And therefore the rebukes that Sir Launcelot did unto many knights causeth them that be men of prowess to beware; for often I have seen the old proved knights rebuked and slain by them that were but young beginners.' Thus they rode sure talking by the way together.

Here leave we off a while of this tale, and speak we of Sir Launcelot du Lake:

CHAPTER 5: *How Sir Launcelot came to the court and heard of La Cote Male Taile, and how he followed after him, and how La Cote Male Taile was prisoner*

That when he was come to the court of King Arthur, then heard he tell of the young knight La Cote Male Taile, how he slew the lion, and how he took upon him the adventure of the black shield, the which was named at that time the hardiest adventure of the world.

'So God me save,' said Sir Launcelot unto many of his fellows, 'it was shame to all the noble knights to suffer such a young knight to take such adventure upon him for his destruction; for I will that ye wit,' said Sir Launcelot, 'that that Damosel Maledisant hath borne that shield many a day for to seek the most proved knights, and that was she that Breunis Saunce Pité took that shield from her, and after Tristram de Liones rescued that shield from him and gave it to the damosel again, a little afore that time that Sir Tristram fought with my nephew Sir Blamor de Ganis, for a quarrel that was betwixt the King of Ireland and him.'

Then many knights were sorry that Sir La Cote Male Taile was gone forth to that adventure.

'Truly,' said Sir Launcelot, 'I cast me to ride after him.'

And within seven days Sir Launcelot overtook La Cote Male Taile, and then he saluted him and the Damosel Maledisant. And when Sir Mordred saw Sir Launcelot, then he left their fellowship; and so Sir Launcelot rode with them all a day, and ever that damosel rebuked La Cote Male Taile, and then Sir Launcelot answered for him; then she left off, and rebuked Sir Launcelot.

So this meantime Sir Tristram sent by a damosel a letter unto Sir Launcelot, excusing him of the wedding of Isoud la Blanche Mains; and said in the letter, as he was a true knight he had never ado fleshly with Isoud la Blanche Mains; and passing courteously and gently Sir Tristram wrote unto Sir Launcelot, ever beseeching him to be his good friend and unto La Beale Isoud of Cornwall, and that Sir Launcelot would excuse him if that ever he saw her. And within short time, by the grace of God, said Sir Tristram that he would speak with La Beale Isoud, and with him right hastily.

Then Sir Launcelot departed from the damosel and from Sir La Cote Male Taile, for to oversee that letter, and to write another letter unto Sir Tristam de Liones.

And in the meanwhile La Cote Male Taile rode with the damosel until they came to a castle that hight Pendragon; and there were six knights stood afore him, and one of them proffered to joust with La Cote Male Taile.

And there La Cote Male Taile smote him over his horse's croup. And then the five knights set upon him all at once with their spears, and there they smote La Cote Male Taile down, horse and man. And then they alit suddenly, and set their hands upon him all at once, and took him prisoner, and so led him unto the castle and kept him as prisoner.

And on the morn Sir Launcelot arose, and delivered the damosel with letters unto Sir Tristram, and then he took his way after La Cote Male Taile. And by the way upon a bridge there was a knight proffered Sir Launcelot to joust, and Sir Launcelot smote him down, and then they fought upon foot a noble battle together, and a mighty; and at the last Sir Launcelot smote him down grovelling upon his hands and his knees. And then that knight yielded him, and Sir Launcelot received him fair.

'Sir,' said the knight, 'I require thee tell me your name, for much my heart giveth unto you.'

'Nay,' said Sir Launcelot, 'as at this time I will not tell you my name, unless then that ye tell me your name.'

'Certainly,' said the knight, 'my name is Sir Nerovens, that was made knight of my lord Sir Launcelot du Lake.'

'Ah, Nerovens de Lile,' said Sir Launcelot, 'I am right glad that ye are proved a good knight, for now wit ye well my name is Sir Launcelot du Lake.'

'Alas,' said Sir Nerovens de Lile, 'what have I done!'

And therewithal flatling he fell to his feet, and would have kissed them, but Sir Launcelot would not let him; and then either made great joy of other.

And then Sir Nerovens told Sir Launcelot that he should not go by the Castle of Pendragon: 'For there is a lord, a mighty knight, and many knights with him, and this night I heard say that they took a knight prisoner yesterday that rode with a damosel, and they say he is a knight of the Round Table.'

CHAPTER 6: *How Sir Launcelot fought with six knights, and after with Sir Brian, and how he delivered the prisoners*

'Ah,' said Sir Launcelot, 'that knight is my fellow, and him shall I rescue or else I shall lose my life therefore.'

And therewithal he rode fast till he came before the Castle of Pendragon; and anon therewithal there came six knights, and all made them ready to set upon Sir Launcelot at once. Then Sir Launcelot fewtered his spear, and smote the foremost that he brake his back insunder, and three of them hit and three failed. And then Sir Launcelot passed through them, and lightly he turned in again, and smote another knight through the breast and throughout the back more than an ell, and therewithal his spear brake. So then all the remnant of the four knights drew their swords and lashed at Sir Launcelot. And at every stroke Sir Launcelot bestowed so his strokes that at four strokes sundry they avoided their saddles, passing sore wounded; and forthwithal he rode hurling into that castle.

And anon the lord of the castle, that was that time cleped Sir Brian de les Isles, the which was a noble man and a great enemy unto King Arthur, within a while he was armed and upon horseback. And then they fewtered their spears and hurled together so strongly that both their horses rashed to the earth. And then they avoided their saddles, and dressed their shields, and drew their swords, and flung together as

ell: a measure of length: 45 inches. *cleped*: called.

wood men, and there were many strokes given in a while.

At the last Sir Launcelot gave to Sir Brian such a buffet that he kneeled upon his knees, and then Sir Launcelot rashed upon him and with great force he pulled off his helm; and when Sir Brian saw that he should be slain he yielded him, and put him in his mercy and in his grace.

Then Sir Launcelot made him to deliver all his prisoners that he had within his castle, and therein Sir Launcelot found of Arthur's knights thirty, and forty ladies, and so he delivered them; and then he rode his way.

And anon as La Cote Male Taile was delivered he gat his horse, and his harness, and his damosel Maledisant.

The meanwhile Sir Nerovens, that Sir Launcelot had foughten withal afore at the bridge, he sent a damosel after Sir Launcelot to wit how he sped at the Castle of Pendragon. And then they within the castle marvelled what knight he was, when Sir Brian and his knights delivered all those prisoners.

'Have ye no marvel,' said the damosel, 'for the best knight in this world was here, and did this journey, and wit ye well,' she said, 'it was Sir Launcelot.'

Then was Sir Brian full glad, and so was his lady, and all his knights, that such a man should win them. And when the damosel and La Cote Male Taile understood that it was Sir Launcelot du Lake that had ridden with them in fellowship, and that she remembered her how she had rebuked him and called him coward, then was she passing heavy.

CHAPTER 7: *How Sir Launcelot met with the damosel named Maledisant, and named her the Damosel Bienpensant*

So then they took their horses and rode forth a pace after Sir Launcelot. And within two mile they overtook him, and saluted him, and thanked him, and the damosel cried Sir Launcelot mercy of her evil deed and saying,

'For now I know the flower of all knighthood is departed

even between Sir Tristram and you. For God knoweth,' said the damosel, 'that I have sought you my lord, Sir Launcelot, and Sir Tristram long, and now I thank God I have met with you. And once at Camelot I met with Sir Tristram, and there he rescued this black shield with the white hand holding a naked sword that Sir Breunis Saunce Pité had taken from me.'

'Now, fair damosel,' said Sir Launcelot, 'who told you my name?'

'Sir,' said she, 'there came a damosel from a knight that ye fought withal at the bridge, and she told me your name was Sir Launcelot du Lake.'

'Blame have she then,' said Sir Launcelot, 'but her lord, Sir Nerovens, hath told her. But, damosel,' said Sir Launcelot, 'upon this covenant I will ride with you, so that ye will not rebuke this knight Sir La Cote Male Taile no more; for he is a good knight, and I doubt not he shall prove a noble knight, and for his sake and pity that he should not be destroyed I followed him to succour him in this great need.'

'Ah, Jesu thank you,' said the damosel, 'for now I will say unto you and to him both, I rebuked him never for no hate that I hated him, but for great love that I had to him. For ever I supposed that he had been too young and too tender to take upon him these adventures. And therefore by my will I would have driven him away for jealousy that I had of his life, for it may be no young knight's deed that shall achieve this adventure to the end.'

'Perdy,' said Sir Launcelot, 'it is well said, and where ye are called the Damosel Maledisant I will call you the Damosel Bienpensant.'

And so they rode forth a great while unto they came to the border of the country of Surluse, and there they found a fair village with a strong bridge like a fortress. And when Sir Launcelot and they were at the bridge there start forth afore them of gentlemen and yeomen many, that said,

'Fair lords, ye may not pass this bridge and this fortress because of that black shield that I see one of you bear, and therefore there shall not pass but one of you at once; therefore choose you which of you shall enter within this bridge first.'

Then Sir Launcelot proffered himself first to enter within this bridge.

'Sir,' said La Cote Male Taile, 'I beseech you let me enter within this fortress, and if I may speed well I will send for you, and if it happened that I be slain, there it goeth. And if so be that I am a prisoner taken, then may ye rescue me.'

'I am loth,' said Sir Launcelot, 'to let you pass this passage.'

'Sir,' said La Cote Male Taile, 'I pray you let me put my body in this adventure.'

'Now go your way,' said Sir Launcelot, 'and Jesu be your speed.'

So he entered, and anon there met with him two brethren, the one hight Sir Plaine de Force, and the other hight Sir Plaine de Amours. And anon they met with Sir La Cote Male Taile; and first La Cote Male Taile smote down Plaine de Force, and after he smote down Plaine de Amours; and then they dressed them to their shields and swords, and bad La Cote Male Taile alight, and so he did; and there was dashing and foining with swords and so they began to assail full hard La Cote Male Taile, and many great wounds they gave him upon his head, and upon his breast, and upon his shoulders. And as he might ever among he gave sad strokes again. And then the two brethren traced and traversed for to be of both hands of Sir La Cote Male Taile, but he by fine force and knightly prowess gat them afore him. And then when he felt himself so wounded, then he doubled his strokes, and gave them so many wounds that he felled them to the earth, and would have slain them had they not yielded them.

And right so Sir La Cote Male Taile took the best horse that there was of them three, and so rode forth his way to the other fortress and bridge; and there he met with the third brother whose name was Sir Plenorius, a full noble knight, and there they jousted together, and either smote other down, horse and man, to the earth. And then they avoided their horses, and dressed their shields, and drew their swords, and gave many sad strokes, and one while the one knight was afore on the bridge, and another while the other. And thus they fought two hours and more, and never rested. And ever Sir Launcelot and the damosel beheld them.

'Alas,' said the damosel, 'my knight fighteth passing sore and over long.'

'Now may ye see,' said Sir Launcelot, 'that he is a noble knight, for to consider his first battle, and his grievous wounds; and even forthwithal so wounded as he is, it is marvel that he may endure this long battle with that good knight.'

CHAPTER 8: *How La Cote Male Taile was taken prisoner, and after rescued by Sir Launcelot, and how Sir Launcelot overcame four brethren*

This meanwhile Sir La Cote Male Taile sank right down upon the earth, what forwounded and what forbled he might not stand. Then the other knight had pity of him, and said,

'Fair young knight, dismay you not, for had ye been fresh when ye met with me, as I was, I wot well that I should not have endured so long as ye have done; and therefore for your noble deeds of arms I shall show to you kindness and gentleness in all that I may.'

And forthwithal this noble knight, Sir Plenorius, took him up in his arms, and led him into his tower. And then he commanded him the wine, and made to search him and to stop his bleeding wounds.

'Sir,' said La Cote Male Taile, 'withdraw you from me, and hie you to yonder bridge again, for there will meet with you another manner knight than ever was I.'

'Why,' said Plenorius, 'is there another manner knight behind of your fellowship?'

'Yea,' said La Cote Male Taile, 'there is a much better knight than I am.'

'What is his name?' said Plenorius.

'Ye shall not know for me,' said La Cote Male Taile.

'Well,' said the knight, 'he shall be encountered withal whatsomever he be.'

Then Sir Plenorius heard a knight call that said, 'Sir Plenorius, where art thou? Other thou must deliver me the prisoner that thou hast led unto thy tower, or else come and do battle with me.'

Then Plenorius gat his horse, and came with a spear in his hand walloping toward Sir Launcelot; and then they began to fewter their spears, and came together as thunder, and smote either other so mightily that their horses fell down under them.

And then they avoided their horses, and pulled out their swords, and like two bulls they lashed together with great strokes and foins; but ever Sir Launcelot recovered ground upon him, and Sir Plenorius traced to have gone about him. But Sir Launcelot would not suffer that, but bare him backer and backer, till he came nigh his tower gate.

And then said Sir Launcelot, 'I know thee well for a good knight, but wit thou well thy life and death is in my hand, and therefore yield thee to me, and thy prisoner.'

The other answered no word, but struck mightily upon Sir Launcelot's helm, that the fire sprang out of his eyen. Then Sir Launcelot doubled his strokes so thick, and smote at him so mightily, that he made him kneel upon his knees. And therewith Sir Launcelot leapt upon him, and pulled him grovelling down.

Then Sir Plenorius yielded him, and his tower, and all his prisoners at his will. Then Sir Launcelot received him and took his troth.

And then he rode to the other bridge, and there Sir Launcelot jousted with other three of his brethren, the one hight Pillounes, and the other hight Pellogris, and the third Sir Pellandris. And first upon horseback Sir Launcelot smote them down, and afterward he beat them on foot, and made them to yield them unto him. And then he returned unto Sir Plenorius, and there he found in his prison King Carados of Scotland, and many other knights, and all they were delivered.

And then Sir La Cote Male Taile came to Sir Launcelot, and then Sir Launcelot would have given him all these fortresses and these bridges.

'Nay,' said La Cote Male Taile, 'I will not have Sir Plenorius' livelihood. With that he will grant you, my lord Sir Launcelot, to come unto King Arthur's court, and to be his knight, and all his brethren, I will pray you my lord, to let him have his livelihood.'

'I will well,' said Sir Launcelot, 'with this, that he will come to the court of King Arthur and become his man, and his brethren five. And as for you, Sir Plenorius, I will undertake,' said Sir Launcelot, 'at the next feast, so there be a place voided, that ye shall be knight of the Round Table.'

'Sir,' said Plenorius, 'at the next feast of Pentecost I will be at Arthur's court, and at that time I will be guided and ruled as King Arthur and ye will have me.'

Then Sir Launcelot and Sir La Cote Male Taile reposed them there, unto the time that Sir La Cote Male Taile was whole of his wounds, and there they had merry cheer, and good rest, and many good games, and there were many fair ladies.

CHAPTER 9: *How Sir Launcelot made La Cote Male Taile lord of the Castle of Pendragon, and after was made knight of the Round Table*

And in the meanwhile came Sir Kay, the Seneschal, and Sir Brandiles, and anon they fellowshipped with them. And then within ten days, then departed those knights of Arthur's court from these fortresses.

And as Sir Launcelot came by the Castle of Pendragon there he put Sir Brian de les Isles from his lands, for cause he would never be withhold with King Arthur; and all that Castle of Pendragon and all the lands thereof he gave to Sir

La Cote Male Taile. And then Sir Launcelot sent for Nerovens that he made once knight, and he made him to have all the rule of that castle and of that country, under La Cote Male Taile; and so they rode to Arthur's court all wholly together.

And at Pentecost next following there was Sir Plenorius and Sir La Cote Male Taile, called otherwise by right Sir Breunor le Noire, both made knights of the Table Round; and great lands King Arthur gave them. And there Breunor le Noire wedded that damosel Maledisant. And after she was called Beauvivante, but ever after for the more part he was called La Cote Male Taile; and he proved a passing noble knight, and mighty, and many worshipful deeds he did after in his life. And Sir Plenorius proved a noble knight and full of prowess, and all the days of their life for the most part they awaited upon Sir Launcelot; and Sir Plenorius' brethren were ever knights of King Arthur. And also, as the French book maketh mention, Sir La Cote Male Taile avenged his father's death.

CHAPTER 10: *How La Beale Isoud sent letters to Sir Tristram by her maid Bragwaine, and of divers adventures of Sir Tristram*

Now leave we here Sir La Cote Male Taile, and turn we unto Sir Tristram de Liones that was in Brittany. When La Beale Isoud understood that he was wedded she sent to him by her maid Bragwaine as piteous letters as could be thought and made, and her conclusion was that, and it pleased Sir Tristram, that he would come to her court, and bring with him Isoud la Blanche Mains, and they should be kept as well as she herself.

Then Sir Tristram called unto him Sir Kehydius, and asked him whether he would go with him into Cornwall secretly. He answered him that he was ready at all times. And then he let ordain privily a little vessel, and therein they went, Sir

Tristram, Kehydius, Dame Bragwaine, and Gouvernail, Sir Tristram's squire.

So when they were in the sea a contrarious wind blew them on the coasts of North Wales, nigh the Castle Perilous.

Then said Sir Tristram, 'Here shall ye abide me these ten days, and Gouvernail, my squire, with you. And if so be I come not again by that day, take the next way into Cornwall; for in this forest are many strange adventures, as I have heard say, and some of them I cast me to prove or I depart. And when I may I shall hie me after you.'

Then Sir Tristram and Kehydius took their horses and departed from their fellowship. And so they rode within that forest a mile and more; and at the last Sir Tristram saw afore him a likely knight armed sitting by a well, and a strong mighty horse passing nigh him tied to an oak, and a man hoving and riding by him leading an horse lade with spears. And this knight that sat at the well seemed by his countenance to be passing heavy.

Then Sir Tristram rode near him and said, 'Fair knight, why sit ye so drooping? Ye seem to be a knight errant by your arms and harness, and therefore dress you to joust with one of us, or with both.'

Therewithal that knight made no words, but took his shield and buckled it about his neck, and lightly he took his horse and leapt upon him. And then he took a great spear of his squire, and departed his way a furlong.

Sir Kehydius asked leave of Sir Tristram to joust first.

'Do your best,' said Sir Tristram.

So they met together, and there Sir Kehydius had a fall, and was sore wounded on high above the paps.

Then Sir Tristram said, 'Knight, that is well jousted, now make you ready unto me.'

'I am ready,' said the knight. And then that knight took a greater spear in his hand, and encountered with Sir Tristram, and there by great force that knight smote down Sir Tristram from his horse and had a great fall.

Then Sir Tristram was sore ashamed, and lightly he

avoided his horse, and put his shield afore his shoulder, and drew his sword. And then Sir Tristram required that knight of his knighthood to alight upon foot and fight with him.

'I will well,' said the knight.

And so he alit upon foot, and avoided his horse, and cast his shield upon his shoulder, and drew his sword, and there they fought a long battle together full nigh two hours.

Then Sir Tristram said, 'Fair knight, hold thine hand, and tell me of whence thou art, and what is thy name.'

'As for that,' said the knight, 'I will be advised; but and thou wilt tell me thy name peradventure I will tell thee mine.'

CHAPTER 11: *How Sir Tristram met with Sir Lamorak de Gales, and how they fought, and after accorded never to fight together*

'Now fair knight,' he said, 'my name is Sir Tristram de Liones.'

'Sir,' said the other knight, 'and my name is Sir Lamorak de Gales.'

'Ah, Sir Lamorak,' said Sir Tristram, 'well be we met, and bethink thee now of the despite thou didst me of the sending of the horn unto King Mark's court, to the intent to have slain or dishonoured my lady the queen, La Beale Isoud; and therefore wit thou well,' said Sir Tristram, 'the one of us shall die or we depart.'

'Sir,' and Sir Lamorak, 'remember that we were together in the Isle of Servage, and at that time ye promised me great friendship.'

Then Sir Tristram would make no longer delays, but lashed at Sir Lamorak; and thus they fought long till either were weary of other. Then Sir Tristram said to Sir Lamorak.

'In all my life met I never with such a knight that was so big and well breathed as ye be, therefore,' said Sir Tristram, 'it were pity that any of us both should here be mischieved.'

'Sir,' said Sir Lamorak, 'for your renown and name I will

that ye have the worship of this battle, and therefore I will yield me unto you.' And therewith he took the point of his sword to yield him.

'Nay,' said Sir Tristram, 'ye shall not do so, for well I know your proffers, and more of your gentleness than for my fear or dread ye have of me.' And therewithal Sir Tristram proffered him his sword and said, 'Sir Lamorak, as an overcomen knight I yield me unto you as to a man of the most noble prowess that ever I met withal.'

'Nay,' said Sir Lamorak, 'I will do you gentleness. I require you let us be sworn together that never none of us shall after this day have ado with other.'

And therewithal Sir Tristram and Sir Lamorak sware that never none of them should fight against other, nor for weal nor for woe.

CHAPTER 12: *How Sir Palomides followed the Questing Beast, and smote down Sir Tristram and Sir Lamorak with one spear*

And this meanwhile there came Sir Palomides, the good knight, following the Questing Beast that had in shape a head like a serpent's head, and a body like a leopard, buttocks like a lion, and footed like an hart; and in his body there was such a noise as it had been the noise of thirty couple of hounds questing, and such a noise that beast made wheresomever he went; and this beast evermore Sir Palomides followed, for it was called his quest.

And right so as he followed this beast it came by Sir Tristram, and soon after came Palomides. And to brief this matter he smote down Sir Tristram and Sir Lamorak both with one spear; and so he departed after the Beast Glatisant, that was called the Questing Beast; wherefore these two knights were passing wroth that Sir Palomides would not fight on foot with them.

glatisant: barking.

Here men may understand that be of worship, that he was never formed that all times might stand, but sometime he was put to the worse by mal-fortune; and at sometime the worse knight put the better knight to a rebuke.

Then Sir Tristram and Sir Lamorak gat Sir Kehydius upon a shield betwixt them both, and led him to a forester's lodge, and there they gave him in charge to keep him well, and with him they abode three days. Then the two knights took their horses and at the cross they departed.

And then said Sir Tristram to Sir Lamorak, 'I require you if ye hap to meet with Sir Palomides, say him that he shall find me at the same well there I met him, and there I, Sir Tristram, shall prove whether he be better knight than I.'

And so either departed from other a sundry way, and Sir Tristram rode nigh thereas was Sir Kehydius; and Sir Lamorak rode until he came to a chapel, and there he put his horse unto pasture.

And anon there came Sir Meliagaunt, that was King Bagdemagus' son, and he there put his horse to pasture, and was not ware of Sir Lamorak; and then this knight Sir Meliagaunt made his moan of the love that he had to Queen Guenever, and there he made a woful complaint.

All this heard Sir Lamorak, and on the morn Sir Lamorak took his horse and rode unto the forest, and there he met with two knights hoving under the wood shaw.

'Fair knights,' said Sir Lamorak, 'what do ye hoving here and watching? And if ye be knights errant that will joust, lo I am ready.'

'Nay, sir knight,' they said, 'not so, we abide not here for to joust with you, but lie here in await of a knight that slew our brother.'

'What knight was that,' said Sir Lamorak,' that you would fain meet withal?'

'Sir,' they said, 'it is Sir Launcelot that slew our brother, and if ever we may meet with him he shall not escape, but we shall slay him.'

shaw: thicket.

'Ye take upon you a great charge,' said Sir Lamorak, 'for Sir Launcelot is a noble proved knight.'

'As for that we doubt not, for there nis none of us but we are good enough for him.'

'I will not believe that,' said Sir Lamorak, 'for I heard never yet of no knight the days of my life but Sir Launcelot was too big for him.'

CHAPTER 13: *How Sir Lamorak met with Sir Meliagaunt, and fought together for the beauty of Dame Guenever*

Right so as they stood talking thus Sir Lamorak was ware how Sir Launcelot came riding straight toward them; then Sir Lamorak saluted him, and he him again. And then Sir Lamorak asked Sir Launcelot if there were anything that he might do for him in these marches.

'Nay,' said Sir Launcelot, 'not at this time I thank you.'

Then either departed from other, and Sir Lamorak rode again thereas he left the two knights, and then he found them hid in the leaved wood.

'Fie on you,' said Sir Lamorak, 'false cowards, pity and shame it is that any of you should take the high order of knighthood.'

So Sir Lamorak departed from them, and within a while he met with Sir Meliagaunt. And then Sir Lamorak asked him why he loved Queen Guenever as he did: 'For I was not far from you when ye made your complaint by the chapel.'

'Did ye so?' said Sir Meliagaunt, 'then will I abide by it: I love Queen Guenever, what will ye with it? I will prove and make good that she is the fairest lady and most of beauty in the world.'

'As to that,' said Sir Lamorak, 'I say nay thereto, for Queen Margawse of Orkney, mother to Sir Gawain, and his mother is the fairest queen and lady that beareth the life.'

'That is not so,' said Sir Meliagaunt, 'and that will I prove with my hands upon thy body.'

'Will ye so?' said Sir Lamorak, 'and in a better quarrel keep I not to fight.'

Then they departed either from other in great wrath. And then they came riding together as it had been thunder, and either smote other so sore that their horses fell backward to the earth. And then they avoided their horses, and dressed their shields, and drew their swords. And then they hurtled together as wild boars, and thus they fought a great while. For Meliagaunt was a good man and of great might, but Sir Lamorak was hard big for him, and put him always aback, but either had wounded other sore.

And as they stood thus fighting, by fortune came Sir Launcelot and Sir Bleoberis riding. And then Sir Launcelot rode betwixt them, and asked them for what cause they fought so together: 'And ye are both knights of King Arthur!'

'Sir,' said Meliagaunt, 'I shall tell you for what cause we do this battle. I praised my lady, Queen Guenever, and said she was the fairest lady of the world, and Sir Lamorak said nay thereto, for he said Queen Margawse of Orkney was fairer than she and more of beauty.'

'Ah, Sir Lamorak, why sayest thou so? It is not thy part to dispraise thy princes that thou art under their obeisance, and we all.' And therewith he alit on foot, and said, 'For this quarrel, make thee ready, for I will prove upon thee that Queen Guenever is the fairest lady and most of bounty in the world.'

'Sir,' said Sir Lamorak, 'I am loth to have ado with you in this quarrel, for every man thinketh his own lady fairest; and though I praise the lady that I love most ye should not be wroth; for though my lady, Queen Guenever, be fairest in your eye, wit ye well Queen Margawse of Orkney is fairest in mine eye, and so every knight thinketh his own lady fairest; and wit ye well, sir, ye are the man in the world except Sir Tristram that I am most lothest to have ado withal, but, and ye will needs fight with me, I shall endure you as long as I may.'

Then spake Sir Bleoberis and said, 'My lord Sir Launcelot, I wist you never so misadvised as ye are now, for Sir Lamorak sayeth you but reason and knightly; for I warn you I have a lady, and methinketh that she is the fairest lady of the world. Were this a great reason that ye should be wroth with me for such language? And well ye wot, that Sir Lamorak is as noble a knight as I know, and he hath ought you and us ever good will, and therefore I pray you be good friends.'

Then Sir Launcelot said unto Sir Lamorak, 'I pray you forgive me mine evil will, and if I was misadvised I will amend it.'

'Sir,' said Sir Lamorak, 'the amends is soon made betwixt you and me.'

And so Sir Launcelot and Sir Bleoberis departed, and Sir Meliagaunt and Sir Lamorak took their horses, and either departed from other.

And within a while came King Arthur, and met with Sir Lamorak, and jousted with him; and there he smote down Sir Lamorak, and wounded him sore with a spear, and so he rode from him; wherefore Sir Lamorak was wroth that he would not fight with him on foot, howbeit that Sir Lamorak knew not King Arthur.

CHAPTER 14: *How Sir Kay met with Sir Tristram, and after of the shame spoken of the knights of Cornwall, and how they jousted*

Now leave we of this tale, and speak we of Sir Tristram, that as he rode he met with Sir Kay, the Seneschal; and there Sir Kay asked Sir Tristram of what country he was. He answered that he was of the country of Cornwall.

'It may well be,' said Sir Kay, 'for yet heard I never that ever good knight came out of Cornwall.'

'That is evil spoken,' said Sir Tristram, 'but and it please you to tell me your name I require you.'

'Sir, wit ye well,' said Sir Kay, 'that my name is Sir Kay, the Seneschal.'

'Is that your name?' said Sir Tristram, 'Now wit ye well that ye are named the shamefullest knight of your tongue that now is living; howbeit ye are called a good knight, but ye are called unfortunate, and passing overthwart of your tongue.'

And thus they rode together till they came to a bridge. And there was a knight would not let them pass till one of them jousted with him; and so that knight jousted with Sir Kay, and there that knight gave Sir Kay a fall. His name was Sir Tor, Sir Lamorak's half-brother.

And then they two rode to their lodging, and there they found Sir Brandiles, and Sir Tor came thither anon after. And as they sat at supper these four knights, three of them spake all shame by Cornish knights. Sir Tristram heard all that they said and he said but little, but he thought the more, but at that time he discovered not his name.

Upon the morn Sir Tristram took his horse and abode them upon their way. And there Sir Brandiles proffered to joust with Sir Tristram, and Sir Tristram smote him down, horse and all, to the earth.

Then Sir Tor le Fise de Vayshoure encountered with Sir Tristram, and there Sir Tristram smote him down, and then he rode his way, and Sir Kay followed him, but he would not of his fellowship.

Then Sir Brandiles came to Sir Kay and said, 'I would wit fain what is that knight's name.'

'Come on with me,' said Sir Kay, 'and we shall pray him to tell us his name.'

So they rode together till they came nigh him, and then they were ware where he sat by a well, and had put off his helm to drink at the well. And when he saw them come he laced on his helm lightly, and took his horse, and proffered them to joust.

'Nay,' said Sir Brandiles, 'we jousted late enough with you, we come not in that intent. But for this we come to require you of knighthood to tell us your name.'

'My fair knights, sithen that is your desire, and to please you, ye shall wit that my name is Sir Tristram de Liones, nephew unto King Mark of Cornwall.'

'In good time,' said Sir Brandiles, 'and well be ye founden, and wit ye well that we be right glad that we have found you, and we be of a fellowship that would be right glad of your company. For ye are the knight in the world that the noble followship of the Round Table most desireth to have the company of.'

'God thank them,' said Sir Tristram, 'of their great goodness, but as yet I feel well that I am unable to be of their fellowship, for I was never yet of such deeds of worthiness to be in the company of such a fellowship.'

'Ah,' said Sir Kay, 'and ye be Sir Tristram de Liones, ye are the man called now most of prowess except Sir Launcelot du Lake; for he beareth not the life, Christian ne heathen, that can find such another knight, to speak of his prowess, and of his hands, and his truth withal. For yet could there never creature say of him dishonour and make it good.'

Thus they talked a great while, and then they departed either from other such ways as them seemed best.

CHAPTER 15: *How King Arthur was brought into the Forest Perilous, and how Sir Tristram saved his life*

Now shall ye hear what was the cause that King Arthur came into the Forest Perilous, that was in North Wales, by the means of a lady. Her name was Annowre, and this lady came to King Arthur at Cardiff; and she by fair promise and fair behests made King Arthur to ride with her into that Forest Perilous. And she was a great sorceress; and many days she had loved King Arthur, and because she would have him to lie by her she came into that country.

So when the king was gone with her many of his knights followed after King Arthur when they missed him, as Sir Launcelot, Brandiles, and many other. And when she had brought him to her tower she desired him to lie by her; and then the king remembered him of his lady, and would not lie by her for no craft that she could do. Then every day she would make him ride into that forest with his own knights, to the intent to have had King Arthur slain. For when this Lady Annowre saw that she might not have him at her will, then she laboured by false means to have destroyed King Arthur, and slain.

Then the Lady of the Lake that was alway friendly to King Arthur, she understood by her subtle crafts that King Arthur was like to be destroyed. And therefore this Lady of the Lake that hight Nimue, came into that forest to seek after Sir Launcelot du Lake or Sir Tristram for to help King Arthur; foras that same day this Lady of the Lake knew well that King Arthur should be slain, unless that he had help of one of these two knights. And thus she rode up and down till she met with Sir Tristram, and anon as she saw him she knew him.

'O my lord Sir Tristram,' she said, 'well be ye met, and blessed be the time that I have met with you; for this same day, and within these two hours, shall be done the foulest deed that ever was done in this land.'

'O fair damosel,' said Sir Tristram, 'may I amend it?'

'Come on with me,' she said, 'and that in all the haste ye may, for ye shall see the most worshipfullest knight of the world hard bestad.'

Then said Sir Tristram, 'I am ready to help such a noble man.'

'He is neither better ne worse,' said the Lady of the Lake, 'but the noble King Arthur himself.'

'God defend,' said Sir Tristram, 'that ever he should be in such distress.'

Then they rode together a great pace, until they came to a little turret, a castle; and underneath that castle they saw a knight standing upon foot fighting with two knights; and so Sir Tristram beheld them, and at the last the two knights smote down the one knight, and that one of them unlaced his helm to have slain him. And the Lady Annowre gat King Arthur's sword in her hand to have stricken off his head.

And therewithal came Sir Tristram with all his might, crying, 'Traitress, traitress, leave that!' And anon there Sir Tristram smote the one of the knights through the body that he fell dead; and then he rashed to the other and smote his back in sunder.

And in the meanwhile the Lady of the Lake cried to King Arthur, 'Let not that false lady escape.'

Then King Arthur overtook her, and with the same sword he smote off her head, and the Lady of the Lake took up her head and hung it up by the hair off her saddle-bow.

And then Sir Tristram horsed King Arthur and rode forth with him, but he charged the Lady of the Lake not to discover his name as at that time. When the king was horsed he thanked heartily Sir Tristram, and desired to wit his name; but he would not tell him, but that he was a poor knight adventurous; and so he bare King Arthur fellowship till he met with some of his knights.

And within a while he met with Sir Ector de Maris, and he knew not King Arthur nor Sir Tristram, and he desired to joust with one of them. Then Sir Tristram rode unto Sir Ector, and smote him from his horse.

And when he had done so he came again to the king and said, 'My lord, yonder is one of your knights, he may bear you fellowship, and another day that deed that I have done for you I trust to God ye shall understand that I would do you service.'

'Alas,' said King Arthur, 'let me wit what ye are?'

'Not at this time,' said Sir Tristram.

So he departed and left King Arthur and Sir Ector together.

CHAPTER 16: *How Sir Tristram came to La Beale Isoud, and how Kehydius began to love Beale Isoud, and of a letter that Tristram found*

And then at a day set Sir Tristram and Sir Lamorak met at the well; and then they took Kehydius at the forester's house, and so they rode with him to the ship where they left Dame Bragwaine and Gouvernail, and so they sailed into Cornwall all wholly together.

And by assent and information of Dame Bragwaine when they were landed they rode unto Sir Dinas, the Seneschal, a trusty friend of Sir Tristram's. And so Dame Bragwaine and Sir Dinas rode to the court of King Mark, and told the queen, La Beale Isoud, that Sir Tristram was nigh her in that country.

Then for very pure joy La Beale Isoud swooned; and when she might speak she said, 'Gentle knight, seneschal, help that I might speak with him, other my heart will brast.'

Then Sir Dinas and Dame Bragwaine brought Sir Tristram and Kehydius privily unto the court, unto a chamber whereas La Beale Isoud had assigned it; and to tell the joys that were betwixt La Beale Isoud and Sir Tristram, there is no tongue can tell it, nor heart think it, nor pen write it.

And as the French book maketh mention, at the first time that ever Sir Kehydius saw La Beale Isoud he was so enamoured upon her that for very pure love he might never withdraw it. And at the last, as ye shall hear or the book be ended, Sir Kehydius died for the love of La Beale Isoud.

And then privily he wrote unto her letters and ballads of the most goodliest that were used in those days. And when La Beale Isoud understood his letters she had pity of his complaint, and unadvised she wrote another letter to comfort him withal.

And Sir Tristram was all this while in a turret at the commandment of La Beale Isoud, and when she might she came unto Sir Tristram.

So on a day King Mark played at the chess under a chamber window; and at that time Sir Tristram and Sir Kehydius were within the chamber over King Mark, and as it mishapped Sir Tristram found the letter that Kehydius sent unto La Beale Isoud, also he had found the letter that she wrote unto Kehydius. And at that same time La Beale Isoud was in the same chamber.

Then Sir Tristram came unto La Beale Isoud and said, 'Madam, here is a letter that was sent unto you, and here is the letter that ye sent unto him that sent you that letter. Alas, Madam, the good love that I have loved you, and many lands and riches have I forsaken for your love, and now ye are a traitress to me, the which doth me great pain. But as for thee, Sir Kehydius, I brought thee out of Brittany into this country, and thy father, King Howel, I won his lands. Howbeit I wedded thy sister Isoud la Blanche Mains for the goodness she did unto me, and yet, as I am true knight, she is a clean maiden for me. But wit thou well, Sir Kehydius, for this falsehood and treason thou hast done me, I will revenge it upon thee.' And therewithal Sir Tristram drew out his sword and said, 'Sir Kehydius, keep thee!'

And then La Beale Isoud swooned to the earth. And when Sir Kehydius saw Sir Tristam come upon him he saw none other boot, but leapt out at a bay-window even over the head where sat King Mark playing at the chess.

And when the king saw one come hurling over his head, he said, 'Fellow, what art thou, and what is the cause thou leapest out at that window?'

'My lord the king,' said Kehydius, 'it fortuned me that I was asleep in the window above your head, and as I slept I slumbered, and so I fell down.' And thus Sir Kehydius excused him.

CHAPTER 17: *How Sir Tristram departed from Tintagel, and how he sorrowed and was so long in a forest till he was out of his mind*

Then Sir Tristram dread sore lest he were discovered unto the king that he was there; wherefore he drew him to the strength of the tower, and armed him in such armour as he had for to fight with them that would withstand him.

And so when Sir Tristram saw there was no resistance against him he sent Gouvernail for his horse and his spear, and knightly he rode forth out of the castle openly, that was called the Castle of Tintagel. And even at the gate he met with Gingalin, Sir Gawain's son.

And anon Sir Gingalin put his spear in his rest, and ran upon Sir Tristram and brake his spear; and Sir Tristram at that time had but a sword, and gave him such a buffet upon the helm that he fell down from his saddle, and his sword slid adown, and carved asunder his horse's neck.

And so Sir Tristram rode his way into the forest. And all this doing saw King Mark. And then he sent a squire unto the hurt knight, and commanded him to come to him, and so he did. And when King Mark wist that it was Sir Gingalin he welcomed him and gave him an horse, and asked him what knight it was that had encountered with him.

'Sir,' said Sir Gingalin, 'I wot not what knight he was, but well I wot that he sigheth and maketh great dole.'

Then Sir Tristram within a while met with a knight of his own, that hight Sir Fergus. And when he had met with him he made great sorrow, insomuch that he fell down off his horse in a swoon, and in such sorrow he was in three days and three nights.

Then at the last Sir Tristram sent unto the court by Sir Fergus, for to spere what tidings. And so as he rode by the way he met with a damosel that came from Sir Palomides, to know and seek how Sir Tristram did. Then Sir Fergus told her how he was almost out of his mind.

'Alas,' said the damosel, 'where shall I find him?'

'In such a place,' said Sir Fergus.

Then Sir Fergus found Queen Isoud sick in her bed, making the greatest dole that ever any earthly woman made.

And when the damosel found Sir Tristram she made great dole because she might not amend him, for the more she made of him the more was his pain. And at the last Sir Tristram took his horse and rode away from her. And then was it three days or that she could find him, and then she brought him meat and drink, but he would none.

And then another time Sir Tristram escaped away from the damosel, and it happed him to ride by the same castle where Sir Palomides and Sir Tristram did battle when La Beale Isoud departed them. And there by fortune the damosel met with Sir Tristram again, making the greatest dole that ever earthly creature made; and she yede to the lady of that castle and told her of the misadventure of Sir Tristam.

'Alas,' said the lady of that castle, 'where is my lord, Sir Tristram?'

'Right here by your castle,' said the damosel.

'In good time,' said the lady, 'is he so nigh me; he shall have meat and drink of the best; and an harp I have of his whereupon he taught me, for of goodly harping he beareth the prize in the world.'

So this lady and damosel brought him meat and drink, but he ate little thereof. Then upon a night he put his horse from him, and then he unlaced his armour, and then Sir Tristram would go into the wilderness, and brast down the trees and boughs; and otherwhile when he found the harp that the lady sent him, then would he harp, and play thereupon and weep together. And sometime when Sir Tristram was in the wood that the lady wist not where he was, then would she sit her down and play upon that harp: then would Sir Tristram come to that harp, and hearken thereto, and sometime he would harp himself.

Thus he there endured a quarter of a year. Then at the last he ran his way, and she wist not where he was become.

And then was he naked and waxed lean and poor of flesh; and so he fell in the fellowship of herdmen and shepherds, and daily they would give him some of their meat and drink. And when he did any shrewd deed they would beat him with rods, and so they clipped him with shears and made him like a fool.

CHAPTER 18: *How Sir Tristram soused Dagonet in a well, and how Palomides sent a damosel to seek Tristram and how Palomides met with King Mark*

And upon a day Dagonet, King Arthur's fool, came into Cornwall with two squires with him; and as they rode through that forest they came by a fair well where Sir Tristram was wont to be; and the weather was hot, and they alit to drink of that well, and in the meanwhile their horses brake loose.

Right so Sir Tristram came unto them, and first he soused Sir Dagonet in that well, and after his squires, and thereat laughed the shepherds; and forthwithal he ran after their horses and brought them again one by one, and right so, wet as they were, he made them leap up and ride their ways. Thus Sir Tristram endured there an half year naked, and would never come in town ne village.

The meanwhile the damosel that Sir Palomides sent to seek Sir Tristram, she yede unto Sir Palomides and told him all the mischief that Sir Tristram endured.

'Alas,' said Sir Palomides, 'it is great pity that ever so noble a knight should be so mischieved for the love of a lady; but nevertheless, I will go and seek him, and comfort him and I may.'

Then a little before that time La Beale Isoud had commanded Sir Kehydius out of the country of Cornwall. So Sir Kehydius departed with a dolorous heart, and by adventure he met with Sir Palomides, and they enfellowshipped to-

shrewd: wicked.

gether; and either complained to other of their hot love that they loved La Beale Isoud.

'Now let us,' said Sir Palomides, 'seek Sir Tristram, that loved her as well as we, and let us prove whether we may recover him.'

So they rode into that forest, and three days and three nights they would never take their lodging, but ever sought Sir Tristram. And upon a time, by adventure, they met with King Mark that was ridden from his men all alone. When they saw him Sir Palomides knew him, but Sir Kehydius knew him not.

'Ah, false king,' said Sir Palomides, 'it is pity thou hast thy life, for thou art a destroyer of all worshipful knights, and by thy mischief and thy vengeance thou hast destroyed that most noble knight, Sir Tristram de Liones. And therefore defend thee,' said Sir Palomides, 'for thou shalt die this day.'

'That were shame,' said King Mark, 'for ye two are armed and I am unarmed.'

'As for that,' said Sir Palomides, 'I shall find a remedy therefore: here is a knight with me, and thou shalt have his harness.'

'Nay,' said King Mark, 'I will not have ado with you, for cause have ye none to me; for all the misease that Sir Tristram hath was for a letter that he found; for as to me I did to him no displeasure, and God knoweth I am full sorry for his disease and malady.'

So when the king had thus excused him they were friends, and King Mark would have had them unto Tintagel, but Sir Palomides would not, but turned unto the realm of Logris, and Sir Kehydius said that he would go into Brittany.

Now turn we unto Sir Dagonet again, that when he and his squires were upon horseback he deemed that the shepherds had sent that fool to array them so, because that they laughed at them, and so they rode unto the keepers of beasts and all to-beat them.

Sir Tristram saw them beat that were wont to give him

meat and drink, then he ran thither and gat Sir Dagonet by the head, and gave him such a fall to the earth that he bruised him sore so that he lay still. And then he wrast his sword out of his hand, and therewith he ran to one of his squires and smote off his head, and the other fled. And so Sir Tristram took his way with that sword in his hand, running as he had been wild wood.

Then Sir Dagonet rode to King Mark and told him how he had sped in that forest. 'And therefore,' said Sir Dagonet, 'beware, King Mark, that thou come not about that well in the forest, for there is a fool naked, and that fool and I fool met together, and he had almost slain me.'

'Ah,' said King Mark, 'that is Sir Matto le Breune, that fell out of his wit because he lost his lady; for when Sir Gaheris smote down Sir Matto and won his lady of him, never since was he in his mind, and that was pity, for he was a good knight.'

CHAPTER 19: *How it was noised how Sir Tristram was dead, and how La Beale Isoud would have slain herself*

Then Sir Andred, that was cousin unto Sir Tristram, made a lady that was his paramour to say and to noise it that she was with Sir Tristram or ever he died. And this tale she brought unto King Mark's court, that she buried him by a well, and that or he died he besought King Mark to make his cousin, Sir Andred, king of the country of Liones, of the which Sir Tristram was lord of. All this did Sir Andred because he would have had Sir Tristram's lands.

And when King Mark heard tell that Sir Tristram was dead he wept and made great dole. But when Queen Isoud heard of these tidings she made such sorrow that she was nigh out of her mind; and so upon a day she thought to slay herself and never to live after Sir Tristram's death.

And so upon a day La Beale Isoud gat a sword privily and bare it into her garden, and there she pitched the sword through a plum tree up to the hilts, so that it stuck fast, and it stood breast high. And as she would have run upon the sword and to have slain herself all this espied King Mark, how she kneeled down and said, 'Sweet Lord Jesu, have mercy upon me, for I may not live after the death of Sir Tristram de Liones, for he was my first love and he shall be the last.'

And with these words came King Mark and took her in his arms, and then he took up the sword, and bare her away with him into a tower; and there he made her to be kept, and watched her surely, and after that she lay long sick, nigh at the point of death.

This meanwhile ran Sir Tristram naked in the forest with the sword in his hand, and so he came to an hermitage, and there he laid him down and slept; and in the meanwhile the hermit stole away his sword, and laid meat down by him. Thus was he kept there a ten days; and at the last he departed and came to the herdmen again.

And there was a giant in that country that hight Tawleas, and for fear of Sir Tristram more than seven year he durst never much go at large, but for the most part he kept him in a sure castle of his own; and so this Tawleas heard tell that Sir Tristram was dead, by the noise of the court of King Mark.

Then this Tawleas went daily at large. And so he happed upon a day he came to the herdmen wandering and lingering, and there he set him down to rest among them. The meanwhile there came a knight of Cornwall that led a lady with him, and his name was Sir Dinaunt; and when the giant saw him he went from the herdmen and hid him under a tree, and so the knight came to that well, and there he alit to repose him.

And as soon as he was from his horse this giant Tawleas came betwixt this knight and his horse, and took the horse and leapt upon him. So forthwith he rode unto Sir Dinaunt and took him by the collar, and pulled him afore him upon his horse, and there would have stricken off his head.

Then the herdmen said unto Sir Tristram, 'Help yonder knight.'

'Help ye him,' said Sir Tristram.

'We dare not,' said the herdmen.

Then Sir Tristram was ware of the sword of the knight thereas it lay, and so thither he ran and took up the sword and struck off Sir Tawleas' head, and so he yede his way to the herdmen.

CHAPTER 20: *How King Mark found Sir Tristram naked, and made him to be borne home to Tintagel, and how he was there known by a brachet*

Then the knight took up the giant's head and bare it with him unto King Mark, and told him what adventure betid him in the forest, and how a naked man rescued him from the grimly giant, Tawleas.

'Where had ye this adventure?' said King Mark.

'Forsooth,' said Sir Dinaunt, 'at the fair fountain in your forest where many adventurous knights meet, and there is the mad man.'

'Well,' said King Mark, 'I will see that wild man.'

So within a day or two King Mark commanded his knights and his hunters that they should be ready on the morn for to hunt, and so upon the morn he went unto that forest.

And when the king came to that well he found there lying by that well a fair naked man, and a sword by him. Then King Mark blew and straked, and therewith his knights came to him; and then the king commanded his knights to: 'Take that naked man with fairness, and bring him to my castle.'

So they did safely and fair, and cast mantles upon Sir Tristram, and so led him unto Tintagel; and there they bathed him, and washed him, and gave him hot suppings till they

straked: sounded a note on the horn.

had brought him well to his remembrance; but all this while there was no creature that knew Sir Tristram, nor what man he was.

So it fell upon a day that the queen, La Beale Isoud, heard of such a man, that ran naked in the forest, and how the king had brought him home to the court.

Then La Beale Isoud called unto her Dame Bragwaine and said, 'Come on with me, for we will go see this man that my lord brought from the forest the last day.'

So they passed forth, and spered where was the sick man. And then a squire told the queen that he was in the garden taking his rest, and repos[ing] him against the sun.

So when the queen looked upon Sir Tristram she was not remembered of him. But ever she said unto Dame Bragwaine, 'Meseemeth I should have seen him heretofore in many places.'

But as soon as Sir Tristram saw her he knew her well enough. And then he turned away his visage and wept.

Then the queen had always a little brachet with her that Sir Tristram gave her the first time that ever she came into Cornwall, and never would that brachet depart from her but if Sir Tristram was nigh thereas was La Beale Isoud; and this brachet was sent from the king's daughter of France unto Sir Tristram for great love. And anon as this little brachet felt a savour of Sir Tristram, she leapt upon him and licked his lears and his ears, and then she whined and quested, and she smelled at his feet and at his hands, and on all parts of his body that she might come to.

'Ah, my lady,' said Dame Bragwaine unto La Beale Isoud, 'alas, alas,' said she, 'I see it is mine own lord, Sir Tristram.'

And thereupon Isoud fell down in a swoon, and so lay a great while. And when she might speak she said, 'My lord Sir Tristram, blessed be God ye have your life, and now I am sure ye shall be discovered by this little brachet, for she will never leave you. And also I am sure as soon as my lord, King

lears: cheeks.

Mark, do know you he will banish you out of the country of Cornwall, or else he will destroy you. For God's sake, mine own lord, grant King Mark his will, and then draw you unto the court of King Arthur, for there are ye beloved, and ever when I may I shall send unto you; and when ye list ye may come to me, and at all times early and late I will be at your commandment, to live as poor a life as ever did queen or lady.'

'O madam,' said Sir Tristram, 'go from me, for mickle anger and danger have I escaped for your love.'

CHAPTER 21: *How King Mark, by the advice of his council, banished Sir Tristram out of Cornwall the term of ten year*

Then the queen departed, but the brachet would not from him; and therewithal came King Mark and the brachet set upon him, and bayed at them all.

Therewithal Sir Andred spake and said, 'Sir, this is Sir Tristram, I see by the brachet.'

'Nay,' said the king, 'I cannot suppose that.' Then the king asked him upon his faith what he was, and what was his name.

'So God me help,' said he, 'my name is Sir Tristram de Liones; now do by me what ye list.'

'Ah,' said King Mark, 'me repenteth of your recovery.' And then he let call his barons to judge Sir Tristram to the death.

Then many of his barons would not assent thereto, and in especial Sir Dinas, the Seneschal, and Sir Fergus. And so by the advice of them all Sir Tristram was banished out of the country for ten year, and thereupon he took his oath upon a book before the king and his barons. And so he was made to depart out of the country of Cornwall; and there were many barons brought him unto his ship, of the which some were his friends and some his foes.

And in the meanwhile there came a knight of King Arthur's, his name was Dinadan, and his coming was for to seek after Sir Tristram; then they showed him where he was armed at all points going to the ship.

'Now fair knight,' said Sir Dinadan, 'or ye pass this court that ye will joust with me I require thee.'

'With a good will,' said Sir Tristram, 'and these lords will give me leave.'

Then the barons granted thereto, and so they ran together, and there Sir Tristram gave Sir Dinadan a fall. And then he prayed Sir Tristram to give him leave to go in his fellowship.

'Ye shall be right welcome,' said then Sir Tristram.

And so they took their horses and rode to their ships, together, and when Sir Tristram was in the sea he said,

'Greet well King Mark and all mine enemies, and say them I will come again when I may; and well am I rewarded for the fighting with Sir Marhaus, and delivered all this country from servage; and well am I rewarded for the fetching and costs of Queen Isoud out of Ireland, and the danger that I was in first and last, and by the way coming home what danger I had to bring again Queen Isoud from the Castle Pluere; and well I am rewarded when I fought with Sir Bleoberis for Sir Segwarides' wife; and well am I rewarded when I fought with Sir Blamor de Ganis for King Agwisance, father unto La Beale Isoud; and well am I rewarded when I smote down the good knight, Sir Lamorak de Gales, at King Mark's request; and well am I rewarded when I fought with the King with the Hundred Knights, and the King of Northgales, and both these would have put his land in servage, and by me they were put to a rebuke; and well I am rewarded for the slaying of Tawleas, the mighty giant, and many other deeds have I done for him, and now have I my warison. And tell King Mark that many noble knights of the Table Round have spared the barons of this country for my sake. Also am I not well rewarded when I fought with the good knight Sir

warison: reward.

Palomides and rescued Queen Isoud from him; and at that time King Mark said afore all his barons I should have been better rewarded.'

And forthwithal he took the sea.

CHAPTER 22: *How a damosel sought help to help Sir Launcelot against thirty knights, and how Sir Tristram fought with them*

And at the next landing, fast by the sea, there met with Sir Tristram and with Sir Dinadan, Sir Ector de Maris and Sir Bors de Ganis; and there Sir Ector jousted with Sir Dinadan, and he smote him and his horse down. And then Sir Tristram would have jousted with Sir Bors, and Sir Bors said that he would not joust with no Cornish knights, for they are not called men of worship; and all this was done upon a bridge.

And with this came Sir Bleoberis and Sir Driant, and Sir Bleoberis proffered to joust with Sir Tristram, and there Sir Tristram smote down Sir Bleoberis.

Then said Sir Bors de Ganis, 'I wist never Cornish knight of so great valour nor so valiant as that knight that beareth the trappers embroidered with crowns.'

And then Sir Tristram and Sir Dinadan departed from them into a forest, and there met them a damosel that came for the love of Sir Launcelot to seek after some noble knights of King Arthur's court for to rescue Sir Launcelot. And so Sir Launcelot was ordained, for by the treason of Queen Morgan le Fay to have slain Sir Launcelot, and for that cause, she ordained thirty knights to lie in await for Sir Launcelot, and this damosel knew this treason. And for this cause the damosel came for to seek noble knights to help Sir Launcelot. For that night, or the day after, Sir Launcelot should come where these thirty knights were.

And so this damosel met with Sir Bors and Sir Ector and with Sir Driant, and there she told them all four of the treason of Morgan le Fay; and then they promised her that they would be nigh where Sir Launcelot should meet with the thirty knights. 'And if so be they set upon him we will do rescues as we can.'

So the damosel departed, and by adventure the damosel met with Sir Tristram and with Sir Dinadan, and there the damosel told them all the treason that was ordained for Sir Launcelot.

'Fair damosel,' said Sir Tristram, 'bring me to that same place where they should meet with Sir Launcelot.'

Then said Sir Dinadan, 'What will ye do? It is not for us to fight with thirty knights, and wit you well I will not thereof. As to match one knight two or three is enough and they be men, but for to match fifteen knights that will I never undertake.'

'Fie for shame,' said Sir Tristram. 'Do but your part.'

'Nay,' said Sir Dinadan, 'I will not thereof but if ye will lend me your shield, for ye bear a shield of Cornwall; and for the cowardice that is named to the knights of Cornwall, by your shields ye be ever forborne.'

'Nay,' said Sir Tristram, 'I will not depart from my shield for her sake that gave it me. But one thing,' said Sir Tristram, 'I promise thee, Sir Dinadan, but if thou wilt promise me to abide with me, here I shall slay thee, for I desire no more of thee but answer one, knight. And if thy heart will not serve thee, stand by and look upon me and them.'

'Sir,' said Sir Dinadan, 'I promise you to look upon and to do what I may to save myself, but I would I had not met with you.'

So then anon these thirty knights came fast by these four knights, and they were ware of them, and either of other. And so these thirty knights let them pass,[1] for this cause, that they would not wrath them, if case be that they had ado with Sir Launcelot; and the four knights let them pass to this intent, that they would see and behold what they would do with Sir Launcelot.

wrath: anger.

And so the thirty knights passed on and came by Sir Tristram and by Sir Dinadan, and then Sir Tristram cried on high, 'Lo, here is a knight against you for the love of Sir Launcelot.' And there he slew two with one spear and ten with his sword.

And then came in Sir Dinadan and he did passing well, and so of the thirty knights there went but ten away, and they fled.

All this battle saw Sir Bors de Ganis and his three fellows, and then they saw well it was the same knight that jousted with them at the bridge; then they took their horses and rode unto Sir Tristram, and praised him and thanked him of his good deeds, and they all desired Sir Tristram to go with them to their lodging; and he said nay, he would not go to no lodging. Then they all four knights prayed him to tell them his name.

'Fair lords,' said Sir Tristram, 'as at this time I will not tell you my name.'

CHAPTER 23: *How Sir Tristram and Sir Dinadan came to a lodging where they must joust with two knights*

Then Sir Tristram and Sir Dinadan rode forth their way till they came to the shepherds and to the herdmen, and there they asked them if they knew any lodging or harbour there nigh hand.

'Forsooth, sirs,' said the herdmen, 'hereby is good lodging in a castle; but there is such a custom that there shall no knight be harboured but if he joust with two knights, and if he be but one knight he must joust with two. And as ye be therein soon shall ye be matched.'

'There is shrewd harbour,' said Sir Dinadan; 'lodge where ye will, for I will not lodge there.'

'Fie for shame,' said Sir Tristram, 'are ye not a knight of the Table Round? Wherefore ye may not with your worship refuse your lodging.'

'Not so,' said the herdmen, 'for and ye be beaten and have the worse ye shall not be lodged there, and if ye beat them ye shall be well harboured.'

'Ah,' said Sir Dinadan, 'they are two sure knights.'

Then Sir Dinadan would not lodge there in no manner but as Sir Tristram required him of his knighthood; and so they rode thither. And to make short tale, Sir Tristram and Sir Dinadan smote them down both, and so they entered into the castle and had good cheer as they could think or devise.

And when they were unarmed, and thought to be merry and in good rest, there came in at the gates Sir Palomides and Sir Gaheris, requiring to have the custom of the castle.

'What array is this?' said Sir Dinadan, 'I would have my rest.'

'That may not be,' said Sir Tristram. 'Now must we needs defend the custom of this castle, insomuch as we have the better of the lords of this castle, and therefore,' said Sir Tristram, 'needs must ye make you ready.'

'In the devil's name,' said Sir Dinadan, 'came I unto your company.'

And so they made them ready; and Sir Gaheris encountered with Sir Tristram, and Sir Gaheris had a fall; and Sir Palomides encountered with Sir Dinadan, and Sir Dinadan had a fall: then was it fall for fall. So then must they fight on foot. That would not Sir Dinadan, for he was so sore bruised of the fall that Sir Palomides gave him. Then Sir Tristram unlaced Sir Dinadan's helm, and prayed him to help him.

'I will not,' said Sir Dinadan, 'for I am sore wounded of the thirty knights that we had but late ago to do withal. But ye fare,' said Sir Dinadan unto Sir Tristram, 'as a madman and as a man that is out of his mind that would cast himself away, and I may curse the time that ever I saw you, for in all the world are not two such knights that be so wood as is Sir Launcelot and ye Sir Tristram; for once I fell in the fellowship of Sir Launcelot as I have done now with you, and he set me a work that a quarter of a year I kept my bed. Jesu defend me,' said Sir Dinadan, 'from such two knights, and specially from your fellowship.'

'Then,' said Sir Tristram, 'I will fight with them both.'

Then Sir Tristram bad them come forth both, 'for I will fight with you.'

Then Sir Palomides and Sir Gaheris dressed them, and smote at them both. Then Dinadan smote at Sir Gaheris a stroke or two, and turned from him.

'Nay,' said Sir Palomides, 'it is too much shame for us two knights to fight with one.'

And then he did bid Sir Gaheris stand aside with that knight that hath no list to fight. Then they rode together and fought long, and at the last Sir Tristram doubled his strokes, and drove Sir Palomides aback more than three strides. And then by one assent Sir Gaheris and Sir Dinadan went betwixt them, and departed them in sunder.

And then by assent of Sir Tristram they would have lodged together. But Sir Dinadan would not lodge in that castle. And then he cursed the time that ever he came in their fellowship, and so he took his horse, and his harness, and departed.

Then Sir Tristram prayed the lords of that castle to lend him a man to bring him to a lodging, and so they did, and overtook Sir Dinadan, and rode to their lodging two mile thence with a good man in a priory, and there they were well at ease.

And that same night Sir Bors and Sir Bleoberis, and Sir Ector and Sir Driant, abode still in the same place thereas Sir Tristram fought with the thirty knights; and there they met with Sir Launcelot the same night, and had made promise to lodge with Sir Colgrevaunce the same night.

CHAPTER 24: *How Sir Tristram jousted with Sir Kay and Sir Sagramore le Desirous, and how Sir Gawain turned Sir Tristram from Morgan le Fay*

But anon as the noble knight, Sir Launcelot, heard of the shield of Cornwall, then wist he well that it was Sir Tristram that fought with his enemies. And then Sir Launcelot praised Sir Tristram, and called him the man of most worship in the world.

So there was a knight in that priory that hight Pellinor, and he desired to wit the name of Sir Tristram, but in no wise he could not. And so Sir Tristram departed and left Sir Dinadan in the priory, for he was so weary and so sore bruised that he might not ride.

Then this knight, Sir Pellinor, said to Sir Dinadan, 'Sithen that ye will not tell me that knight's name I will ride after him and make him to tell me his name, or he shall die therefore.'

'Beware, sir knight,' said Sir Dinadan, 'for and ye follow him ye shall repent it.'

So that knight, Sir Pellinor, rode after Sir Tristram and required him of jousts. Then Sir Tristram smote him down and wounded him through the shoulder, and so he passed on his way.

And on the next day following Sir Tristram met with pursuivants, and they told him that there was made a great cry of tournament between King Carados of Scotland and the King of North Wales, and either should joust against other at the Castle of Maidens; and these pursuivants sought all the country after the good knights, and in especial King Carados let make seeking for Sir Launcelot du Lake, and the King of Northgales let seek after Sir Tristram de Liones. And at that time Sir Tristram thought to be at that jousts; and so by adventure they met with Sir Kay, the Seneschal, and Sir Sagramore le Desirous; and Sir Kay required Sir Tristram to

pursuivants: heralds.

joust, and Sir Tristram in a manner refused him, because he would not be hurt nor bruised against the great jousts that should be before the Castle of Maidens, and therefore he thought to repose him and to rest him.

And alway Sir Kay cried, 'Sir knight of Cornwall, joust with me, or else yield thee to me as recreant.'

When Sir Tristram heard him say so he turned to him, and then Sir Kay refused him and turned his back.

Then Sir Tristram said, 'As I find thee I shall take thee.'

Then Sir Kay turned with evil will, and Sir Tristram smote Sir Kay down, and so he rode forth.

Then Sir Sagramore le Desirous rode after Sir Tristram, and made him to joust with him, and there Sir Tristram smote down Sir Sagramore le Desirous from his horse, and rode his way.

And the same day he met with a damosel that told him that he should win great worship of a knight adventurous that did much harm in all that country. When Sir Tristram heard her say so, he was glad to go with her to win worship. So Sir Tristram rode with that damosel a six mile, and then met him Sir Gawain, and therewithal Sir Gawain knew the damosel, that she was a damosel of Queen Morgan le Fay. Then Sir Gawain understood that she led that knight to some mischief.

'Fair knight,' said Sir Gawain, 'whither ride you now with that damosel?'

'Sir,' said Sir Tristram, 'I wot not whither I shall ride but as the damosel will lead me.'

'Sir,' said Sir Gawain, 'ye shall not ride with her, for she and her lady did never good, but ill.' And then Sir Gawain pulled out his sword and said, 'Damosel, but if thou tell me anon for what cause thou leadest this knight with thee thou shalt die for it right anon: I know all your lady's treason, and yours.'

'Mercy, Sir Gawain,' she said, 'and if ye will save my life I will tell you.'

'Say on,' said Sir Gawain, 'and thou shalt have thy life.'

'Sir,' she said, 'Queen Morgan le Fay, my lady, hath ordained a thirty ladies to seek and espy after Sir Launcelot or Sir Tristram, and by the trains of these ladies, who that may first meet any of these two knights, they should turn them unto Morgan le Fay's castle, saying that they should do deeds of worship; and if any of those two knights came there, there be thirty knights lying and watching in a tower to wait upon Sir Launcelot or upon Sir Tristram.'

'Fie for shame,' said Sir Gawain, 'that ever such false treason should be wrought or used in a queen, and a king's sister, and a king and queen's daughter.'

CHAPTER 25: *How Sir Tristram and Sir Gawain rode to have foughten against the thirty knights, but they durst not come out*

'Sir,' said Sir Gawain, 'will ye stand with me, and we will see the malice of these thirty knights.'

'Sir,' said Sir Tristram, 'go ye to them, and it please you, and ye shall see I will not fail you, for it is not long ago since I and a fellow met with thirty knights of that queen's fellowship; and God speed us so that we may win worship.'

So then Sir Gawain and Sir Tristram rode toward the castle where Morgan le Fay was, and ever Sir Gawain deemed well that he was Sir Tristram de Liones, because he heard that two knights had slain and beaten thirty knights. And when they came afore the castle Sir Gawain spake on high and said,

'Queen Morgan le Fay, send out your knights that ye have laid in a watch for Sir Launcelot and for Sir Tristram. Now,' said Sir Gawain, 'I know your false treason, and through all places where that I ride men shall know of your false treason; and now let see,' [said] [1] Sir Gawain, 'whether ye dare come out of your castle, ye thirty knights.'

trains: enticements.

Then the queen spake and all the thirty knights at once, and said, 'Sir Gawain, full well witest thou what thou dost and sayest; for by God we know thee passing well, but all that thou speakest and dost, thou sayest it upon pride of that good night that is there with thee. For there be some of us that knowen full well the hands of that knight over all well. And with thou well, Sir Gawain, it is more for his sake than for thine that we will not come out of this castle. For wit ye well, Sir Gawain, the knight that beareth the arms of Cornwell, we know him and what he is.'

Then Sir Gawain and Sir Tristram departed and rode on their ways a day or two together; and there by adventure, they met with Sir Kay and Sir Sagramore le Desirous. And then they were glad of Sir Gawain, and he of them, but they wist not what he was with the shield of Cornwall, but by deeming. And thus they rode together a day or two.

And then they were ware of Sir Breunis Saunce Pité chasing a lady for to have slain her, for he had slain her paramour afore.

'Hold you all still,' said Sir Gawain, 'and show none of you forth, and ye shall see me reward yonder false knight; for and he espy you he is so well horsed that he will escape away.'

And then Sir Gawain rode betwixt Sir Breunis and the lady, and said,

'False knight, leave her, and have ado with me.'

When Sir Breunis saw no more but Sir Gawain he fewtered his spear, and Sir Gawain against him; and there Sir Breunis overthrew Sir Gawain, and then he rode over him, and overthwart him twenty times to have destroyed him. And when Sir Tristram saw him do so villainous a deed, he hurled out against him. And when Sir Breunis saw him with the shield of Cornwall he knew him well that it was Sir Tristram, and then he fled, and Sir Tristram followed after him; and Sir Breunis Saunce Pité was so horsed that he went his way quite, and Sir Tristram followed him long, for he would fain have been avenged upon him.

And so when he had long chased him, he saw a fair well, and thither he rode to repose him, and tied his horse till a tree.

CHAPTER 26: *How Damosel Bragwaine found Tristram sleeping by a well, and how she delivered letters to him from La Beale Isoud*

And then he pulled off his helm and washed his visage and his hands, and so he fell asleep.

In the meanwhile came a damosel that had sought Sir Tristram many ways and days within this land. And when she came to the well she looked upon him, and had forgotten him as in remembrance of Sir Tristram, but by his horse she knew him, that hight Passe-Brewel that had been Sir Tristram's horse many years. For when he was mad in the forest Sir Fergus kept him. So this lady, Dame Bragwaine, abode still till he was awake. So when she saw him wake she saluted him, and he her again, for either knew other of old acquaintance; then she told him how she had sought him long and broad, and there she told him how she had letters from Queen La Beale Isoud. Then anon Sir Tristram read them, and wit ye well he was glad, for therein was many a piteous complaint.

Then Sir Tristram said, 'Lady Bragwaine, ye shall ride with me till that tournament be done at the Castle of Maidens, and then shall ye bear letters and tidings with you.'

And then Sir Tristram took his horse and sought lodging, and there he met with a good ancient knight and prayed him to lodge with him. Right so came Gouvernail unto Sir Tristram, that was glad of that lady. So this old knight's name was Sir Pellounes, and he told of the great tournament that should be at the Castle of Maidens. And there Sir Launcelot and thirty-two knights of his blood had ordained shields of Cornwall.

And right so there came one unto Sir Pellounes, and told him that Sir Persides de Bloise was come home; then that knight held up his hands and thanked God of his coming home. And there Sir Pellounes told Sir Tristram that in two years he had not seen his son, Sir Persides.

'Sir,' said Sir Tristram, 'I know your son well enough for a good knight.'

So on a time Sir Tristram and Sir Persides came to their lodging both at once, and so they unarmed them, and put upon them their clothing. And then these two knights each welcomed other.

And when Sir Persides understood that Sir Tristram was of Cornwall, he said he was once in Cornwall: 'And there I jousted afore King Mark; and so it happed me at that time to overthrow ten knights, and then came to me Sir Tristram de Liones and overthrew me, and took my lady away from me, and that shall I never forget, but I shall remember me and ever I see my time.'

'Ah,' said Sir Tristram, 'now I understand that ye hate Sir Tristram. What deem ye, ween ye that Sir Tristram is not able to withstand your malice?'

'Yes,' said Sir Persides, 'I know well that Sir Tristram is a noble knight, and a much better knight than I, yet shall I not owe him my good will.'

Right as they stood thus talking at a bay-window of that castle, they saw many knights riding to and fro toward the tournament. And then was Sir Tristram ware of a likely knight riding upon a great black horse, and a black-covered shield.

'What knight is that,' said Sir Tristram, 'with the black horse and the black shield? He seemeth a good knight.'

'I know him well,' said Sir Persides, 'he is one of the best knights of the world.'

'Then is it Sir Launcelot,' said Tristram.

'Nay,' said Sir Persides, 'it is Sir Palomides, that is yet unchristened.'

CHAPTER 27: *How Sir Tristram had a fall of Sir Palomides, and how Launcelot overthrew two knights*

Then they saw much people of the country salute Sir Palomides. And within a while after there came a squire of the castle, that told Sir Pellounes, that was lord of that castle, that a knight with a black shield had smitten down thirteen knights.

'Fair brother,' said Sir Tristram unto Sir Persides, 'let us cast upon us cloaks, and let us go see the play.'

'Not so,' said Sir Persides, 'we will not go like knaves thither, but we will ride like men and good knights to withstand our enemies.'

So they armed them, and took their horses and great spears, and thither they went thereas many knights assayed themself before the tournament.

And anon Sir Palomides saw Sir Persides, and then he sent a squire unto him and said, 'Go thou to the yonder knight with the green shield and therein a lion of gules, and say him I require him to joust with me, and tell him that my name is Sir Palomides.'

When Sir Persides understood that request of Sir Palomides, he made him ready, and there anon they met together, but Sir Persides had a fall.

Then Sir Tristram dressed him to be revenged upon Sir Palomides, and that saw Sir Palomides that was ready and so was not Sir Tristram, and took him at advantage and smote him over his horse's tail when he had no spear in his rest. Then start up Sir Tristram and took his horse lightly, and was wroth out of measure, and sore ashamed of that fall. Then Sir Tristram sent unto Sir Palomides by Gouvernail, and prayed him to joust with him at his request.

'Nay,' said Sir Palomides, 'as at this time I will not joust with that knight, for I know him better than he weeneth. And if he be wroth he may right it tomorn at the Castle

gules: red (heraldic).

of Maidens, where he may see me and many other knights.'

With that came Sir Dinadan, and when he saw Sir Tristram wroth he list not to jape.

'Lo,' said Sir Dinadan, 'here may a man prove, be a man never so good yet may he have a fall, and he was never so wise but he might be overseen, and he rideth well that never fell.'

So Sir Tristram was passing wroth, and said to Sir Persides and to Sir Dinadan, 'I will revenge me.'

Right so as they stood talking there, there came by Sir Tristram a likely knight riding passing soberly and heavily with a black shield.

'What knight is that?' said Sir Tristram unto Sir Persides.

'I know him well,' said Sir Persides, 'for his name is Sir Briant of North Wales.' So he passed on among other knights of North Wales.

And there came in Sir Launcelot du Lake with a shield of the arms of Cornwall, and he sent a squire unto Sir Briant, and required him to joust with him.

'Well,' said Sir Briant, 'sithen I am required to joust I will do what I may.'

And there Sir Launcelot smote down Sir Briant from his horse a great fall. And then Sir Tristram marvelled what knight he was that bare the shield of Cornwall.

'Whatsoever he be,' said Sir Dinadan, 'I warrant you he is of King Ban's blood, the which be knights of the most noble prowess in the world, for to account so many for so many.'

Then there came two knights of Northgales, that one hight Hugh de la Montaine, and the other Sir Maddock de la Montaine, and they challenged Sir Launcelot foot hot. Sir Launcelot not refusing them but made him ready, with one spear he smote them down both over their horse's croups; and so Sir Launcelot rode his way.

'By the good lord,' said Sir Tristram, 'he is a good knight that beareth the shield of Cornwall, and meseemeth he rideth in the best manner that ever I saw knight ride.'

Then the King of Northgales rode unto Sir Palomides, and prayed him heartily for his sake to 'joust with that knight that hath done us of Northgales despite.'

'Sir,' said Sir Palomides, 'I am full loth to have ado with that knight, and cause why is, for as tomorn the great tournament shall be, and therefore I will keep myself fresh by my will.'

'Nay,' said the King of Northgales, 'I pray you require him of jousts.'

'Sir,' said Sir Palomides, 'I will joust at your request, and require that knight to joust with me, and often I have seen a man have a fall at his own request.'

CHAPTER 28: *How Sir Launcelot jousted with Palomides and overthrew him, and after he was assailed with twelve knights*

Then Sir Palomides sent unto Sir Launcelot a squire, and required him of jousts.

'Fair fellow,' said Sir Launcelot, 'tell me thy lord's name.'

'Sir,' said the squire, 'my lord's name is Sir Palomides, the good knight.'

'In good hour,' said Sir Launcelot, 'for there is no knight that I saw this seven years that I had lever ado withal than with him.'

And so either knights made them ready with two great spears.

'Nay,' said Sir Dinadan, 'ye shall see that Sir Palomides will quit him right well.'

'It may be so,' said Sir Tristram, 'but I undertake that knight with the shield of Cornwall shall give him a fall.'

'I believe it not,' said Sir Dinadan.

Right so they spurred their horses and fewtered their spears, and either hit other, and Sir Palomides brake a spear upon Sir Launcelot, and he sat and moved not; but Sir Launcelot smote him so lightly that he made his horse to avoid the saddle, and the stroke brake his shield and the hauberk, and had he not fallen he had been slain.

'How now?' said Sir Tristram, 'I wist well by the manner of their riding both that Sir Palomides should have a fall.'

Right so Sir Launcelot rode his way, and rode to a well to drink and to repose him, and they of Northgales espied him whither he rode; and then there followed him twelve knights for to have mischieved him, for this cause that upon the morn at the tournament of the Castle of Maidens that he should not win the victory.

So they came upon Sir Launcelot suddenly, and unnethe he might put upon him his helm and take his horse, but they were in hands with him; and then Sir Launcelot gat his spear, and rode through them, and there he slew a knight and brake his spear in his body. Then he drew his sword and smote upon the right hand and upon the left hand, so that within a few strokes he had slain other three knights, and the remnant that abode he wounded them sore all that did abide.

Thus Sir Launcelot escaped from his enemies of North Wales; and then Sir Launcelot rode his way till a friend, and lodged him till on the morn; for he would not the first day have ado in the tournament because of his great labour. And on the first day he was with King Arthur thereas he was set on high upon a scaffold to discern who was best worthy of his deeds. So Sir Launcelot was with King Arthur, and jousted not the first day.

CHAPTER 29: *How Sir Tristram behaved him the first day of the tournament, and there he had the prize*

Now turn we unto Sir Tristram de Liones, that commanded Gouvernail, his servant, to ordain him a black shield with none other remembrance therein. And so Sir Persides and Sir Tristram departed from their host Sir Pellounes, and they rode early toward the tournament, and then they drew them to King Carados' side, of Scotland.

And anon knights began the field, what of King Northgales' part, and what of King Carados' part, and there began great party. Then there was hurling and rashing. Right so came in Sir Persides and Sir Tristram, and so they did fare that they put the King of Northgales aback.

Then came in Sir Bleoberis de Ganis and Sir Gaheris with them of Northgales, and then was Sir Persides smitten down and almost slain, for more than forty horsemen went over him. For Sir Bleoberis did great deeds of arms, and Sir Gaheris failed him not.

When Sir Tristram beheld them, and saw them do such deeds of arms, he marvelled what they were. Also Sir Tristram thought shame that Sir Persides was so done to; and then he gat a great spear in his hand, and then he rode to Sir Gaheris and smote him down from his horse. And then was Sir Bleoberis wroth, and gat a spear and rode against Sir Tristram in great ire; and there Sir Tristram met with him, and smote Sir Bleoberis from his horse.

So then the King with the Hundred Knights was wroth, and he horsed Sir Bleoberis and Sir Gaheris again, and there began a great medley; and ever Sir Tristram held them passing short, and ever Sir Bleoberis was passing busy upon Sir Tristram. And there came Sir Dinadan against Sir Tristram, and Sir Tristram gave him such a buffet that he swooned in his saddle.

Then anon Sir Dinadan came to Sir Tristram and said, 'Sir, I know thee better than thou weenest; but here I promise thee my troth I will never come against thee more, for I promise thee that sword of thine shall never come on mine helm.'

With that came Sir Bleoberis, and Sir Tristram gave him such a buffet that down he laid his head; and then he raught him so sore by the helm that he pulled him under his horse's feet.

And then King Arthur blew to lodging. Then Sir Tristram departed to his pavilion, and Sir Dinadan rode with him; and Sir Persides and King Arthur then, and the kings upon both parties, marvelled what knight that was with the black shield. Many said their advice, and some knew him for Sir Tristram, and held their peace and would nought say. So that first day King Arthur, and all the kings and lords that were judges, gave Sir Tristram the prize; howbeit they knew him not, but named him the Knight with the Black Shield.

CHAPTER 30: *How Sir Tristram returned against King Arthur's party because he saw Sir Palomides on that party*

Then upon the morn Sir Palomides returned from the King of Northgales, and rode to King Arthur's side, where was King Carados, and the King of Ireland, and Sir Launcelot's kin and Sir Gawain's kin. So Sir Palomides sent the damosel unto Sir Tristram that he sent to seek him when he was out of his mind in the forest, and this damosel asked Sir Tristram what he was and what was his name?

'As for that,' said Sir Tristram, 'tell Sir Palomides ye shall not wit as at this time unto the time I have broken two spears upon him. But let him wit thus much,' said Sir Tristram, 'that I am the same knight that he smote down in over evening at the tournament; and tell him plainly on what party that Sir Palomides be, I will be of the contrary party.'

'Sir,' said the damosel, 'ye shall understand that Sir Palomides will be on King Arthur's side, where the most noble knights of the world be.'

'In the name of God,' said Sir Tristram, 'then will I be with the King of Northgales, because Sir Palomides will be on King Arthur's side, and else I would not but for his sake.'

So when King Arthur was come they blew unto the field; and then there began a great party, and so King Carados jousted with the King of the Hundred Knights, and there King Carados had a fall: then was there hurling and rashing, and right so came in knights of King Arthur's, and they bare aback the King of Northgales' knights.

Then Sir Tristram came in, and began so roughly and so

bigly that there was none might withstand him, and thus Sir Tristram dured long. And at the last Sir Tristram fell among the fellowship of King Ban, and there fell upon him Sir Bors de Ganis, and Sir Ector de Maris, and Sir Blamor de Ganis, and many other knights. And then Sir Tristram smote on the right hand and on the left hand, that all lords and ladies spake of his noble deeds.

But at the last Sir Tristram should have had the worse had not the King with the Hundred Knights been. And then he came with his fellowship and rescued Sir Tristram, and brought him away from those knights that bare the shields of Cornwall.

And then Sir Tristram saw another fellowship by themself, and there were a forty knights together, and Sir Kay, the Seneschal, was their governor. Then Sir Tristram rode in amongst them, and there he smote down Sir Kay from his horse; and there he fared among those knights like a greyhound among conies.

Then Sir Launcelot found a knight that was sore wounded upon the head.

'Sir,' said Sir Launcelot, 'who wounded you so sore?'

'Sir,' he said, 'a knight that beareth a black shield, and I may curse the time that ever I met with him, for he is a devil and no man.'

So Sir Launcelot departed from him and thought to meet with Sir Tristram, and so he rode with his sword drawn in his hand to seek Sir Tristram; and then he espied him how he hurled here and there, and at every stroke Sir Tristram well-nigh smote down a knight.

'O mercy Jesu!' said the king. 'Sith the time I bare arms saw I never no knight do so marvellous deeds of arms.'

'And if I should set upon this knight,' said Sir Launcelot to himself, 'I did shame to myself,' and therewithal Sir Launcelot put up his sword.

And then the King with the Hundred Knights and an hundred more of North Wales set upon the twenty of Sir Launcelot's kin: and they twenty knights held them ever together as wild swine, and none would fail other. And so when Sir Tristram beheld the noblesse of these twenty knights he marvelled of their good deeds, for he saw by their fare and by their rule that they had lever die than avoid the field.

'Now Jesu,' said Sir Tristram, 'well may he be valiant and full of prowess that hath such a sort of noble knights unto his kin, and full like is he to be a noble man that is their leader and governor.' He meant it by Sir Launcelot du Lake.

So when Sir Tristram had beholden them long he thought shame to see two hundred knights battering upon twenty knights. Then Sir Tristram rode unto the King with the Hundred Knights and said,

'Sir, leave your fighting with those twenty knights, for ye win no worship of them, ye be so many and they so few; and wit ye well they will not out of the field, I see by their cheer and countenance; and worship get ye none and ye slay them. Therefore leave your fighting with them, for I to increase my worship I will ride to the twenty knights and help them with all my might and power.'

'Nay,' said the King with the Hundred Knights, 'ye shall not do so; now I see your courage and courtesy I will withdraw my knights for your pleasure, for evermore a good knight will favour another, and like will draw to like.'

CHAPTER 31 : *How Sir Tristram found Palomides by a well, and brought him with him to his lodging*

Then the King with the Hundred Knights withdrew his knights.

And all this while, and long tofore, Sir Launcelot had watched upon Sir Tristram with a very purpose to have fellowshipped with him. And then suddenly Sir Tristram, Sir Dinadan, and Gouvernail, his man, rode their way into the forest, that no man perceived where they went.

So then King Arthur blew unto lodging, and gave the King

of Northgales the prize because Sir Tristram was upon his side.

Then Sir Launcelot rode here and there, so wood as lion that faulted his fill, because he had lost Sir Tristram, and so he returned unto King Arthur.

And then in all the field was a noise that with the wind it might be heard two mile thence, how the lords and ladies cried, 'The Knight with the Black Shield hath won the field!'

'Alas,' said King Arthur, 'where is that knight become? It is shame to all those in the field so to let him escape away from you; but with gentleness and courtesy ye might have brought him unto me to the Castle of Maidens.'

Then the noble King Arthur went unto his knights and comforted them in the best wise that he could, and said, 'My fair fellows, be not dismayed, howbeit ye have lost the field this day.' And many were hurt and sore wounded, and many were whole. 'My fellows,' said King Arthur, 'look that ye be of good cheer, for to-morn I will be in the field with you and revenge you of your enemies.' So that night King Arthur and his knights reposed themself.

The damosel that came from La Beale Isoud unto Sir Tristram, all the while the tournament was adoing she was with Queen Guenever, and ever the queen asked her for what cause she came into that country.

'Madam,' she answered, 'I come for none other cause but from my lady La Beale Isoud to wit of your welfare.' For in no wise she would not tell the queen that she came for Sir Tristram's sake.

So this lady, Dame Bragwaine, took her leave of Queen Guenever, and she rode after Sir Tristram. And as she rode through the forest she heard a great cry; then she commanded her squire to go into the forest to wit what was that noise.

And so he came to a well, and there he found a knight bounden till a tree crying as he had been wood, and his horse and his harness standing by him. And when he espied the squire, therewith he abrayed and brake himself loose, and took his sword in his hand, and ran to have slain that squire.

Then he took his horse and fled all that ever he might unto Dame Bragwaine, and told her of his adventure. Then she rode unto Sir Tristram's pavilion, and told Sir Tristram what adventure she had found in the forest.

'Alas,' said Sir Tristram, 'upon my head there is some good knight at mischief.'

Then Sir Tristram took his horse and his sword and rode thither; there he heard how the knight complained unto himself and said:

'I, woful knight Sir Palomides, what misadventure befalleth me, that thus am defiled with falsehood and treason, through Sir Bors and Sir Ector. Alas,' he said, 'why live I so long?'

And then he gat his sword in his hands, and made many strange signs and tokens; and so through his raging he threw his sword into that fountain. Then Sir Palomides wailed and wrang his hands. And at the last for pure sorrow he ran into that fountain, over his belly, and sought after his sword.

Then Sir Tristram saw that, and ran upon Sir Palomides, and held him in his arms fast.

'What art thou,' said Palomides, 'that holdeth me so?'

'I am a man of this forest that would thee none harm.'

'Alas,' said Sir Palomides, 'I may never win worship where Sir Tristram is; for ever where he is and I be there, then get I no worship; and if he be away for the most part I have the gree, unless that Sir Launcelot be there or Sir Lamorak.' Then Sir Palomides said, 'Once in Ireland Sir Tristram put me to the worse, and another time in Cornwall, and in other places in this land.'

'What would ye do,' said Sir Tristram, 'and ye had Sir Tristram?'

'I would fight with him,' said Sir Palomides, 'and ease my heart upon him; and yet, to say thee sooth, Sir Tristram is the gentlest knight in this world living.'

'What will ye do?' said Sir Tristram, 'Will ye go with me to your lodging?'

'Nay,' said he, 'I will go to the King with the Hundred Knights, for he rescued me from Sir Bors de Ganis and Sir Ector, and else had I been slain traitorly.'

Sir Tristram said him such kind words that Sir Palomides went with him to his lodging.

Then Gouvernail went tofore, and charged Dame Bragwaine to go out of the way to her lodging. 'And bid ye Sir Persides that he make him no quarrels.'

And so they rode together till they came to Sir Tristram's pavilion, and there Sir Palomides had all the cheer that might be had all that night. But in no wise Sir Palomides might not know what was Sir Tristram; and so after supper they yede to rest, and Sir Tristram for great travail slept till it was day.

And Sir Palomides might not sleep for anguish; and in the dawning of the day he took his horse privily, and rode his way unto Sir Gaheris and unto Sir Sagramore le Desirous, where they were in their pavilions; for they three were fellows at the beginning of the tournament. And then upon the morn the king blew unto the tournament upon the third day.

CHAPTER 32: *How Sir Tristram smote down Sir Palomides, and how he jousted with King Arthur, and other feats*

So the King of Northgales and the King with the Hundred Knights, they two encountered with King Carados and with the King of Ireland; and there the King with the Hundred Knights smote down King Carados, and the King of Northgales smote down the King of Ireland.

With that came in Sir Palomides, and when he came he made great work, for by his indented shield he was well known.

So came in King Arthur, and did great deeds of arms together, and put the King of Northgales and the King with the Hundred Knights to the worse.

With this came in Sir Tristram with his black shield, and

anon he jousted with Sir Palomides, and there by fine force Sir Tristram smote Sir Palomides over his horse's croup.

Then King Arthur cried, 'Knight with the Black Shield, make thee ready to me,' and in the same wise Sir Tristram smote King Arthur.

And then by force of King Arthur's knights the king and Sir Palomides were horsed again. Then King Arthur with a great eager heart he gat a spear in his hand and there upon the one side he smote Sir Tristram over his horse.

Then foot-hot Sir Palomides came upon Sir Tristram, as he was upon foot, to have overriden him. Then Sir Tristram was ware of him, and there he stooped aside, and with great ire he gat him by the arm and pulled him down from his horse.

Then Sir Palomides lightly arose, and then they dashed together mightily with their swords; and many kings, queens, and lords, stood and beheld them. And at the last Sir Tristram smote Sir Palomides upon the helm three mighty strokes, and at every stroke that he gave him he said, 'Have this for Sir Tristram's sake.' With that Sir Palomides fell to the earth grovelling.

Then came the King with the Hundred Knights, and brought Sir Tristram an horse, and so was he horsed again. By then was Sir Palomides horsed, and with great ire he jousted upon Sir Tristram with his spear as it was in the rest, and gave him a great dash with his sword. Then Sir Tristram avoided his spear, and gat him by the neck with his both hands, and pulled him clean out of his saddle, and so he bare him afore him the length of ten spears, and then in the presence of them all he let him fall at his adventure.

Then Sir Tristram was ware of King Arthur with a naked sword in his hand, and with his spear Sir Tristram ran upon King Arthur; and then King Arthur boldly abode him and with his sword he smote a-two his spear, and therewithal Sir Tristram stonied; and so King Arthur gave him three or four great strokes or he might get out his sword, and at the last Sir Tristram drew his sword, and assailed other passing hard. With that the great press departed.

Then Sir Tristram rode here and there and did his great pain, that eleven of the good knights of the blood of King Ban, that was of Sir Launcelot's kin, that day Sir Tristram smote down, that all the estates marvelled of his great deeds. and all cried upon the Knight with the Black Shield.

CHAPTER 33: *How Sir Launcelot hurt Sir Tristram, and how after Sir Tristram smote down Sir Palomides*

Then this cry was so large that Sir Launcelot heard it. And then he gat a great spear in his hand and came towards the cry.

Then Sir Launcelot cried, 'The Knight with the Black Shield, make thee ready to joust with me!'

When Sir Tristram heard him say so he gat his spear in his hand, and either abashed down their heads, and came together as thunder; and Sir Tristram's spear brake in pieces, and Sir Launcelot by malfortune struck Sir Tristram on the side a deep wound nigh to the death; but yet Sir Tristram avoided not his saddle, and so the spear brake. Therewithal Sir Tristram that was wounded gat out his sword, and he rashed to Sir Launcelot, and gave him three great strokes upon the helm that the fire sprang thereout, and Sir Launcelot abashed his head lowly toward his saddle-bow.

And therewithal Sir Tristram departed from the field, for he felt him so wounded that he weened he should have died; and Sir Dinadan espied him and followed him into the forest.

Then Sir Launcelot abode and did many marvellous deeds.

So when Sir Tristram was departed by the forest's side he alit, and unlaced his harness and freshed his wound; then weened Sir Dinadan that he should have died.

'Nay, nay,' said Sir Tristram, 'Dinadan never dread thee, for I am heart whole, and of this wound I shall soon be whole, by the mercy of God.'

By that Sir Dinadan was ware where came Palomides

riding straight upon them. And then Sir Tristram was ware that Sir Palomides came to have destroyed him.

And so Sir Dinadan gave him warning, and said, 'Sir Tristram, my lord, ye are so sore wounded that ye may not have ado with him, therefore I will ride against him and do to him what I may, and if I be slain ye may pray for my soul; and in the meanwhile ye may withdraw you and go into the castle, or in the forest, that he shall not meet with you.'

Sir Tristram smiled and said, 'I thank you, Sir Dinadan, of your good will, but ye shall wit that I am able to handle him.' And then anon hastily he armed him, and took his horse, and a great spear in his hand, and said to Sir Dinadan, 'Adieu!' and rode toward Sir Palomides a soft pace.

Then when Sir Palomides saw that, he made countenance to amend his horse, but he did it for this cause, for he abode Sir Gaheris that came after him. And when he was come he rode toward Sir Tristram.

Then Sir Tristram sent unto Sir Palomides, and required him to joust with him; and if he smote down Sir Palomides he would do no more to him; and if it so happened that Sir Palomides smote down Sir Tristram, he bad him do his utterance.

So they were accorded. Then they met together, and Sir Tristram smote down Sir Palomides that he had a grievous fall, so that he lay still as he had been dead. And then Sir Tristram ran upon Sir Gaheris, and he would not have jousted; but whether he would or not Sir Tristram smote him over his horse's croup, that he lay still as though he had been dead.

And then Sir Tristram rode his way and left Sir Persides' squire within the pavilions, and Sir Tristram and Sir Dinadan rode to an old knight's place to lodge them. And that old knight had five sons at the tournament, for whom he prayed God heartily for their coming home. And so, as the French book saith, they came home all five well beaten.

And when Sir Tristram departed into the forest, Sir Launcelot held alway the stour like hard, as a man araged that took no heed to himself, and wit ye well there was many a noble knight against him.

And when King Arthur saw Sir Launcelot do so marvellous deeds of arms he then armed him, and took his horse and his armour, and rode into the field to help Sir Launcelot; and so many knights came in with King Arthur. And to make short tale in conclusion the King of Northgales and the King of the Hundred Knights were put to the worse; and because Sir Launcelot abode and was the last in the field the prize was given him.

But Sir Launcelot would neither for king, queen, ne knight, have the prize, but where the cry was cried through the field: 'Sir Launcelot, Sir Launcelot hath won the field this day.' Sir Launcelot let make another cry contrary: 'Sir Tristram hath won the field, for he began first, and last he hath endured, and so hath he done the first day, the second, and the third day.'

CHAPTER 34: *How the prize of the third day was given to Sir Launcelot, and how Sir Launcelot gave it to Sir Tristram*

Then all the estates and degrees high and low said of Sir Launcelot great worship, for the honour that he did unto Sir Tristram; and for that honour doing to Sir Tristram he was at that time more praised and renowned than and he had overthrown five hundred knights; and all the people wholly for this gentleness, first the estates both high and low, and after the commonalty, cried at once, 'Sir Launcelot hath won the field whosoever say nay.'

Then was Sir Launcelot wroth and ashamed, and so therewithal he rode to King Arthur.

'Alas,' said the king, 'we are all dismayed that Sir Tristram is thus departed from us. By God,' said King Arthur, 'he is one of the noblest knights that ever I saw hold spear or sword in hand, and the most courteous knight in his fighting; for full hard I saw him,' said King Arthur, 'when he smote Sir Palomides upon the helm thrice, that he abashed his helm with his strokes, and also he said, "Here is a stroke for Sir Tristram," and thus thrice he said.'

Then King Arthur, Sir Launcelot, and Sir Dodinas le Savage took their horses to seek Sir Tristram, and by the means of Sir Persides he had told King Arthur where Sir Tristram was in his pavilion. But when they came there, Sir Tristram and Sir Dinadan were gone. Then King Arthur and Sir Launcelot were heavy, and returned again to the Castle of Maidens making great dole for the hurt of Sir Tristram, and his sudden departing.

'So God me help,' said King Arthur, 'I am more heavy that I cannot meet with him than for all the hurts that all my knights have had at the tournament.'

Right so came Sir Gaheris and told King Arthur how Sir Tristram had smitten down Sir Palomides, and it was at Sir Palomides' own request.

'Alas,' said King Arthur, 'that was great dishonour to Sir Palomides, in as much as Sir Tristram was sore wounded, and now may we all, kings and knights, and men of worship, say that Sir Tristram may be called a noble knight, and one of the best knights that ever I saw the days of my life. For I will that ye all, kings and knights, know,' said King Arthur, 'that I never saw knight do so marvellously as he hath done these three days; for he was the first that began and that longest held on, save this last day. And though he was hurt, it was a manly adventure of two noble knights, and when two noble men encounter, needs must the one have the worse, like as God will suffer at that time.'

'As for me,' said Sir Launcelot, 'for all the lands that ever my father left me I would not have hurt Sir Tristram and I had known him at that time; that I hurt him was for I saw not his shield. For and I had seen his black shield, I would not have meddled with him for many causes: for late he did as much for me as ever did knight, and that is well known that he had ado with thirty knights, and no help save Sir Dinadan. And one thing shall I promise,' said Sir Launcelot,

'Sir Palomides shall repent it as in his unkindly dealing for to follow that noble knight that I by mishap hurted thus.' Sir Launcelot said all the worship that might be said by Sir Tristram.

Then King Arthur made a great feast to all that would come. And thus we let pass King Arthur, and a little we will turn unto Sir Palomides, that after he had a fall of Sir Tristram, he was nigh hand araged out of his wit for despite of Sir Tristram. And so he followed him by adventure. And as he came by a river, in his woodness he would have made his horse to have leapt over; and the horse failed footing and fell in the river, wherefore Sir Palomides was adread lest he should have been drowned; and then he avoided his horse, and swam to the land, and let his horse go down by adventure.

CHAPTER 35: *How Palomides came to the castle where Sir Tristram was, and of the quest that Sir Launcelot and ten knights made for Sir Tristram*

And when he came to the land he took off his harness, and sat roaring and crying as a man out of his mind. Right so came a damosel even by Sir Palomides, that was sent from Sir Gawain and his brother unto Sir Mordred, that lay sick in the same place with that old knight where Sir Tristram was. For, as the French book saith, Sir Persides hurt so Sir Mordred a ten days afore; and had not been for the love of Sir Gawain and his brother, Sir Persides had slain Sir Mordred. And so this damosel came by Sir Palomides, and she and he had language together, the which pleased neither of them; and so the damosel rode her ways till she came to the old knight's place, and there she told that old knight how she met with the woodest knight by adventure that ever she met withal.

'What bare he in his shield?' said Sir Tristram.

'It was indented with white and black,' said the damosel.

'Ah,' said Sir Tristram, 'that was Sir Palomides, the good knight. For well I know him,' said Sir Tristram, 'for one of the best knights living in this realm.'

Then that old knight took a little hackney, and rode for Sir Palomides, and brought him unto his own manor; and full well knew Sir Tristram Sir Palomides, but he said but little, for at that time Sir Tristram was walking upon his feet, and well amended of his hurts; and always when Sir Palomides saw Sir Tristram he would behold him full marvellously, and ever him seemed that he had seen him.

Then would he say unto Sir Dinadan, 'And ever I may meet with Sir Tristram he shall not escape mine hands.'

'I marvel,' said Sir Dinadan, 'that ye boast behind Sir Tristram, for it is but late that he was in your hands, and ye in his hands. Why would ye not hold him when ye had him? For I saw myself twice or thrice that ye gat but little worship of Sir Tristram.'

Then was Sir Palomides ashamed. So leave we them a little while in the old castle with the old knight Sir Darras.

Now shall we speak of King Arthur, that said to Sir Launcelot, 'Had not ye been we had not lost Sir Tristram, for he was here daily unto the time ye met with him, and in an evil time,' said Arthur, 'ye encountered with him.'

'My lord Arthur,' said Launcelot, 'ye put upon me that I should be cause of his departition; God knoweth it was against my will. But when men be hot in deeds of arms oft they hurt their friends as well as their foes. And my lord,' said Sir Launcelot, 'ye shall understand that Sir Tristram is a man that I am loth to offend, for he hath done for me more than ever I did for him as yet.'

But then Sir Launcelot made bring forth a book; and then Sir Launcelot said, 'Here we are ten knights that will swear upon a book never to rest one night where we rest another this twelvemonth until that we find Sir Tristram. And as for me,' said Sir Launcelot, 'I promise you upon this book that and I may meet with him, other with fairness or foulness I shall bring him to this court, or else I shall die therefore.'

And the names of these ten knights that had undertake this quest were these following: First was Sir Launcelot, Sir Ector de Maris, Sir Bors de Ganis, and Bleoberis, and Sir Blamor de Ganis, and Lucan the Butler, Sir Uwain, Sir Galihud, Lionel, and Galihodin.

So these ten noble knights departed from the court of King Arthur, and so they rode upon their quest together until they came to a cross where departed four ways, and there departed the fellowship in four to seek Sir Tristram.

And as Sir Launcelot rode by adventure he met with Dame Bragwaine that was sent into that country to seek Sir Tristram, and she fled as fast as her palfrey might go. So Sir Launcelot met with her and asked her why she fled.

'Ah, fair knight,' said Dame Bragwaine, 'I flee for dread of my life, for here followeth me Sir Breunis Saunce Pité to slay me.'

'Hold you nigh me,' said Sir Launcelot.

Then when Sir Launcelot saw Sir Breunis Saunce Pité, Sir Launcelot cried unto him, and said, 'False knight, destroyer of ladies and damosels, now thy last days be come!'

When Sir Breunis Saunce Pité saw Sir Launcelot's shield he knew it well, for at that time he bare not the arms of Cornwall, but he bare his own shield. And then Sir Breunis fled, and Sir Launcelot[1] followed after him. But Sir Breunis was so well horsed that when him list to flee he might well flee, and also abide when him list.

And then Sir Launcelot returned unto Dame Bragwaine, and she thanked him of his great labour.

CHAPTER 36: *How Sir Tristram, Sir Palomides, and Sir Dinadan were taken and put in prison*

Now will we speak of Sir Lucan the Butler, that by fortune he came riding to the same place thereas was Sir Tristram, and in he came in none other intent but to ask harbour. Then the porter asked what was his name.

'Tell your lord that my name is Sir Lucan, the Butler, a knight of the Round Table.'

So the porter went unto Sir Darras, lord of the place, and told him who was there to ask harbour.

'Nay, nay,' said Sir Daname, that was nephew to Sir Darras, 'say him that he shall not be lodged here, but let him wit that I, Sir Daname, will met with him anon, and bid him make him ready.'

So Sir Daname came forth on horseback, and there they met together with spears, and Sir Lucan smote down Sir Daname over his horse's croup, and then he fled into that place, and Sir Lucan rode after him, and asked after him many times.

Then Sir Dinadan said to Sir Tristram, 'It is shame to see the lord's cousin of this place defiled.'

'Abide,' said Sir Tristram, 'and I shall redress it.'

And in the meanwhile Sir Dinadan was on horseback, and he jousted with Lucan the Butler, and there Sir Lucan smote Dinadan through the thick of the thigh, and so he rode his way. And Sir Tristram was wroth that Sir Dinadan was hurt, and followed after, and thought to avenge him; and within a while he overtook Sir Lucan, and bad him turn; and so they met together so that Sir Tristram hurt Sir Lucan passing sore and gave him a fall.

With that came Sir Uwain, a gentle knight, and when he saw Sir Lucan so hurt he called Sir Tristram to joust with him.

'Fair knight,' said Sir Tristram, 'tell me your name I require you.'

'Sir knight, wit ye well my name is Sir Uwain le Fise de Roi Uriens.'

'Ah,' said Sir Tristram, 'by my will I would not have ado with you at no time.'

'Ye shall not so,' said Sir Uwain, 'but ye shall have ado with me.'

And then Sir Tristram saw none other boot, but rode against him, and overthrew Sir Uwain and hurt him in the side, and so he departed unto his lodging again.

And when Sir Dinadan understood that Sir Tristram had hurt Sir Lucan he would have ridden after Sir Lucan for to have slain him, but Sir Tristram would not suffer him.

Then Sir Uwain let ordain an horse litter, and brought Sir Lucan to the abbey of Ganis, and the castle thereby hight the Castle of Ganis, of the which Sir Bleoberis was lord. And at that castle Sir Launcelot promised all his fellows to meet in the quest of Sir Tristram.

So when Sir Tristram was come to his lodging there came a damosel that told Sir Darras that three of his sons were slain at that tournament, and two grievously wounded that they were never like to help themself. And all this was done by a noble knight that bare the black shield, and that was he that bare the prize.

Then came there one and told Sir Darras that the same knight was within, him that bare the black shield. Then Sir Darras yede unto Sir Tristram's chamber, and there he found his shield and showed it to the damosel.

'Ah sir,' said the damosel, 'that same is he that slew your three sons.'

Then without any tarrying Sir Darras put Sir Tristram, and Sir Palomides, and Sir Dinadan, within a strong prison, and there Sir Tristram was like to have died of great sickness; and every day Sir Palomides would reprove Sir Tristram of old hate betwixt them. And ever Sir Tristram spake fair and said little. But when Sir Palomides saw the falling of sickness of Sir Tristram, then was he heavy for him, and comforted him in all the best wise he could.

And as the French book saith, there came forty knights to Sir Darras that were of his own kin, and they would have slain Sir Tristram and his two fellows, but Sir Darras would not suffer that, but kept them in prison, and meat and drink they had.

So Sir Tristram endured there great pain, for sickness had

undertake him, and that is the greatest pain a prisoner may have. For all the while a prisoner may have his health of body he may endure under the mercy of God and in hope of good deliverance; but when sickness toucheth a prisoner's body, then may a prisoner say all wealth is him bereft, and then he hath cause to wail and to weep. Right so did Sir Tristram when sickness had undertake him, for then he took such sorrow that he had almost slain himself.

CHAPTER 37: *How King Mark was sorry for the good renown of Sir Tristram. Some of Arthur's knights jousted with knights of Cornwall*

Now will we speak, and leave Sir Tristram, Sir Palomides, and Sir Dinadan in prison, and speak we of other knights that sought after Sir Tristram many divers parts of this land.

And some yede into Cornwall; and by adventure Sir Gaheris, nephew unto King Arthur, came unto King Mark, and there he was well received and sat at King Mark's own table and ate of his own mess. Then King Mark asked Sir Gaheris what tidings there were in the realm of Logris.

'Sir,' said Sir Gaheris, 'the king reigneth as a noble knight; and now but late there was a great jousts and tournament as ever I saw any in the realm of Logris, and the most noble knights were at that jousts. But there was one knight that did marvellously three days, and he bare a black shield, and of all knights that ever I saw he proved the best knight.'

'Then,' said King Mark, 'that was Sir Launcelot, or Sir Palomides the paynim.'

'Not so,' said Sir Gaheris, 'for both Sir Launcelot and Sir Palomides were on the contrary party against the knight with the black shield.'

'Then was it Sir Tristram,' said the king.

'Yea,' said Sir Gaheris.

And therewithal the king smote down his head, and in his

heart he feared sore that Sir Tristram should get him such worship in the realm of Logris wherethrough that he himself should not be able to withstand him.

Thus Sir Gaheris had great cheer with King Mark, and with Queen La Beale Isoud, the which was glad of Sir Gaheris' words; for well she wist by his deeds and manners that it was Sir Tristram.

And then the king made a feast royal, and to that feast came Sir Uwain le Fise de Roi Uriens, and some called him Uwain le Blanchemains. And this Sir Uwain challenged all the knights of Cornwall. Then was the king wood wroth that he had no knights to answer him.

Then Sir Andred, nephew unto King Mark, leapt up and said, 'I will encounter with Sir Uwain.' Then he yede and armed him and horsed him in the best manner. And there Sir Uwain met with Sir Andred, and smote him down that he swooned on the earth. Then was King Mark sorry and wroth out of measure that he had no knight to revenge his nephew, Sir Andred. So the king called unto him Sir Dinas, the Seneschal, and prayed him for his sake to take upon him to joust with Sir Uwain.

'Sir,' said Sir Dinas, 'I am full loth to have ado with any knight of the Round Table.'

'Yet,' said the King, 'for my love take upon thee to joust.'

So Sir Dinas made him ready, and anon they encountered together with great spears, but Sir Dinas was overthrown, horse and man, a great fall. Who was wroth but King Mark!

'Alas,' he said, 'have I no knight that will encounter with yonder knight?'

'Sir,' said Sir Gaheris, 'for your sake I will joust.'

So Sir Gaheris made him ready, and when he was armed he rode into the field. And when Sir Uwain saw Sir Gaheris' shield he rode to him and said,

'Sir, ye do not your part. For sir, the first time ye were made knight of the Round Table ye sware that ye should not have ado with your fellowship wittingly. And perdy, Sir Gaheris, ye knew me well enough by my shield, and so do I know you by your shield, and though ye would break your oath I would not break mine; for there is not one here nor ye that shall think I am afeared of you, but I durst right well have ado with you, and yet we be sister's sons.'

Then was Sir Gaheris ashamed, and so therewithal every knight went their way, and Sir Uwain rode into the country.

Then King Mark armed him, and took his horse and his spear, with a squire with him. And then he rode afore Sir Uwain, and suddenly at a gap he ran upon him as he that was not ware of him, and there he smote him almost through the body, and there left him.

So within a while there came Sir Kay and found Sir Uwain, and asked him how he was hurt.

'I wot not,' said Sir Uwain, 'why nor wherefore, but by treason I am sure I gat this hurt; for there came a knight suddenly upon me or that I was ware, and suddenly hurt me.'

Then there was come Sir Andred to seek King Mark.

'Thou traitor knight,' said Sir Kay, 'and I wist it were thou that thus traitorly hast hurt this noble knight thou shouldst never pass my hands.'

'Sir,' said Sir Andred, 'I did never hurt him, and that I will report me to himself.'

'Fie on you false knights,' said Sir Kay, 'for ye of Cornwall are nought worth.'

So Sir Kay made carry Sir Uwain to the Abbey of the Black Cross, and there he was healed.

And then Sir Gaheris took his leave of King Mark, but or he departed he said, 'Sir king, ye did a foul shame unto you and your court, when ye banished Sir Tristram out of this country, for ye needed not to have doubted no knight and he had been here.' And so he departed.

CHAPTER 38: *Of the treason of King Mark, and how Sir Gaheris smote him down and Andred his cousin*

Then there came Sir Kay, the Seneschal, unto King Mark, and there he had good cheer showing outward.

'Now fair lords,' said he, 'will ye prove any adventure in the Forest of Morris, in the which I know well is as hard an adventure as I know any.'

'Sir,' said Sir Kay, 'I will prove it.'

And Sir Gaheris said he would be advised, for King Mark was ever full of treason; and therewithal Sir Gaheris departed and rode his way. And by the same way that Sir Kay should ride he laid him down to rest, charging his squire to wait upon Sir Kay; 'And warn me when he cometh.'

So within a while Sir Kay came riding that way, and then Sir Gaheris took his horse and met him, and said, 'Sir Kay, ye are not wise to ride at the request of King Mark, for he dealeth all with treason.'

Then said Sir Kay, 'I require you let us prove this adventure.'

'I shall not fail you,' said Sir Gaheris.

And so they rode that time till a lake that was that time called the Perilous Lake, and there they abode under the shaw of the wood.

The meanwhile King Mark within the Castle of Tintagel avoided all his barons, and all other save such as were privy with him were avoided out of his chamber. And then he let call his nephew Sir Andred, and bad arm him and horse him lightly; and by that time it was midnight. And so King Mark was armed in black, horse and all; and so at a privy postern they two issued out with their varlets with them, and rode till they came to that lake.

Then Sir Kay espied them first, and gat his spear, and proffered to joust. And King Mark rode against him, and smote each other full hard, for the moon shone as the bright day. And there at that jousts Sir Kay's horse fell down, for his horse was not so big as the king's horse, and Sir Kay's horse bruised him full sore. Then Sir Gaheris was wroth that Sir Kay had a fall.

Then he cried, 'Knight, sit thou fast in thy saddle, for I will revenge my fellow!'

Then King Mark was afeared of Sir Gaheris, and so with evil will King Mark rode against him, and Sir Gaheris gave him such a stroke that he fell down.

So then forthwithal Sir Gaheris ran unto Sir Andred and smote him from his horse quite, that his helm smote in the earth, and nigh had broken his neck. And therewithal Sir Gaheris alit, and gat up Sir Kay. And then they yode both on foot to them, and bad them yield them, and tell their names other they should die.

Then with great pain Sir Andred spake first, and said, 'It is King Mark of Cornwall, therefore be ye ware what ye do, and I am Sir Andred, his cousin.'

'Fie on you both,' said Sir Gaheris, 'for a false traitor, and false treason hast thou wrought and he both, under the feigned cheer that ye made us! It were pity,' said Sir Gaheris, 'that thou shouldst live any longer.'

'Save my life,' said King Mark, 'and I will make amends; and consider that I am a king anointed.'

'It were the more shame,' said Sir Gaheris, 'to save thy life; thou art a king anointed with cream, and therefore thou shouldest hold with all men of worship; and therefore thou art worthy to die.'

With that he lashed at King Mark without saying any more, and covered him with his shield and defended him as he might. And then Sir Kay lashed at Sir Andred, and therewithal King Mark yielded him unto Sir Gaheris. And then he kneeled adown, and made his oath upon the cross of the sword, that never while he lived he would be against errant-knights. And also he sware to be good friend unto Sir Tristram if ever he came into Cornwall. By then Sir Andred was on the earth, and Sir Kay would have slain him.

'Let be,' said Sir Gaheris, 'slay him not I pray you.'

'It were pity,' said Sir Kay, 'that he should live any longer, for this is nigh cousin unto Sir Tristram, and ever he hath been a traitor unto him, and by him he was exiled out of Cornwall, and therefore I will slay him,' said Sir Kay.

'Ye shall not,' said Sir Gaheris; 'sithen I have given the king his life, I pray you give him his life.' And therewithal Sir Kay let him go.

And so Sir Kay and Sir Gaheris rode their way unto Dinas, the Seneschal, for because they heard say that he loved well Sir Tristram. So they reposed them there, and soon after they rode unto the realm of Logris.

And so within a little while they met with Sir Launcelot, that always had Dame Bragwaine with him, to that intent he weened to have met the sooner with Sir Tristram; and Sir Launcelot asked what tidings in Cornwall, and whether they heard of Sir Tristram or not. Sir Kay and Sir Gaheris answered and said that they heard not of him. Then they told Sir Launcelot word by word of their adventure.

Then Sir Launcelot smiled and said, 'Hard it is to take out of the flesh that is bred in the bone;' and so made them merry together.

CHAPTER 39: *How after that Sir Tristram, Sir Palomides, and Sir Dinadan had been long in prison, they were delivered*

Now leave we off this tale, and speak we of Sir Dinas that had within the castle a paramour, and she loved another knight better than him. And so when Sir Dinas went out on hunting she slipped down by a towel, and took with her two brachets, and so she yede to the knight that she loved, and he her again.

And when Sir Dinas came home and missed his paramour and his brachets, then was he the more wrother for his brachets than for the lady. So then he rode after the knight that had his paramour, and bad him turn and joust. So Sir

Dinas smote him down, that with the fall he brake his leg and his arm. And then his lady and paramour cried Sir Dinas mercy, and said she would love him better than ever she did.

'Nay,' said Sir Dinas, 'I shall never trust them that once betrayed me, and therefore as ye have begun so end, for I will never meddle with you.'

And so Sir Dinas departed, and took his brachets with him, and so rode to his castle.

Now will we turn unto Sir Launcelot, that was right heavy that he could never hear no tidings of Sir Tristram, for all this while he was in prison with Sir Darras, Palomides, and Dinadan.

Then Dame Bragwaine took her leave to go into Cornwall, and Sir Launcelot, Sir Kay, and Sir Gaheris rode to seek Sir Tristram in the country of Surluse.

Now speaketh this tale of Sir Tristram and of his two fellows, for every day Sir Palomides brawled and said language against Sir Tristram.

'I marvel,' said Sir Dinadan, 'of thee, Sir Palomides, and thou hadest Sir Tristram here thou wouldst do him no harm; for and a wolf and a sheep were together in a prison the wolf would suffer the sheep to be in peace. And wit thou well,' said Sir Dinadan, 'this same is Sir Tristram at a word, and now mayst thou do thy best with him, and let see now if ye can skift it with your hands.'

Then was Sir Palomides abashed and said little.

'Sir Palomides,' then said Sir Tristram, 'I have heard much of your maugre against me, but I will not meddle with you as at this time by my will, because I dread the lord of this place that hath us in governance; for and I dread him not more than I do thee, soon it should be skift.' So they peaced themself.

Right so came in a damosel and said, 'Knights, be of good cheer, for ye are sure of your lives, and that I heard say my lord, Sir Darras.'

skift: manage. *maugre*: ill-will.

Then were they glad all three, for daily they weened they should have died.

Then soon after this Sir Tristram fell sick that he weened to have died; then Sir Dinadan wept, and so did Sir Palomides, under them both making great sorrow. So a damosel came in to them and found them mourning.

Then she went unto Sir Darras, and told him how that mighty knight that bare the black shield was likely to die.

'That shall not be,' said Sir Darras, 'for God defend when knights come to me for succour that I should suffer them to die within my prison. Therefore,' said Sir Darras to the damosel, 'fetch that knight and his fellows afore me.'

And then anon Sir Darras saw Sir Tristram brought afore him. He said, 'Sir knight, me repenteth of thy sickness, for thou art called a full noble knight, and so it seemeth by thee; and wit ye well it shall never be said that Sir Darras shall destroy such a noble knight as thou art in prison, howbeit that thou hast slain three of my sons, whereby I was greatly aggrieved. But now shalt thou go and thy fellows, and your harness and horses have been fair and clean kept, and ye shall go where it liketh you, upon this covenant, that thou, knight, wilt promise me to be good friend to my sons two that be now alive and also that thou tell me thy name.'

'Sir,' said he, 'as for me my name is Sir Tristram de Liones, and in Cornwall was I born, and nephew I am unto King Mark. And as for the death of your sons I might not do withal, for and they had been the next kin that I have I might have done none otherwise. And if I had slain them by treason or treachery I had been worthy to have died.'

'All this I consider,' said Sir Darras, 'that all that ye did was by force of knighthood, and that was the cause I would not put you to death. But sith ye be Sir Tristram, the good knight, I pray you heartily to be my good friend and to my sons.'

'Sir,' said Sir Tristram, 'I promise you by the faith of my body, ever while I live I will do you service, for ye have done to us but as a natural knight ought to do.'

Then Sir Tristram reposed him there till that he was amended of his sickness; and when he was big and strong they took their leave, and every knight took their horses, and so departed and rode together till they came to a cross way.

'Now fellows,' said Sir Tristram, 'here will we depart in sundry ways.'

And because Sir Dinadan had the first adventure, of him I will begin.

CHAPTER 40: *How Sir Dinadan rescued a lady from Sir Breunis Saunce Pité, and how Sir Tristram received a shield of Morgan le Fay*

So as Sir Dinadan rode by a well he found a lady making great dole.

'What aileth you?' said Sir Dinadan.

'Sir knight,' said the lady, 'I am the woefullest lady of the world, for within these five days here came a knight called Sir Breunis Saunce Pité, and he slew mine own brother, and ever since he hath kept me at his own will, and of all men in the world I hate him most; and therefore I require you of knighthood to avenge me, for he will not tarry, but be here anon.'

'Let him come,' said Sir Dinadan, 'and because of honour of all women I will do my part.'

With this came Sir Breunis, and when he saw a knight with his lady he was wood wroth. And then he said, 'Sir Knight, keep thee from me!'

So they hurled together as thunder, and either smote other passing sore, but Sir Dinadan put him through the shoulder a grievous wound, and or ever Sir Dinadan might turn him Sir Breunis was gone and fled.

Then the lady prayed him to bring her to a castle there beside but four mile thence; and so Sir Dinadan brought her there, and she was welcome, for the lord of that castle was her uncle. And so Sir Dinadan rode his way upon his adventure.

Now turn we this tale unto Sir Tristram, that by adventure he came to a castle to ask lodging, wherein was Queen Morgan le Fay; and so when Sir Tristram was let into that castle he had good cheer all that night.

And upon the morn, when he would have departed, the queen said, 'Wit ye well ye shall not depart lightly, for ye are here as a prisoner.'

'Jesu defend!' said Sir Tristram, 'for I was but late a prisoner.'

'Fair knight,' said the queen, 'ye shall abide with me till that I wit what ye are and from whence ye come.'

And ever the queen would set Sir Tristram on her own side, and her paramour on the other side. And ever Queen Morgan would behold Sir Tristram, and thereat the knight was jealous, and was in will suddenly to have run upon Sir Tristram with a sword, but he left it for shame.

Then the queen said to Sir Tristram, 'Tell me thy name, and I shall suffer you to depart when ye will.'

'Upon that covenant I tell you my name is Sir Tristram de Liones.'

'Ah,' said Morgan le Fay, 'and I had wist that, thou shouldst not have departed so soon as thou shalt. But sithen I have made a promise I will hold it, with that thou wilt promise me to bear upon thee a shield that I shall deliver thee, unto the Castle of the Hard Rock, where King Arthur hath cried a great tournament, and there I pray you that ye will be, and to do for me as much deeds of arms as ye may do. For at the Castle of Maidens, Sir Tristram, ye did marvellous deeds of arms as ever I heard knight do.'

'Madam,' said Sir Tristram, 'let me see the shield that I shall bear.'

Then the shield was brought forth, and the field was gules with a king and queen therein painted, and a knight standing above them upon the king's head, and the other upon the queen's.

'Madam,' said Sir Tristram, 'this is a fair shield and a mighty; but what signifieth this king and this queen, and that knight standing up both their heads?'

'I shall tell you,' said Morgan le Fay. 'It signifieth King Arthur and Queen Guenever, and a knight that holdeth them both in bondage and in servage.'

'Who is that knight?' said Sir Tristram.

'That shall ye not wit as at this time,' said the queen.

But as the French book saith, Queen Morgan loved Sir Launcelot best, and ever she desired him, and he would never love her nor do nothing at her request, and therefore she held many knights together for to have taken him by strength. And because she deemed that Sir Launcelot loved Queen Guenever paramour, and she him again, therefore Queen Morgan le Fay ordained that shield to put Sir Launcelot to a rebuke, to that intent that King Arthur might understand the love between them.

Then Sir Tristram took that shield and promised her to bear it at the tournament at the Castle of the Hard Rock. But Sir Tristram knew not that that shield was ordained against Sir Launcelot, but afterward he knew it.

CHAPTER 41: *How Sir Tristram took with him the shield, and also how he slew the paramour of Morgan le Fay*

So then Sir Tristram took his leave of the queen, and took the shield with him.

Then came the knight that held Queen Morgan le Fay, his name was Sir Hemison, and he made him ready to follow Sir Tristram.

'Fair friend,' said Morgan, 'ride not after that knight, for ye shall not win no worship of him.'

'Fie on him, coward,' said Sir Hemison, 'for I wist never good night come out of Cornwall but if it were Sir Tristram de Liones.'

up both their heads: on both their heads.
paramour: as a lover.

'What and that be he?' said she.

'Nay, nay,' said he, 'he is with La Beale Isoud, and this is but a daffish knight.'

'Alas, my fair friend, ye shall find him the best knight that ever ye met withal, for I know him better than ye do.'

'For your sake,' said Sir Hemison, 'I shall slay him.'

'Ah, fair friend,' said the Queen, 'me repenteth that ye will follow that knight for I fear me sore of your again coming.'

With this this knight rode his way wood wroth, and he rode after Sir Tristram as fast as he had been chased with knights.

When Sir Tristram heard a knight come after him so fast, he returned about, and saw a knight coming against him. And when he came nigh to Sir Tristram he cried on high, 'Sir knight, keep thee from me!'

Then they rashed together as it had been thunder, and Sir Hemison bruised his spear upon Sir Tristram, but his harness was so good that he might not hurt him. And Sir Tristram smote him harder, and bare him through the body, and fell over his horse's croup. Then Sir Tristram turned to have done more with his sword, but he saw so much blood go from him that him seemed he was likely to die, and so he departed from him and came to a fair manor to an old knight, and there Sir Tristram lodged.

CHAPTER 42: *How Morgan le Fay buried her paramour, and how Sir Tristram praised Sir Launcelot and his kin*

Now leave to speak of Sir Tristram, and speak we of the knight that was wounded to the death. Then his varlet alit, and took off his helm, and then he asked his lord whether there were any life in him.

'There is in me life,' said the knight, 'but it is but little; and therefore leap thou up behind me when thou hast holpen me up, and hold me fast that I fall not, and bring me to

daffish: stupid.

Queen Morgan le Fay; for deep draughts of death drawen to my heart that I may not live, for I would fain speak with her or I died: for else my soul will be in great peril and I die.'

For with great pain his varlet brought him to the castle, and there Sir Hemison fell down dead.

When Morgan le Fay saw him dead she made great sorrow out of reason; and then she let despoil him unto his shirt, and so she let him put into a tomb. And about the tomb she let write: HERE LIETH SIR HEMISON, SLAIN BY THE HANDS OF SIR TRISTRAM DE LIONES.

Now turn we unto Sir Tristram, that asked the knight his host if he saw late any knights adventurous.

'Sir,' he said, 'the last night here lodged with me Ector de Maris and a damosel with him, and that damosel told me that he was one of the best knights of the world.'

'That is not so,' said Sir Tristram, 'for I know four better knights of his own blood, and the first is Sir Launcelot du Lake, call him the best knight, and Sir Bors de Ganis, Sir Bleoberis, Sir Blamour de Ganis, and Sir Gaheris.

'Nay,' said his host, 'Sir Gawain is a better knight than he.'

'That is not so,' said Sir Tristram, 'for I have met with them both, and I felt Sir Gaheris for the better knight, and Sir Lamorak, I call him as good as any of them except Sir Launcelot.'

'Why name ye not Sir Tristram?' said his host, 'For I account him as good as any of them.'

'I know not Sir Tristram,' said Tristram.

Thus they talked and bourded as long as them list, and then went to rest. And on the morn Sir Tristram departed, and took his leave of his host, and rode toward the Roche Dure, and none adventure had Sir Tristram but that; and so he rested not till he came to the castle where he saw five hundred tents.

bourded: jested.

CHAPTER 43: *How Sir Tristram at a tournament bare the shield that Morgan le Fay delivered to him*

Then the King of Scots and the King of Ireland held against King Arthur's knights, and there began a great medley.

So came in Sir Tristram and did marvellous deeds of arms, for there he smote down many knights. And ever he was afore King Arthur with that shield. And when King Arthur saw that shield he marvelled greatly in what intent it was made; but Queen Guenever deemed as it was, wherefore she was heavy.

Then was there a damosel of Queen Morgan in a chamber by King Arthur, and when she heard King Arthur speak of that shield, then she spake openly unto King Arthur:

'Sir King, wit ye well this shield was ordained for you, to warn you of your shame and dishonour, and that longeth to you and your queen.'

And then anon that damosel picked her away privily, that no man wist where she was become. Then was King Arthur sad and wroth, and asked from whence came that damosel. There was not one that knew her nor wist where she was become.

Then Queen Guenever called to her Sir Ector de Maris, and there she made her complaint to him, and said, 'I wot well this shield was made by Morgan le Fay in despite of me and of Sir Launcelot, wherefore I dread me sore lest I should be destroyed.'

And ever the King beheld Sir Tristram, that did so marvellous deeds of arms that he wondered sore what knight he might be, and well he wist it was not Sir Launcelot. And it was told him that Sir Tristram was in Petit Britain with Isoud la Blanche Mains, for he deemed, and he had been in the realm of Logris, Sir Launcelot or some of his fellows that were in the quest of Sir Tristram that they should have found him or that time. So King Arthur had marvel what

picked: went.

knight he might be. And ever Sir Arthur's eye was on that shield. All that espied the queen, and that made her sore afeared.

Then ever Sir Tristram smote down knights wonderly to behold, what upon the right hand and upon the left hand, that unnethe no knight might withstand him. And the King of Scots and the King of Ireland began to withdraw them. When Arthur espied that, he thought that that knight with the strange shield should not escape him. Then he called unto him Sir Uwain le Blanchemains, and bad him arm him and make him ready.

So anon King Arthur and Sir Uwain dressed them before Sir Tristram, and required him to tell them where he had that shield.

'Sir,' he said, 'I had it of Queen Morgan le Fay, sister unto King Arthur.'

So here endeth this history of this book, for it is the first book of Sir Tristram de Liones, and the second book of Sir Tristram followeth.

NOTES TO VOLUME I

ABBREVIATIONS

C. Caxton's edition.
W. Winchester Manuscript.

PREFACE

1. *Godfrey of Bouillon:* a leader in the first crusade, who became ruler of Jerusalem.
2. *Polichronicon:* a Latin historical work of Ranulf Higden (d. 1364), a Benedictine monk. An English version by John Trevisa was published by Caxton in 1482.
3. *Galfridus in his British book:* Geoffrey of Monmouth's *History of the Kings of Britain*, written *c.* 1135.

BOOK I

ch. 4 1. At this point nobody except Uther and Merlin know who Arthur is.

ch. 7 1. Malory refers to Arthur's knights as 'of the Round Table', although Arthur has not yet been presented with the Round Table (cf. Book III, ch. 1). Probably he did this out of habit.

ch. 9 1. According to Malory's later account (Book I, ch. 25) Excalibur is also the name of the sword which Arthur receives from the Lady of the Lake.

ch. 10 1. C: *do.*

ch. 11 1. *he* refers to Arthur.

ch. 15 1. Moris de la Roche nevertheless reappears later in the fighting (cf. ch. 17). For an explanation of how the reading here could have arisen from textual corruption, see Vinaver, p. 1292, n. 8–9.

2. C: 'one of the best knights'.

3. *Bleoberis.* This character is apparently distinct from Bleoberis de Ganis. He does not reappear.

ch. 20 1. The sense is obviously defective here. A better reading is found in W: 'but and I might prove it, I would wit whether thou were better ...'

2. How Ulfius and Brasias got to know about Arthur's origins is not explained.

ch. 23 1. C: 'the mights'.

BOOK II

ch. 4 1. C: 'said Balin'.
ch. 6 1. C: 'came ride'.
ch. 14 1. C: *ouer;* W: *one.*
ch. 15 1. Malory later implies (ch. 8) that Balin carries two swords, but this is not assumed here. Malory has probably taken 'Knight with the Two Swords' literally where it is meant to be a title. See Vinaver, pp. 1315, n. 84. 29–30, and 1321, n. 89. 10–11.
2. W. has the less startling and obviously better reading: 'and for the most party of that castle was dead through the dolorous stroke. Right so lay King Pellam and Balin three days.' See Vinaver, p. 1317, n. 85. 13–15.
ch. 16 1. *And King Pellam . . . dole, tray and tene.* This passage does not appear in any of Malory's known sources. It is imperfectly harmonized with the later account of the Grail story. Galahad, son of Launcelot, is here confused with Galahaut the Haut Prince; cf. Book XIII, ch. 4, and Book XVII, ch. 1.
ch. 19 1. cf. ch. 16. n. 1.

BOOK III

ch. 2 1. *twenty and eight knights.* This should be forty-eight, leaving the two vacant seats which Arthur remarks on (Book III, ch. 4).
ch. 10 1. C: 'and'.
ch. 12 1. *Hontzlake of Wentland* is distinct from Ontzlake, who plays a prominent part in the episode of Arthur and Accolon in Book IV.
ch. 13 1. *Brian of the Isles* as described here does not seem consistent with the warlike character Brian de les Isles who appears as the enemy of Arthur in Book IX, ch. 6. Probably the two are meant to be distinct.
ch. 15 1. The passage which follows is an original passage of Malory's, notable for its outline of knightly behaviour. In place of *always to do ladies, damosels and gentlewomen succour, upon pain of death,* W. has: *strengthe hem in hir ryghtes, and never to enforce them.*

BOOK IV

ch. 5 1. *a branch of an holy herb.* Vinaver (p. 1342, n. 132. 14–17) has shown how this rather puzzling reference could be due to Malory's mistaking of the word *branke,* used in his source in the literary sense of a subdivision of a cycle of stories.
ch. 15 1. *armyvestal.* This word does not occur elsewhere, and the sense can only be conjectured from the context. It may be intended

to mean 'warlike', and could be an attempt to make sense of W.'s equally obscure *amyvestyall*.

ch. 17 1. *certain cause* not in C.

ch. 20 1. C: *make*.

ch. 24 1. *knight of the Table Round*. However, Marhaus has not yet been made a knight of the Round Table. Cf. Book IV, ch. 28.

ch. 28 1. This mistaken assertion may be the result of confusion of Pelleas and King Pelles.

BOOK V

The source for this part of the story is the English alliterative poem *Morte Arthure*. Caxton has considerably reduced the alliterative cadence.

ch. 2 1. *Cateland*: Catalonia. Not all place-names in the account of Arthur's campaign which follow are capable of identification, and the forms of some have obviously arisen through misunderstanding.

ch. 3 1. Baudwin and Constantine are two characters created by Malory to replace Mordred, who in other versions of the story is here appointed as Arthur's deputy. But Malory keeps the story of Mordred's treachery until the final book.

ch. 12 1. *Pleasance*: Placenza; *Petersaint*: possibly Pietrasanta; *Port of Tremble*: Pontremoli.

BOOK VI

ch. 4 1. *white monks*: Cistercians.

ch. 10 1. *adventurous or lecherous*. The two adjectives are clearly incongruous. The reading in W. showss that there must have been confusion with the word *advoutrers* ('adulterers'). See Vinaver, p. 1421, n. 270. 34–36.

ch. 13 1. C: 'he'.

ch. 16 1. *rownsepyk*. No satisfactory explanation of this form has been suggested. It is best explained as a corruption of W.'s rowgh spyke ('rough spike').

BOOK VII

ch. 2 1. The story of 'La Cote Male Taile' is told in Book IX.

ch. 7 1. C: *merueylled*.

ch. 9 1. *Wade*. The legend of Wade, a famous hero of antiquity, is mentioned by many medieval writers, including Chaucer (*Merchant's Tale*, 1424.). In Scandinavian writings he appears as a giant, the father of Wayland.

Tristram is here referred to as a grown man. An account of his birth and early life appears later, at the beginning of Book VIII.

ch. 15 1. C: *encreased.*

ch. 20 1. C: 'of Sir Gawain'.

ch. 22 1. C: *Syr.*

ch. 26 1. W: 'And if so be that he be a wedded man that wins the degree he shall have a coronal of gold.' C.'s variant is probably due to a misreading, since the 'degree' at a tournament would only be awarded to a knight. See Vinaver, p. 1438, n. 341. 22–4.

ch. 27 1. *himself* refers to 'beauty'.

ch. 28 1. *encountered* not in C. 2. C: 'Launcelot'. 3. C: 'Green'.

ch. 32 1. *The Brown Knight Without Pity,* who meets his death here, is clearly identical with Breunis Saunce Pité, who appears in later books. Cf. notes to Book VII, chs. 2 and 9 above.

ch. 34 1. W: 'Sir Gareth met with her'.

BOOK VIII

ch. 1 1. *wife* not in C.

ch. 12 1. C: 'he that'.

ch. 16 1. *keep* not in C.

ch. 17 1. C.'s 'where ye beat' is not consistent with the previous account of the tournament in Book VIII, chs. 9 and 10. W: *he.*

ch. 24 1. In making Isoud's mother give the potion to Isoud herself, C. has creaed a strange inconsistency, since thte episode which followes clearly depends on Isoud's being unaware of the magic power of the potion. The mistake has probably arisen from a misunderstanding. In W. the sense is clear: 'then the queen Isode's mother gave Dame Grangwaine unto her to be her gentlewoman, and also she and Gouvernaile had a drink of he queen and she charged them ...' See Vinaver, p. 1462, n. 411. 35–412. 2.

ch. 25 1. C: 'mine'.

ch. 28 1. C: *a gyaunt that fought*: an obviously corrupt reading. See Vinaver, p. 1463, n. 418. 13. W. has *whyche* instead of *that,* and Vinaver suggests as the original reading *whyght* ('mighty').

BOOK IX

ch. 22 1. *them pass* not in C.

ch. 25 1. W: 'said Sir Gawain'.

ch. 35 1. C: *Tristram.*

GLOSSARY OF PROPER NOUNS

The following list contains only the major proper nouns and those likely to cause difficulty.

Accolon of Gaul, lover and champion of Morgan le Fay.
Agloval, brother of Percival.
Agravain, son of King Lot of Orkney.
Agwisance, King of Ireland, father of Isoud.
Alice la Beale Pilgrim, wife of Alisander le Orphelin.
Alisander le Orphelin, son of Boudwin and nephew of King Mark.
Almain, Germany.
Andred, cousin and enemy of Tristram.
Anglides, wife of Boudwin and mother of Alisander le Orphelin.
Aries, the cow-herd whose wife was mother of Tor.
Astlabor, father of Palomides.
Avelion, territory of the Lady Lile.
Avilion, isle of, home of Gringamore.
vale of, valley to which the queens carry the dying Arthur.
Bagdemagus, King of Gore, cousin of King Uriens.
Balan, brother of Balin.
Balin le Savage, 'the Knight with the Two Swords'.
Ban, King of Benwick, father of Launcelot du Lake.
Baudwin of Britain, appointed as viceroy during Arthur's Roman campaign; later a hermit.
Beaumains, nickname given by Kay to Gareth.
Bedevere, brother of Lucan.
Bellengerus le Beuse, son of Alisander le Orphelin.
Benwick, realm and city of King Ban.
Bernard, father of Elaine, maiden of Astolat.
Berrant le Apres, 'the King with the Hundred Knights'.
Blamor de Ganis, brother of Bleoberis.
Bleise, Beerlin's master, chronicler of Arthur's reign.
Bleoberis de Ganis, brother of Blamor.
Borre, son of Arthur and Lionors.
Bors de Ganis, son of King Bors of Gaul.
Boudwin, brother of King Mark; father of Alisander le Orphelin.
Bragwaine, servant of Isoud.
Brandegoris, King of Strangore.
Brandiles, one of the knights delivered from Turquin by Launcelot.

Brastias, knight of the Duke of Tintagel, afterwards of Arthur; hermit in the Forest of Windsor who offers hospitality to Launcelot.

Breunis Saunce Pité, enemy of Arthur's knights, identical with the *Brown Knight Without Pity*.

Breunor, knight of the Castle Pluere (Book VIII, ch. 24).

Breunor le Noire, called 'La Cote Male Taile' by Kay.

Brian of the Isles, sworn brother of Meliot of Logris (Book III, ch. 13); probably distinct from *Brian de les Isles*, lord of the Castle of Pendragon and enemy of Arthur.

Cador of Cornwall, leader in Arthur's army, father of Constantine.

Camelerd, realm of King Leodegrance.

Camelot, Arthur's residence, identified with Winchester.

Carados, King of Scotland.

Carados of the Dolorous Tower, brother of Turquin.

Carbonek, city and castle of the Grail.

Clariance de la Forest Savage, knight defeated by King Lot in the war against the eleven kings.

Clarivaus, King of Northumberland.

Clarrus of Cleremont, supporter of Launcelot.

Claudas, king, enemy of Ban and Bors.

Clegis, leader in Arthur's army.

Colgrevaunce of Gore, knight who fights against the eleven kings; slain by Lionel.

Constantine, son of Cador; king after Arthur.

Corbin, see *Carbonek*.

Cradelment, King of North Wales.

Dagonet, Arthur's fool.

Damas, knight who imprisons Arthur (Book IV).

Dinadan, companion of Tristram.

Dinas, seneschal of King Mark.

Dodinas le Savage, knight of Arthur's court.

Dornard, son of Pellinor.

Ector, foster father of Arthur.

Ector de Maris, brother of Launcelot.

Elaine, wife of King Nentres.

Elaine, daughter of King Pellinor and the Lady of the Rule.

Elaine, wife of King Ban.

Elaine, daughter of King Pelles; mother of Galahad.

Elaine le Blank, the maiden of Astolat, daughter of Bernard.

Eliazer, son of King Pelles.

Elizabeth, wife of Meliodas and mother of Tristram.

Epinogrus, son of the King of Northumberland.

Ettard, unfaithful lover of Pelleas.

Eustace, Duke of Canbenet, one of the eleven kings who oppse Arthur.

Evelake, pagan king, receives the baptismal name of *Mordrains*; cured by Galahad.

Excalibur, Arthur's sword.

Florence, son of Gawain.

Gahalatine, supporter of Launcelot.

Gaheris, son of King Lot; brother of Gawain.

Galagars, chosen by Pellinor to be a knight of the Round Table.

Galahad, son of Launcelot and Elaine.

Galahad, baptismal name of Launcelot.

Galahaut the Haut Prince, lord of Surluse.

Gales, Wales

Galihodin, king 'within the country of Surluse'.

Galihud, one of the knights delivered from Turquin by Launcelot; takes part in the quest for Tristram.

Galleron of Galway, knight of the Round Table, one of the twelve who join Agravain.

Gareth, son of King Lot; called Beaumains by Kay.

Gawain, son of King Lot; nephew of Arthur.

Gingalin, son of Gawain.

Gore, realm of King Uriens.

Gouvernail, attendant of Tristram.

Griflet le Fise de Dieu, knight of Arthur's court, chosen by Pellinor to be a knight of the Round Table.

Gringamore, brother of Lyonesse.

Grummor Grummorson, Scottish knight (Caxton's conflation of two characters).

Guenever, daughter of Leodegrance and wife of Arthur.

Harry le Fise Lake, one of the three knights of the Round Table who fight Breunis Saunce Pité.

Harsouse le Berbeus, defeated by Alisander le Orphelin.

Hebes le Renoumes, knight of Launcelot's kin; squire to Tristram.

Helin le Blank, son of Sir Bors.

Herlews le Berbeus, slain by Garlon (Book II, ch. 12).

Hermance, King of the Red City.

Hervis de Revel, chosen by Pellinor to be a knight of the Round Table.

Hontzlake of Wentland, knight slain by Pellinor.

Howel, King of Brittany, father of Isoud la Blanche Mains; possibly identical with Howell, Duke of Brittany, whose wife is murdered by a giant (Book V, ch. 5).

Idres, King of Cornwall.

Idrus, son of Uwain.

Igraine, mother of Arthur.
Ironside, name of the Red Knight of the Red Launds.
Isoud, La Beale, daughter of King Agwisance of Ireland; wife of King Mark of Cornwall.
Isoud la Blanche Mains, daughter of King Howel of Brittany; married to Tristram.
Kay, the Seneschal, son of Ector and foster brother of Arthur.
Kehydius, son of King Howel of Brittany; falls in love with La Beale Isoud.
King with the Hundred Knights, The, see *Berrant*.
La Cote Male Taile, 'The Ill-Tailored Coat' – nickname given to *Breunor* by Kay.
Lamorak de Gales, son of Pellinor.
Lanceor, son of the King of Ireland.
Launcelot du Lake, son of King Ban of Benwick.
Lavaine, son of Bernard of Astolat.
Leodegrance, King of Camelerd, father of Guenever.
Lile, Lady, of Avelion, enemy of Balin.
Lionel, nephew of Launcelot.
Liones, territory of Tristram.
Lionors, daughter of Sanam and mother of Borre.
Listinoise, kingdom of Pellam and Pellinor.
Logris, a kingdom of Great Britain ruled by Arthur.
Lot, King of Lothian and Orkney.
Lovell, son of Gawain.
Lucan the Butler, knight of Arthur's court, son of Corneus.
Lynet, sister of Lyonesse.
Lyonesse, sister of Lynet; rescued by Gareth.
Margawse, wife of King Lot.
Marhaus, brother of the Queen of Ireland; slain by Tristram.
Mark, King of Cornwall, uncle of Tristram.
Meliagaunt, son of Bagdemagus.
Meliodas, King of Liones, father of Tristram.
Meliot de Logris, cousin of Nimue (Book III); wounded by Gilbert the Bastard and healed by Launcelot (Book VI); joins Agravain's plot against Launcelot (Book XX).
Merlin, magician and soothsayer.
Mondrames, a misreading of *Mordrains*, q.v., treated as a separate character (Book XIII, ch. 10).
Mordrains, see *Evelake*.
Morgan le Fay, wife of Uriens; sister of Arthur.
Nacien, an ancestor of Launcelot.
Nacien, hermit, a descendant of Joseph of Arimathea.
Nentres, King of Garlot.

Nimue, called 'the chief Lady of the Lake'; caused the death of Merlin; married Pelleas.
Ontzlake, brother of Damas.
Ozana le Cure Hardy, knight of Arthur's court.
Palomides, the Saracen, son of Astlabor and brother of Safer.
Pellam, of Listinoise, father of Pelles; 'the Maimed King', injured by Balin with a magic spear (Book II, ch. 15) and later healed by Galahad (his great-grandson).
Pelleas, lover of the Lady Ettard; accompanied Guenever on her Maying expedition; married Nimue.
Pelles, son of Pellam and father of Elaine, mother of Galahad; also called 'the Maimed King'; wounded as a result of drawing the mysterious sword (Book XVII, ch. 5).
Pellinor, of Listinoise, father of Lamorak.
Percival de Gales, one of the three Grail knights.
Perimones, name of the Red Knight.
Persant of Inde, name of the Blue Knight.
Pertelope, name of the Green Knight.
Priamus, son of a pagan prince who rebelled against Rome; brother of Dinas.
Rience, King of North Wales.
Sadok, friend of Alisander and Tristram.
Safer, brother of Palomides.
Sagramore le Desirous, a knight of Arthur's court.
Sangrail, the Holy Grail.
Segwarides, enemy of Tristram.
Selises of the Dolorous Tower, nephew of the King with the Hundred Knights.
Strangore, kingdom of Brandegoris.
Surluse, realm of Galahaut the Haut Prince.
Tor le Fise de Vayshoure; le Fise Aries, son of Pellinor and Aries' wife.
Tristam de Liones, son of Meliodas; nephew of King Mark.
Turquin, enemy of Arthur's knights.
Ulfius, knight of Uther Pendragon.
Uriens, King of Gore.
Urré of the Mount, Hungarian knight; comes to Arthur's court to be healed.
Uther Pendragon, father of Arthur.
Uwain le Blanchemains; les Avoutres, son of King Uriens. (Treated as two separate characters, Book X, ch. 11.)
Waste Lands, Queen of the, aunt of Percival; one of the queens who bear away the dying Arthur.

GLOSSARY OF PROPER NOUNS

Nimue, called the Damsel of the Lake: caused the death of Merlin; married Pelleas.
Outlake: brother of Damas.
Ozana le Cure Hardy: knight of Arthur's court.
Palomides: the Saracen knight, [illegible] and brother of Safere.
Pellam, of Lystenoyse: father of Pelles, the Maimed King; injured by Balin with a magic spear (Book II ch. 15) and later healed by Galahad [illegible].
Pelleas: lover of the Lady Ettard; accompanied Guenevere on her Maying expedition; married Nimue.
Pelles: son of Pellam and father of Elaine, mother of Galahad; also called the Maimed King; wounded as a result of drawing the magic sword (Book XVII ch. 5).
Pellinore, of [illegible]: father of [illegible].
Percival de Galis: one of the three Grail Knights.
Persaunt: one of the [illegible] Knights.
Pertolope of [illegible]: one of the [illegible] Knights.
Perymones: one of the [illegible] Knights.
Priamus: a pagan prince who fought against Gawain; [illegible] of [illegible].
Ryons: King of North Wales.
Sadok: friend of Alisaundir and Tristram.
Safere: brother of Palomides.
Sagramore le Desyrus: a knight of Arthur's court.
Sarras: the Holy [illegible].
Segwarides: brother of Palomides.
[illegible]: the Dolorous Tower, overthrown by the King with the Hundred Knights.
Surluse: Kingdom of [illegible].
[illegible]: realm of Galahaut the Haut Prince.
Tor: le Fise de Vayshoure, or le Fise Aries, son of Pellinore and Aries' wife.
Tristram de Lyones: son of [illegible], the nephew of King Mark.
Turquine: enemy of Arthur's knights.
Ulfius: knight of Uther Pendragon.
Uriens: King of Gore.
Urry of the Mount of Hungary: knight, comes to Arthur's court to be healed.
Uther Pendragon: father of Arthur.
Uwayne les Blaunche Maynys, the Avoutres, son of King Uriens; [illegible] accidentally slain by Gawain (Book XVI, ch. 11).
Wade, Lady: Queen of the [illegible] of Northgalis, one of the queens who bore away the dying Arthur.

GLOSSARY

abode	v. pret.	withstood
abought	v. pret.	paid for
abrayed	v. pret.	started up
accord	n.	reconciliation
adoubted	p. p.	afraid
adventure	n.	fortune, chance, hazard
affiance	n.	trust
afterdeal	n.	disadvantage
against	prep.	in the presence of
aknown	ppl. adj.	aware
allow	v.	to commend
almeries	n. pl.	libraries
alther	adj. gen. pl.	of all
and	conj.	if
apayed	ppl. adj.	pleased
apel	v.	to impeach, accuse
appeach	v.	to accuse
appertices	n. pl.	feats
aretted	p. p.	reckoned
arson	n.	saddle bow
assoil	v.	to absolve
astonied	p. p.	stunned
attaint	ppl. adj.	exhausted
avail	n.	advantage
avaled	v. pret.	lowered
aventred	v. pret.	set (spear) in position for a charge
avoid	v.	to leave, send away
avow	v.	to admit, promise
awke	adj.	back-handed
awroke	p. p.	avenged
bachelor	n.	young knight
bain	n.	bath
bated	v. pret.	abated
battle	n.	battalion
bawdy	adj.	dirty
beams	n. pl.	bugles
bee	n.	ring, bracelet
be	v. pres. pl.	are
behest	n.	promise
behight	v. pret.	see *behote*

behote	v.	to promise
behove	v.	to be necessary
benome	p. p.	taken away
beseem	v.	to befit, appear
beseen	adj.	looking, having an appearance
beskift	v.	to thrust off
bestad	p. p.	biset
bestial	n.	cattle
betake	v.	to entrust
betaught	v. pret.	commended
bevered	v. pret.	trembled
bewared	p. p.	bestowed
bezant	n.	gold coin
blee	n.	complexion
bless	v. reflex.	to cross oneself
bobaunce	n.	boasting
boistous	adj.	unsophisticated, rough
boot	n.	remedy
borow	n.	pledge
	v.	to rescue, ransom
bounty	n.	goodness, favour
bourd	v.	to jest
brachet	n.	bitch-hound
braid	n.	attack
brain-pan	n.	skull
brast	v. pret. and p. p.	burst
brim	adj.	fierce
broached	v. pret.	pierced
brose	n.	a kind of broth
bruise	v.	to shatter, hurt
bur	n.	broad ring on a spear to protect the hand
burgh	n.	town
bushment	n.	ambush
by	prep.	about
caitiff	n. as adj.	miserable
cantel	n.	piece
cast	v.	to intend, imagine
cedle	n.	letter
cere	n.	wax
chaflet	n.	platform
champaign	n.	plain, field
charge	n. and v.	command

cheer	n.	entertainment, appearance
clean	adj.	excellent, pure
	adv.	completely
cleped	v. pret.	called
cleyght	v. pret.	seized
clip	v.	to embrace
cog	n.	broadly built ship
coif	n.	close fitting cap
complished	p. p.	filled
conceit	n.	judgement
conjour	v.	to urge
conversant	adj.	living
cording	n.	agreement
cost	n.	side
costed	v. pret.	followed
couch	v.	to lower spear for attack
courage	n.	desire
courtelage	n.	court-yard
covin	n.	conspiracy
cream	n.	chrism
credence	n.	message
cunning	n.	ability
daffish	adj.	stupid
damage	n.	grief, injury
damosel	n.	maiden
danger	n.	power
dawe	v.	to revive
deal	n.	part
debonair	adj.	gracious
deem	v.	to judge
defend	v.	to forbid
defendant	n.	defence
defile	v.	to afflict, put to shame
degree	n.	prize at a tournament, honour, rank, condition
delibered	p. p.	considered
deliverly	adv.	neatly
depart	v.	to divide
dere	v.	to harm
descrive	v.	to interpret
device	n.	arrangement, conversation
devise	v.	to think about
devoided	v. pret.	dismounted
devoir	n.	endeavour

devour	v.	to make away with, destroy
dight	v. pret. and p. p.	furnished, prepared
dindled	v. pret.	trembled
dint	n.	blow
diseased	adj.	weary
disperpled	p. p.	dispersed
dispoil	v.	to undress
dissever	v.	to distinguish
distained	p. p.	dishonoured
dole	n.	lamentation, sorrow
domineth	v. pres. 3 sg.	holds sway
doubt	n.	fearful thing
	v.	to fear
drenched	p. p.	drowned
dress	v.	to set in position, prepare, step forward
dretch	v.	to harrass, disturb
dromond	n.	large ship
duress	n.	affliction
dwell	v.	to delay
dwined	v. pret.	wasted
eagerness	n.	violence
eft	adv.	again
ell	n.	a measure of length: 45 inches
eme	n.	uncle
enchafe	v.	to make warm
endlong	adv. and prep.	along
eneled	p. p.	anointed
enewed	ppl. adj.	coloured
engine	n.	evil device
enow	adj.	enough
enprise	v.	to undertake
entreat	v.	to negotiate
erst	adv.	before
estures	n. pl.	rooms
eure	n.	fortune
evenlong	adv. and prep.	along
fain	adv.	gladly
	adj.	glad
faiter	n.	imposter
fare	v.	to act, behave
fault	v.	to lack

feute	n.	track
fewter	n.	rest for spear
	v.	to fix a spear in its rest
fiance	n.	promise
flacket	n.	flask
flemed	v. pret. and p. p.	put to flight
foin	n.	thrust
force	n.	strength, might
no force		that does not matter
fordeal	n.	advantage
fordo	v.	to render powerless
forfend	v.	to forbid
forfoughten	ppl. adj.	weary with fighting
forthink	v. reflex and impers.	to regret
gad	n.	rod
gainest	adj. superl.	quickest
gar	v.	to cause
gat	v. pret.	got, begot
gisarme	n.	battle-axe
glasting, glatisant	adj.	barking
graithed	v. pret.	prepared
grame	n.	harm
gramercy		many thanks
greces	n. pl.	stairs
gree	n.	victory
guardrobe	n.	wardrobe
guise	n.	custom
gules	adj.	(heraldic) red
habergeon	n.	coat of mail
halp	v. pret.	helped
halse	v.	to embrace
handsel	n.	gift
hete	n.	reproach
hie	v. reflex.	to hasten
hight	v. pres. and pret.	to be called
hill	v.	to cover
holden	p. p.	held
holpen	p. p.	helped
hough	n.	back part of the knee joint

houselled	p. p.	given the sacrament
hove	v.	to remain, wait
intermit	v.	to concern oneself
item	adv.	likewise, also
iwis	adv.	indeed
jesseraunte	n.	coat of armour
keep	v.	to care, guard
kemp	n.	warrior
kind	n.	nature
kindly	adj.	natural
large	adj.	generous
laund	n.	glade
layne	v.	to conceal
lazar-cote	n.	hut for lepers
lears	n. pl.	cheeks
leech	n.	physician
let	v.	to cease, prevent
leve	v.	to believe
leve	adj.	pleasing, dear
lever	adv. comp.	more gladly, rather
lewd	adj.	ignorant, boorish
licours	adj.	lecherous
lightly	adv.	quickly, easily
like	adv.	equally
limb-meal	adv.	limb from limb
list	v.	to wish
lith	n.	joint
long	v.	to belong
loth	adj.	unwilling, hateful
loos	n.	renown
lotless	adj.	without harm
lune	n.	leash for a hawk
lusk	n.	idle lout
lust	n.	wish
lygement	n.	alleviation
maims	n. pl.	wounds
mainten	n.	manner of life
makeless	adj.	matchless
maugre	n.	ill-will
	prep.	in spite of

measure	n.	moderation
medley	n.	conflict
meet	adj.	suitable, useful
mesel	n.	sickness
mette	v. pret.	dreamed
meyne	n.	retinue
mickle	adv. and adj.	much
minever	n.	fur trimming
mishaply	adv.	by misfortune
mister	n.	need
morte	n.	death
mote	n.	note on a horn or trumpet
	v. pres. 3 sg.	might
mountenance	n.	amount, space
ne	adv. and conj.	not, nor
nesh	adj.	soft
nis	v. pres. 3 sg.	is not
nobley	n.	pomp
notforthan	adv.	nevertheless
	conj.	although
noyous	adj.	troublesome
oftsides	adv.	often
or	conj. and prep.	before
ordain	v.	to arrange, appoint, command
ordinance	n.	command
orgulity	n.	pride
orgulous	adj.	proud
other	conj.	either, or
ouch	n.	clasp
ought	v. pret.	owed, possessed
outcept	v.	to except
out-take	v.	to except
overthwart	adj., adv. and prep.	slanting, askew, perverse, crosswise, across
paltock	n.	doublet
parage	n.	lineage
paramours(s)	adv.	as a lover
pareil	adj.	equal
passing	adv.	exceedingly
paynim	n.	pagan
paytrels	n. pl.	breast armour for a horse
pensel	n.	small pennon

perclose	n.	enclosure
perdy	adv.	indeed
peron	n.	large block of stone
pick	v. reflex.	to go away secretly
piller	n.	plunderer
plain	adj.	open, regular
plenour	adv.	with the full number
plumb	n.	block
point	v.	to lace
pounte	n.	bridge
press	n.	crowd
pretend	v.	to pertain
prize	n.	capture
puissance	n.	power
purfle	n.	trimming
purfled	p. p.	trimmed
pursuivant	n.	herald
purvey	v.	to provide
	reflex.	to prepare oneself
quarrel	n.	short arrow
quest	n.	judgement
quit	adj.	free
	v.	to repay, avenge
	reflex.	to acquit oneself
range	n.	line of battle
rase	v.	to tear, slash
rash	v.	to dash, slash, drag violently
rasure	n.	destruction
raught	v. pret.	reached
raundon	n.	force
rechate	n.	calling back the hounds
reck	v.	to care
recreant	adj.	surrendering, cowardly
rede	n.	advice
	v.	to advise
reney	v.	to deny
retray	v. reflex.	to draw back
rivage	n.	shore
roted	p. p.	practised
rush	v. trans.	to drag, smash
sacring	n.	consecration
sadly	adv.	soundly

sale	n.	hall
samite	n.	a rich silk material, often inter-woven with gold or silver threads
sarpe	n.	chain
scathe	n. and v.	harm
scomfit	v.	to defeat
selar	n.	canopy
semblable	adj.	comparable
sendal	n.	fine cloth
seneschal	n.	steward
senship	n.	censure
sewer	n.	serving-man
shaftmon	n.	hand-breadth
shaw	n.	thicket
shend	v.	to disgrace
	[p. p. *shent.*]	
shenship	n.	disgrace
shower	n.	misfortune
shrewd	adj.	mischievous, wicked
sib	adj.	related
siege	n.	seat
siker	adj.	sure
sikerness	n.	assurance
sith, sithen	adv.	then
	conj.	since
skift	n.	fate
	adj.	rid
	v.	to manage
slade	n.	valley
slake	n.	ravine
	v.	to abate
sodden	p. p.	boiled
sond	n.	messenger
sooth	adj.	true
	n.	truth
speed	v.	to succeed
	[p. p. *sped*]	
spere	v.	to ask
sperhawk	n.	sparrow-hawk
sprent	v. pret.	sprinkled
stale	n.	position
stalled	p. p.	put, installed
stead	n.	place
steven	n.	occasion, assignation, voice
stigh	n.	path

stint	v.	to cease, put an end to
stonied	p. p.	see *astonied*
stour	n.	battle
strait	adj.	narrow, confined
straitly	adv.	severely
strake	n.	signal with hunting horn
	v.	to sound a note on a horn
strong	adj.	severe
sue	v.	to follow
surcingle	n.	girth for a horse
swallow	n.	whirlpool
swapped	v. pret.	struck
sweven	n.	dream
swough	n.	swoop
tailles	n. pl.	taxes
take	v.	to give
tale	n.	reckoning
tame	v.	to pierce
tatch	n.	quality, habit
tene	n.	grief
thilk	demons. adj.	that
thrang	v. pret.	thrust
thrulled	v. pret.	pierced
till	prep.	to
tofore	adv., conj. and prep.	before
trace	v.	to go, pass, pursue
trains	n. pl.	enticements
trapper	n.	trapping
traverse	adv.	crossways
tray	n.	sorrow
trist	n.	hunting station
trow	v.	to think, believe
truss	v.	to bundle, equip
ubblye	n.	oblation
umbecast	v. pret.	cast around
umberere	n.	visor
umbre	n.	shadow
unadvised	adv.	rashly
undern	n.	about 9.0 a.m. or later
unnethe(s)	adv.	scarcely
up	prep.	on
utas	n.	octave; eighth day after festival

ventail	n.	vent
wag	v.	to shake, totter
wage	v.	to pay
wait	n.	watchman
	v.	to watch, be careful
wallop	v.	to gallop
wan	v.	to grow dark
wanhope	n.	despair
wap	v.	to lap
warison	n.	reward
warn	v.	to prevent
ween	v.	to think
whether	pron.	which of two, whichever
wide-where	adv.	far and wide
wield	v.	to possess, control
wight	adj.	stalwart
wist	v. pret.	see *wit* v. (1)
wit	v. (1)	to know
	v. (2)	to blame
wite	n.	blame
wittily	adj.	cleverly
witting	n.	knowledge
witty	adj.	wise
wood	adv.	madly, fiercely
	adj.	mad
woodness	n.	madness
worship	n.	worth, honour
	v.	to honour
wot	v. pres.	see *wit* v. (1)
wrack	n.	strife
wrast	v. pret.	wrenched
wrath	v.	to anger
wroken	p.p.	see *awroke*
wrothe	v. pret.	twisted
yard	n.	branch
yede, yode	v. pret.	went

MORE ABOUT PENGUINS, PELICANS, PEREGRINES AND PUFFINS

CLASSICS IN TRANSLATION IN PENGUINS

☐ ***The Treasure of the City of Ladies***
Christine de Pisan

This practical survival handbook for women (whether royal courtiers or prostitutes) paints a vivid picture of their lives and preoccupations in France, *c.* 1405. First English translation.

☐ ***La Regenta*** **Leopoldo Alas**

This first English translation of this Spanish masterpiece has been acclaimed as 'a major literary event' – *Observer*. 'Among the select band of "world novels" . . . outstandingly well translated' – John Bayley in the *Listener*

☐ ***Metamorphoses*** **Ovid**

The whole of Western literature has found inspiration in Ovid's poem, a golden treasury of myths and legends that are linked by the theme of transformation.

☐ ***Darkness at Noon*** **Arthur Koestler**

'Koestler approaches the problem of ends and means, of love and truth and social organization, through the thoughts of an Old Bolshevik, Rubashov, as he awaits death in a G.P.U. prison' – *New Statesman*

☐ ***War and Peace*** **Leo Tolstoy**

'A complete picture of human life;' wrote one critic, 'a complete picture of the Russia of that day; a complete picture of everything in which people place their happiness and greatness, their grief and humiliation.'

☐ ***The Divine Comedy: 1 Hell*** **Dante**

A new translation by Mark Musa, in which the poet is conducted by the spirit of Virgil down through the twenty-four closely described circles of hell.